Spirits Do Not Rest

Heartbreak at Wounded Knee

MARGARET LUKAS

First edition
Printed in the United States of America

ISBN: 978-1-950251-22-3 paperback
ISBN: 978-1-950251-23-0 Ebook

Cover illustration by Ellie Maxwell.
Cover design by Ellie Maxwell and Lucy Arnold.

Published by The National League of American Pen Women, Inc.
PEN WOMEN PRESS
Founded in 1897, the National League of American Pen Women, Inc. is a nonprofit dedicated to promoting the arts.
NLAPW, Inc. 1300 17th Street NW, Washington, D.C. 20036-1973;
www.nlapw.org

Endorsements

Spirits Do Not Rest: Heartbreak at Wounded Knee is a profound story of compassion and love. I felt every frozen gust of wind, every ache of guilt and hope. The novel is not only historically rich but spiritually resonant-a novel that reminds us redemption often comes where we least expect it.
> —Alecia Heidemann, *Western Nebraska Observer*

"What a great book. The portrayal of Native people is well researched and compassionate.

The history is right on."
> —Cindy Krafka, Professor of Native American Studies, University of Nebraska-Omaha. Sicanju Lakota Nation (Rosebud).

Historical Page-Turning Novel
Spirits Do Not Rest: Heartbreak at Wounded Knee

Margaret Lukas' historical novel, *Spirits Do Not Rest: Heartbreak at Wounded Knee,* is one of the most consequential works of fiction being released this year. Readers, along with Lukas' young protagonist Lauder Ellison, step into a critical moment in American history of the West, learning the hard way about American mistakes born out of ignorance and cruelty, resulting in a massacre of over 300 native peoples, including many innocent women and children. Like our young country in 1890, Lauder often blunders, showing unintentional prejudices, yet we root for her to discover the truth and greater humanity in herself. While this chapter in the history of the West is well-documented, the incredible story behind the dates and facts are not well known, but they remain essential to understanding not only our past but where we stand as a country today.
> —Nancy Avery Dafoe is the author, editor, and poet of 15 books, including *Yet in the Land of the Living* and *Socrates is Dead Again.*

I loved this book! A white woman encounters Native Americans who are in a difficult situation. As a result, her concern and empathy grow throughout the story. Beautifully written!
> —Margaret Hines,Sicangu Lakota
> *Who Cries for Mother Earth.*

To my husband, children, and grandchildren,
whose support has never faltered,

and to my parents, Stanley and Irene Loeffler,
who deserve being listed here, and lastly,

to the hundreds of thousands of Native American
children who suffered abuse, and even death,
in Indian boarding schools.

Contents

Preface

GROWING UP NEAR an Indian Boarding school in Genoa, Nebraska, I was fascinated by the abandoned and haunted buildings and the thought of how many children had been pulled from their families and spent their childhoods there. At one time, there were over 500 in residence. My grandfather, born in 1880, passed down stories of his encounters with Native Americans, and those stories, too, piqued my interest about people, said to be different from me, yet who had lived on the very ground where I stood. Grandfather, who never had a negative thing to say about Native Americans, a strikingly unpopular opinion during his life, was ten years old when the Wounded Knee massacre happened and papers across the country carried the news with various depths of concern for accuracy. I wrote *Spirits Do Not Rest: Heartbreak at Wounded Knee* to bring awareness to a massacre we cannot afford to forget, and to pay tribute to a people, who at that time, were misunderstood and abused.

One

November 1890. Riding across Nebraska, Lauder Ellison's hand jerked under the train's rocking. Ink splatters tracked across her journal page, but she didn't mind. At twenty-two and free — at least for now — she was Hermes, traveling between mortal and immortal worlds.

"Forty-five miles an hour," the porter had answered her earlier question. The speed thrilled her, though as the daughter of a railroad executive, she knew modern engines had the capability of reaching higher numbers. The concern was safety.

The farther west we go, Lauder wrote, *the more likelihood of flooding or blowing sand burying tracks in quarter mile sheets; rails trampled by cattle herds driven over them; even Indians now that they are on the warpath again, using horses and pulling rails off ballasts.*

She settled back into the velvet seat, loosened the silk scarf around her neck, and stared out the window at the great span of blue sky. Thoreau, her favorite author, had written on the vanity of a person who'd sit down to write when he had "not stood up to live." She had dared to stand up to live and look at the mess she had gotten herself into.

Past tense, she assured herself. She was escaping shame and Father's wrath by moving nearly five hundred miles from Omaha. "Pine Ridge

Indian Reservation," she whispered. She loved the sound of the four long words. A place to hide until the tempest blew over. If ever it did.

The prairie stretched beyond the train window, mile after mile of wind gusts raking dried grasses. A tendril of smoke in the distance made her wonder if, in this modern age, an earth lodge still remained. She dipped her pen. *How is it that a child can live as subterranean as a mole? Floors and ceilings made of dirt.*

She shut her journal and gave the cap of her ink bottle a hard twist. A child could live in one of the city's finest homes with well-respected parents, but behind those stately doors live year after year in terror. Then one could flee, she reminded herself. Of her own volition, a young woman could board a train and escape.

She had, though not without acting impulsively yet again, stolen her mother's greatest treasure: the music box belonging to Babette, the child who'd died only three days before Lauder's birth. At Pine Ridge, Lauder vowed, I will have the thing shipped back, and that will be the end of it. She fingered the scarf around her neck. "Buy it," Babette said the afternoon the silk caught Lauder's eye in a shop window. Mother wasn't the only one who spoke with the dead.

The nearly empty touring car felt suddenly ominous. Throughout the journey, people exited, and people boarded at nearly every stop. Now, on the last leg of the trip, the destination Rushville, Nebraska, she was one of only four passengers. General Brooke, commander of the Department of the Platte, had stood in Father's library and spoken of the "white folks running from the Dakotas." Still, she had expected more travelers. An old man with a cough sat in the back of the car beside a woman as elderly as himself. He wore a long coat and stowed his tall hat on an overhead shelf. The woman wore a fashionable coat, though not with an additional fur-trimmed capette like Lauder's. But, like Lauder, she kept her hat with its tall feathers firmly on her head. The only other passenger was a young female, her skin the copper of native peoples, the color of Lauder's dear Nurse in whose arms Lauder had wept, saying good-bye.

The young woman, looking ill at ease, sat a couple of seats farther down the aisle and across. Windows at her left, while Lauder's windows were at her right. The arrangement placed them squarely in the other's line of sight. The woman kept her gaze on the prairie, allowing Lauder furtive looks.

Was she eighteen or nineteen? Younger? Older and closer to Lauder's age? She appeared nervous and kept her badly worn carpet bag tucked between herself and the wall panel. Even then, one brown hand clutched the handles as though she believed one of her three fellow passengers had thievery on his mind. If the bag contained the woman's entire belongings, if she had no trunks stored on the train (Lauder had two, both quite large), then she didn't own much. Her small hat, little more than a beret, lacked a single ornate plume and looked sent from a mail-order house. Not acquired from a millinery shop. Her coat was plain and mannish, but on her small feet, as if to speak for the whole, she wore elaborately beaded moccasins that rose up over her ankles and disappeared somewhere above the hem of her skirt.

A door opened, and a commotion of voices in foreign tongues rolled in. Lauder turned. In the car behind, a throng of poorly dressed people crowded onto wooden seats and spilled into the aisle: immigrants. Bags and boxes covered the floor around their feet, even filled their laps. They shouted over one another to be heard, and children cried. She knew a portion of these were people the railroad courted from across the ocean with elaborate flyers. Even sent callers to stand on foreign street corners: "Bumper crops, mild climates, free land." Others had come from states east on the same promises of land the government had confiscated after breaking up the Great Sioux Reservation.

A man, thin in the face, stepped through carrying a bundled quilt with long wooden handles poking out the top. Had he brought his shovel, hoe, and rake all the way from Dusseldorf? He spied the empty seats and motioned to others behind him. A woman and four children stumbled in on his heels. A girl of about thirteen, two younger boys, and the smallest, another girl of four or five with fine, tangled hair. Their clothing, a woody mix of dull grays and rough browns, heralded poverty. They smelled of fatigue, dusty hope, and days without a bath. Crowding into two adjoining seats, they stared off.

The elderly couple grumbled, their tongues tsking. The family clearly hadn't paid for upholstered seats and room to relax their elbows, and the wealthy couple would remind them. Was there no compassion even for the children? Lauder wondered. She pitied them all, including the man who now looked over his struggling family. If his dreams of a new life failed, he failed them. He'd brought them on the promise of free or nearly free land, but did he know the Sioux reservation had been broken up over a year ago? How many of those millions of acres had already been sold or given away? Still, here the family was, tired and hungry, and Lauder knew there was no way to send them, or the throngs like them, back. Space had to be made.

She looked away. Writing accounts of immigrants and their hardships, though she would never seek to publish again, did not interest her. The last remaining and fast-disappearing Indian chiefs, especially the wild ones like Sitting Bull, did. With a start, she remembered the craniometer in her case. Father wanted, nay demanded, she send him measurements of native head sizes to support his theories on the superiority of the white race. She would not.

The train reached Rushville under a cloudless, cold sky. Lauder deboarded with her leather case but remained on the platform until the porter had pulled both trunks from the baggage car. She couldn't lose her clothing in one and certainly not her books in the second.

Hollering from down the street startled her. Rushville was a long stretch of dirt with hastily constructed unpainted buildings. And with as many canvas tents with pans and wares hanging on ropes and banging in the wind. Wood and canvas both seemed to shudder, and men who looked as if they'd not bathed in weeks loitered and hawked goods around doorways, rain barrels, wagons, and pack-laden mules. Not a woman in sight, though she dared not think over-much about the activity inside the trembling tents or behind the second-story windows with their shabby lace curtains. She backed into the shadows and closer to the safety of the station house.

No escort waited for her, and fear began clutching her chest. The correspondence she received clearly stated that Agent Moyer would send someone to accompany her safely to the agency. With the heightened tensions over the Ghost Dancing and Sioux threatening war, she had expected five or six men in military uniforms waiting on horseback, alongside a covered coach for her. Instead, she was left unaccompanied. Suppose no one came at all, and she found herself stuck overnight, needing to find safe lodging? She would not walk into the hullabaloo that was Rushville. She fingered the large bead on the end of her twelve-inch hat pin, took a steadying breath, tucked the ends of her silk scarf tighter into her coat collar, and hurried inside and out of sight.

The room was empty but for the Indian woman, her bag on her lap and her hands still clutching the handles. Lauder's heart dropped further. They were two women alone. Even the porter who had pulled her trunks from the train had just as quickly reboarded, not bothering to be sure they were safe. Suppose a band of men from that lawless chaos down the street descended on them?

With her knees feeling shaky, Lauder took the second bench. The Indian watched one window, but Lauder, having no idea from which direction she could expect rescue, looked right and left. Straightaway upon reaching the agency, she would write General Brooke explaining in detail the distress she had been put through. She would hold him accountable just as she would Agent Moyer and the headmistress at the school where she was to teach. All three were responsible.

"This is unacceptable," she muttered.

A glance. Soft, dark eyes that quickly looked away.

Deciding to speak required consideration and caution. Suppose the native carried a knife in her skirts and misunderstood Lauder's friendliness for a threat?

"Good day." Even to herself, Lauder sounded embarrassingly meek.

The woman nodded, equally cautious, a slight furrow in her sable brows. Her attention swung back to the window where the train was departing, leaving empty tracks and an even emptier prairie.

"I Miss Lauder Ellison." She tapped her chest. How to mime her reason for being there? "I teach," she pretended to hold a pen and write.

"I am Mina. You will teach at the agency day school?"

"Why yes." Lauder lifted her chin. She had not only communicated effectively, word of her arrival must have passed across the reservation. Though that fact made her tardy conveyance even more disheartening. "I," Lauder tapped her chest again, then pointed at Mina, "teach you?"

Sorrow passed over Mina's face. She turned back to the window and the empty road.

Had it been the mention of school that upset her? Lauder wondered. And ought she break the rules and offer her a ride to Pine Ridge? Lauder had received clear instructions by post on several matters, one being that she must not interfere in personal issues with her students or the reservation families. Her role was to teach and enforce "all rules of conduct as laid down by the headmistress, Mrs. Streamist." Offering a ride to the girl, woman — Lauder still couldn't decide — clearly broke the rules. Also, Mina was waiting for someone who was surely on his way.

An old wagon came into view, and Mina rose. Her lips pressed, the bottom one shaking slightly as her eyes searched the couple riding high on the seat.

Breath knotted in Lauder's lungs. She was about to be left alone.

The wagon, pulled by a single skinny black horse, stopped beside the tracks, and Mina stared at the couple as if through the fog of time. Clutching her bag, she hurried out.

An elderly man and a woman with skin just as dark as his, probably one of his numerous wives, stepped down from the weather-bleached buckboard. Poorly dressed, the couple rushed to Mina with hugs and high-pitched greetings.

Sadness sank through Lauder; her parents never expressed such overt love. But I was lucky all the same, she reminded herself. I had Nurse. Many children in the classic works of literature don't have a single elder to love them.

She turned from the reunion, searched for any sign of her escort, and, seeing none, fought growing fear. I am Lauder Ellison. I will not give in to my emotions in the first hour of my arrival.

The man left off hugging Mina and opened the depot door. He leaned in, his face craggy, and his eyes fell on Lauder. "Come."

She swallowed too quickly and coughed, catching her breath. Had Mina begged her a ride? She shook her head. "No, thank you." What sign language for NEVER!? Agent Moyer would appear at any moment with a dozen soldiers. Perhaps General Brooke himself would come for her. Shoulders back, she told herself, smile, show no fear. "I'm waiting for my escort." She enunciated her next words slowly and clearly, "Soldiers come for me. Men have orders."

"I orders. Come."

Two

SHOCKED, LAUDER DREW in a sharp breath. This man, an Indian, with command in his voice, left no doubt: He was her escort to the reservation.

Not waiting on her, he turned back, letting the door blow shut behind him. He lifted her first trunk onto the back of his wagon and shoved it forward. Her second caused him to struggle, and Mina grabbed one handle. Together they hoisted. When it was squarely on the wagon's platform, Mina climbed in and pulled while he shoved. They chuckled with the effort, the bottom of Lauder's new trunk scraping over splintered and rough planks.

Lauder forced herself to stand. Her knees needed wrestling to hold her weight. How could Agent Moyer and Mrs. Streamist have thought so little of her welfare? The agency was nearly twenty miles away, which meant over four hours riding in the open. She ought to stay right there and take the first train back to Omaha. She wouldn't. She couldn't. And since she couldn't, she had no choice but to go with these people. Though she had no proof she wasn't being taken hostage to be sold to a warrior for his fourth wife, or that a mile or two out of town, they wouldn't push her off to die, while they rode away with her clothes and all her books. And possibly her scalp.

She grabbed her carrying case and marched out to join her future.

The threesome, knowing where to step and grab, climbed aboard, chatting and filling the wagon seat. Mina turned back, frowned to see Lauder still standing on the depot platform. She reached over the seat to pat the top of one of the trunks. "Sit here." Still clutching her satchel as though it contained the Queen's diamonds, she stared at Lauder. Then, with a word to the woman sitting beside her, she climbed over the seat and sat on the trunk. "Come."

Lauder glanced about for some sort of stool or aid to use as a step.

"Your knees," Mina said.

"My coat." She managed not to mention its cost.

Mina frowned.

With no other option, Lauder lifted the wool over her knees, and certain she looked like Mother's dog clawing to reach Mother's too-high bed, she crawled onto the back of the wagon, sacrificing her skirt. Also, expensive.

They rode. The cold winds ruffled the ends of Lauder's scarf, worked between the buttons of her coat, and threatened to take her hat despite the long pin. The hard trunk beneath her grew increasingly uncomfortable, and the land she had admired from inside the train stretched eerily into a vacuous distance. No secure streets with rows of houses and trees, no trolleys running in every direction, and no comforting crowds. Someone would hear of the needless stress she'd been put under.

The frozen road rolled up and down the hills while the cold bit Lauder's ears and burned her toes through her thin shoes. Mina seemed not to experience discomfort. She often lifted her face to wind gusts as if they were caresses. The older woman sitting on the wooden seat noticed how Lauder shivered and handed back a striped blanket. Sharing the additional warmth, she and Mina squeezed shoulder to shoulder and hip to hip. Conversation increased in starts and stops but relaxed mile by mile with the swaying and close proximity.

"Blackbird is aunt," Mina said.

"And his name?"

"Plants Corn."

"I mean his real name. How I should address him."

Mina's brow wrinkled. "Address him by his name: Plants Corn."

The man in his patched clothing matched that of the poor immigrant farmer on the train, sans the smell of needing to bathe. But this man, though Indian, was too plain to be a chief. She had hoped to find exotic Indians, and her first introduction was to these ordinary people. He, with his grey hair, wore not a feather, spot of face paint, or regalia of any sort. She, with glossy black hair, was wrapped in a simple wool blanket, her back to them. Neither were of the stuff she had hoped to find and write about, although that writing would never see publication.

Mina pulled a hand from the folds of the blanket and panned the vista. "Ancestors."

Lauder wasn't sure how to respond. The comment seemed more prayer and greeting than an attempt at conversation. "The Sioux believe—"

"I am Lakota," Mina said. "The land is ancestor."

Again, Lauder wasn't sure how to answer, though she was happy at having been stopped before she demonstrated how little she knew about the Sio… Lakota.

"Your people," Mina continued, "do not share even their corpses with the land."

Shoulder to shoulder with a near stranger, a Lakota, who might still have a knife buried in her skirts, the comment felt sharp edged. "You mean our use of coffins?" She smiled. "We take our dead bones seriously."

Out over the prairie that Mina admired, Lauder saw only emptiness. Newspapers in Omaha printed daily accounts of uprisings, or rumors of uprisings, but she suspected the reports were exaggerated, if not entirely false. She didn't want her life threatened, but she wanted wide-eyed experiences for her journals. Though, she reminded herself yet again, that she would never seek publication. She would write for herself because the thing that ruined her was also the only thing that could save her.

In the old wagon, the road rutted and battered by the weight of thousands of troops and endless supply wagons, Lauder and Mina were jolted in unison, knocked shoulders, bounced as one, and settled the same.

Mina explained she was returning to the reservation she had not seen since being taken away as a small child. She had come now, "for my people. I come also for the gift of my ancestors' healing."

Mina had nodded at Plants Corn and Blackbird, but Lauder understood her people meant far more than just the two. "Healing," she repeated Mina's word. She dared not ask more. She wasn't Lakota, and she had no hope of the land healing her. Could time? Time to think and plan what to do next with her ruined life.

When Mina once again lifted her face to a gust of wind and the sun hanging low in the west, Lauder did the same. Would exposing her face so, result in her first freckle? As a child, Nurse had only let her read in the garden early mornings or evenings when the sun's rays were less direct. Even given the limited hours, Nurse insisted Lauder wear wide-brimmed bonnets and long sleeves. Her hands in small white gloves. It had not been Mother who cared if Lauder's skin freckled, but Nurse, watching the little alabaster figure in Babette's music box, who had hoped to make Lauder a child Mother could love.

Lauder had prided herself on being a rebel against society's strictures on women. But sitting with her face exposed to the wind for the first time, she realized with a shameful blush how conventional her life had been. Tucked safely inside her books, inside the house on Omaha's Gold Coast, inside her job teaching high school literature, she had lived nearly as bound by convention as Mother. Not any longer. Life was grabbing her by the shoulders once again and giving her a great shake.

"I, too, will teach at the day school," Mina said.

"The same as I?" Lauder needed to force her mouth closed. She had so proudly announced her appointment, had without thought believed she spoke to someone lower in rank. She tapped fingers on her knees, tried to upright her emotions, and think of something other than her embarrassment.

As their conversation progressed, Lauder grew increasingly surprised by their similarities: age, sex, and occupation. Given that Mina had been away from the reservation most of her life, both were also green to the place. Neither had met Agent Moyer whom they imagined must be a dashing man, or the head mistress whom they imagined had a nose like a sweet potato. *And we both carry stones,* Lauder thought.

"I fear my people will not want me," Mina whispered.

The comment and the whispering surprised Lauder. With the wagon's rattling and the wind's gusting, they already struggled to hear the other. Did Mina not want her aunt and uncle to hear her confession? Which could only mean she feared they would disapprove of her reasoning.

"They took me from my family." Mina kept her voice low. "Boarding school. At the age of four." She dropped her face in her hands, illustrating how as a small child she had wept. Then she mimed ripping at her chest and tearing out her heart. On flattened palms, she extended the offering.

Imagining the bloody, plucked organ, Lauder nearly gagged. She pulled the blanket higher under her chin. *I don't belong here,* she thought. *I lack the soul.*

Mina's gaze lingered on a bit of Lauder's fur-trimmed coat. "Why have you come?"

"I wanted to become a great writer. I hope to meet famous chiefs like Sitting Bull."

Plants Corn turned his head, spoke over his shoulder. "Many miles. When grass is green, we go."

Lauder's eyes widened. "Thank you. That would be splendid." She turned back to Mina. "He really knows Sitting Bull?"

A nod, though Lauder saw the disappointment in Mina's eyes. A moment earlier, she had asked a heartfelt question, and Lauder hadn't given an equally heartfelt answer. But she wasn't ready to disclose the reason she had come, and she likely never would be.

"Uncle's mothers live at Standing Rock," Mina said, "near Sitting Bull. Many relatives are there."

Happy for the turn from Mina's deeper question, Lauder ignored the reference to Plants Corn's mother in the plural. "Your uncle is related to Sitting Bull?"

"Sitting Bull is cousin to Uncle. Spotted Elk, the army calls him Big Foot, is also cousin." She paused, "You do not write of your own good chiefs?"

Lauder stumbled on the thought. "Who do you consider is a good white chief?"

"Only General Crook." Mina put her hands on her cheeks and fluttered her fingers to demonstrate Crook's bushy chops. "He never lied to us."

Troubled by another thought, Lauder pressed her shoulder into Mina's. The age of Plants Corn put him far past the age of the current troublemakers terrorizing people, but a few decades ago? "Did your uncle fight at Custer's Last Stand?"

Three

"PLANTS CORN DEFENDED his people," Mina said. "Warriors from many tribes defended the people at the attack at Greasy Grass."

How strange, Lauder thought, to think of Custer's Last Stand as the attack at Greasy Grass. Entirely omitting the name of the famous general who had died there. Like the maps she and Father had drawn, the angle of perception changed everything.

"Plants Corn, Crazy Horse," Mina went on over the wagon noise, "thousands fought."

Lauder took a quick glance back over her shoulder. Stooped, worn coat, slouchy soiled hat. He seemed hardly the stuff of exciting history.

"Is that not true of white men?" Mina asked. "Do they not fight when their families are attacked?"

The question came with such a flat expression, Lauder wondered if Mina mocked her.

"Uncle raided when young," Mina went on quickly, her tone soft again. "He stole horses, warred, counted coups. Killed white soldiers. He will war no more. War with whites kills his people."

Lauder considered. Even at the time of the battle, some fourteen years earlier, Plants Corn would not have been a young man. Though surely, every man with the strength to lift a gun or a bow would have done so to protect his family. "Is that when he took up his name? Telling everyone that henceforth, he'd be known as a farmer?"

"Thirty warriors died at the battle," Mina's concerns drifted beyond Lauder. "Nearly as many women and children. I was a small girl, already away at school. I was not there to press my knife into a white soldier's throat."

"Slicing someone's throat?" Lauder hoped to lighten the mood. "Hemlock is cleaner." She huddled closer. "My father never fought in any conflict, but he and I have made many maps of Civil War battlefields."

"You know maps?"

"I am an official member of the Civil War Map Club."

"That is good?"

"It's grown boys playing." The six members loved war talk and battlefield maps, but when the Civil War broke out, young men then, none rushed as had thousands of others to enlist. Now, older, chests puffed, they studied maps with little symbols that represented fifty dead, a hundred, a thousand. Small keys that trivialized the carnage while the men pontificated on the past from the safety of the present. Yet, Lauder had prided herself on her growing understanding of cartography and even on Father's insistence that she attend the meetings.

"Maybe you will become a warrior," Mina said. She glanced at Lauder's hat and frowned. "Maybe no."

The blanket, pulled up over their heads like a shared hood, flattened the shoulder-wide brim of Lauder's winter hat, and she knew the tall, stylish feathers were broken. The sensibility of Mina's narrower and deeper hat was obvious. "In the milliner's shop," she offered, "it was lovely."

For several long moments, Mina did not speak. "My parents," she said finally, "died of sorrow."

Mina's openness, when their relationship was so new, moved Lauder, but she knew two people didn't literally die of sorrow. Likely, the couple had died of alcoholism. If Mina didn't wish to admit that sad fact, she had every right to omit it. "I'm sorry for their deaths."

"I was sent away to school. If they had allowed me to stay, if I had been there ... maybe then."

"You mustn't blame yourself." Surely Mina appreciated having learned to speak English and the ways of white culture. "The government is saving the Ind… Lakota."

"I want the memory of my parents in a great fight for me."

Lauder understood. She had grown up feeling responsible for Babette's death though Nurse explained time and time again that when Babette died, Lauder's birth was still a few days away. *My head knows I'm not guilty*, she thought, *but my heart won't forgive me.*

"You have run away," Mina said.

Was it so obvious? "General Brooke sent me." Another half-truth, but she still had her own questions about being there and the speed with which she had arrived. "'I want to live deep and suck out the marrow of life.' Have you read Thoreau?"

"A man may use many words and say few things."

"You're joking. *Walden* is amazing. And what about you? Besides your people, why are you here, at this time?"

"I applied in the spring and received a letter. 'No openings.'"

"A rejection letter." Their developing friendship, surely it was a developing friendship, delighted Lauder. "I've more than a few of those."

"I had education," Mina lifted Lauder's wrist, pushed back the cuff of her coat, and tapped the exposed flesh. "But not this. White skin."

Mina wore no gloves, yet the finger she used to touch Lauder was warm. "Even with the education," Lauder asked, "skin color matters on the reservation?"

"We are educated to serve whites, not to join them as equals. An educated Lakota is still a Lakota. Then last month, a letter. 'Come immediately.'"

"You shouldn't be nervous. You belong here."

"Many will resent my years with whites, thinking me weak and favoring their ways. Others will be jealous of my years with whites." She sighed, smiled. "I am like your Thoreau. I talk much."

Wind continued to ripple the dry grasses while the sinking sun painted the tips rose and copper. The wagon passed three ragged children picking up pieces of coal half buried in snow and putting the dark bits into rusty pails.

Mina threw the blanket off her shoulders and asked something of Blackbird.

"She says," Mina interpreted, "Man Afraid needs many fires. The wagons bounce, drop coal."

"Little girls out in this weather?" Lauder shook her head. "It'll be dark soon, and they're out here picking up scraps of coal?" What parent allowed it? "They must be freezing."

"Come," Mina said. She jumped off the rolling wagon and began searching along the road's snowy edge.

The wagon stopped, but Lauder remained sitting. She could not jump as had Mina. She was sure to break a leg. And she couldn't climb back in without once again risking her coat and making a fool of herself. Watching Mina, she shrugged off her guilt: Mrs. Streamist would not approve of the behavior. Besides, did the children really need to scavenge with their small hands for chunks of coal? To her knowledge, no newspapers were reporting that families suffered without heat.

One of the girls, seven or eight years of age, stopped hunting to stare at Lauder. A seeing so deep that after a few moments, Lauder needed to grip the sides of the trunk to keep from toppling.

Mina found and dropped chunks of coal in each bucket before starting back.

The staring girl continued to stare. Lauder stood, unwrapped the blanket and held it out over the side of the wagon. The girl, her eyes even keener now, started forward, wind like a ghost walking beside her. She accepted the wool cautiously. As the wagon pulled away, the other two children rushed, and they dropped together on the frozen ground. Knees touching like sisters, they wrapped themselves in the blanket, sharing the remaining bit of Lauder and Mina's warmth still in the wool.

"I'm sorry, the blanket wasn't mine," Lauder said as Mina settled beside her again. "I felt so guilty and wanted to do something. I'll replace it." And before Mina could answer, "I came to live. To find myself." She would make Pine Ridge her Walden. And when her time ended, she would be healed enough to face the world again. Hadn't Thoreau gone into the woods to save himself? And hadn't he returned changed?

As the agency finally came into view, the wagon rolled for nearly a half mile along Sibley tents stretched across an open field. Smoke rose from countless fires and soldiers in long coats crowded around them or milled about in a commotion of activity and noise. Among them, other men plied cameras on tripods. In the distance, a second company drilled, their gun barrels and bayonets flashing in the fading sunlight. At the sight, Mina drew in sharp sucks of air. She had picked up her satchel after the children, but now she put it on the floor of the wagon and tried to hide it behind her feet. Her heels pushed the soft bag against the trunk, and she pull the hem of her skirt down so that only the toes of her beaded moccasins remained visible.

The massive buildup of weaponry, horses and men made Lauder shudder as well. The accumulation proved the army not only had the ability to slay every Lakota on the reservation, but down to a man, it was prepared and willing to do so. And she well knew this show of force had come at enormous cost to the government. For Father there would be more imported liqueurs, Cuban tobacco, and elephant-hide settees. When next she could, she would open her journal and write: *A thousand wolves have been brought to circle the warren. To fix the rabbits in a panic of obedience.*

Mina, trembling harder as the wagon rolled closer to the massive military presence, pressed her shoulder against Lauder's as they had while sharing the blanket. Her nearness created a wall of their backs, and wide-eyed, she peeked quickly over her shoulder to be certain neither relative watched. With shaking hands, she brought her satchel back to her lap and opened it hurriedly to draw out a small bundle wrapped loosely in green calico. She paused before opening the flaps of fabric and revealing a grass basket. "Take," she whispered.

"Me?" The basket, small enough to cup in Lauder's hands, and with its loose weaving, reminded her of a bird's nest. An old nest from the previous year and rejected by this year's brooders. A thing the gardener would rake onto a shovel and incinerate as yard waste.

Mina's shoulder pressed. "Please, take."

Please no, Lauder thought. I don't want that in my bag with my night shirt and intimate laces. It might carry mites or some other flea-like insect.

"Please." Mina's eyes filled, and she pointed at Lauder's case. Her voice still a whisper though the army added even more noise to the horse's clopping and the wagon's rumbling. "My mother."

Lauder tried refusal again. If the basket held such significance, why pass it to a near stranger? She tipped her head in Blackbird's direction. "Your aunt?"

"Please."

I don't want it, she kept from saying.

"Spirits do not rest," Mina said, "while their sacred objects are in the hands of thieves."

"Perhaps ... your chief? Red Cloud?"

"No time." Mina's eyes fixed on the basket as if listening to the object itself. Then without sound, only moving her lips. *Please.*

Goosebumps tracked across Lauder's shoulders. She saw not just the basket in Mina's hands, but the heart from earlier, blood running. She opened her satchel, not understanding, but feeling the absoluteness of what she must do. Afterall, the railroad and Father, and she as heir of her father's money lust, were an arm of the massed troops and the terror they brought Mina.

Lauder set the wrapped bundle carefully atop Babette's music box and the craniometer. Such a bizarre collection of objects. What did they all mean?

"White women's possessions are safe," Mina said. "Not torn away."

Refastening her traveling bag, Lauder wondered what gift she might give in return for the blanket she had passed to the children and the basket. She had not actually been gifted the basket, thankfully, though she had been gifted with being seen as a worthy keeper until Mina calmed enough to have it back. Still, wasn't it the custom with Indians to exchange gifts? She fingered the silk scarf around her neck. Blue in honor of Babette.

"Babette preferred blue," Mother so often said. As if the child, dead two decades, through her love of blue in every hue, proved a superiority Lauder could never match. Bragged of the dead child as if Babette's love of blue proved she, Mother, had birthed at least one worthy child.

As much as the color honored a sister Lauder would never know, she also loved the stars. They reminded her of the large armillary standing on a three-foot pedestal in Father's library. The armillary's nine rings depicted the Earth and its interplay with the planets and promised that, without variation, month after month, year after year, millennium after millennium, the heavenly bodies orbited in rotations discovered in the time of Galileo and Kepler. The armillary promised that despite all the appearances of chaos in the world, the universe had retained a set order for billions of years, was ordered now, and would always be so ordered.

Slowly, Lauder took the Oriental silk from her neck and, despite her coat and the lace collar on her dress, felt instant cold air claw at her neck. She handed the blue, studded with stars, to Mina.

Mina nodded in appreciation and wrapped the scarf around her neck. Her gaze dropped again on Lauder's case as though seeing through to the more valuable basket.

"I'll take care of it," Lauder said. "Until you're ready." Mina's fear for the nest of thatch seemed exaggerated, but newspapers reported attacks on Indian villages, the killing of even women and children, and the burning down of every lodge. Thus, destroying any object deemed unworthy of confiscation.

The wagon rolled on at the same slow pace down Pine Ridge Road. Lauder quivered with cold, huddled in on herself, her frozen hands, despite her gloves, covering her frozen ears. Mina hadn't spoken since giving the basket, and in her ensuing silence, the sad reasons for her having to give up the treasured item continued to trouble Lauder. White women's possessions are safe, she'd said. The comment heavy in its truthfulness. I've been chosen, Lauder told Babette, based on the color of my skin, not on the virtue of my soul.

Plants Corn stopped the wagon, and rank odors touched Lauder's nose. She had read Dickens and others who described the wretched poor in picturesque detail, but no novel had prepared her for this creature. She dragged her hands from her ears down to cover her mouth and nose. Breathed in the perfume of her soft kid gloves. The thing, a bear-like form on the ground, was slumped against a grey post. Surely a man, sunken in layers of ragged furs, his chin affixed in stupor to his chest. Ropes of long, snarled hair fell over his shoulders and face, leaving only a couple of inches on one cheek exposed. Chestnut as day-old coffee.

Blackbird shouted. The bear remained motionless and mute.

Mina stood as if to jump down again and approach him.

"No," Lauder grabbed her arm. "He's dangerous."

Blackbird called again, then spoke to Plants Corn.

"Your aunt knows him?" Lauder asked.

"He sits here," Mina answered, disappointment in her voice. "Therefore, he's one of the people."

"But look at him. Why did we stop?" Omaha surely had its vagrants and drunkards — though Lauder doubted any looked this bad — but the police kept them ushered into the bowels of the city, away from polite society. "Keep him away from me."

Mina's gaze dropped to Lauder's case.

"Please," Lauder said. It wasn't necessary to say more. She would protect the basket, and Mina would protect her from this creature.

After a few words to Plants Corn, though Lauder didn't know what Mina said, he shook the reins, and they rolled on.

Lauder turned several times to look back and make certain the entity, more an apparition, was not running down the road after them. She tried to settle her nerves by studying the buildings as they came abreast. After Rushville's chaos, she had feared what the agency might be like and was relieved to see the order: two trading posts, a post office, a harness shop, a hotel. Other buildings appeared in good condition, while still others looked as though they'd stood in the wind and beneath a bleaching sun for decades. Some with no signage looked bleak beside those sporting large lettering on wooden plaques. Men of both races wore civilian clothing, rode in buckboards or on horses. Soldiers at ease walked with their breaths puffing white in the cold. A brown skinned woman in a long calico dress and a blanket around her shoulders carried a large basket that appeared full of laundry.

Lauder dared not look at Mina, who in her nervousness, twisted and pulled on the ends of the fragile silk scarf, worrying them as if they were strips of leather. Was it just the army's huge presence that frightened her, or did the street, closed in on both sides feel like a trap?

Perhaps it was seeing the woman; a laundress now for the dirty clothing of whites.

At the far end of Pine Ridge Road, a small and lonely-looking church sat on a low hilltop. The sun, bleeding still lower in the west, cast a coral tinge over the whitewashing. Lauder swallowed, her throat dry. The agency was bookended by the vagrant on one side and the church on the other. Both filled her with foreboding. Growing up, she had learned to keep alert for impending danger. She had learned to read the lines around Mother's mouth and sense when Mother was about to say something hurtful — though Mother cut and chiseled her words down to as few syllables as possible. She had learned, too, to know when a snowstorm would arrive twenty-four hours later, drop six feet of snow; when the house at the end of the block would catch fire; when the last cook was about to spill grease that would burn her leg so severely she never returned to the house. Most importantly, she had learned to excuse herself from the library when the papers on Father's desk angered him, made him grind his teeth on his pipestem and land stern eyes across the room onto her.

Four

PLANTS CORN STOPPED the wagon again, this time in front of a one-story building. The sign over the door read: *Indian Agent.* Lauder, with her feet numb and her legs stiff with cold, no longer cared about her coat or skirt or how unladylike she presented herself. She dropped to the end of the rough wagon bed and scooted off.

Plants Corn, with Mina's help, unloaded the two trunks, and before Lauder had gotten her bearings, the wagon began pulling away, her scarf with its bright stars fluttering around Mina's neck. She wondered at how quickly the family fled — was Mina so afraid? — and continued to watch their retreat. Reaching the end of the road, Plants Corn stopped the wagon, climbed down, and half lifted, half dragged the wretched creature to the back. She watched still as Mina reached for the hapless elbow, helped pull the brute aboard, and lay him out. That reaching for what had scared Lauder stung like a slap of rejection and shattered what she had believed was a budding friendship. Despite all the ways they were the same, deep and broad distances separated them.

She turned away, stood alone on the windy street. People went about their business, but none were interested in her. She had expected a formal escort from Rushville, which hadn't happened. She had also expected a well-attended reception on her arrival at the agency:

adults and children gathered on the street, waiting for her with happy greetings. She shifted her hat into place, touched broken feathers no longer reaching a fashionable height, but sticking out like wayward horns. She would not lose her composure. She gripped her case, forced her tremulous knees and numb feet up the two steps to Agent Moyer's office. Freezing, she barely retained control of her body, but she had her books, her soul, and her hopes for redemption.

A dark-skinned man in a navy coat with a six-point badge on his chest, stepped so quickly in front of her they nearly collided. Indian Police or guard, he'd been sitting so still until that moment, she'd not noticed him until his lunge stopped her.

She took a frightened step back. "I'm here to see Agent Moyer."

He looked down on her. His eyes, even darker than his skin, held her fixed.

"It's all right," a man stepped through the office door. "I've got her."

Without a nod of greeting or word of apology for having frightened her, the Indian turned back to his cold chair.

"Welcome to Pine Ridge, ma'am," her savior said. He stood a foot taller than her, broad shouldered, and with hazel eyes that took her in.

Disappointed, Lauder thought the eyes said.

"You must be Miss Ellison."

"Yes, Miss Lauder Ellison."

He looked up the street after the receding wagon. "She didn't stay."

Having registered his disappointment on seeing her, she now saw his disappointment over Mina's leaving. "They were very anxious to depart." She wouldn't mention they'd picked up the indigent. "My instructions were clear: Visit Agent Moyer's office upon arrival. I'm sure she received the same instructions." Why the quick, harsh feelings toward Mina? Was it that she had not obeyed the rules? Or that she cared about the bum? Or was it that the tall man at Lauder's side, disappointed in her, was eager to see Mina?

The man's gaze lifted from Lauder's face to her crushed hat and back to her eyes. "Welcome to the agency. I'm Dak, right hand gopher to Agent Moyer."

Too cold and too nervous to care what a man named Dak or

gopher thought of her, she motioned to the door. "Agent Moyer must be inside."

"This way."

Leaving the cutting cold outside and stepping into the office, the room felt not just overly warm but thick with heat and cigar smoke. Smaller than she expected, the place held a roaring stove and two desks. The largest desk sat prominently in the center, facing the door. A man, certainly Agent Moyer, paying no attention to the fact she had entered, scratched his signature on what looked like a letter. He worked a cigar between his lips, then flicked the ashy end over a cast iron frying pan littered with cigar butts smoked and chewed to within an inch of their cheap lives. He dipped his pen and went on signing the next form or letter. Beneath his work, a long strip of brown paper covered the desktop. The very sort of paper the butcher used to wrap the roasts and legs of lamb Cook carried home in her basket.

Dak pointed to a chair in front of Agent Moyer's desk. "Miss, have a seat."

She wanted to insist she would stand until she was formally received but sit she must, or her shaking knees would put her on the floor. With her bag at her feet, she sat erect, waiting.

The office touted a clutter of violence. Rifles, upright in a frame, stood ready to be snatched at a moment's notice. The back wall screamed aggression as well: horns, antlers, moose paddles, and animal heads of every size. In the center, the head of a wild boar: a gaping mouth with razor-sharp yellow teeth reaching back to the dark maw of its throat. A long red tongue as thick as her forearm lulled over the side of its mouth, and yellow tusks scored from its jaws. The lower tusks, as long as eight inches, rose above the snout. Dull eyes aimed directly at her.

What sort of men could work happily under such butchery? Nowhere in the room lay a hint of grace: curtains, rugs, paintings, or books. Nowhere a photograph of a wife or child.

She tried to remain calm despite the day's disappointments coiling in her, and now the agent's continued rudeness. Not addressing her, only scratching his signature again, licking a dirty thumb for moisture, and flicking up the corner of the next sheet. Reading nothing of the papers he signed, lapping his stained thumb, dipping his pen, and signing. He had a round face with little ears. Or was it the plumpness of his face that made the ears seem small? Shine marked his receding hairline, the loss making an M pattern, though she knew he was only thirty-six. He chomped again on the rancid-smelling cigar. A mustache, badly in need of a barber, hung scraggly over the end of the cigar, covering his top lip and nearly the lower. He wore his suit coat with only the top button closed, hugging his throat.

Dak, who had taken a seat at the second desk pushed against a side wall, spoke louder than necessary. "He'll be right with you."

The comment, its volume obviously directed at Agent Moyer, told her the one named Dak or gopher or handsome possessed enough manners to recognize Agent Moyer's lack of them.

Pale and with a pinched, nervous look around the eyes, Agent Moyer continued his signing. His mouth full of cigar and his self-important scowl, said he had no time for the bother of a woman. He'd signed one of the instructional letters she had received, so he well knew she was to arrive today, and he'd certainly been behind Plants Corn and the old wagon rather than a comfortable, formal, and secure passage for her. Now this rudeness: another affront. Or did he suppose his flurried scratching somehow impressed her, and so he'd go on, demonstrating his importance? General Brooke had spoken of the agent's letter writing, how the man feared for his life, and continuously begged Washington for troops. This unimpressive man, and yet his office gave him the power to wield incredible influence, including bringing in thousands of troops.

At his desk, Dak sat in profile and was hopefully too busy to notice her furtive glances. His jaw held a late afternoon shadow, but in contrast to Agent Moyer, he looked well-groomed. Father and his ilk all wore mustaches, goatees, or mutton chops on their fleshy faces. Dak's face wasn't just lean and shaved that morning, his tan skin proved he spent more hours under sunlight than lamplight. She guessed him a few years older than herself, and something else. She needed a moment and caught the motion of his shoulder muscles moving under his shirt when he pulled open a drawer with hands strong and accustomed to physical labor. She knew then what unsettled her. He was an outside man. She came from a world of inside men who paid workers to garden and drive their carriages. Dak spent more time outdoors doing physical labor than at a desk wielding a pen. He was an imposter.

"Sir," Dak turned to Agent Moyer, restating the obvious. "Miss Ellison has arrived." At Agent Moyer's mutter, he went on, "Miss Ell--ison, sent to us under the command of General Brooke."

Agent Moyer appeared pulled from a trance. He flicked fresh ash from his cigar into the frying pan. "Yes, yes, General Brooke."

"She won't last."

The voice, coming from a shadowed corner behind her, made her jump. A man, one casual arm thrown over the back of his chair, eyed her. Older than Dak with hints of silver hair kissing his temples, he, too, was handsome. But his eyes held a bright glint with the self-satisfied air she had seen in the suitors her parents invited to the house. An assumption that his being male, she would naturally swoon over him. And, his having waited and watched her for long moments before making himself known, was also rude. "Good afternoon," she managed.

Agent Moyer slapped a hand on the papers he'd signed and growled at the man. "General Brooke needs them thieves caught. Find the red devils."

Dak rose and took the sheets Agent Moyer held thrust in the air. "It could have been anyone," he said. "There's no proof it was Lakota. This place is crawling with sight-seekers, reporters, soldiers, do-gooders."

Agent Moyer scowled. An expression etching his face, as if to demand who but Lakota would steal from him. Or why was there a woman in his office, or why hadn't Dak already disposed of said woman?

"Miss Ellison," Dak said for the third time.

"Ellison," Agent Moyer coughed gray smoke.

"A friend of General Brooke?" the man in the corner asked.

"I'm sorry," she turned, "I didn't catch your name."

He stood finally, approached with spurs on his boots tingling, and reached for her hand. "Sgt. Atlock."

He was tall, trim, and looked official in his army shirt. A belt of shiny bullets hung low on his hips and all but framed his groin. She drew her gaze quickly back to his face. Despite his lack of manners, his being well-armed and capable-looking helped ease some of the tension

Lauder had felt since stepping off the train in Rushville. Smiling, she gently pulled her hand from his grasp.

"Expected two," Sgt. Atlock said. "A squaw, but we weren't expecting nothing like you."

Agent Moyer's eyebrows flared. "Another redskin on my reservation?"

"She's qualified," Dak said. "Needed."

Agent Moyer glowered. "Bringing in more? I never signed nothing like that."

Dak kept his eyes on the papers before him. "The form must have gone out before you arrived."

Sgt. Atlock leaned against the corner of Agent Moyer's desk, crossed his arms over his chest, and stared at Lauder. Had he moved to that location to get a better look at her, or so she would have a better look at him? If it were the latter, she didn't mind. Between him and Dak, South Dakota men could make her stay a whole lot more enjoyable.

"Might be," Agent Moyer's attention finally settled on Lauder, "General Brooke don't understand the situation. It ain't certain how long I'll have a need for you."

Lauder shifted in her chair, her hopes dropping.

"Congress plans to close reservation schools," Agent Moyer said. "Put 'em where they can be taught proper. Boarding schools."

"Close the schools?"

Dak opened a second drawer, removed nothing, and shut it with more force than necessary.

"'Fore they close the doors," Agent Moyer continued, "there is a thing I need. That be a name for each one. Not some gibberish. A name a man can say. Christian."

"I'm not sure I understand."

"A census. Every ward."

"Of course." She nodded, wondering why upper-level students did not already have Christian names he could say? Wasn't that done when a child first began school? Most troubling was the possibility of the school closing. She had escaped Omaha, survived the journey from Rushville, she was exhausted, and she wasn't boarding a train back. Her heart began to drum, the boar on the wall leered down at her, pinned her, and made her heart drum louder. The noise growing in her ears. She had only ever seen pictures of wild boars, yet the night before General Brooke visited the house, while she sat reading in Father's library....

...the walls of the agent's office slid back and away.

The clock chimed two a.m. in Father's library, and the last of the evening's coals shifted behind the ornate fireplace grate. Reading alone and late into the night normally filled Lauder with pleasure. Books opened onto a world vaster than her otherwise safe life with her parents, servants, and students in her classroom squirming with disinterest.

Tonight's reading wasn't helping. The worst had happened. The day's post had brought the latest edition of the *American Historical Journal,* and there was her plagiarized article. "No!" She had confessed to her plagiarism weeks ago, writing a long letter of retraction and apology to the editorial staff the moment she received notification of its acceptance. She had only pulled the ruse after they'd refused half a dozen legitimate articles. More, always with the same form letter: "We regret to inform you…" and the closing, "thank you for your efforts."

She never submitted efforts; she submitted highly researched articles. The rejections made her lament what males, their hair slicked back from their horsey faces, decided her expertise wasn't worthy of publication. That she wasn't good enough. She knew what lay behind her rejections: her sex. The journal editors did not care what a female had to say. Their magazine was above the banal mentality of women.

She had acted to prove that point. And the journal had published the article. Not a word of it original. Not a word hers. Father could never know. How many of his contemporaries had already read the monthly, realized they had read whole paragraphs before, and were considering how they would broach the subject with Father?

She lifted her book again. One more page. She would try to settle her nerves and then get some sleep. How many times had she read *Walden?* Was this the third? The fourth? Thoreau's words had the power to reshape the world in her mind, and at the moment, she needed nothing more.

Her index finger caught the corner of the next sheet and turned.

A coarse black string slid down the page. The filament as startling as if it were a roach scurrying from light. Then the alarm of the eight-inch thing moving from the page into her lap. She froze. What was it? A hair from a buffalo, the stiff whisker of a wolf or wild boar? The possibilities sent shivers racing up her arms. How had the offense found its way into the house, let alone the library and into one of her favorite books?

Five

IN AGENT MOYER's office, the three men studied Lauder as though she had fainted while they watched and each helplessly waited for her to recover.

"You all right?" Dak asked.

"Exhausted." She wanted to disappear. How long had she been away, staring into space? "I'm quite all right." She dared not look at the boar again, the sight of which had transported her. The first time she flew — how else to think of the bouts where she was lifted from one place to the next like a wind-blown leaf the experience frightened her. That first time, she had been working on a Civil War battlefield map with Father, concentrating, shutting out all else but the graphic in front of her, her pencil shading in a hillside. Suddenly, considering the dead, her heart began rapping against the walls of her chest, drumming harder until she felt light-headed, and then … she was on that hillside slick with blood and torn bodies.

"Agent Moyer," the words rushed, and she prayed her face wasn't flaming with embarrassment, "I'm also here to act as your personal recorder." She hadn't planned to lie, but if the school closed, she needed a reason for being allowed to stay.

"Personal recorder?" A twitch of his top lip. The cigar following in kind.

"These are especially troubling times." She had already gotten herself in over her head. "Varied accounts of the uprisings and dancing come from every sector. General Brooke believes a non-military observer, someone without a newspaper affiliation and bias would be useful." She sounded more the liar with each word.

"Washington," Agent Moyer nodded at the other two men. "I knew they'd want my papers."

"Even official papers," she rushed on, "are far from the full story of a man's valor."

Each man held a different expression: Dak's doubting, Sgt. Atlock's accepting, but Agent Moyer's a mix of surprise and worry. The bags under his tired eyes held dusk, but his curiosity was piqued.

She motioned to the butcher paper. "General Brooke, while a guest of my father, enjoyed the maps Father displayed. He'll be interested in yours, as well."

"You hear, men? My maps. General Brooke."

She wanted safely out of the office before she hung herself yet again with more lies. Would she never learn her lesson? "My role will be twofold," there was no stopping now, the horse had bolted, "teaching, and should the school close, documenting your efforts and many achievements."

Stretching to his full five-and-a-half-foot stature, Agent Moyer punched two fingers onto the butcher paper and spoke in Sgt. Atlock's direction. "My maps'll be official government records."

What could Lauder do but stick to her story? "Maps are prized by historians. My father and I are students of cartography."

Agent Moyer's brow twitched quizzically.

This time at Dak, who turned slightly, amusement in his eyes. "Map making, Sir."

Her comment would have angered Father, who thought himself a professional and she a mere pupil of cartography. And she wasn't sure if Dak wanted to laugh at Agent Moyer or her? Agent Moyer for his part may have questioned the meaning of cartography, or just as likely questioned the possibility of a woman being familiar with the word.

"I've been to medical college," Agent Moyer said and leaned over the butcher's wrap before any questions were raised about why he wasn't currently practicing medicine, or how the education he touted applied to the current conversation. "I expect General Brooke will be along to look."

Lauder stood, approached the desk. He carried the same pride as Father when displaying his maps, considering himself an authority, even quasi-proprietor over the territory he rendered in ink.

"Right here," he rapped, "dancing. Planning attacks, thinking we ain't watching, ain't mapping. Not being schooled in war, Miss Ellison, there's a term you ain't likely heard." He paused. "Trojan horse."

Had he read about the Greeks and their attack on Troy or heard the term in passing? She wasn't sure it applied to the current situation, but standing in the too-warm office in her coat and capette and with her broken hat, she was in no position to challenge. She dared not ask or even lift her eyes from his map.

Sgt. Atlock returned to his chair, pulling it from the corner to one of the two windows. The last rays of the sinking sun cast a sheen around his head. He stretched his right leg out to its full extent, then his left, and languidly crossed his ankles as he settled back, all but reclining in the straight-backed chair, his long body on full display. "We've been waiting half the afternoon for you to show up." His voice rolled down his torso. "Ain't no hurrying a redskin. Blood slow as slugs."

Lauder fought to maintain a pleasant expression, though the pain of biting her tongue was wrenching. Waiting half the afternoon? All of them had been leisurely waiting in their warm office, and not one of them had bothered to come for her?

Spittal glistened as Agent Moyer's lips moved. "My records, hey?"

"I'm sure," Lauder said, "you're in need of an unbiased, truthful account of your fine work. The newspaper reporters out there," she nodded toward the front windows, "answer to bosses. Military correspondents to their superiors. I'll answer only to you."

"My own correspondent?" A dark flake of ash dropped from his cigar, settled onto the butcher paper. He thumbed it flat. "Dak here helps with the whatnots, but he ain't a secretary. Men around here are busy."

"You ain't a spy for Brooke?" Sgt. Atlock asked.

Lauder hoped her smile looked genuine. "Whyever would General Brooke wish for a spy?"

"I wrote a full report on the robbery," Agent Moyer replied. "He don't blame me?"

"I've no idea." She heard tapping, realized it was her own foot, and stopped. "General Brooke's correspondences are confidential, and he demands the same of our arrangement. It's not to be spoken of." She included each man with a nod around. "You aren't to mention my work even to him."

A chuckle from Sgt. Atlock. "Wouldn't never know redskins broke in and wiped the place clean. I hear Dak here, patched up the damage real nice for you."

Dak ignored the mention of his name and continued reading the papers on his desk, but Agent Moyer bent lower over his map. "Private lodgings, General Brooke's orders."

"The place of a robbery?" she asked.

The night General Brooke drank port in Father's library and agreed to write a letter recommending her for one of the abandoned teaching posts, she had asked him to arrange private lodgings. But the site of a break-in? And given the wretched man for whom Plants Corn had stopped the wagon, maybe she shouldn't be alone. "I'll be safe?"

"More troops here now," Agent Moyer puffed, "than fought in the whole god-damned war against the Mexicans."

Lauder's day thus far had been a series of emotional and exhausting squalls. Now, still in her coat and hat, the thick heat from the stove added to that exhaustion. "If I could," she said, "I'd like to be shown to my accommodations." She wanted to face them straightaway, find something to eat, change into more comfortable clothing, and work on her journals. She had several impressions she planned to record before retiring, and if she found the strength, she would also write General Brooke. The morning was soon enough to tour the school and meet the headmistress.

"You'll start with the ghost dancing," Agent Moyer said. "Write how savages are planning war."

Dak stirred.

"Perhaps tomorrow," Lauder suggested. "If I could only—"

"Ones we already conquered turning wild again."

She needed to gather herself, finish her ruse, and get away. "Agent Moyer, the Ghost Dancing would be an excellent place to start. My composition notebooks are deep in a trunk outside. Perhaps tomorrow—"

"Write," Agent Moyer said, "how they threaten the safety of every white man, woman, and child." He reached over the frying pan and flicked his cigar. Ashes dropped onto the stew.

Lauder's stomach rolled.

"The land belongs to white men now," Agent Moyer continued. "Men who'll plow and plant like God intended."

Sgt. Atlock remained stretched out, his long body asking for attention. "She's too pretty to be a writer."

His disparaging the word writer carried to Lauder's ear the barb of a woman wannabe. A female supposing she has something worth saying. She coached herself; don't let him goad you into saying something you'll regret. "I've been told I'm too attractive for many things." She smiled. "Even too attractive to suffer fools."

Sgt. Atlock was a predatory fox grooming his coat, and Agent Moyer too full of pomp, though it did not mask his insecurity. But Dak? What could be said of him? He disapproved of the other two men just as he disapproved of her.

Agent Moyer waved a hand in Dak's direction. "Get my map of the agency." When Dak retrieved the map from amongst several rolled and leaned in a corner, the agent flung the sheet across his desk, covering the map of the reservation.

The topographic symbols were so amateurishly drawn, they looked to Lauder like the efforts of a child. "Your work, Sir?"

Dak glanced at her, warning in his eyes.

The map crunched under Agent Moyer's rapping. "Mess hall down here. School here." He went on, pointing out buildings Lauder had seen when coming up the road and could see now through the windows. "You'll be staying here." A single sharp tap. "Right here."

The lopsided square he'd drawn indicated a spot nearly directly across Pine Ridge Road. From where Lauder stood, she imagined that with a good slingshot she could send a stone hurling to the door. But rather than pointing out the window, the new agent would have her attention on his ill-drawn map.

"The varmints didn't get any guns," he said. "You write that nice and clear. No guns stolen from Agent Moyer."

Shadow spread up the desk and over the map. A man in a battered hat with a blanket around his shoulders peered in the closest window. The guard who had all but accosted Lauder was nowhere to be seen.

Agent Moyer yanked open a top desk drawer and pulled out a pistol. "Who the hell?" he barked at Dak.

"Unarmed." Dak pushed back his chair, the four legs scraping the plank flooring. His hands splayed the air in a calming gesture. "The man's a friendly."

"Wanting more food?" Agent Moyer cussed. "Thinking I'm fool enough to increase rations? He's likely killed his cow."

Dak crossed to the door, his hand on the doorknob. "They're starving. They'd butcher trees if their children could eat them."

"Write," Agent Moyer looked directly at Lauder, "how they'll eat their only cow. Now you tell me, how they going to have a spring calf without a cow."

"But if their children are starving today," Lauder suggested, "there'll be no one to feed in the spring."

Agent Moyer looked to Dak. "What's he want?"

"He came yesterday," Dak said. "He's asking permission to trade a horse with his brother."

"Never saw the bastard before."

"You were visiting the grumper, Sir."

The agent's small ears turned an angry red. "Hell, I can't even shit in peace without a damned redskin needing me."

"If two grown men," Lauder began, "wish to—"

"Wards!" Agent Moyer cut her off. Bright spittle flew past the wet end of his cigar. "Wards. Write that down. Crazy redskins fighting the government at every turn."

Over the week in preparation for coming, and to distract herself from her reason for needing to do so, Lauder spent every free hour reading anything she could find on the Sioux. She learned the tribes had been considered intelligent, responsible, and well enough educated in economics to sign treaties that cost them millions of acres of land. But now, men like Plants Corn were considered too stupid to trade a horse?

The man at the window pulled back as Dak stepped out and greeted him. They stood talking, wind ruffling the blanket and Dak's hair, hatless, as well as the sleeves of his shirt, coatless. He is the man who actually runs the office, Lauder decided. She couldn't hear well enough to make out the words, only Dak's low and friendly tone. Respectful of the man being refused an audience with Agent Moyer.

"Tell him I'm busy," Agent Moyer shouted from behind his desk, his gun still in his hand. "Come back tomorrow." He turned to Sgt. Atlock, "That one, he a dancer? I ain't letting no dancers trade horses."

Seargent Atlock sat up straight, tipped back his chair, and peered through the window. "That old goat? Dance?"

"The messiah craze." Agent Moyer returned his gun to the drawer, rolled the top map, and referred again to the one beneath. "Atlock found them Ghost Dancing here."

Lauder turned. "You're a scout?"

"Finest around."

She wondered about the stories he could tell. And as Dak shook hands with the petitioner outside, she wondered about his stories.

"Miss Ellison," Sgt. Atlock said when the Lakota had left and Dak returned, "I'll show you to your cabin." He started as if he meant to stand, but stopped. "Them your trunks out there?"

"I have two."

"Ain't them too big for you?"

She hesitated, exhaustion rolling over her shoulders again, heavier this time. Was he joking, or was he actually suggesting she ought to carry her own luggage?

His eyes narrowed. "You brought crates you can't handle?"

Ought she give him a good look at the sharp end of her hat pin?

"I'll take her over." Dak lifted his coat and hat from a peg on the wall. "And her trunks."

Sgt. Atlock settled back into his chair. "Atta boy," he said to Dak, a man every bit his size.

Six

WALKING ACROSS PINE Ridge Road with Dak, Lauder felt a growing uneasiness. Night was descending rapidly, as if the world were lidding, and she was about to be left alone. She carried her satchel, while Dak carried the first of her trunks propped on one shoulder. She had not considered the possibility of being expected to haul her own trunks. Nor had any member of her household expected such a thing. "Thank you."

"Ma'am."

One word.

Behind them, Agent Moyer locked the office door, and he and Sgt. Atlock started off in the direction of the hotel.

"Will they wait for you?"

"For dinner?" Dak had left his heavy coat unbuttoned for the short distance, though he wore his hat and gloves. "I'll eat at home."

"She's waiting for you?"

"She's keeping supper warm."

Clutching her satchel, Lauder used the other hand to keep her skirt hem off the icy, rutted road. Of course, he's married, she told Babette. Look at him. Which was just as well. He was cold as an apple fresh from the cellar and not the least bit interested in her. And I'm not interested in him; I didn't come to further complicate my life.

"Your name's unusual. I've not heard Dak before."

He shifted the chest. "Family bible says Dakota. Had three brothers who butchered it."

He spoke of brothers in the past tense, and she wouldn't pursue that line of questioning. A conversation about lost siblings was too heavy. "You don't mind your name?"

"Dak Thomas? Never thought to mind." They stepped over a wide wagon rut, then a second. "Lauder's one I haven't heard."

"It's a butchering of two names. My mother's name is Laura, my father's Sander. I think it was their attempt at a treaty." She paused. "More likely, the name was given as a punishment for my being born at all. Bad timing and then female."

Dak gave her a sidelong glance.

"Well, it isn't pretty," she added.

"That's a lot of fuss over a name."

"I mean, it's odd. Not male or female. It's certainly not feminine like… Babette."

"Babette? A showgirl?"

"Really? You think Babette sounds like a showgirl?"

He didn't answer. He probably thought her yammering, and she resisted saying anything more as they finished crossing. They stepped onto the wooden planks elevating them from the dirty road, and she stood in front of what would be her lodgings. Drab, weathered, and disappointing. She tried to relax by running a gloved hand along the seal fur trimming on her capette. She was Lauder Ellison, a lady. "Sgt. Atlock said you waited half the afternoon for my arrival." He looked quizzically at her, but she determined to press on. Her facts needed to be accurate before she wrote complaints to General Brooke. "Yet no one came to escort me?"

Just below his hat, two small lines scored between his eyes. "I sent Plants Corn."

"You?"

"I trust him more than anyone around here."

"Well—"

"I figured it best for his niece. She's never seen my face and an army escort…hell, that would have scared her."

Embarrassment flushed Lauder's cheeks, and she was relieved that in the descending darkness, he couldn't see the blush. Given the way Mina reacted to the soldiers, Dak had been right to send her uncle. A kindness to Mina, but what about her? She pushed the thought away. Dak had done the wise thing. Even sending a second convoy for her would have frightened Mina, and the two of them would never have gotten acquainted.

He set her trunk down, pulled a key from his coat pocket, and opened the door into a space so utterly dark she had no sense of its dimensions. Her heart hammered against her ribs.

"Give me a sec." He struck a match from a tin case in his breast pocket and went inside.

When light from two lanterns showed the way, Lauder stepped through. One room, small and cold. Primitive. So sparsely furnished it was nearly uninhabitable. A coal stove matched the one in Agent Moyer's office and vented with a large pipe snaking up through the ceiling. She walked a few steps in, keeping her back to Dak to hide the dismay on her face. Her fingers trailed over the corner of a desk, the back of a chair, neither piece with so much as a carved scroll on a leg. A narrow bed and a four-drawer dresser with a mirror just as plain. She swallowed on seeing a basin bowl and pitcher. "No running water?"

"Pump's out back. Grumper's a bit farther." He pulled her trunk to the back wall. "If that's your preference, don't forget your lantern. The way ain't lit."

The air in her lungs caught. He had used the word grumper earlier. "Do you mean I'm to—"

Hell, he thought. What does a lady from Omaha call a shit hole?

She found breath. "There's no water closet?" Another breath. "Perhaps in the hotel?" She had never used a horrid, outside facility, though once at a school picnic in a park, she had opened a door on one. The smell alone made her nearly pass out. A rotting wooden frame over a hole in the ground. Spiders and wood roaches. She had slammed the door.

"There's also a pot under your bed."

Stunned, she sank onto the bed with its dark, army-issued blankets, and shook her head. What about bathing? Had Father thought of these things? Mother must have; she had been pink with anger on hearing a daughter of hers would join "natives." "The things you'll see," she said. "And you, with your susceptible temperament. You won't be able to endure."

Mother was right, Lauder thought. I can't stay here. This cell couldn't be her quarters. What had she done? She was an educated woman but entirely unprepared for this world, where one used a… grumper.

"Women can be hired for your laundry," Dak said, "but your face tells me you'll not be here long enough to soil a pair of knickers."

She glared.

"Sorry. Didn't mean disrespect."

She was disappointing him. Disappointing herself. "However mean your life," she said softly, "meet it and live it; do not shun it and call it hard names. The setting sun is reflected from the windows of the almshouse as brightly as from the rich man's abode."

Dak's eyes questioned.

"Thoreau."

"You telling me I do need to lug in that second trunk?"

"I'll help."

He lifted a hand signaling she was to stay there and tossed the key he'd used onto the desk as if the cursed thing burned his pocket. He stepped out, leaving the door open.

She bit the inside of her cheek. She wouldn't shed a single tear. Exhaustion would let her sleep the night, and in the morning with the sun shining again, everything would be better.

Even with the door left wide, the room felt suddenly crowded and closed as a tomb. Her heart squeezed, and she rushed for the door just as Dak stepped from the darkness and back inside.

He grunted under the weight of her trunk. "You brought gold bars?"

"Books to share with my students." She ignored the surprised look on his face. "You're sure I'm safe here?"

"That stick of lumber in the corner, keep it across the door. You'll be safe enough."

Enough? A relative safety?

Dak put the second trunk along the back wall beside the first and rolled his neck in relief. He squatted at the stove and opened the small door to where he had laid crumbled paper, bits of tree bark, and kindling. The whole fashioned like a tiny teepee. He lit a match, held it between his fingers to the paper, then tossed the stick in. "Won't be long, the place'll heat right up."

A stove she must keep burning? She hugged her arms close to her body and sank again onto the bed. "It's cold. Someone should have lit that fire earlier."

Dak said nothing. He needed a teacher, not someone thinking a military escort should have been sent to fetch her and an underling have warmed her room. Wasted a stove full of coal to spare her ten minutes of discomfort. What game did General Brooke play? She was something to look at, but he didn't need a stunner. The school needed a mule who, for the last decade, hadn't had the guts to look in a mirror. Not a debutant on holiday. He slid open the air vent beneath the combustibles. "There's some getting used to coal stoves and keeping them lit. A fire needs air."

Lauder moved to look over his shoulder as he demonstrated a lever.

"This vent is your regulator."

As the paper at the bottom crackled and the bark began to curl, he stood, unfolding into the air. She wouldn't let his closeness and looks unnerve her. "Now you just dump coal on the top," she said, "and shut the door. I've got it from here."

"The fire needs to be plenty hot. We'll give it a few minutes before adding coal."

She knew Cook never left the stove door open. An open door prevented cakes and pies from baking. She didn't wish to sound superior, but if Dak was testing her, she didn't want to appear the fool. "Close the door. Everything will heat faster."

"A fire needs air," he repeated, slower this time. He'd laugh if he wasn't afraid for her. "Once it's going, you can feed enough air in from the bottom."

She sensed disquiet in the set of his shoulders and in the stance of his long legs. Disappointment or pity? And what more to say to this man, alone with her in her sleeping quarters? "It's very clean." The place was at least that. "Thank you for fixing it up for me."

"There was a second window." He lifted a hand, his thumb pointing. "A couple of older boys from the school helped me cover the whole thing, putting a second wall over the first. Snug the place up."

She would miss the window.

"That being north and with winds coming down from Canada, you'll be glad of the extra insulation."

"Agent Moyer is quite concerned about the thieves who broke in."

Agent Moyer. Her putting the title in front of the name every time she said it made him itch. Same as her thinking he'd fixed up the place specifically for her. He hadn't. Wasn't anything wrong with her liking the room, but thinking he'd done it just for her wasn't the whole of it. He'd also needed to cover up the terrible truth.

"The thieves broke through the absent window?" she asked.

He pulled off his gloves, shoved the tops into a back pocket. Why did she need to be doubly sure of every detail? "You planning to write about the robbery? Best leave it alone."

She had no plans to seek publication again, but private writing was just that: private. "Mr. Thomas, I appreciate your concern, but I'll write as I wish."

He'd never seen eyes so blue. She was innocent, thinking Brooke had shown her some kind of favor in giving her a teaching position. He'd sent her to hell. "The window was torn clear out. Frame and all."

She didn't care a wit about his stupid wall, but what else to say? "A whole new wall?"

"The place wasn't built for people."

She would ask no more questions. Carrying on a conversation with Babette from a realm away was easier than doing so with this man standing in front of her.

He added more kindling to the growing fire. Easiest to keep his back to her. Maybe she was right, and he ought to have started the stove hours ago and avoided being stuck there nursing flames. She was naïve and wouldn't last, but he'd see her sent home alive, not frozen in a box. Having to replace her though, admitting another teacher had left, drew attention to the school, threatened it. "Get tough," he wanted to tell her, but there wasn't a need. Living here would harden her up quick. He couldn't stop that, but all the same, he was sorry for her. Women weren't built for surviving the West. They broke too easily. His mother and grandmother were proof enough.

He eyed the trunks he'd lugged in for her. The leather straps, like belly straps on a saddle, were cinched tight. The leather new and unyielding. Someone stronger than her had jammed the strips in through the buckles and forced the prongs into fresh holes. "You opened those since you left home?"

Father's driver had brought the trap from the carriage house. He'd come to her room and carried her trunks down and out. He was the one who must have fastened the buckles, but they were only buckles. She needed to prove she wasn't entirely helpless and bent down to the first strap. Unyielding. She knelt, refusing to admit defeat, and tried again. "I've opened them before," a lie, "but my hands and the leather are cold. They'll warm." If need be, the blasted leather could be cut with the first knife she found.

"Ma'am." He ignored her refusal, dropped to one knee beside her, and tugged at the hard leather. He wanted to scold her as had Atlock. You brought luggage you can't open?

Lauder watched his strong fingers knead and work out the leather, telling her she couldn't have opened them even with a knife. She stood. Thus far, she was failing the entire endeavor and felt like cursing or weeping. She wanted him gone so she could sleep. She needed hours of slumber to dull the edges of this new and frightful world. In the morning, she told herself again, everything will be better.

Her trunks were carried in, opened, and the fire was lit. She needed nothing more from the man. "Thank you," she said. "I can manage from here."

"The commissary is a bit past the hotel. You ought to go now. They're apt to close up."

Lauder's stomach clenched with hunger, but she didn't feel confident enough to step into the darkness alone. "Are Sgt. Atlock and Agent Moyer there?"

"Wouldn't count on it. Most nights they eat at the hotel." He watched her hesitation. "Could be a couple of the other teachers are there. You could introduce yourself."

"Mrs. Streamist?"

"She eats at home."

"Mina?" If Mina were there, Lauder would go.

"She'll have commissary rights, but my guess is she's eating with her aunt and uncle."

"Who do not have commissary rights?" She glanced at the sole remaining window. She still trembled remembering the Indian guard at Agent Moyer's door. Suppose more like him roamed in the dark? And there'd been the horrid creature at the end of the road. "You and I," she swallowed, a shoulder shrugging as if a refusal wouldn't really matter, "we could go."

"Sorry, I need to get home."

"There's no reason to be sorry."

He'd give her credit for the pluck, though it wouldn't be enough. "I could walk you down." A full two hours of farm chores waited: cows needed milking, steers needed hay pitched, pigs and chickens needed grain, and everything needed water. Grandma, too, would be at the window, wringing her hands, waiting for a horse to come riding down the lane, praying he's the man in the saddle. "I could make introductions, but then, I'd best head home. Chores waiting."

The room was still too cold to remove her coat, but the fire helped. "How far away are those important chores?"

"Two miles. Give or take one."

"Then you'd better get going."

"Atlock is Moyer's hired gun," Dak said, his gaze steady. "Stay away from him."

The warning and quick turn in their conversation surprised Lauder. "I will associate with whomever—"

"He's a rake. Supplies whiskey to the Lakota."

"Isn't that against the law?"

"Laws out here are for those who bother keeping them. There aren't enough tin badges to round up land grabbers and murderers. Not much interest in someone selling whiskey."

She lifted a hand for the reassurance of her scarf. Absent. "But

Agent Moyer? He must know what's going on, and he doesn't see the situation as serious?"

"If he isn't looking, he isn't seeing."

"Why isn't he looking?"

She was something to rest his eyes on. "Every drunken Lakota can be held up as proof the people aren't worthy of keeping their land or of the annuities they receive. Treaties signed or not. Moyer also likes his spy walking around their camps. His eyes open to anything needing reported. Especially government property."

"You surprise me, Mr. Thomas, you don't seem interested in the thieves being caught."

"You been warned about Atlock."

She removed her gloves, flattened them one beside the other atop the dresser. Sgt. Atlock had sunned himself in the window, but she could handle his type. "Thank you for your concern. I'm quite sure, however, that I can take care of myself."

From the corner of an eye, Dak watched as she removed her hat, a contraption half the size of a bushel basket with feathers sticking out like arrows. Her shoes on the other hand were no bigger than bread buns and the leather thin. "I hope one of those trunks contains a decent pair of boots. The temps here can spend a month at minus thirty, forty."

She feigned concern about where best to keep her hat. Men still wrote accounts of a recent infamous blizzard. Was it two, perhaps three years back?

"Children's blizzard," he said. "Two years ago. Killed over five hundred."

"My warmest things are being sent," she lied.

"You got a third trunk coming?"

She pursed her lips. "Perhaps I will write about the break-in. Agent Moyer certainly considers the loss of goods a major crime."

Dak took a small shovel from the scuttle, shoved it into the hard chunks of coal. "Moyer hadn't been here a month when the break-in happened. He's worried about how that looks. His reputation."

"How much was taken?"

"The main commissary is a quarter mile up." He looked around, tamped down the sorrow he felt every time he stepped into the place. "In here, he kept a private little storehouse for himself. Bribes for others."

"You don't like the man, and you're disrespectful of the office."

"Agents come in every stripe," Dak said. She was afraid and had no understanding of the agency. There wasn't a reason for him to say more.

Lauder paced and regretted having spoken so frankly. What was wrong with her? Dak, however, had been gentleman enough to say little. "Let's pray Sgt. Atlock finds the thieves. I don't want them breaking in again."

He shook a light layer of coal across the fire. "They're long gone."

"How can you be certain? You don't know who they are."

He nodded at her hat on the dresser top. "You got anything better?"

"First my shoes and now my hat."

"That hat does nothing but draw attention you don't need. Tomorrow, one of the traders can fit you."

Kind one moment, brash the next. "What sort of hat do you suggest?"

"Something that covers your head, not just your topknot."

She touched her hair. Nurse would laugh at the coiffure being referred to as a topknot. "I'll see to my clothing, Mr. Thomas. Perhaps you know when I'm to start teaching."

"Tomorrow."

The straps on her trunk of books thankfully hung free. Despite her fatigue, she needed to come up with lesson plans yet that evening. "Of course, though I hadn't thought so soon."

"You won't be needing those." His gaze followed hers to the trunk. "Not sure many of your students speak English."

"Then how can I teach them?" This posed another obstacle for which she was woefully unprepared. "After years in school, why do they not understand and speak English?"

"You have the littlest ones," Dak said. "First years."

Her breath drew in. "There's been a mistake, I teach high school literature."

He sifted on more coal. "Five- and six-year-olds."

Lauder crossed her arms, clutched tight. She taught high-school literature. Dak hadn't made the announcement with any hint of malice, but he also hadn't given any hint that her assignment could be changed. Being assigned the youngest constituted a professional slap. Coming to Pine Ridge she'd also fled classrooms where assigning the great classics met with students rolling their eyes, as if the masterpieces were better suited for their grandparents? She had looked forward to native students who'd be enthralled by those same texts and her learned discussions. Was she being punished because General Brooke appointed her, and she had not gone through proper channels as had Mina?

"Vocabulary, numbers," he said. "You'll get the hang of it."

"That, Mr. Thomas, is my entire orientation? Vocabulary and numbers?" And her books? Abandoning the classics was abandoning her foundation. Only temporarily, she promised herself. "I'll teach where I'm needed. This explains why Agent Moyer asked me to assign names. The children are relatively new to the school, and the previous teacher must not have taken the time to assign names."

"No rush," Dak said. "They're partial to their names."

Again, she wondered what Agent Moyer would say to Dak's attitude. She glanced at the bed wishing she could stretch out, close her eyes, and think, but she was a lady and he a man. She would do nothing suggestive. "Was it Agent Moyer who decided on my placement?"

"The headmistress," Dak answered. "Mrs. Streamist." That answer was close enough to the truth. And now that he'd met her, he felt certain she'd be good for the little ones. Quiet voice, something pleasant to look at, not a wart on her face. "If you have a problem, I'm usually in Moyer's office."

"If I have a problem, I'll discuss it with the headmistress." If there was nothing to be done about her low placement, still she had other reasons for coming to the reservation. Though Dak could answer one question. "Mina…," she concentrated a moment on relaxing her throat, "what grade will she teach?"

"Older ones."

Her pride was wounded, but she agreed Mina should have older students. Mina knew Lakota language and culture. Though, of course, language and culture were to be schooled out of the students.

"Mrs. Streamist is a bit," Dak rubbed the back of his neck as if he could scrub off an irritation, "forgetful. She can get confused. You have a problem with her, I'd rather you came and saw me. Not Moyer."

His dark eyes pierced and wanted agreement, but she hesitated. She was there by a stroke of luck, and she wouldn't do anything to jeopardize her stay, which meant going to the proper authorities when required. Dak was a man overstepping his rank. "I understand Mina and I are replacing teachers who fled frightened by the threats of uprisings. Can you tell me anymore?"

"Frightened. A man and wife. They rode out the morning after the break-in."

"When did General Brooke hear?"

Dak wondered if he needed to add dangerous to her list of traits? "Between writing half a dozen letters every day to Washington, Moyer regularly wires General Miles and General Brooke. He likely sent a telegram the day it happened. Used their leaving to bolster his cry for more troops."

"Do you think they fled afraid of the uprisings? Or were they possibly the thieves?"

"Let it go. The robbery's got nothing to do with your teaching." He looked again at the stove. "I'll give the fire another minute."

His back to her, she watched him. He'd dropped his hat on the floor beside the stove, and his wavy hair brushed the top of his ears. She was coming across as terribly righteous but that was fear, too. She couldn't explain the stress she had been carrying on her back and in her stomach since seeing her plagiarized article, but she could at least mind her manners. "Mr. Thomas, thank you for everything. And for how ungrateful I must seem, I apologize."

"No need." He turned. They were getting off on the wrong foot, and he couldn't blame her for the whole of it. She wasn't the brawny countrywoman he'd hoped for, and he hated being in the shed where there had already been one disaster. She wanted him gone, but he wasn't wanting to find her frozen one morning before she took her pretty little skirts back to Omaha. "I'll stay until that's going good and strong. Without a fire, you won't make it."

He seemed overly concerned about the fire and her having heat but pressing him on the matter felt rude.

"You a church goer?" he asked.

Another quick switch in the direction of their conversation. "I'm not." Only one sort of woman admitted they didn't attend religious services, and a rung below that was the woman who admitted it boldly.

"The government," Dak went on, "gives the schools to churches. The Mission School was given to the Catholics, ours here on the agency grounds went to the Episcopalians."

"Is Red Cloud Episcopalian?"

"Catholics got him first." She'd opened her coat, pushed it partially off her shoulders. She wore lace around her neck, but the naked inch he saw at the top revealed skin smooth as the cream he poured in his coffee. "Episcopalians, needing to pat themselves on the back for their great charitable work, are heading in to check on how their money is being spent."

"Is it all right that I'm not a churchgoer?"

"General Brooke sent you. You've got the job."

She glanced again at the trunk holding her books. Nary a one would be considered a Christian text. "At one time, my parents were believers, but after losing a child, they decided God hadn't properly repaid them for their attendance. Or for the contributions they'd dropped in collection baskets."

"It'd help if you taught the children to recite a few religious words, but you don't have much time. The next delegation'll arrive before Christmas.

She sighed. Teach very small children, most of whom couldn't even speak English, religious words. Not as something to help them, or that they'd understand, but to impress outsiders.

'The church gauges the school's success on those kinds of performances," Dak said. He reached for his hat. "Don't mess with the ash pan. I'll empty it in a day or two."

"Thank you, but I'm sure I can clean out my own ashes."

Dak let out a low, slow breath. "Stick your shovel in too far, try to lift out too much ash, and it's likely to puff up over the top of the coals. Smother the fire."

Despite urging him to go, she wanted him to stay. But the longer he did, moving back and forth in front of the stove, the more guilt she felt for keeping him. She opened her satchel for the busyness of something to do. Mina's basket! There was no telling where it had been. Hidden amongst infested furs, hanging from a tree? She lifted out the bundle and placed it on the desk. Hurrying back, she removed the music box and the craniometer. Her white nightgown, still in the case, looked clean, no dark, crawling specks, though she wished she could give it a hard shake. She couldn't, however, pull out the intimate garment with Dak in the room.

"What's that?" Dak's eyes locked on the craniometer.

His manner and impropriety jabbed her. "It's a scientific tool for measuring the size of heads."

His gaze lifted onto her.

Clearly, he knew the device's purpose and hadn't needed to ask. She fought the blush rising on her cheeks. "It's science. It measures the cranium, bregma to lambda, for instance." She touched the crest of her skull, then the back. "Phrenology has fallen into disrepute, but Father hopes to see a resurgence in the study." Her loathing of the field was personal. She had been forced to sit too many times, the cold jaws clamped onto her head while Father related the sad news to the members of the Civil War Map Club that her head size had not improved. But her hatred of the contraption didn't mean the science was either sound or unsound. "There are thirteen bumps on the skull used to measure brain size and development."

He turned away. The shovel scraped again, metal on the metal hod, as he lifted out coal.

"Take as many measurements as you can," Father had instructed. "Be exact. Accuracy is the mark of a true scientist."

Father had no idea about her true purpose for going. She had wanted to insist that her stay on the reservation would be only for a few months, hardly time for a child to have any measurable growth. Though maybe it wasn't growth that interested him, but comparing the head sizes of Indian children to statistics gathered on Negro and Chinese of the same age. Did Father believe proving a deficiency in the Indian meant they could be exterminated without guilt? How much more land would that open to the railroads? How much more profit and honor for Sander Ellison?

"I've banked the fire," Dak said. He wouldn't question her intentions, but he'd keep an eye on her. "That ought to see you 'til morning."

"Banked?"

"Stacked the corners. The coal'll fall in as needed." He moved the bottom lever again, opening and closing the vent. "If you're cold, let in more air, it'll burn hotter. If you're warm enough, close this some. Less air, less burn. Don't waste your fuel."

"I've no plans to use the craniometer. It's Father's."

He lifted his hat from the floor. Pressed it tight on his head.

She knew what he was thinking; she'd brought it along, hadn't she? She disappointed him, but she disappointed herself as well. She ought to have thrown the thing into the first available receptacle. Being with Dak reinforced her fears: Suppose she failed reservation life, too? And yet, she wouldn't leave. After lying to Agent Moyer, she had no choice but to do whatever else was necessary to save herself from returning home.

"Get yourself something to eat. When you're back, drop that bar across the door." He pointed again to the lumber plank leaning in the corner. "Don't open until daylight. I'll see you at school in the morning."

"I'll be safe?"

He buttoned his coat, pulled the collar up along the back of his neck. He wanted to take her into his arms, lift her onto the bed. "I wouldn't leave you if I didn't trust you'd be safe. Just remember to drop the bar."

She heard concern but charged with the care of a shipment of cabbages, she felt certain he'd give the vegetables as much attention.

One hand on the doorknob, he hesitated. "If you'd rather spend your first night with the other teachers?"

Her trunks were there, he'd already built a fire, making himself late for who-knew-how-many chores, and his wife had his dinner waiting. She wouldn't ask him to locate a wagon and take her to a new location at this hour. "I'm perfectly fine. Thank you."

He respected her feigned courage. A lady like her ought to be set up at the hotel but rent for a room wouldn't fit in any Episcopal budget, and some of the worst men he'd ever laid eyes on roomed there. Including Atlock. He touched his hat brim. "Night then."

Seven

LAUDER FITTED THE bar across the door and heard Dak step away only after the plank settled. She peeked around the shade drawn over her window, watched him cross the road, mount a horse, and ride off. She remained standing there, suddenly wide awake with fear. Her stomach growled, but darkness hugged the ground deep and feral. She would rather starve than go out into the untamed night. She used the key Dak left on the desk and locked the door, though he'd implied the bar was an adequate measure. Taking the lantern off the desk, she put it on the dresser with the second one and dragged the desk, scraping it over the plank flooring and directly in front of her door. She carried the lantern back. Nurse, who lived with a fear of fire, would be proud of her caution.

Though nothing appeared to crawl from the straw basket, Lauder would leave it on the desk: best to keep the thatch in plain sight. It wasn't just a possible insect infestation, the object held an eeriness, a felt thing, not entirely inanimate. Was it this aliveness Mina would not have locked away in a museum? Would not risk to the hands of an unfeeling curator who might discard it? There were likely thousands of baskets, not only of the same size and of the same grasses, but in better shape.

Thankfully, Mina wasn't expecting Lauder to keep it for long. Mina only wanted a caretaker for a few days. A week at most. Once she calmed down, the keepsake would be returned.

She set Babette's music box on the desk, as well. What did it say about her that she had stolen and brought along the memento of a dead sister? She'd see the box was mailed back to Mother, but for now, the box was a balancing presence to the ominous basket.

The two items added to her bramble of roiling thoughts, and no matter how much she wished for the escape of sleep, she was wide awake. Somewhere in the insistent, charted, and unchanging rotations of the Earth, the fabric had torn. She opened her journal feeling she must make a full accounting of the sickening event that had brought her to the reservation. Only Nurse knew the truth. Not these pages, as if they required the most of her. She dipped her pen.

When the monthly journal arrived in the mail, and I found my article had been published despite my retraction, my heart dropped away. I'd confessed my shame to the journal editors at having plagiarized and explained in a long letter why I'd so dishonestly submitted an article that wasn't mine.

"Kind Sirs," I wrote in part, "my deepest apologies for my deceit. From the first hour that article left in the post I've prayed and even believed you would not find my submission worthy of your distinguished journal. In which case, the matter would be over, and my deceitfulness of no consequence. As you have accepted the piece, I must ask your forgiveness for my unprofessional actions."

Lauder paused, dipped her pen, touched the nib to the lip of the bottle, dipped again. *I did not add in the letter, DO NOT PUBLISH. Wasn't that understood? Then that very night, after seeing the article in print, a feral whisker dropped from my book. Today, in Agent Moyer's office, hanging predominantly on the wall, a boar's head. Ugly, and yet, surely it means Pine Ridge is exactly where I must be.*

She considered and dipped the pen. *What I did not write to the editors is that I won't live in a beautiful home with half a dozen staff waiting on me and spend my days as bitterly unhappy as my parents. I'll remain unmarried and as such, I will need a livelihood beyond teaching.*

She put her pen down. The boar's whisker, Babette's music box, and Mina's basket were all a gathering of ghosts. Especially the nesting of dead grasses with its tiny strands of mysterious black fibers. She pulled one free, her hands feeling suddenly shaky, and her heart knocking. She held the fiber over lantern flame, watched it coil, smoke, and disappear.

Hair!

Her hands flew back and away. She stood, took quick and retreating steps. The hair undoubtedly belonged to Mina's dead mother. Lived for Mina still. Nurse saved both Mother and Lauder's hair, as if saving some aspect of their breath and spirit. Had the practice started after Babette's death? A child Nurse must have loved and felt she'd not saved? Why else but for protection, pull hair from combs, hairbrushes, pillow covers? Did Nurse's Old-World mythologies and Lakota traditions have kindred roots?

Lauder sank onto the small bed and stared into her new quarters. The night before General Brooke's visit, when the coarse hair slid down the page of her book and into her lap, she'd stood and shook out her skirt before racing up the stairs for her bedroom. At the top of the stairs, the faint sound of Babette's music box stopped her. She stood in the hallway listening to the sound from behind Mother's closed door. Afraid to knock, she considered taking the stairs up to the third floor and Nurse. Nurse would be awake, pacing in her tiny room, her ancient feet sliding over her worn rug. Sliding rather than lifting the space of a breath because at this hour the wee ancestors stole souls through soles. Nurse would welcome Lauder, but she didn't deserve the weight of Lauder's mood. Instead, Lauder continued standing outside Mother's door, wanting to cry out, Mother, I need you. I'm in such trouble. She hadn't. The tinny tune meant it was Babette Mother wanted, not her. Not her, who days before being born was the reason Mother was in bed that afternoon with Nurse tending her. Leaving Father unchaperoned time with Babette.

Confined for the night in her new quarters on the reservation, Lauder fisted her hands and struck the bed. The stove Dak lit burned evenly, but the room felt suddenly colder and draftier. She busied herself for bed and sleep — her only possible escape from the new unease she felt. She stepped out of her traveling clothes, pulled her nightgown over her head, and removed the pins from what Dak had called her topknot. With long strokes she brushed her hair, then studied the brush. She was never sure why Nurse kept strands of hair or the depth of the woman's seeing. What disaster did Nurse hope to ward off by ferreting the strands? Ought Lauder save her own? Begin growing protection against…what?

She turned down one lantern but left the second burning low. Nurse, fearful of a lantern being tipped over, and a spray of flame bursting across the room, would object. Lauder, however, would not be startled awake later and find herself in utter darkness. She crawled into bed. Rough cotton and the scratch of wool blankets. She hugged her knees and tried to calm herself.

A stirring along the back wall made her start and hold herself tighter. The sound came again, right there in the room with her, and yet she saw nothing. The wall's flat surface and new paint reflected only the slightest sense of shifting lantern light.

The sound came again.

Horrid! Mice, maybe rats, in the walls! She threw back her blankets, slammed shut the lids on both trunks, then hesitated, listening, turning to take in the whole room. Babette? Nurse? The basket on her desk, woven through with the hair of the dead, sent her back into bed.

Eight

IN THE MORNING, a rumbling thunder woke Lauder. She hurried to the window. A long line of cavalry in great coats, their faces high and declarative were arriving. Horses with shiny flanks and hooves pounded the snowy, frozen ground. The parade seemed endless and then the spectacle of nearly as many wagons loaded with supplies, horse drawn, then mule drawn, and the slowest, drawn by oxen sometimes in teams of six. "The cost of all this," she said to Babette. "Hooray for Agent Moyer and the success of all his letter writing."

The passing spectacle blocked most of the view of Agent Moyer's office and Dak who might be moving around inside. She wished she could go back and tear up yesterday's lies the way she tore up horrid stories. Claiming to be Agent Moyer's private recorder. Oh God, reducing herself in front of him, Sgt. Atlock and Dak. Even using the word valor. And all of it with a straight face. Had she still not learned to think before she acted?

She turned from the window to face the small and sparse room. No homier in daylight. Could she live with so little? There'd been the childhood summer when she snuck away from Nurse in the afternoons and into the barn brimming with unwanted things: a dozen velvet dinner chairs no longer to Mother's liking, three-foot vases, a myriad of expensive and discarded objects stacked and draped with sheets grown dusty. Winding her way through, she dropped onto a soft elephant-hide settee and napped. There, she had dreamed of wild things: giraffes, tigers, elephants. Mother had frowned when it was uncrated and ordered it carted to the barn, off to the far edge of the property. The replacement settee arrived months later, dyed in what Mother considered a "truer blue." Lauder saw no difference in the shading, and she quit lifting the heavy metal latch on the storage barn, no longer napped in the dusty place that could make her sneeze. And although she loved to curl up on the new leather, she no longer dreamed of wild creatures.

She fought an urge to return to bed. She wouldn't give into it; she was still young and despite all her mistakes thus far, she had a long life ahead of her. She needed to dress and discover the day. Dak needed to be found and informed of the scratching in the wall. In nailing new lumber over the old, he'd created a nesting space large enough for something nocturnal.

She dressed and pulled back her hair, hoping that without Nurse's help, she was still getting it up into something reasonably fashionable. Though more important was proving to Dak and whomever else that she was prepared for winter in South Dakota. She pulled the three tall and broken feathers from her hat and set it smartly on her head. It wasn't to Dak's liking, but no lady appeared in public without a hat.

A plate of food sat on her front stoop. Under the cloth, she found biscuits and a thick slice of ham. The gift might have come from anyone, but only Dak knew she had been too frightened to search out the mess hall. She ate greedily.

The trader's shelves held candles, kerosene, coffee grinders, sorghum syrup, bolts of blue and gray serge, along with various hardware she could not name. She held a pair of boots, plain leather, plain soled, and put them down. She would not wear footwear ugly enough for a man, even if they were in a woman's size six. She moved on, saw nothing suitable for her.

"Lauder," Babette scolded, "if not fine enough for you, then for what sort of woman are they meant?"

She picked up the boots again and considered a coat. It was heavy enough to fight off a South Dakota winter but lacked a modern cut and sported not an inch of fur.

The proprietor approached. "You must be married to one of those army officers."

"Why, actually," she smiled, "I'll be teaching at the school."

He scowled at her burgundy coat, the fitted bodice and flaring skirt, the capette with its seal trim. "Well, deary, it ain't likely I carry anything that'll interest you."

His beard hung to the middle of his chest, and she wanted to give it a hard yank. I'm not your deary, she managed to avoid saying. I'm not your wife, not your child, and not your underling. Then because he continued to watch her, her confidence faltered. "I am considering the coat."

He walked away with a dismissive shrug.

She studied the dark wool. Would she still be Lauder Ellison wearing such a thing? Every woman knew fashion hid flaws and insecurities from public view. Maybe more importantly, hid them from the wearer. Was her spirit so thin that in the unattractive coat she would be unattractive even to herself?

Boots and coat in hand, she started for the counter. Gold thread in a small basket of black and navy spools stopped her. Golden as the stars in the scarf Mina now owned. The spool had likely fallen into a shipment of threads and needles coming from who knew how far away. She had no use for the thread, other than as a reminder of Babette.

At a second shop, she purchased a hat. "A Montana," the man at the money till said. The five-inch-wide brim would give protection against the sun and wet weather and featured a long string that fit under her chin. "A stampede string," he said of the leather. The flat-topped black wool sank nearly over her eyes, but a long hat pin would keep it high enough.

First impressions were lasting impressions. This being her first day, when she had not yet met Mrs. Streamist and the other teachers, her finest attire was best. How better to cover her wounded pride at being assigned to teach the youngest in the school? She returned her purchases to her quarters for another time. Before leaving, she picked up the music box. Without a single book to share, she had at least the dancer and music. Something to show the children.

Standing in the schoolyard an hour later, the cold chilling even her lungs, she studied a massive oak, the only tree in the yard. A thin coat of ice laced its branches, and the low easterly sun lit the tree with an explosion of light. In a letter to Nurse, she would explain how the symbol marked her first day with hope.

Five yards away, Mina stood in her coat and hat. Long hair that had been pinned up the day before, now streamed down her back. The silk scarf, its golden stars sun-bright against her brown cheeks, looked as though the finery had been made for her.

The two of them had just left Mrs. Streamist's office. The small woman had sat behind a large desk, her elderly head a bit tremulous on her small shoulders, but her intent keen. "The Bible reminds us," her eyes on a printed sheet in front of her, "do not spare the rod. For what are seven-times-seven strikes a day if the reward is eternal life?"

Lauder had glanced at Mina who stood stoic, looking directly through the elderly woman with an arrow-straight gaze. Lauder had never struck a child, and Mina's stance stated not only had she never done so, in her boarding school days, she'd received many blows. Mrs. Streamist didn't look capable of raising her hand either, and yet, the admonishment. The necessity of reading it. Likely, Lauder tried to reassure herself, the headmistress had one sheet from which she'd read since the school's opening. Without deviation.

Mrs. Streamist's eyes lingered overlong on Mina. "You are to be a role model of good womanhood."

Lauder's stomach sank. Good womanhood? What was that? And why was it said only to Mina?

Mrs. Streamist's attention swung to Lauder. "Do not show favoritism. No child under the age of five is permitted in the school."

The other three teachers were introduced and Mrs. Streamist led them all outside. "You will stand here," she said to Mina. And walking farther, a shawl tied under her chin, "Miss Ellison, you will stand here." Not waving a hand, "You over there, and you over there." Walking them to their places as if to X's fixed on a theatre stage. Now, the five teachers stood rooted across the front of the school.

Spinster Salem had introduced herself as that, as if her spinsterhood were a medal or a biography. At the sight of Mina's beaded moccasins, Spinster Sarah had crossed herself, her index finger touching her forehead, each shoulder, then her heart.

Greta, a large Norwegian woman, felt much like the oak tree. Her hat, a wool pail with beaver skin around the brim and with skin flaps over her ears, made Lauder wonder if she'd done the trapping and skinning herself. She spoke with such a strong accent, she sounded as if she chewed the English words in her mouth and spit them out in pieces. A string of "gut," and "thak," and "umps" might mean something like "very nice." Or "you're at my school," or "I sleep with a knife."

Lastly was Dolly, who'd made Lauder's eyes widen. Waxed eyebrows and glossed lips and cheeks. She wore a black hat with a large satin rose of the same funeral color over her right ear, and a brim curling just above her brows. Though not as large as Lauder's, the hat set off the woman's henna hair, a color somewhere between copper and pink. She stood with a tortured stance. Breasts and buttocks pushed out, whale bones slaving under the strain of holding her in the shape of a brittle S. She hardly looked the model of 'good womanhood.' To Spinster Salem's crossing herself and Greta's "Gut, yaw," Dolly had given a cloying, "Miss Ellison." Making Lauder thankful she had chosen to wear the burgundy, no matter Dak's opinion.

Lauder wanted to dismiss all the teachers except for Mina and herself, as ineffective. Mrs. Streamist approached the seventy-year mark or had already left it behind. Spinster Salem and Greta had to be over forty, and Dolly not a Sunday younger. But the women Lauder would discredit had taught at the school for years, and they were staying even with the danger. They also had the more advanced classes, while she had been tasked with only numbers and letters. As though they matched the degree of her education. Boarding the train in Omaha and throughout that ride, she had believed her smart-looking clothing and education set her apart. Yet in less than twenty-four hours, after riding to the reservation in the poorest of conveyances, witnessing the miserable creature board Plants Corn's wagon, and humiliating herself in Agent Moyer's office, cracks rattled that foundation.

Children arrived alone or with chaperones, on foot or in wagons, even on bare-backed skinny ponies. As the adults who accompanied them caught sight of her and Mina, the two new faces, their expressions covered a wide range of emotion from pleasant to disinterest to resentment. The last was unsettling. Didn't every parent want their child to have an education? Was there anything more basic? A wagon pulled to the edge of the schoolyard and stopped under the tree. Half a dozen children jumped off the back, their faces ranging in browns from coffee to bronze. When the driver jumped off as well, his short legs bending at the knees as he landed on the frozen ground, Lauder's mouth opened. Was he as old as ten or eleven? No child so young should be handling a horse and wagon. Had no parent on the reservation lost a child under a carriage wheel?

She reached into her pocket and palmed the spool of gold thread. Children handling dangerous animals, the rules she must follow, her pitiful quarters, and the thousand and more troops doing drills in the distance all made her feel as though she inhabited a sort of liminal warp of time and space.

Students grouped around their teachers, the smallest children gathering around Lauder. A near dozen faces with hair and wide eyes as black as Nurse's onyx looked up at her. In Omaha, she'd not known any children this small. The wonder and belief in these eyes brimmed with an innocence the craniometer could not measure. One girl kept back from the others. Standing stock-still, the child kept her gaze down, looking as if she expected to be found guilty of some infraction. And yet, Lauder noted, she would not run.

Seeing her fear, her struggle to be invisible, her waiting for what the adult in charge wanted from her, clutched Lauder's throat. She had been that child, standing in front of Mother or Father. Guilty of being so much less than they expected of her.

"It's all right," Lauder stepped closer, leaned down to the child. Was trying to soothe her considered favoritism? Would Mrs. Streamist, who watched with steely eyes, consider it an infraction? "Don't be afraid," Lauder whispered, one hand squeezing the spool deep in her right pocket. The other clutching the silk lining in the left. She couldn't be certain the child understood the words, but she surely understood a calming tone. "Don't be afraid."

Mrs. Streamist, in her coat and still with a shawl over her head and tied under her chin, rang a large bell and motioned for Lauder's class to enter. There would be order: No one entered the building, despite the cold, until the bell sounded, and they'd enter one orderly class at a time. The children who'd gathered around Lauder followed her inside in regimental file.

Nine

To Lauder's right in the classroom, a row of windows gave the only light. Behind her, a large slate and above the slate, the room's only décor: an American Flag painted on a wood slab. The desks were built for two, and a stove like the one in her quarters was lit and warming the room. The children hung their coats and blankets on a row of pegs. They'd known to do that, but now they stood staring at her. Britches and dresses spotted with patches but scrubbed clean. Their bodies thin, and their eyes alive with trepidation: a hope they would be treated with kindness, and a niggling fear they would not be.

Lauder had once seen a small sepia print of Nurse: a child with dark eyes full of mystery and a life not yet lived. The child in the picture was beautiful, just as were these children standing before her. Beautiful without exception. Not one with a mouthful of crooked teeth, a snarl on his lips, or eyes crossed in boredom. They watched her with innocent eyes.

How could she give these children even half of what they needed when her duty was to drive out the very innocence she recognized? Drive out the teachings of their ancestors and replace that with the mores of the white race? Standing in Father's library with him and General Brooke, the night the portly army officer accepted an invitation to the house, she had not imagined teaching small children that their very beings were flawed. As she had been taught of her own person. Teaching literature to older students, she gave them the value of the texts they read. With these children she could only give the value of herself, and what was that?

"Good morning," a small boy startled her.

"Good morning." Her voice lacked confidence. "Good morning," she said again with more volume.

The words echoed back to her: "Good morning." Tiny voices, singsong and lilting, which said rehearsed words, and that the children didn't know their meaning. Practiced, taught, perhaps by the previous teacher. Perhaps by parents wanting their little ones to show respect to the new teacher in the hope that the teacher will treat their children in kind.

They remained standing in a near huddle, the shyest with her eyes on the toes of her worn brown shoes. Their waiting must have been the previous teacher's rule: Stand until I give the command to sit. With the desks built for two, Lauder didn't want to assign seats that possibly paired them uncomfortably.

"Sit wherever you'd like."

They stared, faces quizzical and doubt creeping from one to the next. These are the first-years, Lauder reminded herself. School had started for them weeks earlier, and then they may have lost weeks between the time of their teacher's fleeing and Lauder's arrival. At any rate, now in the latter part of November, they still spoke little English, which meant their parents weren't using it at home.

"Good morning." This, coming again from the little fellow who'd first issued the greeting.

Did he know more English than just the two words? "What is your name?"

"Richard."

"Richard is a very good name. Tell them..." how could he without speaking his native language? She didn't care. "Tell them we will play a game. I'm going to turn around and count to fifteen. While I count, everyone should sit." She spread her hands, indicating the whole room. "It's a game, tell them. They may sit anywhere they want."

She turned around feeling better. "One, two..." she counted.

They whispered amongst themselves, passing the information along, but only whispering, not boldly speaking their native language. They were animated, having fun, pushing desks — she hadn't expected that. But given their delight, the day was starting off a success. "Fourteen, fifteen." She turned back. The desks were pushed along the walls and in the cleared space, the children sat on the floor in a circle, their faces beaming.

"Very good," she laughed at herself. They'd already bested her, and she loved seeing them in a circle. They appeared relaxed, and they could see each other's faces, not just the backs of their heads. "Very, very good." She pulled her chair from behind the teacher's desk and nudged it between two students. With paper and pencil, she sat in front of them. "Now, I must learn your names."

"No!" A loud screech cut the air. "Wrong."

Lauder jumped as Mrs. Streamist, conjured from thin air, burst through the door.

"Not allowed." The headmistress stomped around the outside of the circle clapping angry hands. "No circles!"

Lauder's heart whipped as the children scrambled to their feet with startled faces, some looking ready to cry. "I only meant for them to feel comfortable."

"Your first day." Mrs. Streamist looked as frightened as the children. "You must establish the rules." She clapped again, still loud and fast. "No circles."

The haste with which the children worked at pushing desks back in line alarmed Lauder. "Right now," Father clapped and bellowed in her ears. "You will learn, if you have to stand there all night."

Lauder was sorry. She couldn't stand on one foot while he poked at her ribs. She must learn, and she must not tell Nurse how Father was teaching her to be special. Not ordinary like other men's children.

"Straight rows!" Mrs. Streamist panted.

"It's alright." Dak hurried into the room. A hand to his hat, removing it. "Mrs. Streamist," his voice calm, "I'll see to this."

"Always their circles," Mrs. Streamist nearly wept. "Their pagan circles. We can't have it."

"Good morning, Miss Ellison," Dak said. "I'm happy to see you survived your first night." While two children were needed to move a single desk, Dak grabbed two at a time and pulled them into line. He smiled at the children as he did so, and despite how quickly he worked, he looked calm, his face relaxed, and his whole person exuding quiet. He stood close to the elderly woman, head and shoulders above her, tipping his head down to look steadily into her eyes. "Let's go to your office. Everything is fine here."

"Look at them," Mrs. Streamist said. "Like wooden figures. They lack the mental development for facial expressions."

Lauder saw children frozen in fear, eyes filling, lips trembling. The girl who'd been most afraid hung her face so low there was no way to see if she was crying or closing her eyes so hard she saw only blackness.

"They know," Mrs. Streamist slumped against Dak. "They know."

His face shadowed, and with an arm around the woman's shoulders, he led her from the room.

They know what? Lauder wanted to scream. She didn't actually care about the little secret they shared, but she did wish to scream. The familiarity between Dak and the headmistress was also unsettling. She walked down the center aisle, tried to smile at each child, and again she felt thrown back into her past. She was six or seven, alone with Father in the library, the door closed, her stomach so tight she might be sick. The other adults in the house asleep, or deaf, or miles of not-caring away. "One foot," Father shouted. "Stand straight. Try harder or you'll never amount to more than salt."

"Miss Ellison." Dak stood in the doorway. "Carry on." He gave the class a reassuring smile and a few words in Lakota.

She appreciated his help, though speaking in Lakota broke a school rule. Why wasn't Mrs. Streamist clapping and shouting at him, "English! Only English!"

With her chair returned behind her desk and Dak gone, Lauder took a deep breath. She was shaking. Her leniency had placed the children in a vulnerable position and all within her first minutes. She wanted to lay a hand on the shoulder of the girl who would not run despite crippling fear, but she didn't trust her legs to carry her there, and doing so would call attention to the child's distress. Let her have a private moment. For now, Lauder needed to know what Dak had said to the children. Had he joked with them, made her the object of his witticism, called her green? "Richard, please, what did Mr. Thomas say?"

The boy smiled. "Mr. Dak like circles."

She wished she were alone, if only for a second, so she could drop her face into her hands and, for that brief second, regroup. She appreciated Dak's concern for the children and for ending the situation so quickly, she did, but telling them he also liked circles contradicted Mrs. Streamist and somehow made Lauder feel weak for not having done so. How far did he imagine his reach extended?

Movement at the window made her turn. The top of a small head in a grey knitted cap and a pair of dark eyes peeked over the sill. "Come," she motioned. The child was late, lucky for him, though he must have heard Mrs. Streamist's yelling. "It's all right," she motioned again. The old bat is gone, she wanted to add.

Seconds later, the boy stepped cautiously into the room holding the hand of a girl even younger. She thought the boy at about five years of age, but the girl didn't look much past three. She couldn't be sure of any of their ages, and a child, half-starved since birth, would not be the same size as the plump children she saw in Omaha on the trolley or being pushed in prams.

Coming down the aisle, the girl wasn't just holding the boy's hand, but clinging like an appendage to his side. The tail of the dirty blanket she wore over her coat dragged on the floor. Her hair, a medium brown to his black, and her skin several shades lighter, made Lauder suspect she was a half-breed. "Good morning," she said. "What are your names?"

The boy touched his patched coat front, gave a small bow. "George."

George? An assigned name like Richard? In this case a tribute to a Founding Father? But in his fear, he'd given the name as if handing over a paper proving his right to be there. Or begging for it. "Is this your sister?"

"Little Rose most quiet."

The girl remained half hidden behind him, one eye peering around at Lauder.

This was surely the child Mrs. Streamist had warned about in their earlier meeting. The headmistress had expected George would try and sneak her in. "George," Lauder spoke gently, "you can stay, but she cannot."

"Little Rose most quiet."

"I'm sorry. But according to the rules, she's just too young." Though, of course, Lauder thought of Mina's torn heart, Little Rose wouldn't be too young for boarding school.

George's face fell further. "Little Rose," he begged, "most quiet."

Lauder felt cruel. "How old is she?"

Tears filled his eyes, and he tried to blink and refuse them. "Angry-face teacher gone."

Lauder wasn't sure if he referred to the teacher who had fled or to Mrs. Streamist. Either way, with a new teacher, George had dared to come, hoping for acceptance. "It's not my rule." Lauder's hands were shaky again. "I can't change the rules. Little Rose must go home."

Did he understand? She wouldn't put the burden of explaining on Richard; he didn't deserve that. Ought she run into the next room, fetch Mina to explain in Lakota? The two children didn't move, though all hope had drained from George's face. He looked at his sister, and still fighting back tears, he gave a tiny shake of his head.

"Little Rose is just too young. Are your parents outside?"

George gave the same resigned shake of his head. Still holding his sister's hand, he turned her, and they started back down the aisle.

Lauder's anguish increased. Ought she try and find Dak or take the children to Mrs. Streamist the very person they'd tried to avoid? The cold outside was brutal, and the small pair had only just entered. Both their noses ran, and Little Rose's fairer cheeks were red and chapped. Even if George could be persuaded to stay in the classroom, his sister couldn't be sent out into the cold alone. Where were the parents? George was far too young to be responsible even for himself and far too young to be responsible for someone even younger. He needed to be in school, but if his sister couldn't stay, he wasn't going to either. "Wait," Lauder said.

George stopped, so that his sister did, too. His back still to Lauder, he scrubbed his eyes of tears he didn't want her to see and turned back. A sob like a tiny bubble in his throat caught. "Little Rose most quiet."

Every child in the room watched the pair, and they watched Lauder. "You can stay," she said. "For a few minutes only, just to warm up."

He stared uncertain. She found her legs, hurried down the aisle. "For now. Stay and get warm."

He broke into a smile so large it startled Lauder. No, I don't mean always, she thought. Don't put your trust in me. "Only a few minutes. I can't promise more."

Little Rose tugged at her brother's coat sleeve. He leaned, listened to her whispering in his ear, and looked sheepishly back at Lauder. His eyes red.

"What did she say?"

"She wishes you hug her."

"Hug her? Me?" Lauder shivered. She came to the reservation to teach literature, including novels like *Great Expectations*. She knew Pip's story and the poverty in Victorian times, but she hadn't expected such needy children to ever be looking up at her.

Little Rose dropped George's hand and stood stiff, waiting to be hugged.

With her arms tight to her sides and despite wearing several layers of clothing, the little girl felt even smaller than she looked. And though she had requested Lauder's embrace, she stood stiff, not relaxing a muscle. She needs more than a hug, Lauder thought. She needs Nurse, hours in someone's loving lap. "I'm not promising," Lauder managed. Letting them stay was a horrible act of defiance, but she didn't care. She was angry at Mrs. Streamist for bursting into the room and treating her and the children with such disrespect. She pushed a desk into a back corner, motioned for the pair to sit there, and returned to her desk in front. If Mrs. Streamist came through the door and down the aisle, she'd see the pair. But if the next time she was curious, she only peeked into the room from the hall, the children would not be in her line of sight. Hopefully, seeing all was well, the headmistress would leave.

Lauder pulled back her shoulders. I'll try and hide them only until the midday meal, she told herself. That was the best she could do. See them warmed and fed.

"I am," she touched her chest and looked over the now weary faces,

"Miss Ell-ison. Now I must learn who has names and who does not." She dreaded the thought of her assignment.

"Names a man can say," Agent Moyer had instructed. Each name she assigned would mean a piece of their identity lost. And a nudge into white society and out of their own.

Two boys raced into the classroom, their worn shoes clapping on the wooden floor as they rushed down the aisle, not stopping until they'd bumped into the front of Lauder's desk. Grins stretched across their faces.

"Well, good morning," she said. Were children going to stream in the morning long? But the little fellows with their bright smiles were welcome. Their joy was a tonic the classroom needed.

They looked at each other to coordinate their greeting and spoke in harmony. "Good morning."

The same practiced words but with earnestness that said they were happy to be there. "Welcome to my classroom."

The taller of the two, perhaps six months older, nodded. His companion continued to beam, his eyes full of an adoration that seemed to be for her, the world, and himself. Lauder's heart swelled. A child so loved, he was the richest of children with an infectious confidence. She wanted to ask if perhaps he'd hug her. "What are your names?"

"Badger." The taller touched his chest. He'd pulled off his coat to show a clean white shirt. Worn and hanging in the shoulders, the sleeves were too long for his small size, but had been tucked under at his wrists and basted. A stitch that could be taken out each time he needed an inch of sleeve to be let down.

"Badger," she repeated his name.

He lifted his hands in the air, made claws of his fingers, and mimed an animal scratching and digging.

So dear was his gesture, as though he'd patiently and necessarily explain a badger to his naive teacher, she thanked him. She would not tell him his name wasn't good enough. Would not tell him he needed to be a Richard or a George. Not today. "Yes. I understand. I won't forget. Badger."

The other lad, with his grin still wide as if saying, I'm the dearest boy in the world, waited.

She turned to him, thinking, Yes, you are exactly that. "What is your name?"

"Much Wind," Badger said.

"Well, Much Wind," she nearly needed to sit on her hands to keep from reaching out and laying a palm on the boy's cheek, "I won't forget your name either."

Badger twisted at the waist and pointed to the seat of his companion's britches. "Much Wind." He pinched his nose and scrunched his face to mime a stink.

Behind the boys, children snickered. Little Rose looked to her brother but covered her mouth with both hands to keep from making even a happy sound.

"Please take seats." Lauder motioned to a desk up front. She would keep them close. "I'm happy you're here."

Badger wasn't finished. He pointed to Much Wind, then out the window to the small church on the hill.

"Much wind in the church?" Lauder kept her voice low, struggled not to show her amusement.

Badger placed his hand on Much Wind's belly and rubbed.

Lauder's enjoyment dissipated. Could the little lad have stomach issues that required a doctor? Possibly early signs of dysentery? Ought she speak to Mrs. Streamist, ask if something should be done? Or would her concern be considered interfering?

The boys smiled at each other and rushed to the desk she indicated. With her paper still clean, she considered her original plan: Write the name of each child as they were known to their family and some physical feature. That night, alone in her residence, there would be time to match them with proper names. Saint George had slain a dragon, and there was George Washington, and Richards had been English kings, and there was some ancient story of a Saint Richard and a dropped chalice. But Saint Badger and Saint Much Wind? She hated the thought of taking away their very personal names and the identities attached to them, but she reminded herself that the names would only apply at school. Sitting before her were the lucky ones who'd go home in the afternoon to families who'd addressed them by their Lakota names.

She carried the sheet of paper and pencil to George. "For Little Rose." Back in front of the room, she drew Babette's music box from her bag and smiled as eyes widened. She wound the key, and like hurrying to a sweet elixir, the children rushed forward and crowded around. Even George, comfortable enough to join the others, came running, which meant Little Rose did as well. Lauder pulled the pair in front of the others and hoped Little Rose's small stature hid her from any eyes peering through the door.

The tiny ballerina twirled. Was music allowed?

"Tutu," Lauder said, pinching her skirt at the hip, pulling it out, and pointing at the dancer.

"Moccasins," Richard said of the ballerina's shoes.

Without heels and softly molded to the foot, the pointe shoes did resemble hide shoes. "Yes, that is right." The children were relaxed again, and she was communicating effectively with them. She turned the key a second time, cupped her ear so that they all listened intently to the music. What an excellent teaching tool the box proved to be; an introduction both to ballet and classical music. Two treasures of white culture.

Badger touched the dome, framed his face with his hands, then mimed framing Lauder's face and pointed back at the ballerina.

"No," she nearly laughed, "that's not me." Clowning, she made a clumsy and ungraceful leap, her arms in the air. A failed fairy. She had never thought of herself as resembling her dead sister, Mother's little girl with "golden hair and blue eyes. Lovely as an angel." Any comparison would have been sacrilegious. But here were fresh eyes seeing her in the figurine. Extraordinary. Could the craniometer, shoved far under her bed, measure the difference in a brain where appreciation had been given the lobe space to grow?

"Beautiful," she looked to the most fearful little girl standing at the edge of the group. She'd think of her as She-Stands-Brave. "You are beautiful.

"Richard, tell them what I'm saying." Walking around the children, she touched each child on the head and looked deeply into the child's eyes. "Beautiful."

"Hopa," Richard repeated. "Hopa. Hopa."

The clamor of three dozen troops suddenly thundering down Pine Ridge Road made Badger and Much Wind duck and crouch. Every child had nearly the same frightened reaction, cowering to the floor.

"Just noise," Lauder said. "Nothing to fear. Richard, tell the class there is no danger. No trouble. No harm."

She got them seated only after the troops had passed. The fear they'd shown was tragic. There could be no peace between the races if the children, like Mina, held such fear of the soldiers. If she was to help them co-exist peacefully with whites, that had to include an appreciation of and a trust in the soldiers.

Ten

Mrs. Streamist, in her coat and with the same grey shawl tied under her chin, walked down the school's hallway toward the exit, ringing her massive bell.

George jumped from his seat before Lauder realized the bell meant the school day was ended. He looked to her for help and, seeing none, grabbed up his sister's hand and their winter things. They ran.

"Wait," she yelled to their backs. "Go with the others, mix in with them."

Too late. As the other children filed from the room, Lauder rushed to the window. Mrs. Streamist held George by the collar and Little Rose, even in terror, still clung to him. Badger, Much Wind, She-Stands-Brave, and the others hurried away, wide of Mrs. Streamist and the shawl billowing angrily around her head. Her words were indistinguishable to Lauder, but George and Little Rose's faces spoke fear. Mrs. Streamist finished her scolding and let go of George, and the children ran, George still carrying their coats and the blanket with the dirty hem.

I'm responsible for that, Lauder thought. I let it happen. If she could only go back. There'd been the knock at the classroom door a couple of hours earlier. A man with a basket who'd not spoken, only lifted the basket in a sort of salute and set it down. On his arms four other baskets of the same size. Looking inside, her heart dropped. Not an apple, a carrot, an egg. Only slices of day-old white bread. Passing out the bread, shame washed over her, and with each little hand reaching eagerly for the paste, her shame grew. The need to send George and Little Rose home forgotten.

Would she ever see the brother and sister again? Lying on the desk they used was the sheet of paper Lauder had given Little Rose. Had it been left in their haste, or had George feared letting his sister take what might be property of the school?

Horses, front and back, covering nearly every inch. Drawings surprisingly good for such a young child. Lauder couldn't be sure, but she thought the pictures were all the same horse. Some large, some only half an inch high, but always the same. A horse, its right front leg lifted, its tail billowing, and stark ribs scoring its side. That detail struck Lauder hardest. A child, so young, aware of a horse's ribs.

Mrs. Streamist entered looking offended and pale. The bell fisted at her side. "Rules, Miss Ellison. Rules."

"I'm sorry, but if I hadn't let Little Rose stay, George would have left, as well. She was most quiet." Lauder held out the paper. "All day, only drawing, not a peep out of her."

"Rules. We must have rules."

Lauder swung her hands behind her back, clasped them. For Mrs. Streamist, the school might not be held together by mortar, boards, and nails, but by her rules. Don't make trouble, Lauder thought. Repent. Beg. "I'm terribly sorry."

"Spare the rod," Mrs. Streamist said, "and lose the child."

Lauder didn't understand how letting Little Rose sit beside her brother and spend the day drawing in the warmth of the classroom mattered so much. Did Mrs. Streamist suppose busy mothers with shopping on their minds were going to start dropping off their children for teachers to tend?

"I hoped you could fulfill your duties," Mrs. Streamist said.

"I assure you, I can."

"Indian children require the strictest discipline. You must command respect."

Lauder imagined a taut wire of fear running through the woman's words. Had she been reprimanded for leniency with the school's standards?

"You abandoned your post in Omaha," Mrs. Streamist said. "I expect you will leave us."

Lauder didn't answer. She'd not thought of herself as having abandoned her job in Omaha. General Brooke's letter ranked above prior commitments.

"Prayers," Mrs. Streamist said. "Numbers, vocabulary. Teach them the correct names for cups, blankets," she looked around, desperate for objects to include, and at the paper in Lauder's hands. "Horses. Teach them words and how the objects are used."

"Used?" Didn't the children already know how to use cups, blankets, and horses? "Keep the curriculum small?" She wanted to pace but forced herself to remain still. "I see my mistakes."

"Agent Moyer," the bell in Mrs. Streamist's hand trembled, "I must go and see him. He must know I'm following every rule."

"You mean to report me? Please. That's not necessary."

"The circle." She waved a pale hand, indicating the floor where the children had sat. The motion stirred the bell, the clapper rounded the mouth.

For all the woman's scolding, once again the sternness seemed to Lauder more rooted in fear than anger.

"I'm headmistress."

"Yes," Lauder said, "of course. But please, this is my first day. I don't want Agent Moyer doubting me before I've been given a chance to learn the rules." She would see the agent herself and explain the misunderstandings before he heard them from Mrs. Streamist. And if necessary, gush over his maps and beg for tales of his valor.

"Howard must know," Mrs. Streamist said.

Agent Moyer's first name? In which case, he and Mrs. Streamist also had a surprising familiarity. Frustrated, Lauder smoothed her hands down her hips. "There's no need to speak with him. This can remain our secret." She leaned in, tried to turn the conversation playful. "Everyone has a secret."

Mrs. Streamist's sallow face turned even more ghostly. A suck of air. "What do you know?"

"Nothing, please." Lauder's hands rose. "I was only jesting. I'm sorry, I meant no disrespect."

The headmistress turned, headed for the door.

Your backside, Lauder thought. She regretted upsetting the woman, though of course, everyone did have a secret. Obviously, Mrs. Streamist, who could now be heard in the next room scolding Mina, considered hers larger and more important than most. If only she knew.

Mina entered minutes later, her face tight and her arms crossed. The scarf of stars cowled around her neck. "That tree out there," she pointed to the large oak at the edge of the schoolyard, its arms now bare and darkly etched against a cold sky. "Students asked about my ancestors, and I told them that was one."

"Mrs. Streamist heard? Do you think she stood outside our doors listening?" Of course, she had. "Did you apologize?"

"Lie? Surrender into more ways of killing?"

"I don't understand."

"We die without our ancestors. They must not be taken from us."

"We need to be careful. Not make trouble on our first day." Though she was also guilty, her offences had come from trying to do right by the children. "You can't teach the old superstitions."

"Superstitions." Mina huffed the word. "A white word. For a tiny world."

"I'm sorry," Lauder said, "I didn't mean to offend you." She was apologizing within minutes of having apologized to Mrs. Streamist. She considered again all the ways she and Mina were similar: age, sex, occupation, single, new to the agency and school. Then there was the mother basket Lauder was temporarily guarding. Wasn't their relationship developing into a sort of not-by-blood sisterhood? Lauder wished it so. "Please obey the rules. I don't want you to lose your position."

"And that wretched flag," Mina pointed to the replica painted on old boards hanging on the wall behind Lauder's desk. "All the years I was forced to stand in front of it. And now here, too, children are forced to honor the symbol of their oppressors."

Honor the symbol of their oppressors? Lauder was accustomed to seeing the stars and stripes. Omaha was replete with flags, but she had never considered what it symbolized to conquered people on a reservation.

"I'm to teach the children," Mina went on, "as I was taught: to pay homage to those who destroy us?"

"Mina ..."

"Does it not touch you that killers force children to place their hands over their hearts and swear loyalty to them? Killers who at this very minute are striving to starve those children and put them into graves."

"It's just not that simple."

"Isn't it?"

"Please don't make trouble."

"It is not the Lakota who make trouble. Trouble comes to us."

Lauder wanted to reach out and embrace Mina, but they stood apart. "I know your boarding school experience was painful."

"School the children into believing animals do not speak, and the hills are only rugs of grass to be walked on. Teach them that this world is dead, and the only life is in the next, sitting at the feet of a supreme white man."

Lauder reached for Mina's hand and felt relief when it was not pulled away. "Please. We've both had rough first days; we need to give this a chance."

"I cannot tell them to look down on the words and teachings of the elders. Must even our stories be destroyed?" Wet fire burned in her eyes. "Who can wish such a world on them?"

"You've only just returned. Give yourself time."

Mina took a long, slow breath. Exhaled just as slowly. "Do not worry." She smiled. "Maybe I'll dance through the night to help my spirits."

The illegal Ghost Dance? Sgt. Atlock was reporting the locations of the dancers, and Agent Moyer mapping them. "Don't joke about that."

Mina pulled her hand away, offered her wrists as if to say, arrest me.

"I'm serious," Lauder said. Mina hadn't been in Agent Moyer's office, hadn't heard his surprise at learning an Indian had been hired to teach. Which meant Dak likely slipped the form in the agent's correspondence at an opportune time, knowing the man would scratch on a signature without attention. "Please be careful. Maybe I should put in a good word to Agent Moyer on our behalf."

"Not on mine," Mina said.

"Only inform him that Mrs. Streamist, should she come to him, misunderstands our good intentions."

"You'll speak to the man who could have me removed?"

"I'd be careful. And I have an excuse for going. I want to see about bringing a couple of soldiers into my class. The children are frightened of the men, and I think if a couple came for a short visit, it would help."

Mina's frown deepened. "Do not teach children to play with snakes."

"The men out there are just men. If there's ever going to be peace, the two races need to quit fearing each other."

"Whites will have peace only when the Lakota are all dead."

"You and I can begin teaching peace to our students."

"Is it you, Lauder Ellison, who single handedly will save the children?"

"I'm not saying that."

Mina moved to the doorway, stopped, and looked back. "Do not teach children to trust the enemy."

Eleven

L AUDER LEFT THE school and hurried down the street with her anger building. She rushed past Lakota, military, and civilians, but paid no more attention to them than to the cold. Ahead of her, Dak had stepped out of his office and onto the road. He stood in front of a group of young men riding barebacked ponies. Eight. All wearing winter gear bought from traders, but with the dark skin and fierce burning eyes that told Lauder they were Sioux.

"Since the time of our grandfather's grandfathers," the leader swore, "our people lived on this land. We owe debt to elders, to the land, to our grandchildren's grandchildren." He pointed around to the gang on horseback. "We are men who will fight."

Despite their heavy clothing, Lauder saw lean-bodies. Skilled hunters certainly, but if they were finding any game, they were passing the meat to weaker people. Their necks were corded with anger and hunger. Their eyes dark with it. She feared they'd reached the outer edge of what they would endure, and when the last inch of restraint gave way, they would be devils.

"You are men," Dak said. He let the acknowledgment settle. "If I thought it were possible to reclaim the land, I'd ride and fight with you."

The leader's horse, as lean as its rider, snorted, stomped impatiently on the frozen ground.

"Red Cloud has seen the cities east," Dak said. "He tells you the truth, you cannot win war against the white invasion." He swung his arm toward a military camp in the distance. A sea of white Sibley tents. "You can't win against that."

The man spat at Dak's feet, kicked his horse's flanks and rode so close to Dak the horse's withers knocked him. Dak regained his balance, stood his ground again, his feet planted in silence.

Lauder held her breath as the small band of riders followed their leader, forming a single file, each passing so close his horse brushed against Dak. As they rode away, she gave a sigh of relief and stepped through the door Dak held for her.

No one sat behind Agent Moyer's large desk, but the macabre animal heads hung in their place. "They're troublemakers," she said of the riders.

"They are men, warriors." He turned the chair she'd used the day before, indicated she should sit. "This land holds the bones of their ancestors. I know what that is, but I can't do a damn thing to help. Now, they're sick and starving."

She felt certain he ached to join the angry group. Her heart shuddered at the thought. "They're going to get themselves killed." And riding with them, she didn't say, you'd get yourself killed.

"Five thousand soldiers," Dak cussed, "and a million more to be called up if it comes to that."

She wasn't ready to sit. "Then you know their resistance makes no sense."

"There's living things can survive a cage and living things that can't."

Her stomach clenched. Dak had met the militants, man-to-man, leaving the office to greet them unarmed, though he could have easily grabbed one of a dozen guns. Standing amongst them, he'd spoken the truth, though had he not, thinking them simple enough to trick with false promises, their horses would have trampled him.

He motioned again to her chair. "How'd you get on with your stove?"

The scene on the street still had her feeling edgy, and her own complaints suddenly childish. But she had not come for herself; George and Little Rose needed help. "My stove is fine, thank you."

His eyes questioned. "And the rest of your day?"

"I need to speak with Agent Moyer about that."

"Something happen? You being chased?"

Marching down the street, she had not meant to give that impression. It was important that she come across as mature and capable. She sat. "I'm here to speak with Agent Moyer."

Dak considered. If it were possible, Lauder looked even prettier today. She wasn't wearing the hat like a goose nesting on her head, and her hair looked less stacked like cordwood. The change wasn't all good. The day before, she'd stood with her shoulders thrown back, and now they looked softer, less sure. He hated seeing the change. She had no business being there, and he needed to be careful. He had no business admiring what he could never have. Only a fool raced down a road that led nowhere. "If you need help—"

"I don't." She didn't need physical help of the sort he provided. Mrs. Streamist was an administrative issue and required Agent Moyer. She pushed her hands into her coat pockets and took a steadying breath. "I've kept the stove going just fine, and I'm capable of finding the mess hall."

"But you haven't yet?"

She kept from asking if he'd brought the food. If he had, food cooked by his wife, she didn't want to know. She wanted to lean against him, have his arm come around her as it had with Mrs. Streamist. "If you could tell me when Agent Moyer is to return, I'll come back at the appropriate hour."

He pulled a watch from a pocket on his slim hip. "Should be any minute. How about a cup of coffee? It tastes even worse than it smells, but it's hot."

She watched as he drew his desk chair a respectful two and a half feet from hers. Caught with her eyes on him, she glanced away to the grizzly wall and then to a gun case.

"You needing to borrow a firearm?"

The ease in his manner made her wonder if he'd been expecting her.

"Well," she began, "I know an old biddy who needs shot. You'd best keep the firearms away from me."

He flinched. Not visibly, but she caught an unquiet twitch just beneath his skin. He carries a wound in his chest, she told herself. Did everyone? Mina certainly did, as did Little Rose. And though Mrs. Streamist hadn't earned compassion, she, too, carried something heavier than just righteousness.

"What happened?" Dak asked. "The children all right?"

"This is a concern for Agent Moyer."

"Moyer," the name dragged from Dak's mouth, "rode out with General Brooke to see Red Cloud."

"The chief?" She wished she'd been invited. "Why did they go?"

He held her gaze. Their going didn't concern her, though she was likely thinking of her record keeping. "Sioux are fleeing to the Black Hills. Army says they're massing and Red Cloud needs to help bring them back."

"I suppose Sgt. Atlock went as well?"

"When Moyer rides out, he takes his hired gun."

His answer sounded irritated. "I only asked out of curiosity. The meeting sounds important, but you didn't go?"

"Things around here," he glanced to the window behind her, "need watching."

With so many soldiers on the agency grounds what threat did Dak suppose required his presence? And what did he think his one gun could add?

He clapped his hands on his knees and stood. "I offered you coffee."

The stove held a charred pot and two tin cups sat at the side. She had no idea whose lips had last been on the tin cups or when they'd last been washed, if ever. "No, thank you."

"Probably smart." He poured himself a cup and sat again. "I'm happy to pass on your concerns about the school."

She wanted to tell him everything, but she wouldn't. "I believe the proper protocol would be to wait for Agent Moyer."

"Suit yourself."

In the ensuing silence, her brain said, leave, but her body said, no way.

Dak reached down, setting his coffee on the floor beside his chair. He leaned slowly forward, purposefully, his elbows on his knees and his hands hanging in front. "What happened?"

A wind gust scraped over the roof and rattled down the stove pipe. The noise like rasping, first here, then there.

"Little Rose and her brother George," Lauder found herself saying. "Do you know the two children? They came to school half-frozen and begging to be allowed to stay. Mrs. Streamist sent them off."

"They're off? She hasn't kept them?"

"Why ever would she keep them?" Lauder shifted in her chair. "I'm sure they'll never come close to the school again."

He leaned back, his coffee cooling on the plank flooring, his attention drawn again to the window. "There she goes."

Lauder turned to see Dolly walking by, a package under her arm.

"She's headed to the post office," Dak said. "Lately, she mails right and left."

Lauder bit her tongue. Did Dak watch every time hip-swinging Dolly pranced past his window? Watch her wiggle and red lips?

"I'd like," Lauder went on, "for Agent Moyer to grant both children permission to attend. They are very well behaved." She had been told not to form attachments, and here she was on the first day. "It's a small request, but I'm afraid it must be granted."

His brows scrubbed. "Or what? I'll be packing those trunks of yours back to Rushville?"

She felt certain he considered her weak, ready to run at the first conflict. Thankfully, the hat Dak thought foolish was still in her classroom. "If Agent Moyer can't help me, perhaps General Brooke can."

"The general?" He reached for his cup, took a swallow. "Students who aren't attending risk being sent to boarding school. You don't want to involve Brooke. If the boy's skipping, I'll talk to his father."

"He won't attend without Little Rose. In my gut," Lauder made a fist and pressed it to her stomach, "I trust that little boy. If he insists on staying close to his sister, not having her at home without him, he must have a good reason."

"Mrs. Streamist all right?" Dak asked. "I can run up there."

Lauder gripped the arms of the chair. She wanted to stay there in the aura of this man, but she forced herself to stand. This wasn't about the headmistress, and he ought to be more concerned about Little Rose. "Mrs. Streamist is fine. I'll watch for Agent Moyer and speak to him when he returns."

"What else?"

Lauder had no intention of confiding further in Dak. She didn't know if she could trust him; handsome wasn't a character trait.

He motioned for her to sit again. "Please."

She sat.

"I'd much appreciate it, Miss Ellison, if before you talked to Moyer, or Brooke, you told me what Grandma has done."

Lauder felt her lips part in surprise. "Grandma? Mrs. Streamist is your grandmother?" She wanted to storm out. "I should have been told."

"Why is that? Why should you have been told, Miss Ellison?"

"Please, Mr. Thomas, quit using my name like that." She threaded her hands in her lap, rubbed one thumb with the other. "I should have been informed, that's all."

"After one day? What difference does it make whether you know or don't know? It's not a secret. I bring her in most mornings. Take her home most afternoons."

"Had I known," Lauder began. She sounded awful even to her own ears, but she couldn't stop herself. "Had I known, I would not have come trumpeting in here like a wounded goose and called your grandmother a biddy."

He suppressed a grin.

Did he agree with her wounded goose assessment, the disrespectful biddy comment, or did he think her altogether laughable? Still, her not having been informed of the relationship carried the sting of an ambush. The very sort of trap Father liked to spring on her. Keeping her constantly unsettled. "I've been informed," she said, "that agency jobs are often acquired through nepotism. I ought to have considered family ties."

One side of his mouth curled, relaxed. "You're here because of General Brooke."

"It wasn't nepotism. I made the decision on my own. The general had spent the day with Father at the railroad office downtown, contracting special trains to move an army," embarrassment had her rambling, "a thousand horses, and a million pounds of equipment. Father asked him to dinner and to be a guest at a meeting of his Civil War Map Club."

"All right."

Her argument was thin, even proved Dak's point. She couldn't stop there. "General Brooke mentioned teachers leaving, and suddenly I was saying I wanted to go."

"That quick?"

She was impulsive, from the frying pan to the fire, but that wasn't Dak's business, and he didn't need to know every detail. "I'm saying it wasn't nepotism; it was my decision to come."

"And here you are."

"It was one letter General Brooke had an aide write. Business with Father, that's all."

She felt as pinned as the boar's head. Of course, it was nepotism, and they both knew it. "I'm sorry."

"Miss Ellison," he recalled the letter, "for the benefit of science and its future service to mankind, will document the sizes and shapes of Lakota children's craniums."

Her tongue stuck to the back of her teeth. It is a science, she wanted to say, but it wasn't. Not any longer. Father wouldn't give it up, but the scientific community labeled phrenology pseudoscience. "I didn't know General Brooke included that in his letter. Then you saw the craniometer." She would not tear up. "As I've said, I have no intention of subjecting a child to that contraption."

"Glad to hear it."

"I've wasted enough of your time. Thank you."

"What happened at school?"

She studied Dak. "Agent Moyer isn't due to return, is he?"

"We can hope it's days."

We? Hardly an endearment, but maybe it proved he'd taken her word on the children and the craniometer. "You're Dak Thomas, she's Streamist."

Dak sipped the bitter coffee. It wasn't Lauder's business, and he didn't like confiding in strangers. Hell, wasn't anyone he liked confiding in, but she was something to look at, and if she did stay more than a week, she needed to understand the situation. "She and Grandpa were Mathis, but after Grandpa died, she married Streamist. My mother's maiden name was Mathis; she married a Thomas."

"Of course."

"After my mother died," Dak said, "then Grandpa, Grandma struggled to run the farm and raise us four boys. All of us ornery, busy beating up each other, too young to bring in an egg from the hen house without breaking it. She wasn't strong enough to plow or throw feed. And not with four rascals she didn't dare turn her back on."

"She married a Mr. Streamist. I understand."

"He courted her in sheep's skin, making himself useful, and Grandma believed he was the only way she could keep us together."

"But that didn't work?"

He ran his fingers through his hair. "Grandma didn't marry a man. She married a fist. The only effort that abuser ever showed was in running off my brothers." He sighed. "I'm telling you this to explain why she forgets things from one day to the next unless it's something that's made a mighty impression on her. Her saying, the children lacked the mental development for facial expression?"

"Yes."

"She read that in a widely published report. At the time, it made her weep. Now, it's stuck in her mind."

Was he suggesting Mrs. Streamist was going mad? Still, the two of them were talking, and she felt bolstered by the ease in their conversation. "What happened to your parents?"

"My parents were my grandparents."

She wouldn't ask more.

"Each brother Streamist run off," Dak said, "a kid with nowhere to go, took a chunk out of Grandma. Carved out a slab of flesh, a rib bone. Pieces of her that never grew back."

"She couldn't stop him?"

"He threatened the younger ones still left. She had no weapons against that." He stopped. He'd said more than enough. Lauder had gotten him talking, but she had to know the reasons for easing up on Grandma. Better that she heard it from him.

"You survived."

"I was ten when the bastard," Dak hesitated, rearranged his thoughts, picked a word, "died."

"I'm sorry. And now you stay because Mrs.… I mean your grandmother, needs you?"

He pulled on his chin. "I need her. The Lakota honor their elders, and in every case, they are better for it. So long as she lives, I'll care for her."

Lauder made a quick count of the numbers. Mrs. Streamist had experienced the loss of Dak's parents, the deaths of two husbands even if one was more fist than man and the loss of three young grandsons. Lauder couldn't know how many others there'd been, but she knew each death in a family changed the lives of those still living. Death sent sadness crawling around the house like the deceased's ghost. It brought sadness, blame, and a myriad of other emotions. Even now, this conversation about death made her feel uneasy and weepy. And what of the genocide the children in her classroom were experiencing? Grandparents, parents, siblings. Such a volume of loss for their young hearts. "I care deeply for those children."

"You surprise me. People usually need time to see color isn't a person."

I've had plenty of time, she thought. Twenty-two years of Nurse's care and companionship. Though the only secret she meant to keep was her plagiarism, her family was too complicated to explain. Boulders needed broken down, examined, and words found. She took a breath. "The school term still has five months to go, and I mean to—"

"Your goal is only to finish the term?"

"I…I don't know." The thought of committing for five months had felt like five years.

"However long you're here, don't use that time destroying the school."

"I have no such intentions." What a thing for him to say. "But the emotional welfare of the children is as important as teaching the English word for cup. Which is why Mrs. Streamist running into the room and frightening them and demanding that George and Little Rose be sent off, made me want to speak to Agent Moyer."

"Watch yourself. Around here, trying to do good, it's just as easy to cause harm."

"Mr. Thomas."

"Grandma's failing fast. Life's piled up on her, and she's just received another shock. One as hard as any."

"Then you know she shouldn't be around children."

"She needs watching, sometimes talked off a roof." Guilt rapped against his ribs. When someone needs your care, counts on it, and you let them down, the harm done rests on your shoulders.

He's carrying pain, Lauder thought again, in the way trees can grow around chunks of iron while no one imagines a lost tool lies hidden in the trunk.

"The Office of Indian Affairs," Dak's jaws tightened, "has petitioned Congress, claiming reservation day-schools aren't serving the country. Boarding schools supposedly are better at assimilation. Taking children from their homes, entirely away from the influence of native-speaking parents and elders is supposedly garnering better results."

Agent Moyer had said as much. She thought of the natural joy and wonder on the faces of the children in her classroom. The result of living in loving families. Mina, on the other hand, carried a deep emptiness as a result of her boarding school experience.

"The government," Dak continued, "is damned proud of their schools." He took his cup, set it hard on the small table by the stove, coffee sloshing over the rim. "They've got to justify the expense for those massive barracks."

Thinking of George and Little Rose being separated in a boarding school made Lauder's stomachache. Tearing them apart would crush them both. "Is that even legal?"

"You need to ask?" Dak shook his head. "In a country where slavery was legal, and half the country was willing to die to keep it so? Where the red man's legally slaughtered, even given blankets carrying smallpox?" his voice trailed off. He wasn't innocent.

Lauder moved to the window, wanting to look out onto a wider space and think. Cold crept through the glass and around its loose edges. "Doesn't the effort to close the school make having an effective headmistress all the more important?"

"All day schools are being watched, but we've stepped in front of the line. Two teachers leaving, the break-in, the dancing. A headmistress needing to be replaced could push us into closure."

"I see."

"If Grandma were removed and the school did stay open, it's not likely you'd want to meet her replacement. A child hater, a Sioux hater, an abuser of the worst kind? With Grandma gone, I wouldn't have an ounce of control over what went on."

"And Agent Moyer wouldn't step in if there was abuse?"

"Moyer's first choice is having the doors nailed shut. Shipping the children to boarding schools. The fewer the Lakota on his reservation, the better. What sort of abuse he'd tolerate, if it were reported to him, hard to say. But I know across the country abuse in Indian schools is ignored. Even cheered on."

"They're children."

He watched her, standing in profile, not realizing how he wanted to take her in his arms. He grabbed the frying pan on Moyer's desk and dumped the mess into the stove. "That shit stinks." And then, "Children grow into adults. If they've been broken like horses, they're easier to control."

"That's the point of the boarding schools? Break children as though they are wild animals?"

"Half. The other half happens here. Take a man's child, and he'll eat out of your hand, hoping to get his kid back."

"Children as hostages?"

"I don't want Moyer's attention on the school. With him already wanting the doors closed, and Grandma being a ... what was your word? Biddy?"

"I've apologized. Can we forget that?" The larger question was her loyalty; was it to the children or to Agent Moyer? She knew what Father and General Brooke would say. "Can't you put one of the other teachers in charge without it being a big, marked affair?" She had no idea which of the three would be better. "Just slip someone else in?"

"Not possible," Dak said. "The commission keeps records, school inspectors, and delegations are routine visitors. I don't know how long Grandma can keep it together, but the safest thing right now is just trying to hold the fort. A day at a time, if need be."

"The school is the reason you're here, not off with the others. You don't like leaving Mrs. Streamist unwatched."

Dak wondered if she knew about the death rates at boarding schools. How half the students died as a result. Hunger, disease, abuse, or they took their lives. Sometimes years later. And the half who survived the schools survived halved. "So, we agree. Any attention Moyer puts on the school threatens the school."

The thought of being in a conspiracy with Dak warmed her. "You're stuck here as long as there's a need for the school. Haven't you ever wished you could just ride away?"

"You ask a lot of questions.

"That was the last one."

"There are days. But I hear a man can't outride himself."

"I suppose your wife," she felt nervousness tracking along a line in her throat, prayed he didn't notice the catch in her voice, "has family close by. She wants to stay in the area, too?"

"You're awfully curious." His eyes said he saw through her veiled question. "As much as I love Grandma, taking a woman into that house wouldn't work. She'd need skin tough as boot bottoms."

Relief at his not being married was followed by embarrassment for having asked. What to say, now? "Men take women into all sorts of homes. Even dirt dugouts."

"True enough. A flash of skirts around here and a dozen bastards line up to see if she's half as pretty as their horse. Some ain't that particular."

"And you?"

"I'd prefer a face a smidgen less horsey." He glanced off and back. "It's tough in these parts. White women don't belong here."

"And red women?"

"They've got no choice."

Lauder moved for the door, determined this time to leave. He was single and not interested in a white woman. Did he have eyes for Mina?

He'd made sure to get her back on the reservation. "I won't speak to Agent Moyer," she said. "You bring back George and Little Rose."

"Did you assign names?"

"I thought I wasn't to hurry."

"The delegation is likely to ask. Hearing Christian names feels like souls on the road to salvation. But no hurry."

She wanted to mention Mina hadn't been saved by her schooling, but decided against bringing her friend's name into the conversation. "Thank you. I'll try and work with Mrs. Streamist."

"Every day we keep those doors open; the students are a day older. That isn't much, but it's a day."

Twelve

THE SUN HAD set a full hour earlier, and the temperature hung well below freezing. The mess hall held men in civilian clothing as well as military officers, some with wives.

Nearly three weeks had passed since Lauder's arrival, but she still wasn't accustomed to dining in a boisterous crowd, and the place still looked foreign. More so in the evenings with darkness blacking out the windows, lamps throwing shadows across the space, and the voices of so many men all swirling with a combative air, needing to be heard over the others.

Mina had chosen their table as she was wont to do, picking one in the back corner. Spinster Salem, Dolly, and Greta had chosen a table in the middle of the room and closer to one of the stoves.

"Of the three," Lauder nodded at the women, "who's your favorite?"

"Greta, absolutely. Blackbird said she loved a Lakota man, and he'd asked her to be a wife. Some say she lived with him and his three wives for a time in the teepee, but she took up too much room, and the wives sent her away."

"Would even three women have the nerve to run her off?"

"I'd want no part of that."

"Maybe she left because she couldn't stand their chattering. Someone should ask her what really happened."

"Not me," Mina said.

Lauder put down her fork, turned her feet out from beneath the table. "Then I will."

"She once had a lad misbehaving in her class." Mina spooned a single bean in her mouth and said no more until she'd chewed and swallowed. "Without touching the fellow, Greta lifted him and the chair he sat on, over her head."

"Really?"

"He was fourteen."

"Really?"

"With one hand."

"Well, never mind." Lauder brought her feet back under the table. "If I ever get the chance, I'll ask Red Cloud if he knows the husband."

Mina put down her spoon. "Have you spoken with Red Cloud?"

"I know he doesn't live far," Lauder said, "but Dak warned me against going. He says angry people from all over the reservation are coming into camp close to him."

"Dak's right."

Lauder wasn't sure she understood. "You mean someone angry might harm me?" There'd been the band of men who'd nearly ridden their horses over Dak. "Or do you think Red Cloud wouldn't welcome me?"

"Red Cloud has many worries. Perhaps he would not welcome the time your visit would require. Perhaps he would consider you a thief."

"Thief? I would write about him only for my journal."

"His time for your journal? And what would you write? Lauder Ellison's opinion of Red Cloud as washed through her history and her beliefs. Your people, however, will believe you wrote the man."

"No. I'd promise—"

"Promise?" Mina cut her off. "Red Cloud says of all the promises whites have made him, they've only kept one. They promised to take the land, and they did."

Mina's words and her tone sounded close to anger. Lauder wanted to ask what was wrong, but changing the subject seemed best. "This morning, a couple of willing soldiers visited my class. At first Badger and Much Wind were scared." She ought to have prepared the children more before the soldiers walked in. It hadn't been just the boys; most of the children had been afraid. "The men stayed nearly an hour," Lauder continued, "let the boys touch their guns, and a couple of girls pulled their beards. By the time they left, the class was marching behind them like ducklings."

Mina's stare stung.

"Don't look at me like that. It was a great success. There must be trust between the races."

Chairs scraped, cutlery scratched against plates, voices rose over the tops of others.

"My class listens as I say the Pledge of Allegiance." Lauder caught herself and stopped. Mina was not in favor of children being forced to honor the flag. "I'm sorry. I'm trying to explain how when I started, I made mistakes right and left. I'm still making them, but I'm feeling better. I think I'm doing better."

Mina lifted another bean, studied it and tipped her spoon, the bean dropping back onto her plate. "Three more from my room are too sick to attend."

"I've lost two," Lauder said. "And you? Are you ill? Once again, you've only nibbled."

"People are dancing tonight. I'm going to join them."

"Ghost dancing?" A shiver ran up Lauder's spine. She looked around, making sure no one heard. "You're risking everything." The idea was also offensive to their relationship: Mina associating with militants, willingly living in a world separate from Lauder's. "You could be arrested. You'd lose your job."

"It's dancing and prayer."

Lauder leaned in, whispered. "Dancing is against the law."

"All those years in school. The drums, the dancing, they were stolen from me. I will dance with my people and my ancestors again tonight."

Their variant cultures cut a rift between them that Lauder wished wasn't there. She had been promising herself that after so long they were close as sisters. "Did you say dance again?"

"This is the second night. Has Atlock, the fool, reported our location?"

On most days, Lauder listened to Agent Moyer for nearly an hour and wrote down his ramblings. Which meant interacting with Dak, as well. She rarely missed an afternoon. Sgt. Atlock came and went. "He was off somewhere yesterday and returned late this afternoon. I haven't heard his report. He might have told Agent Moyer where to make the next little X on his map. If he did—"

"We will not stop. Dancing and prayer are all we have left."

Lauder's eyes moistened. How could Mina think about opposing Agent Moyer and five thousand troops? Breaking the law when her employment, maybe even her life, was at risk? "It's too dangerous."

With a quick glance over her shoulder, Mina took in the room. White men with meanness riding their faces, regimented uniforms, guns and bullets strapped to their hips. "Do you not see this? Danger is the reason we dance."

"I should have brought you into my classroom. Had you see that white soldiers are only men."

"Come with me," Mina urged. "See that we dance because we seek to live."

Lauder's heart sped. "No. And you shouldn't go either. Riding off in the night when it's so dangerous. You're asking for trouble."

"Night or day. No difference. With our women, white men do not need the cover of darkness."

Lauder studied the sad eyes behind Mina's dark lashes. "I wish I could take you away from here. We would move somewhere safe, find teaching jobs, discuss books in safe, carpeted rooms."

"Do not worry," Mina said. "I'll wear my Indian ears that hear for miles and use my Indian eyes that can see into tomorrow."

"Yeah, and with your Indian horse that walks on clouds without making a sound. Very funny."

Mina leaned farther over her plate. "I want you to come, watch a dance, see that we are not murderous."

"I can't. I can't lose this job. I don't even know where I would go."

Mina took moments to herself. "Mother's basket is safe," she said slowly. "You are kind to keep her."

The food on Lauder's plate no longer interested her. "I wouldn't let anything happen to …her." Surely Thoreau had some words of wisdom about being too meek to support a not-by-blood-sister, but

Mina's proposal was too dangerous. "The dancers are being blamed for everything. The army means to destroy them."

"If you won't come for me, come for your journal."

"Risk a thousand soldiers descending on us with rifles firing?" She concentrated on the stars around Mina's neck. Was there a way, mythical, ghostly, in the same way that Lauder flew to battle fields, that Babette could fly via the scarf and attend the dance? Could she help protect Mina?

"I want you to see," Mina tried again, "how your newspapers lie."

"I know they lie. The truth makes less money."

Mina's eyes reflected her disappointment.

"Even if dancing were legal," Lauder insisted, "I can't tonight. I'm working on a story."

Evenings throughout the week, Lauder had been working on a story. Writing, scratching through, rewriting. If there was no future for her as a historian, maybe she could write fiction and publish under a pen name. But fiction didn't excite her, and the plot was both hopelessly muddled and trite. She blamed her lack of concentration on the restless stirring in the back wall, how word of her plagiarism was hitting Father, and dreaming about Dak. His eyes said he cared about her, but he kept his heart shut away. Which was fine. Perfectly fine. She didn't need a man, and she wasn't staying. But Dak made her loneliness heave and burn.

"You do not act for Lauder. Perhaps your stories beg for you to stand up."

As Mina spoke, Lauder watched the way she wrapped one end of the scarf around her fingers. Tight and absentmindedly as her words threw down a gauntlet. But didn't real friends do exactly that? Challenge you? Push you to be brave? "I am standing," Lauder insisted. "Coming to the reservation took standing up." She hadn't confessed her plagiarism to Mina. She would. When there were words. When her character was large enough to admit its shame.

Mina drew a clean white rag from her bookbag and flung it over her cupped palm. With her plate close, her body blocking her actions from the room, she hurriedly scraped the meat, potatoes, and beans into the well. In a flash, all was wrapped and in her bag. Her plate clean.

The same pocketing had happened the previous night. And perhaps the one before. Lauder had thought then that Mina intended to give Plants Corn and Blackbird the treat of variety in their diet, but tonight's fervent pocketing felt more intense. Was she bringing home food so that they could eat at all? "You aren't ill?"

"I am not ill."

The food stash wasn't much, and Mina's contract included an evening meal, but taking food off the premises might be seen as stealing. Every time Lauder sat in front of Agent Moyer, pen in hand taking down his ramblings, he remarked on the robbery and how, "every redskin's a thief."

Lauder's foot tapped the floor under the table, and she quieted it with a firm hand on her knee. Maybe by returning to the discussion of her classroom, she could distract Mina from wanting to dance. "Today was nice. The little fellows I'm always talking about, Badger and Much Wind, and no, I haven't assigned Christian names yet, asked if soldiers could visit again."

"You are dangerous."

"We can do a great service in teaching them trust."

"I will dance."

"If there's fear, there's going to be confrontation. We must do what we can to bridge the two races."

Mina didn't answer.

"Do you want to know what the boys said?"

Mina waited.

"'Happy soldiers. Soldiers much fun.' Now, tell me that's not a good thing."

"I will dance."

Lauder reached across the table and grabbed Mina's wrist. Shapeless forms crouched in her. "Please."

Dolly's laugh rang out, and Lauder turned to see her chortling at their handholding. A laugh that had the room look briefly at her and then to the subject of her laughter.

Mina tried to pull away, but Lauder held tight. "There's something evil about that woman."

Sgt. Atlock entered the hall and looked around. He noticed Lauder, nodded, but went to Dolly, passing tables of military who neither spoke to him nor lifted a finger in acknowledgment. He clasped a hand on Dolly's shoulder.

"Look at that," Lauder whispered. "The two of them touching in public. Before the eyes of God."

As quickly as Sgt. Atlock approached Dolly, he left and headed for Lauder's table.

"Here he comes," she said. "Coming to flirt with me."

"Perhaps he comes for me."

"You know him? Stay away from him."

"Miss Ellison," Sgt. Atlock stood at the table, "how's Moyer's little reporter?"

Before Lauder managed a proper eyeroll, he turned to Mina. "You ready to sell those moccasins?"

"Not for sale."

"Find a price."

"I've said before. There is no price."

He nodded, but nothing in his expression said acceptance.

"No price," Mina said again.

What is it, Lauder wondered, that had Sgt. Atlock's eyes narrow? Did he want the moccasins that badly, or was he angry that a red woman thought she had the right to deny him anything? Even after his suggestion that she name her price? "Sgt. Atlock," Lauder cut in, "Would you please walk me back to my lodge? It's very dark." She needed to separate the two before their conversation grew more heated and Mina said something that could result in serious trouble.

Mina rose. "I must go."

With Sgt. Atlock standing just there, Lauder couldn't apologize again to Mina or attempt to explain further why she wouldn't attend the Ghost Dance. And she couldn't beg yet again for Mina not to go. Taking her time, Lauder pulled her coat from the back of her chair, secured each button, then her hat, sticking through the thirteen-inch pin, giving Mina time to exit the mess hall and be away.

Dolly's daggered looks followed them out the door.

With their breaths cloudy in the cold night air, they passed the post office and the trader's store. All the while Sgt. Atlock talked, and all the while she heard nothing. Mina was dancing.

"It's a wide country," Sgt. Atlock droned. "First, we defeated the redskins east of the Mississippi...."

The longer he pontificated, the more Lauder tried to tune him out, and the happier she was for the darkness that hid the ire on her face.

"Then Mexico tried to take California," he sermonized.

What? Did he read, or did he spend his life supposing and listening to idiots?

"The Sioux didn't even mind none of that," he continued. "The goldrush. That's what finally pissed them off. They'd thought themselves the last of the great, free Indians." His voice boomed. "The unconquered warriors. Civil War breaks out, and redskins believe whites'll end up killing each other off."

He's Father all over again, Lauder thought. Albeit a better-looking version, and I'm right back in the library being taught for my own good.

"What do you think of that?" he asked. "Them hoping we all die?"

"I think I'd hope the same thing."

"Well then, you ain't such an educated woman after all."

She reached up with a mental hand and poked him in the eye. "We took everything. Left them land that's semi-desert and told them to grow corn on it."

"You're right about the land. Round here, there ain't enough rain in a decade to keep your tongue wet. But hell, they're the ones calling this whole damn area 'sacred.'"

As a lady, she wouldn't tell him to shut up, but he had expounded too long on his brilliance. "I understand you just returned from a scouting mission. Anything important I should add to Agent Moyer's records?"

"You've never seen and won't never see a redskin harnessed to a plow. If they ain't going to farm, there ain't a reason for them to have farmland."

"Father has money sitting in the bank. That doesn't mean someone else has the right to take it because he isn't using it. And actually," she said, "the Sioux were using the land. They were pasturing wild game and buffalo. And despite how arid the land is, many are trying to farm. Dak says Red Cloud and his people, and the chief the army calls Big Foot, are trying to farm." She wondered about Plants Corn. Surely he, as his name professed, wanted it known he'd given up fighting and meant to farm.

"This here's a war, darling."

"The government should be sending the promised annuities. Children are dying."

"It's a war."

Her reasoning stopped at his ears. He cared nothing for her opinions, especially if they interfered with his more important ones. A man in love with himself, he didn't want to talk with her; he wanted to talk at her.

"Sioux thinking themselves better," he went on, "because they're the last ones the army's getting around to."

"It's really not 'them they're getting around to,' is it? It's the land."

He slowed even more. Looked down at her. "Being the last buffalo run off a cliff don't make you any luckier than the first."

"Hope isn't wrong."

"Long as you ain't Indian," he laughed. "If you are, it's a goddamn waste of time."

Pick up your fancy boots with your fancy spurs, she wanted to tell him, and walk. This wasn't a summer night with the two of them out for an after-dinner stroll. "No one," she said, "can blame the Lakota for wanting their families to survive. The treaties were all lies."

"Now hold on," Sgt. Atlock stopped. "Those papers got the reds to quit killing white folks going west. Now we got trains instead of wagons, and it's safe to pass through."

"So, honoring the treaties is no longer necessary?" She rocked foot to foot. "They've served their purpose?"

"The government ain't a stone building. Every election we got new leaders. Every Congress has a right to rule its way."

Lauder tightened the stampede string on her hat. Loosened it.

Tightened it again. "Treaties were signed. What about the nation's honor?"

"Whites got it rough, too," Sgt. Atlock said. "Hell, fighting dust and drought and wives hanging themselves from windmills."

Lauder started forward. "Promises were made."

"You ain't listening." He was at her side. "Hostiles out there dancing, attacking homesteads, hiding out from the army. Ain't all that breaking treaties, too?"

She wished Dak were there. Arguing with this man was pointless. He had no intention of even considering another point of view. The more she said, the wider he opened his mouth with utterances he supposed splendid and impressive.

His spurs jingled. "We're getting 'em. Every treaty makes a smaller pen."

"People aren't horses."

"You ain't going to last here."

"You're condescending."

"You ain't got the backbone for hard."

"That's doubly condescending."

"You mean to survive," his brows creased, "you best start growing some grit. Railroads are hammering down track faster 'an rats breed. Reds ain't seen it all yet."

On the train to Rushville, Lauder had seen the packed railcar of foreigners with dreams of owning land swirling in their eyes. And a little girl with tangled hair hungry and wanting a bed to sleep in. "The whole situation is miserable."

"'Course it is. Whole world's hungry.'"

She walked faster, wanting to leave Sgt. Atlock behind. Father liked to brag how railroad wealth built cities: banks, iron works, businesses, schools, even churches. And how the wealth of cities built the country. But the treaties? She wanted things right or wrong. She wanted all things that affected Dak, Mina, and the school to be right. Everything else to be wrong. No grey area.

Passing the hotel, noise came from between it and the Wagon and Repair Shop. Window light from the hotel shone dimly on a patch of dark alleyway. Lauder could make out the broad shoulders of a man in an army-issued coat, his pants sagging so low only his wide-spread legs kept them from dropping entirely to the ground. He seemed to be thrusting himself in and out against the wall. Then a naked thigh in his hand, and the dark and vacant eyes of a young woman staring out over his shoulder. An Indian woman looking as though in a stupor as the man grunted and drove.

Lauder couldn't move. The woman wasn't fighting or showing any signs of distress, but her stare proved she was beyond consenting. What name for this when she wasn't present? Wasn't it still rape? "Do something," she hissed at Sgt. Atlock.

He grabbed her elbow, pulled her forward. "Nothing to see there. You break it up, you'll cheat her out of her quarter."

Lauder pulled free. "We must stop it. Have the man reported."

Sgt. Atlock grabbed her arm for a second time, jerked her forward. "Ain't nothing there but a soldier sowing his oats."

Just as she tried to twist free, the soldier slumped for a moment, stepped back and shook his member into his pants. The woman's dress dropped, and she disappeared into the deep darkness.

Lauder needed several feet of walking before she could speak. She thought of the soldiers camped around the agency. "Thousands," General Brooke had said, and Agent Moyer, "More than fought in the Mexican American War." All that male energy cleaned guns, drank too much cheap whiskey, slapped down cards in losing games, dreamed of women or took them. "That wasn't just a man sowing oats. You may have noticed a woman was there, too."

"Squaws come for it."

"If they do, it's because they're starving and have already been robbed of personhood. They don't 'come for it' because they want some white soldier to poke his…."

He chuckled, waiting for the word she'd use.

She loosened the top button on her coat. He made her blood boil even in freezing weather. "Whites have reduced the women. It's a form of female slavery."

"Hold on—"

"I haven't finished. It's also white men who bring their whoring diseases to the reservations."

"You're awful friendly with the one wearing my moccasins."

"So? And they aren't your moccasins. She's not selling them."

"That beadwork says she's damn near militant."

"Because she still owns something beautiful? Because she still elects to honor her heritage?"

"It ain't their custom to wear them like Mama's knitted socks."

"She likes them. Whites are individuals. They don't all act in the same way. Don't you suppose Lakota are also individuals?"

He lifted his chin, scratched his jaw. "There ain't been a war in history where soldiers ain't had a bit of fun with women."

He's a monster, Lauder thought. "The past is not a moral compass. What about the children soldiers leave behind?"

"Spoken like a woman."

The sound of his spurs reminded her of the tiny bells on Pou-sa's collar. Announcing where he was at all times. But the bells weren't Pou-sa's idea. Coming abreast of her cabin, she rushed for the door latch. "That soldier back there, he won't even know if she bears his child."

"Wouldn't be no child of his." Atlock used a middle finger to push his hat an inch higher above his brows. "Men's seed all stirred up with a dozen others; what's born ain't one man's."

She squinted at him. Perfect features but for his loathing eyes. "That's not science. That's nonsense."

"That there's a proven fact."

Tall, strong, and with all the white matter between his ears of a post. No argument could penetrate the wood. The pity was that he believed his nonsense, and his morals were based on it. How many children had he fathered, never believing he'd fathered one? "The Lakota," Lauder pointed back into the darkness and toward the alley, "those the army labels militants and destroyers, they are fighting for that woman, too. They are dancing for her." She stepped inside. "Good night, Sgt. Atlock."

"That back there, you and me ought to give it a try."

"Never." Such a crude, dishonorable man to speak to her in that way. "Never."

"Miss, that there's a challenge."

Slapping him would require touching him, and she wouldn't, even through a glove. It would also mean getting so close he could grab her. She had not thought of him as dangerous before, albeit, his swampy imagination wasn't a surprise. With a stirring unease, she thought him dangerous, now. "Never."

"One day—"

"Clean out your ears. Never."

She slammed the door, dropped the bar across, and paced, still in her coat and hat. Out there in the winter night, a woman's body and soul had been used like lamp oil. The victim had walked away, but with less of herself. "I'm sorry," she addressed Mina's basket. "I should have gone to dance with her."

When she'd settled enough, she opened her journal. Writing always calmed her. *Little Rose, that innocent little creature, does she have a white father who doesn't know, or care that she exists? Atlock justifies male brutality by believing a child can be sired collectively, leaving individual men free of responsibility. He believes a child can have many fathers, and thus, no father at all.*

The noise she often heard startled her. Tonight, it was louder, more insistent. Her heart chugged. The bar lay securely across the door, shutting out danger, but what of the ghostly danger inside with her? "Who's there?" She stood, turned in a circle: desk, bed, dresser, stove. And the back wall with its fresh paint. "Who's there?"

Thirteen

LAUDER WOKE THE next morning feeling pinned to her bed. She searched the past night's dreams for what she could recall, but the gray wasn't there. It lay ahead in this world. Something large and foreboding crawled over the cold hills toward the agency. Had something happened to Mina?

Stepping out of her quarters later, the morning sun in the east gave light but no heat. She shivered even in her heaviest clothing. In front of the agency office, Dak stood with a group of men, military and civilian. His being there meant he'd already dropped off Mrs. Streamist and started the school's stoves. She was later than she had realized; children would be gathering.

Seeing her, Dak left the men and crossed the road so readily, she felt he'd been keeping one eye on her door.

"Morning." The more time he spent near her, the harder he had to fight himself to keep his heart in check. "You all right?"

"Something is wrong," she said. "Do you feel it?" He did, she realized. Nervousness had him standing out in the cold and crossing the road to her. "Air changes right before tragedy."

Her nervousness spooked him. He wanted to ask if she'd been woken in the night by anything in the cabin, but that was impossible, and he didn't want to hear her possible answer. "You sleep okay?"

"I don't know what it is. Nothing. Maybe everything."

"Long as you're clear." He wanted to open her door, take her inside, barricade them, and stand guard. But against what?

"Hey!" A shout from one of the men.

"Coming." And to Lauder, "Ranchers. Figuring if the army needs their beef, they'll charge three times the going rate."

"And the army," she answered, "will gladly pay it to feed soldiers while claiming there is no money to feed starving Lakota children. But then, this whole mock of a situation is about profit, isn't it?"

He glanced across the road again.

"Go." The word felt pulled from her stomach. "I'm late for school and renaming the children." She had a list of names: Judith, Michael, Martha, James, but imagining those on the innocent faces made her squeamish. "Christian names," she mimicked Agent Moyer, "no nonsense. No gibberish." Though to the children, the names would all be gibberish.

Rushing on to school, she looked for the vagrant hooded and slumped at his post, a beast in dirty furs, his head buried on his chest and likely hiding a face full of scars. He wasn't there, never was in the morning, and she supposed Plants Corn had taken him in for the night, kept him from freezing. Or was it a community of people who made sure the poor creature was safe?

Plants Corn. There was a name an agent could say. Since meeting the man, the name had bothered Lauder. Was it a native name given to him? Or a name that identified him to whites as a friendly and obedient? Or a joke on whites who preferred simpleton tags?

Seeing Mina in the school yard, standing at her assigned spot, Lauder rushed over. "You're safe. Thank God."

They stepped a few feet from Mina's students, a looser group of children than Lauder's class and talking amongst themselves.

Mrs. Streamist watched them. As did Dolly.

"No cavalry attack," Mina said, "only prayers and dancing."

"I'm sorry for being an alarmist, but I worried—"

"Then stop." Mina smiled, her face bright. "Our prayers are heard."

"Shh," Lauder whispered. "Keep your voice down."

"We held hands and danced in a circle."

Lauder wasn't certain why having danced in a circle mattered, though Mrs. Streamist could no doubt give a thorough explanation.

"We were one, a hand in each of my hands." She swayed slightly. "One in the darkness, one with the fire, one in motion. The people, the earth, even our deceased relatives."

"Deceased?"

"Dancers fell into dream and saw their dead. They shared their stories."

Babette? If Lauder had gone, might she also have fallen into trance and for the first time seen her sister? The vision would have changed her forever.

"Being with them," Mina said, her eyes filling, "the ancestors' tears streamed down our faces." She paused as if only in that moment did the realization fully touch her. "I am one with my people."

The words held such emotion, Lauder's own eyes misted. "Of course you are. They love you."

"We are roots of one tree."

"I'm happy for you."

"Yet you carry sadness." Mina paused. Then kindly, "My not-by-blood sister."

Exactly, Lauder thought. The dancers are your real blood relatives. Family I can never be.

"The fire," Mina said, "and dancing with our four-legged brothers." And to Lauder's quizzical look. "The drums. The skins of our brother the buffalo live and speak to us."

"I understand." She understood that in dancing, Mina experienced a oneness with her people that had been denied all her years in boarding school. Mina had come home to the reservation and relatives. A bond stronger than that of her new friendship with a white associate.

"Good morning," Richard called across to Lauder. Then Much Wind and Badger, laughing as though their foolish teacher had lost her way and needed reminding she belonged with them.

"Sorry," she said to Mina. "Must go." Her students gave her a much-needed excuse to take her struggling emotions and hurry to them.

Later, near the end of the school day, after the meal of a thick slice of white bread, which Lauder loathed, she stood at the window looking out at the tree. She hated the bread most because the children ate it greedily, supposing the bread, likely made of rancid flour, food.

The seven boys lay sprawled on the floor, cheering as two of them competed, spinning walnut-sized wooden tops. George, amongst them, and Little Rose at his side, silently drawing pictures of the same skinny horse she'd drawn endless times. Other girls stood at the blackboard playing with chalk while still others sang and clapped their hands on their knees. She-Stands-Brave watched them with earnest eyes. The child never gathered around the others, never entered the school excited, as did many. Always hesitant, still, she never let her fears stop her.

Lauder crossed her arms over her chest. The Episcopal delegation was scheduled to arrive in four days. The last day before Christmas break. She began the day determined to assign English names, but hour by hour she'd kept them to herself as the foreboding she felt moved closer. Unable to continue counting games or showing pictures and having the children repeat the English word after her, she'd had Richard tell them they could play. And so far, Mrs. Streamist, with her fearful all-seeing eyes and ears hadn't burst into the room clapping and insisting children must not play.

Across the school yard, the tree, soldiers in a far field, a sky ice blue, everything looked normal. Nothing sinister or new to see, but she felt no more reassured. The day thus far had been a stretch of fractured hours. Should she have gone with Mina to the Ghost Dance? A sister would have gone, given support. At least one reporter had attended a dance, sat on the sidelines, watched, and wrote an account for his newspaper. Agent Moyer hadn't run him off the reservation. Had she refused to go afraid of committing an illegal act or was her real fear that of being the only white woman amid two, even three hundred Lakota? Or had she feared seeing Mina with her people and not needing her white friend? Whatever the reason, it had been her limitation, and she had failed Mina.

The boys' sudden burst of cheering and yelling pulled Lauder from her mulling. Much Wind's wooden top wobbled erratically in its last rotations and fell over while his opponent's top spun on. He flopped back onto the floor as if he'd been shot. The endearing smile, a little boy in love with life, remained. Other small fellows who'd been cheering for him were as loud as those who cheered for the victor.

"Boys, quiet," Lauder said. "Mrs. Streamist will be coming."

Dak rapped on the doorframe.

He was exactly the balm her jittery nerves needed and she smiled. He came every day, often more than once, pretended to fuss with stoves, wandered through the hallway. She knew he checked on his grandmother and needed to assure himself all was well, but the frequency of his visits, and his way of lingering a long moment outside her door was proof he had growing feelings for her.

"Miss Lauder, a moment."

She saw it then. His expression, the serious, just below the smile he gave to the children. "Now?" she asked. She wouldn't ask what was wrong, and Dak wouldn't share frightening news in front of the children, but they sensed his tension. Girls stopped singing and clapping. Little Rose came to her knees to lean more heavily onto George. Much Wind pocketed his top. Lauder wanted to promise she'd be right back, but a broken promise was worse than no promise. "Continue your games," she said.

"Trouble come?" Badger asked.

"Everything is fine." She tried to offer a broad smile as she stepped into the hall.

"Moyer wants you," Dak said.

"Now? I can't leave the children. Tell him I'll be there when the parents arrive."

"Have them go into Mina's room."

"That urgent?"

Dak's eyes said, yes.

At Mina's door, Lauder's students in a bunch behind her, she spoke calmly into the room. "If they may, my students would like to join you. I'm to see Agent Moyer."

Mina nodded, her gaze full of question and sliding over Lauder to Dak deeper in the hallway.

I'm sure it has nothing to do with your dancing, Lauder wanted to say, but she had no way of knowing. "What's happened?" she whispered as soon as she'd ushered the children inside and stood alone with Dak.

"Grab your things. Sitting Bull is dead."

"My gosh. What happened." Plants Corn had promised to take her in the spring to see the chief, and given that Sitting Bull was related to Mina's uncle, he was also related to Mina. "I should tell her."

Dak grabbed her forearm. "The news might send the school into a panic."

"I want her to hear it from me."

"Make quick work of Moyer and come back. We should let the children hear the news at home. Let their families decide how."

Leaving without telling Mina felt dishonest. Another betrayal. And it was hard to know who Dak was protecting. His grandmother from falling into a panic? The children? Possibly, Sitting Bull's death wouldn't mean much to the children, though certainly a few would be upset. If there was weeping in the school, the news would pass like flood water from one room to the next. She wanted to be the one her children needed at this time, but with a pang of sorrow, she knew she wasn't the one who could best help them. They needed their parents.

With a quick glance at Mrs. Streamist's closed office door, they hurried out, Lauder rushing to keep up with Dak. It wasn't just Sitting Bull's death that had her stomach sinking. Feeling loss for a stranger wasn't possible, but she knew the death lifted a large boot over the heads of so many. People across the reservation would be crestfallen. The fearful would be more fearful. The dejected more dejected. And thousands of tense soldiers would be even more tense. "What will happen now?"

"Hard to say. Quite a few died today. Could be nothing, could be the first battle of the war. In which case, you'd be safer in Omaha."

"Aren't we passed that?"

He wanted to wrap an arm around her. She didn't belong anywhere near danger, but she was right. "Yup. Passed that."

As they neared Agent Moyer's office, the American flag above the door snapped in the wind. Mina was right. The stars and stripes symbolized ownership. Land conquered and a new government in power over its subjects. She shivered. An in-your-face flaunting.

"What," she asked, "does Agent Moyer expect me to write that every reporter on the reservation isn't going to write?"

"Word for word what he tells you. Not what paper bosses want."

"His version."

"You're his personal clerk."

I'm not, she thought. But for every hour she sat in his office, listening to him stew and boast, she gathered more facts and details about issues across the Sioux reservations. Her body of notes grew. Not that she could ever use them. She'd murdered that career.

"Sitting Bull," Dak said, "was shot at Standing Rock. Reporters are killing their horses getting there for the scoop. Moyer needs someone here to tell his story."

She felt a sudden jab of panic. "He's not wanting my notes sent to General Brooke or General Miles, is he?"

"Would that be so bad?"

"I don't want my name on anything. Besides, no one would believe anything I wrote."

"Of course they would. How many reporters have had General Brooke in their homes?" Dak stretched out a hand, moved it across the space in front of him indicating a headline. "General Brooke's Female Protégé Writes Stirring Account of Sitting Bull's Death."

"General Brooke has forgotten I exist."

Her fear surprised Dak, but now wasn't the time to ask for an explanation. "La Flesche and the *Omaha Herald* won't be flattering. Moyer hopes you'll do better."

Lauder pressed a fisted hand against the ache in her stomach. "It feels like the whole world is falling. As though people are falling out of trees. Falling and never landing."

Without breaking stride, Dak wrapped an arm around her shoulder, pulled her close. "It is all right. Don't make yourself sick."

She closed her eyes. It was the first, real physical expression of affection he'd shown her. Or did it only show his fear? In the stress of Sitting Bull's death, had he forgotten himself? Her dread increased, and at the sound of a long groan, she flinched. A wooden sign swung from a rusted metal arm. The sound grated, moaned. "I thought it was that vagrant."

"There's no reason to fear John."

"John?" The man had a name. Biblical. "Easy for you, Mr. Six-Foot Plus with a gun tucked in his trousers."

They reached Agent Moyer's office, but one of the policemen guarding the door, stepped off the walk and spoke to Dak. "Moyer," Dak told Lauder with irritation, "wants you to wait until the fellows inside leave."

"So, I don't hear that version?"

As they waited, Lauder watched a skinny reporter she had seen too often. He stood in the middle of the road, his arms crossed smugly over his chest. A Lakota man stood in fringed leather leggings two yards away with his rifle lifted and aimed. A third man with a camera on a tripod, his head under black drape, sighted them in his lens, "Closer, closer," he motioned the Lakota. "Right there. Hold still."

The smugness on the reporter's face, the staged scene, as though the reporter were fearlessly facing a murderous savage, made Lauder cringe. There he supposedly stood, a big, brave man facing a savage's pointed gun. Would women see the picture in the press and swoon at his courage? Would men wish their lives held the adventure that demanded such gallantry? She lifted her hands and clawed the air as Badger had done to demonstrate a badger digging. "If I only could."

Dak chuckled. "Whose eyes you going for?"

"I'd make the circle. Get all three."

A young man with braids bouncing on his shoulders, surprised them, galloping his horse down the road, riding between the photographer and his subjects, the horse's flanks inches from the thin, wooden legs of the tripod. He rode on to the school despite the curses rained on his back. There, he jumped off his horse before it had come to a complete stop.

"Word's out," Dak said. "The commotion'll roll Grandma over. I need to get her out of there."

"I'll go with you. I want to see Mina."

"Calm Moyer's feathers first."

"Not telling her about Sitting Bull's death is a betrayal."

"Moyer's ranting. If you don't go in there, he's likely to storm the school looking for you."

"Which will frighten your grandmother. I hate being told what to do, but you're right."

Moments earlier he'd steadied her, and she felt emboldened. "You know what I really wish?"

Already turned for the school, he paused, turned back.

"I wish you and I could get away from here."

His eyes softened. She didn't know what she was saying. He couldn't leave with her any more than he could reach the gold at the end of a rainbow.

Two students were being hurried out of the school. At least one classroom knew of the death, and he wanted to get his grandmother home in case all hell broke loose at the agency. She would not survive another tragedy. "I need to get up there."

"Go," she said. "I can handle myself."

The door to Agent Moyer's office opened and two men rushed out, small notebooks in their hands, hats already back on their heads. She entered the smells of gun oil, the grime and dust of old taxidermy, and the stink of Agent Moyer's cigar. His gun lay on the corner of his desk. The day before, he'd looked gaunt with sleeplessness and worry. Now his cheeks had a fiery flush.

She drew out her notebook and pen. *Sitting Bull is dead,* she wrote. Only that morning Mina had been filled with joy, confident the dancers' prayers had been heard. The timing of that, and now this death, felt especially hopeless: punishment for the act of faith.

"Standing Rock Agency," Agent Moyer began, his eyes on Lauder, making sure she was writing. "That goddamned troublemaker is dead. General Brooke's ordered troops to stand at the ready. Tents down, they'll sleep in the cold, weapons under them."

Lauder wrote. She wondered at Agent Moyer's anxiety.

"It weren't mine," he stressed. "Weren't mine taking out Custer's murderer."

"Thousands of warriors were at the Greasy Grass," she said. "Why is Sitting Bull considered his murderer?"

"Whole country knows he was."

Which meant to Lauder that one newspaper created the label, and its popularity had been repeated and spread across the country to the masses wanting to believe that very thing.

"Ain't no Indian," a fleck of wet tobacco landed on Agent Moyer's shirt front, "has got any cause to come for me."

She tried to concentrate on getting his words down though she was a fraud, had been since the first afternoon she arrived. But how to end it?

"You writing that clear?"

Mina had told Lauder that many Lakota read the newspapers and passed on the information to those who didn't. Did he suppose her words would be published and would quell the anger of any Sioux who believed him responsible?

"Those troops out there are mine," he said. "I done that to save the good white folks around here, but Sitting Bull, now that blood ain't on my hands."

Her pen scratched.

"Looky here," he leaned over the map on his desk, rapped the sheet.

She stood, saw the clear outline of the Nebraska-South Dakota border near the bottom. A large square above that line had the initials P.R. A square closer to the top of his map and the South Dakota-North Dakota border was labeled S.R. "Pine Ridge and Standing Rock," she answered. Was it the distance between the two he wanted her to grasp, how his jurisdiction didn't reach that far north? Between the two points, a large area was hashed through with dark lines. "What's this?"

"That there is their winter holdout."

"The Badlands."

"Reds plan on taking another couple hundred to hide in there. Plan to hole up the whole rest of the winter. There'll be no way to flush them out."

"Does it matter so much if they do?"

"Army wants this ended."

She sat again, wanting away from the smoke he puffed in the air without ever bothering to turn his head.

"You ain't met the old bastard."

"Sitting Bull?" He hadn't asked a question; he'd made a statement.

A new unease made her wonder if she was being watched. "I'd hoped to meet him in the spring."

"Sour faced. Hostile. A goddamned dancer, but we got him."

"We, Sir?"

He shook his head. "Weren't me. That don't mean I'm not celebrating. Reds did it themselves."

Her stomach flopped. "His own people killed him?"

"General Miles's been telegraphed. You write how I ain't sorry for what happened, but it weren't my doing. His own people took him out."

How would she tell Mina? Sitting Bull's own people. Just as had happened with Crazy Horse? "I have it down correctly. His people. Your hands are clean."

The door swung open, and Sgt. Atlock stepped through on a rush of cold air. "Miss Ellison. How's our little reporter?" He dropped his hat on Agent Moyer's desk, unbuttoned his coat, and flung it wide like an invitation. "Dak wagered you wouldn't last a week, but look at you, decked out like we got ourselves our own Calamity Jane."

His forwardness made her grit her teeth. Our little reporter. Our own Calamity Jane. Had he forgotten their last meeting? She was not his, and she would never forget his disgusting, earlier proposition. The look in his eyes, even now, held a threatening weight as if he would indeed find a way of bedding her. She stood. "I should get back to the school."

"Sit down," Agent Moyer ordered. "I need you to stay on the side of the whites."

She sat. It was a strange remark, as was Sgt. Atlock's reaction: a nearly imperceptible twitch and recovery. A trace of guilt in his eyes.

Am I being watched because I eat with Mina and not the old teachers? "Of course, Sir." She couldn't risk angering the man by spitting out a string of words that would make Calamity Jane blush.

Sgt. Atlock pulled a letter from his pocket, flopped it on the desk in front of her. "Fellow over at the post office says it's been there a few days."

She recognized the script, the point at the top of the d, the rash swoops in the l's, and the whole of it showing Father's pen pressed hard into the envelope. She left it where it lay.

Sgt. Atlock moved to the window, lifted a newspaper from the chair, and sat. He shook out the broad sheets for easier reading. "Ochre covered mementoes of a fast-vanishing race."

Lauder fixed her eyes on the letter.

"Emaciated bodies," Sgt. Atlock read on, "and particularly their ill-nourished nerves."

"Sir?" she said to Agent Moyer, "is that all?"

The pop of a chuckle from Sgt. Atlock. "Here's one for you. 'Squaws,'" he read, "'dance until perspiration mixes the streaks of varied colored paint upon their faces and makes them look like a three-cent calico dress on a rainy day.'"

She glared at him. That's how Mina's dancing was seen? The people's last straw of hope that their children might live, mocked so shockingly in the paper? "Hideous."

"You heard our man Moyer here," Sgt. Atlock said. "It ain't wise to get too friendly with a red. Ain't a one of them can be trusted. Can't trust which ones are sneaky enough to teach by day and go off dancing at night."

Lauder stuffed Father's letter into her pocket and squeezed the spool of gold she'd begun to carry everywhere.

Fourteen

MINA'S CLASSROOM WAS empty. Deep cold already infiltrating the space.

Only Greta remained at the school. Her stove quieting, she sat at her desk holding a book, but she stared over the top, lost in thought. A large iron key lay on one corner of the desk.

Dak had left the key, trusted her. "You've heard then?" Lauder asked.

Greta answered what sounded like, "Red Cloot, Big Fooot, only stilt living."

"Did Dak take his grandmother home?" Lauder asked. No answer. "Were you able to speak with Mina? Is she all right?"

Not receiving an answer, Lauder walked down one line of empty desks, up the next. She wanted to know what Greta thought would happen now, but the woman hadn't answered the previous questions, and whatever she said would only be one more speculation. Dak had already said it could be nothing or the first battle of the war. "You've been left to lock up?"

She bit her bottom lip at Greta's silence. The woman's large hips spread over the sides of the seat, her arms in the sleeves of her dress stressed the seams. All mass, all business. Whatever happened, Greta would handle that, too. "Goodnight then."

Greta closed the book she hadn't been reading. "Goot night."

Lauder hesitated, wanting to slake her nerves by shaking conversation out of the woman, but unless Greta initiated it, Lauder knew she couldn't so much as shake the woman's hand.

Throughout the evening, not having seen Mina or Dak again, Lauder tried to read, but the words were only ink on a page. She wouldn't open Father's letter, but she tried to write one to Nurse. Attempt after attempt. Nurse would never receive the missive, at least not before Father opened it and read it. And a letter to Nurse might make him even more resentful of the dear woman. "Babette," she confessed to the music box, "I should have written him and Mother by now, but what would I write? There is too much that can't be said yet. Perhaps can never be said."

Lauder slept little. The wind howled; the world outside so angry, it silenced the critters in her back wall. Weepy with loneliness, she finally rose in the predawn light, added a bit of coal to the stove, and dressed hurriedly close to the heat. With a blanket around her shoulders, she sat in the gloom. Her pen and ink idle. Not even Babette's music box could offer assurances, and Lauder turned to the basket. Mina said that while dancing, she had felt the tears of her ancestors. As though ancestors had inhabited her body, used her heart and eyes to weep. How thin the veil between the dead and Mina.

"Watch over your daughter," she whispered to the basket. "Keep her safe."

Snow filled the air when, finally, she could use the excuse of school to leave. Blowing icy crystals stung her face, and she didn't know how much of what felt like sand was new and how much was being scraped from frozen drifts between buildings and the piles of snow proprietors scooped from their stoops. The savagery of the cold held warning, but she couldn't understand it. She'd lost so much of her childhood intuition, or perhaps, she lacked the nerve she once had to see what waited just ahead.

No horses stood shivering in front of Agent Moyer's office to say Dak was inside. She hurried on, needing the school and out of the wind.

The school door opened, which meant at least Greta with her

key was inside. Though Lauder wanted the balm of company, she avoided the room upstairs and the untalkative Greta. Stirring the ashes in her stove, she shoved a tight twist of newspaper into the warmth. Thankfully, there was enough heat still in the coals, and flame rose.

She paced, waited. Had she done anything else in the hours since Sitting Bull's death?

Dak's wagon finally entered the yard, and she backed from the window just far enough that he couldn't see inside. His presence meant routine, normalcy, a new school day beginning. One in which she needed to put her fears and what Mother called her "irrational enthusiasms" aside.

He stopped the horse, lifted off a fur, bear or buffalo, stretching across his and his grandmother's lap. He hurried around, grabbed Mrs. Streamist by the waist, and lifted her off as though she were a child.

Why bring her at all? Lauder wondered. Because at school she believed she still mattered, and Dak wouldn't deny his grandmother that? Because he could watch her better here, not worry about her wandering off through a pasture? Because, though Agent Moyer never set foot in the school, he watched and waited for the day the aging headmistress no longer did?

"Morning," Dak grinned through the classroom door as the pair walked by. "Give me a minute. I'll be back to get your stove going."

Mrs. Streamist looked especially sallow, but she walked on toward her office with a determination Lauder admired.

Dak returned a few minutes later. "You're early."

"I couldn't sleep. I wanted plenty of time to speak with Mina before school." And with you.

He dropped his hat on the desk nearest the stove and looked in. "She's gone. The threesome has a ten-day leave."

"What do you mean, gone?" A wave of panic made her slap her arms across her chest and hold tight. "She can't have just left." Without saying good-bye?

"For only ten days. Can you take a few of her students? I'll send a couple to each room."

"With all that's going on, and," she waved a hand at the window, the snow, and the tree's swaying branches, "in this weather?"

Her intensity surprised him. "They know how and where to shelter."

"Ten days? In this?" She was repeating herself. "All those people you told me about dying in the cold."

"They weren't Sioux." His surprise shifted into concern. "You sleeping okay?"

"I'm not falling apart if that's what you're asking. But Mina and I are friends." She wouldn't mention how much that friendship mattered and how much she had believed it also mattered to Mina. Was Mina's utter disregard, not a word about leaving, because Lauder had refused to attend the stupid, illegal Ghost Dance?

Dak watched her and spoke hesitantly. "They left last night. I'll have Moyer sign off on it. I'll convince him it's better not to raise any dust. Sitting Bull and all."

"You granted them leave without first speaking to your superior?"

She looked close to tears. He closed the stove door. "Fire's going strong."

"Where did they go?"

"After relatives."

"Is it safe to be out there?"

He considered her; she was all but stomping her feet. "Not if you're reading the papers."

"Ten days, a dangerous trip and not even a goodbye?" She lifted her hands to stop him from speaking. "Don't say it. I don't want to hear what you're thinking. It's just, I thought Mina might have wanted to tell me something that important."

"It's ten days. Their needing to hurry didn't have anything to do with you."

Precisely the point. She walked to her desk. Walked back. "When did they decide this?"

"They came out to the house last night. Packed up, needing to go."

Mina had been wearing the scarf, Lauder was sure. "It is a little stardust caught, which I have clutched."

His eyes narrowed.

"Thoreau," she said. This man in front of her, the tip of his nose still flushed from the cold, who Mina had gone to, who devotedly lifted his apple-doll of a grandmother from his wagon, had let the threesome just ride off despite the danger. As though he were in charge of the entire agency. Men and their supposed right to do as they please. "You just gave them permission? Without first telling Agent Moyer. Your superior."

"We've covered that. What's gotten into you?"

"Nothing, Mr. Thomas. I'm just saying you had no right to let them go."

"They aren't wards."

"How dare you!"

"Whoa. I meant to mock Moyer."

"Agent Moyer is not here."

Dak wasn't sure exactly what angered her, but he wanted to pull her into his arms, make them both happy. There wasn't a drop of blood in him not begging for that to happen. He could crush her with how tightly he wanted to hold her.

She stepped forward, flung her arms around his neck, stood on tiptoe, and kissed him hard on the lips. Her arms were shaking, unwilling to let go. "That's so I don't slap you."

He laid his larger hands over hers, squeezed them, brought them down slowly, and with eyes full of unreadable sorrow, returned them to her sides.

Embarrassed, she stepped back. Before she could say more, the school's front door opened, footsteps and voices started down the hall.

Spinster Salem went by the door with a nod, but Dolly, with a package in her arms, stopped and came in. "Mr. Dak," her eyes bright, "I'll be expecting you in my room soon."

"Every morning," he said.

Dolly looked from him to Lauder, a little upturned twist at the edges of her red lips, as if she knew Dak had just resisted the ill-given advance. She took her time stepping out, cooed over her shoulder at Dak, "I'll be waiting." Then, turning back, she held out the package. "Are you heading to the post office today? Could you mail this?" she simpered. "Please?"

His lips stretched, but the smile he gave was flat. "Often as you go, you'll find the place."

She tucked the package back under her arm, gave a cold shrug, and swayed out.

Listening to Dolly's heels clicking down the hall, Lauder wondered what it was between the woman and Dak.

Dak palmed his hat, kept it hanging at his side. "You suppose her students are learning anything? Probably best they don't learn a damn thing from her."

Lauder smoothed her hands down her hips as she wanted to soothe her emotions. She'd embarrassed herself with the misguided kiss and was even more embarrassed by his rebuttal.

"Lauder…" Dak started and stopped. He'd hurt her. He was sorry. He wanted to spend an hour telling her everything, but she'd hightail off the agency if he did. Stick to business, he told himself. "Grandma's struggling this morning. I think more than anything, she's worried about the delegation. Hopefully, being here, at the school, she'll come around."

All business, Lauder thought. She could be as cold. "With Mrs. Streamist so stressed, Sitting Bull's death, and all the angst about the dancing and troops, isn't the reservation too dangerous for visitors?"

"I telegrammed two days ago suggesting the same. No response yet. It's Christmas bringing them. Bearing gifts for the underlings."

"It may be that he who bestows the largest amount of time and money on the needy is doing the most by his mode of life to produce that misery." She gave a strained smile. "Thoreau."

"You got a headful of his sayings?"

"I do."

"Fair warning." He tapped his hat against his leg. "You get a bunch of nosey church folk trampling around the school with no idea what's what, looking for problems because finding something wrong swells them up." He sighed. "Anything can happen."

"Anything? A bad report that could land on a desk at the Bureau of Indian Affairs?"

His expression said yes. And more. She wondered if something dreadful had happened on a previous visit. Asking might sound as if she cared. She wouldn't ask.

Fifteen

AT THE END of the afternoon, with the children dismissed and the schoolyard emptying, Mrs. Streamist returned inside to stand at Lauder's door. Swathed in winter wear, her face pinched. "She didn't come?"

"Miss Mina? No," Lauder admitted. "Dak gave her permission for a few days off."

Mrs. Streamist's eyes held questions as if searching for something she might have been told several times. "She's dancing."

"I'm sure she's not dancing. Dak," Lauder would use the name again knowing Mrs. Streamist trusted him. "Dak allowed her to visit relatives. She'll be back after Christmas."

"No dancing." Mrs. Streamist's head gave a small, tremulous shake.

"Mina is not dancing." She hoped her face substantiated the lie.

A dark-skinned woman Lauder had seen before sitting on a buckboard outside the school, stepped into the doorway. "Good afternoon," Lauder said.

The woman nodded, a pleasant look of greeting, but said nothing.

"Oh, you're Richard's mother," Lauder said, happy to be meeting her. "I've seen him get into your wagon."

Another nod, her expression still pleasant.

"Your son is a wonderful student."

"Thank you."

Mrs. Streamist started for the door. "Take me home."

The familiarity between the two told Lauder that Richard's mother often took the headmistress home. "Where's Dak?" she asked.

Mrs. Streamist mumbled, her back still to Lauder. Richard's mother followed.

Watching them leave, loneliness reared over Lauder again. There was so much, even now, that she didn't know about the community and their relationships with one another. A society flourished around her, but she wasn't a part of it. "I'm not alone," she drew herself up, "I have the children." Still, she wanted to enter Mina's room, drop into a seat, and weep in the emptiness.

Only when Greta appeared in the doorway holding up a key indicating she meant to leave, did Lauder gather her things. The wind had gone down, and the temperature had fallen throughout the school hours. She crossed the school yard, her breath white and crystallizing. She was a fraud, a liar, and she didn't want to be alone with her own company. She considered going with Greta in the opposite direction, but doing so would also mean Dolly and Spinster Salem.

At the far end of Pine Ridge Road, what looked like the lump of a dead animal was slumped against a post. Dak had said, "John." With or without a name, the vagrant still scared her. Who, she wondered, given Mina and her family were gone, would help the creature in out of the cold? Not her. The agency swarmed with people, someone else would come to his aid.

Agent Moyer's horse stood tied in front of his office, a skim of snow tracing its back. The man who spent too many days off hunting with his nephew, now was holding fast to the protection of the agency, lest a Sioux thought him responsible for Sitting Bull's death. She disliked the man, but he would know Dak's whereabouts, and she didn't want to spend the rest of the day alone. She also wanted to confess that she was not sent to document his achievements. Sooner or later, the truth would be found out, and the longer the lie went on, the worse the consequences would be. She'd not yet read Father's letter, and suppose he wrote Agent Moyer a letter, informing him of her plagiarism. Or suppose Father arrived one day, accusing her of the same and demanding her reasons for not sending him the head measurements his work required. Wouldn't it be better if she confessed all now? But suppose she did, and she was sent straight away? What of the school? And what of the mother basket? What of Dak? He frustrated her, and she feared they would likely never be together, but she would not lower the guillotine blade on that hope. Not yet.

She nodded at the guard in his blankets, the tip of a rifle barrel just visible. Her comings and goings were so frequent, he no longer hesitated about letting her enter.

Agent Moyer's topcoat was unbuttoned, his shirt wrinkled, and his receding hair begged washing and a comb. He looked not just unkempt but in need of sleep. "You got your report all wrote up?"

"Nearly so. I'd like to ask a few more questions."

"A man," he rapped on his latest map, "knows the miles between two things, he can figure out other miles. Making maps takes some learning."

It was best to sound impressed, stay small, accept being taught. She couldn't today. "Cartography with the technicalities of triangulation," she began, "and a broader understanding of coordinates, as well as a land-surveyor's ability to read topography, are all concepts requiring an understanding of nuanced and polysyllabic terms." She forced a shudder. "No female mind can grasp it."

"Ain't no cause to sell yourself short," he said. "You been trained to read and write both."

"Thank you, Sir."

"Just signed a pass for that friend of yours." He glanced towards Dak's desk and a sheet of paper. "Ten-day leave. If they ain't leaving 'till tomorrow, they got nine. My signature says this is day one."

"Why only ten?"

"I ain't signing for no longer."

And Dak knows it, she thought. "They must have gone to Sitting Bull's funeral."

Agent Moyer pinched the remaining scrap of cigar in his mouth and dropped the chewed butt into the frying pan. "Ten days. After that, they's hostiles on the loose."

The wet, brown stub lay inert and looked like a deposit from

Pou-sa. "They aren't hostiles," she said. "Mina teaches here. You know her uncle; he brought me from Rushville."

"Weren't me sent him. Dak."

"At any rate, you know they are not hostiles."

"Ten days," Agent Moyer repeated. "They come back in eleven, the army'll arrest them. That won't be my business."

The boar head taunted. "Mina's needed at the school."

Agent Moyer scrunched his brow. "She ain't needed if she can run off for ten days. Could be that school can't keep teachers and ought to be shut down."

There it is, Lauder thought. Mina's absence would be used as additional fodder for reasons why the school should be closed. He likely hoped Mina had joined the hostiles and would be arrested. *Schools, churches, rations,* she would add to her journal, *none are about saving a single Sioux. They are the great cover-up designed to let whites sleep at night.* "Christmas break is Friday," Lauder said, "and she'll be back when the school reopens. She's missing only a few days of teaching."

Knowing her friend and her friend's relatives would be labeled hostiles, even if a blizzard dropped twelve inches of snow and made wagon travel impossible, trembled her breath. The threesome was guilty of being Lakota. It was only a matter of time until Agent Moyer's law got around to them.

"Ten days," he repeated.

"They're mourning. They're not children."

"My legal wards. Same thing."

The more she argued, the more he enjoyed his rebuffs. She softened her tone, hoping to soften his anger. "Agent Moyer, we just don't know what sort of ceremony Sitting Bull's family will have in his honor. Suppose an observance and the long ride to and from takes longer?"

"Indians acting up over every little thing. Good white folks scared. It's up to me; got to keep 'em safe."

This little man, Lauder thought, with his big cigar and bigger ears, isn't keeping anyone safe. "Sitting Bull was killed by his own people. What is it you fear?"

"It ain't the old chief getting himself kilt. It's the dancers screaming at the dead to rise up. It ain't human, calling up the dead to attack us."

Did he really believe their dancing would resurrect the dead?

"They come swooping in here, how we going to survive that?"

The dead? Did the man even hear what he was saying? What sort of weapons did he suppose the dead wielded?

"Ain't going to be no funeral," Agent Moyer said. "Army stuck the body in the ground. Already forgot where."

"An unmarked grave?"

He fingered the gun, his thumb brushing the trigger. "That squaw teacher? You think she come to Pine Ridge to anger my Indians? If she thinks she—"

"No," Lauder blurted. Sgt. Atlock's reading rang in her ears. "Squaws with face paint dancing until perspiration made them look like three-cent calico dresses on a rainy day." People across the country had read the description. Believed it. Used it to justify their hate. Coming into the agent's office had been a rotten idea. She needed to get away.

"You ain't getting involved where you shouldn't?" Despite his short stature, he tilted his head in such a way as to look down his nose at her. "You ain't thinking you can make friends with an Indian? Ain't no trusting a redskin. Never."

"Miss Mina is my colleague. She's educated, wise, and her students love her. Thank you, I'll leave now and finish my report."

"The old lady?" Agent Moyer asked. "Dak's grandma? She struggling to run the school?"

Spinster Salem lacked the initiative to speak against Mrs. Streamist, and Greta never would. Who then? Dolly. Agent Moyer wanted even more information and was fishing for something that would help in his crusade to close the school. "Mrs. Streamist runs a tight ship," Lauder said. "She's extremely effective."

He gave her a patronizing look. "Hope you didn't see nothing of what happened this morning."

She refused to give him the satisfaction of asking for details. She wanted to return to her cabin. Even to the scratching in the walls, the music box, the basket with the hair of the dead.

"Soldiers out there going crazy waiting for action," Agent Moyer said. "Crack of dawn, a couple dozen of 'em stripped to their boots and ran a near quarter-mile foot race."

"Today? In the cold?"

His chuckle was manly. "Won't be a one of 'em sires again. But that bit of fun roused the blood in the whole bunch. You best not write about men running 'round without their britches."

"You can trust I won't."

"What I'm saying," he'd grown serious again, "all this waiting ain't natural. You leave a bunch of fellows loitering days stretching into weeks, there's no telling what might happen once they's loose."

The look in his eyes chilled her.

Sixteen

EN ROUTE TO Mrs. Streamist's Christmas dinner, Lauder rocked in
the back of Dak's wagon with Spinster Salem, Greta, and Dolly.
They sat on kitchen chairs, the legs roped to the wagon sides. Dak
had come for her first, and she had wanted to sit on the seat beside
him, but he'd helped her board via a stool to the back. She understood.
Stopping to retrieve the other three at the small house they shared, this
arrangement showed no hint of favoritism.

A milder front drifted across the prairie under a blue sky and
kept temperatures just above freezing, a welcome relief from the last
few days of severe cold. Wearing two ankle-length bloomers and two
chemises under her dress and coat, along with a quilt Dak brought, she
was warm. Her distress lay deeper. Dolly and Spinster Salem talked,
Greta said nothing, and Lauder's thoughts clung to Father's letter. She
ought to have destroyed it straightaway and not opened the scratched
sheet. Father was "gravely "disappointed in her failure to send measurements." The next line slowed her even more. "I allowed you to go."
Allowed. Ownership. A daughter as property.

Included in the envelope was a page ripped from the *American
Historical Journal,* its editors extending an apology to their readership
for an article published the previous month. They claimed they had
printed the article in good faith — had they really? — not knowing

the author had plagiarized its entirety. In the half-page statement, they included her name twice: Miss Lauder Ellison of Omaha.

As though that pain and disgrace were not enough, Father had sprawled angrily across the page: Do Not Return!

Did he mean forever? Would he never forgive her? Not for the damage she had done to herself, but for the damage to his name. Do Not Return! Three words. Stab. Stab. Stab.

The wagon rolled over a rut, and with the bounce, Spinster Salem gave a small scream.

"Sorry, ladies," Dak called over his shoulder. "Daydreaming."

Dolly stared at Lauder as if something burned on the tip of her tongue. Lauder ignored her, imagining the household in Omaha. At that hour, Mother and Father would still be in their dressing gowns, waiting to change into finer clothes for the guests who would arrive in the afternoon to wish them Christmas cheer. After, they'd dress again in formal dinner attire for the dozen more exclusive guests with whom they would feast and party late into the night. All this while Cook and the young maid, along with extra help hired for the evening, rushed to make every course perfect, and keep every wine glass, champagne flute, and brandy snifter tended. This, after a week of cooking, decorating, and planning, all choreographed to please. Even Pou-sa would be freshly bathed and in a collar of red jewels. The importance of the Ellison's Christmas. And the unimportance of those who made it so. The blasphemies of wealth.

Admitting the truth eroded the memories of her childhood even further. There had been pain and cruelty, and yet now, so far away, she remembered her home as the place where she had belonged. Good and bad, but home all the same. No longer. There'd been no Christmas invitation, no eagerness to see her ever again. *Do Not Return!* Father wrote, the script an angry flourish.

As the wagon rolled over the snowy road, and the conversation wandered from topic to topic, Lauder did her best to smile, nod, and make appropriate comments, but at every lull in the chatting, her thoughts returned to the loss riding in her stomach. Her parents didn't want her at their Christmas table. Even if she could somehow erase the shame of plagiarism, her coming to the reservation embarrassed

Mother, who would not have withstood guests asking Lauder question after question about her life amongst Indians.

Dak slapped the reins and shouted at his team of horses. "Get on there!"

Startled, Lauder turned. Halfway down a long lane, Mrs. Streamist, without a coat or her trusty shawl, rushed toward them, a wobbly limping, her dress blowing against her legs, her eyes wide with alarm.

Reaching her, Dak jumped off the wagon, stripped off his coat, wrapped it around his grandmother's shoulders, and after a moment of comforting, lifted her onto the seat. At the house, he carried her inside.

Lauder sat stunned, wondering if the day was cancelled, and how they were to get back. Greta untied the rope securing them and, using the stool, stepped purposely off. Dolly followed as if a king's red carpet were thrown out before her. Sister Salem and Lauder looked at each other and, not knowing what else to do, followed.

They entered the kitchen where Dak squatted at his grandmother's side. He'd pulled a chair to the stove, opened the oven door, and set her close to the warmth. He clasped both her hands in one of his. It stopped their shaking, but her shoulders shook, and tears tracked down her trembling face as she wrestled to gain control. "Grandma," his voice soothing, "there isn't a one of us doesn't forget himself time to time."

Lauder wished they'd stayed in the wagon until they'd been summoned.

"You've dressed the goose," Dak's eyes full of concern, he continued holding his grandmother's hands, "made rolls, set the table, same as every year." He leaned in, gave her a warm kiss on her cheek. "You're all right." A second kiss and a warmer squeeze of her hands. A whisper. "I've got you."

Mrs. Streamist nodded, her eyes pleading with his. She studied her grandson a while longer, wiped her face with a handkerchief, tucked the moist lace into the sleeve of her dress, and stood. "I have Christmas guests."

Lauder blinked her eyes dry. Babette, she whispered in her head, imagine going through this decline in front of everyone. Mrs. Streamist is the bravest woman I know.

"Goot," Greta said, the word hitting like a judge's gavel. She handed

Dak his coat and flicked a hand in the direction of the door as though having a man in the kitchen were a bother.

He looked from his grandmother to Lauder. His gaze lingering.

"We're good," she said. "The ladies have everything under control."

Mrs. Streamist closed the oven door, stood before a pot of green beans, and began shaking salt over them. "Grandma," he gently squeezed the shaker from her hand, "I'm going to throw a little feed. I'll be just outside." He waited to be sure she understood. "I won't be long."

"Same as every year," she said. "I can fix my Christmas dinner."

While Greta carried in the chairs, Spinster Salem and Lauder tried to make themselves useful. They stirred pots that didn't need stirring, checked the table settings, fussed, made pointless and distracting chatter. When Lauder noticed a pan of peeled, uncooked potatoes, she pulled them onto the stovetop.

Mrs. Streamist yanked them off. "Same as every year. I can fix my Christmas dinner."

"Of course," Lauder said. She tried to cover her error by joking about the need to feel useful.

Dolly watched the proceedings with such intensity, her eyes appeared crisp, missing nothing.

With the chairs carried in, Greta rejoined them, her large frame crowding the small kitchen even more. They watched Mrs. Streamist too closely, expected errors, jumped in quickly when she began to salt her garden beans again. Their scrutiny compounded her struggle to regain composure.

"I think the four of us are only getting in the way," Lauder said.

"Yaw, yaw," Greta shooed them into the next room.

The other teachers knew the parlor from Christmases past, but Lauder took it in slowly. Dak, she decided, might want more modern things, but he let his grandmother keep the house and her memories, as she would. Needlepoint cushions on the chairs showed years of wear and harkened to a past when a younger Mrs. Streamist, Mrs. Mathis at the time, had lived a finer life with Dak's grandfather. The rug too, was worn thin. Frayed strings hung around the edges and reminded Lauder of the rug in Nurse's attic room. She resisted the urge to slide out of her chair onto the floor as she had done countless times to sit at Nurse's knees.

"The church folks aren't coming," Dolly announced. She alone remained standing, studying the objects in a curio cabinet. "Agent Moyer had Dak send a telegram. I'm sure he scared the Christmas fuss out of them."

"When did you hear?" Lauder tried to sound casual. Had she heard about the delayed visit from Sgt. Atlock? Dak wouldn't have had a reason to tell her, and the two were never alone. Were they?

Dolly gave her a long, syrupy look, and turned her attention back to the cabinet, opening the glass doors and inspecting the contents with more scrutiny. "Miss Ellison, you have no family wanting you home for the holidays?"

A comment, masked as a question, meant to provoke. "My parents are heartbroken," Lauder lied happily. Dolly deserved nothing better. "I've also received invitations from other relatives and friends, but my responsibilities lie here." *Do Not Return!* Father's sprawled words burned in the back of her eyes, but even before the letter, going home for the holidays hadn't been an option. How could she leave without an absolute surety Plants Corn, Blackbird, and Mina were safe? And a week in Omaha without Dak? There was also the tension on the reservation and the threat of her not being able to return should General Miles order all white, non-military from the reservation. Or suppose Father had her locked away, even as far as an asylum? But staying meant not seeing Nurse. Since coming to the agency, Lauder missed satin sheets, indoor water closets, but she missed nothing as much as she missed Nurse. She missed sleeping at night knowing that Nurse on the floor above was awake and pacing. A night spirit that did not sleep.

Spinster Salem leaned in Lauder's direction. "What does Agent Moyer say about Red Cloud's visitor?"

"You mean people camping around his house?" She glanced at Dolly just as the woman's hand dove into her dress pocket and just as quickly came out. She hadn't seen Dolly take anything from a shelf, she hadn't seen anything in Dolly's hand, and the pocket in question looked flat. My dislike of the woman, Lauder assured herself, doesn't make her a thief.

Dolly carefully closed the cabinet doors and took a chair. She had pinked her cheeks, reddened her lips, and washed fresh henna through her hair. For Dak? Lauder wondered. Sitting between resolute Greta and cardboard-plain Spinster Salem, Dolly looked like a Christmas bulb. Though despite her efforts at camouflage, Dolly, the bulb, had clearly seen a long string of Christmases.

The bulb glowed. "Sgt. Atlock informed me of Red Cloud's visitor."

Lauder cleared her throat. "What are you referring to?"

On a jittering tray, Mrs. Streamist interrupted with cups of tea. Cups Lauder had seen poured and sitting on the tray when they first walked into the kitchen nearly half an hour earlier. "Thank you," she reached for one.

"Poor woman," Dolly whispered and set her cold cup down as soon as Mrs. Streamist had left again. "The man," she rushed back to her news, "went to Red Cloud claiming he was Jesus Christ and–"

"He claimed to be our savior?" Spinster Salem's eyes nearly crossed in her head.

"Indians are all in a tizzy," Dolly went on, "believing their dancing has called Him down in the flesh."

"A false Messiah!" Spinster Salem crossed herself.

Greta watched, listened.

"Red Cloud," Dolly went on, commanding the room again, "let the imposter sleep at his house. The man even removed his shirt and showed scars he claimed were from his crucifixion. The army's run him off, but it's too late."

"Why too late?" Lauder asked.

Dolly pulled back, as though the answer to Lauder's question was obvious. "The Indians believed it."

One of Greta's feet in sturdy, ankle-high shoes tapped the rug with a soft, irritated thudding.

Spinster Salem fanned herself with her hand. "Ghost shirts and now a false prophet."

"There's no help for them now," Dolly said. "They had their chance. Now things are too bad. Sitting Bull killed and renegades breaking into the houses of anyone who doesn't join them. Burning cabins, stealing, destroying the property of their own people."

Lauder swallowed. Had Sgt. Atlock told her that? Dak? Or had she read it? And if true, what did it mean for Mina? "Most of what's written is lies. Newspapers trying to stir up fears."

Spinster Salem gave a condescending look. "Much of the reporting hasn't been true. But now, things are catching up to the reporting. The papers were right all along, just early."

Lauder hurried to swallow before she spat cold tea across the room. When Mina returned, the two of them would laugh about the comment until their sides hurt. If Mina returned. If she was all right.

"Miss Ellison," Dolly said, "you must know your friend is in peril."

"I do know."

"Which side are they on?"

"The wrong side," Lauder said. "They're too militant for some, not militant enough for others."

"That's bad," Spinster Salem sighed. "They must stay on the right side."

Thankfully, Mrs. Streamist reappeared in the doorway, her face flushed and her eyes looking confused. "Someone must fetch," she faltered. "Howard is shoeing a horse in the barn."

Lauder stood before Dolly could do so. "I'll go for Howard. I'm happy to fetch him."

The saddest part of Mrs. Streamist's struggle, Lauder felt sure, was that today she couldn't deny her slipping mind. Her guests had witnessed her wandering in the cold, and that witnessing added to her emotional devastation. How much luckier she'd be if her mind were totally gone. So that she was unaware of the decline, had no memory, and no dread of the future.

Seventeen

LEAVING HER HAT behind, but wearing the heavy coat she appreciated, Lauder hesitated on the covered porch, letting the breeze blow over her face. The surrounding hills wore windswept bare spots, but there in the quieter valley of the farm, the snow lay a foot deep. A long windbreak of staggered firs, some nine or ten trees thick, stood on the north side of the house, helping to shield the clapboard home. Given the size of the firs, Lauder knew Dak's Grandfather Mathis must have planted the thicket, but smaller ones amongst the stately proved Dak maintained the stand, removing the damaged or dead and planting new when necessary.

She followed his boot-trodden trail through the snow to where he carried two buckets of corn still in their husks. A dozen cows milled along a trough, and she stopped at the split rail. "Dinner is ready."

He finished emptying his pails, loss written on his face. "She's never done something like that."

"And she may never again."

He came to the fence. "I can't risk it."

"You can't be with her every minute," Lauder said. "You've got," she looked over the cattle and a corral with half a dozen horses, "the farm, the agency, the school."

"Can't leave her alone again; can't risk it," he repeated, slower. "Suppose I hadn't come home right then?"

She wanted to ask what he knew about a messiah and hostiles burning down the homes of the peaceful, but at the moment, his thoughts were consumed by his grandmother.

"It's hard out here," he said. "Ma, now her."

"It can be hard everywhere."

He didn't answer, only leaned his arms on the top rail. She imagined his thoughts rolling out and far beyond the moment. "A penny for your thoughts."

His attention returned. "You'd be overpaying."

Seeing his grandmother and his worry for her had him in a rare, raw mood. "She's returned to herself," Lauder tried.

The Adam's apple in his throat, rose, settled. "Maybe it was always going to end this way. The West isn't a place for a woman."

There was nowhere else Lauder wanted to be. "That's just your belief. It doesn't make it so."

He nodded toward the house. "Well, there's your proof."

"And your mother? Is that what happened to her?"

"After my old man rode out, she brought us all here."

"And your grandparents raised you? How old were you?"

He hesitated. "She took a rope to the barn."

"Oh no. I'm sorry." How did one survive a mother hanging herself? She leaned, her shoulder touching his, the fence between them, the contact brief. Dak's mother had also been Mrs. Streamist's daughter. How did one survive losing a daughter to suicide?

Along the trough, cows chewed slowly, teeth grinding.

Lauder had always suspected her mother was a different woman before losing Babette. For everything that happened after that tragedy, maybe Mother was no more responsible for her actions than was Mrs. Streamist. "I hope," Lauder said, "you don't blame yourself for your mother's death." She carried plenty of blame both for Babette's death and for the sad life that death laid over Mother. And so, why had she taken the music box? What was that but an attempt to fight against the blame and guilt she felt?

"The dead can't be blamed," Dak said. "A person gets sick. A mind goes the same as a heart, a leg. Suicide is just one of a hundred ways the body takes you out."

The conversation depressed Lauder. "It's Christmas, a day of good cheer. We'll concentrate on that."

"At one time," Dak said, "Christmas was quite a holiday around here." He motioned over a pasture. "Teepees, twenty, thirty, forty people."

"Lakota? For Christmas?"

"We feasted at different times throughout the year. One blizzard had twenty people camping on our floor for nearly a week. To a young kid, that was a swell time. There weren't any white boys living close. When my Lakota friends came, and my brothers let off beating me up, it was a holiday."

Just beneath his hat, a breeze ruffled a curl of hair along the top of his ear. "But that all ended?"

"After Grandpa died," he said, "and Streamist moved into the house, he greeted anyone riding bareback with a shotgun. Told them to get off his property. When the bastard died, two good friends returned. We did a lot of fishing and hunting. Having noisy boys around again helped Grandma, too."

"Do you still see them?"

"They got nipped."

She waited, afraid of what he would say next.

"Boarding school."

"I'm sorry. Before the reservation school opened?"

"Just a year before the agency was moved here. Wouldn't have mattered. They wanted to hunt, ride their horses, not be cooped up in a school."

"They didn't return after graduation?"

He leaned heavily on the fence. "They beat one to death. The other took a rope into a schoolyard shed."

"Like your mother?" The question came quickly, breathy. She had not meant to verbally make that association.

"I've wondered," Dak said. "Did hearing Ma's story from me help him make the decision?"

"And your other friend? Did someone go to prison for killing him?"

Dak yanked off his gloves like he couldn't stand the confinement. Held them in his right hand, slapped them into the palm of his left. Again. "The report said he died during the night. Unknown causes. A young fellow who'd been there got word to the family. 'Beaten so bad he'd needed carried to his bed.'" Dak cleared his throat. "The hanging happened a few days later."

"Terrible." She thought of her little boys: Richard, George, Badger, Much Wind, and the others. The possibility of them going through something so horrific made her bite her bottom lip. "Their deaths must also have affected your grandmother."

"Like a bullet shattering glass."

"How old were you?"

"Twelve."

Her stomach shuddered. She needed to say something. "So, you're twenty-six."

"You sure?" His brows lifted. "I'm not sixty-six? Eighty-six?"

"Losing your friends is part of your dedication to the school and helping Mina get her job so she could return here."

He tipped his head in the direction of the house. "She's more qualified than a couple of those in there. And if she wants to be on the reservation, she deserves to be."

"No matter how painful your life," Lauder spoke slowly, "millions suffer more."

"Thoreau?" Dak asked.

"Lauder. Who's spent her life feeling sorry for herself." She hoped he didn't hear that as a plea for attention or sympathy. "I still wish I'd been able to tell Mina about Sitting Bull. I know that sounds self-important, supposing she should hear the news from me. She's grieving; she hardly cares about this white woman's sorrow."

"She's your friend. That isn't about white or red."

"Actually," Lauder said, "so much seems to be exactly that. There's no end to all the dumb things I say."

"No one comes here knowing a tenth of what they suppose they know. We try, learn a little bit, and then try harder the next time."

"I'm worried about her getting back safely. Is there anything you can do?"

"She's with Plants Corn. I can't do better than that."

She was glad for Dak's confidence, if only she shared it.

"We best go in," he said.

She didn't move. They were having a real conversation. When would that happen again? "All of this land must have been reservation."

"If you're wondering if Grandpa cheated or stole to get the land, it didn't begin like that."

She heard the release of a tight breath.

"When Grandpa came the Sioux welcomed him. They traded cattle, furs, smoked, and feasted together. They thought him a fool for building a house and staying in one place, but not in terms of him taking their land. The plains were endless."

"But you own the land now?"

"Own?" he hesitated. "For all I do know, living right here, there are a thousand things I don't. I was three when the Fort Laramie Treaty was signed, and the Sioux Reservation was formed."

"Your grandfather was still welcome?"

"He came in the 1820's. When the Boseman Trail opened, he'd already been here nearly forty years. Whites began pouring in, poisoning streams, killing game, bringing diseases. The army followed, building forts all along the trail. Red Cloud led a war against that and won."

"I love that he won."

"It didn't last. They forced the Fort Laramie Treaty on him, and things got worse real quick. Gold was found in the Black Hills, the railroads kept coming, and claims were being filed on the land. Somewhere in those years, Grandpa filed."

"He had to save his home from whites. What about the school?"

"The treaty included building schools and a teacher for every thirty students. When the agency was moved so close to us, Grandma filed papers, did what she needed to get certified to teach. McGillicuddy was the agent then, a big friend of Crazy Horse. He was happy to give Grandma a job. Maybe he knew her past, maybe he was happy to get at least one post filled. There weren't many around wanting to teach. The work helped her, but the past is catching up."

"This was after your Grandfather Mathis died?"

"She believes he's still here. She's never wanted to leave, and she needed the teaching money, pittance as it is. The agency moving so close was a godsend. Through those trees," he pointed, "Grandpa's grave. Ma's. Grandma's planning on resting with them."

Two crosses stood as white and as bright as the snow around them.

"Grandpa broke bones planting trees," Dak continued, "digging the well, building a house and barn. If I tied up Grandma, hauled her off, and abandoned the place, the land wouldn't go to the Lakota. It'd fall to a white man who'd feast on Grandpa's labor. I'm not doing that. But own?" He shook his head. "The place doesn't always feel that way."

"Everything across the reservation feels hopeless."

"If I handed the farm over to a Lakota, he wouldn't be able to keep it. He'd be targeted. The people just lost millions of acres, and not a thing they could do about it. There'd be fourteen ways to swindle a red man out of this place. Hell, outright killing him would be the quickest. Broad daylight, if you wanted to get to bed on time. My life's here, but far as I'm concerned, this land is still red land. They are welcome to ride it, hunt it, pray on it. I'll make no claim against them."

"As I said, 'hopeless.'"

He lifted his hat, let a breeze comb hair off his forehead, and replaced it. "You ever witnessed a prairie fire? The heat, the fumes, the speed the flames travel? It's Hell roaring through. But the fuel runs out, the rains come, the fire meets a river. The Sioux are being burned down, but I've got to believe that fire will end at some point. They're some of the strongest, best people on this earth. When the ashes cool, they'll rebuild in ways you and I couldn't guess."

"You believe that?"

"It gets me out of bed in the morning."

"You've got a lot of faith. I can hear my father saying, 'White expansion is saving the west from savagery.'"

"I wouldn't want to speak against your father, but I imagine he and I would come to fists."

"My father wouldn't fight. He's a paper warrior. Believes he's king of all the land he maps, and the railroad can confiscate." She wanted to tell Dak about the letter, ease her heart by having him share in the knowing, but she couldn't. "I suppose my father is a lot like Agent Moyer."

"Moyer came with good intentions, even if he didn't know what the hell he was doing. He lost his nerve day one. Maybe it was day two. It's only getting worse."

"Now, Sitting Bull's death."

"Realizing he's in over his head only has him digging his heels in deeper."

"Father again," Lauder said, "who rants on the benefits of phrenology no matter what the experts say. He knows it's a disproven science, but that only makes him more stubborn. He'll stick with his lies. He's invested in them, and heaven be damned."

Dak lifted the loop holding the gate closed and stepped through. "Moyer won't last long. Maybe things'll start improving that quick."

"You think he's going?"

"They call him Young Man Afraid of Indians. And his endless letters begging for troops have got to be angering Washington."

Lauder stepped aside as Dak came through.

"He isn't sleeping," Dak continued. "All but locks himself away. He's a tick ready to bust. Red Cloud's already campaigning for a new agent. I don't know what tomorrow holds, and now Grandma." He sighed. "But I know if we lose the school, we'll never get those children back. Even if the doors reopen in a year or two, those gone are gone."

"We stay the course. One day at a time."

"Something like that."

She admired him. He'd been through plenty, and now there was his fear for his grandmother. Yet, he'd fight on. "Who are you?"

His eyes narrowed. "I'm the bastard you never wanted to meet."

Her heart constricted. Generous one minute, he shut her out the next. "You can be such an unfriendly bloke, and bloke is not really my word of choice. Why wouldn't I want to meet you?"

He closed the gate. Secured it.

"On second thought," her hand slipped into her coat pocket, and she grasped the gold thread, "don't bother answering that."

Cows at the trough shuffled against one another.

She started for the house. "Keep your secrets. I don't want to know." If they were so bad, she didn't. She had plenty of her own. "You'd think we could at least be friends."

He took quick steps to catch up. "Maybe that's it, right there. Maybe we can't be just friends."

His attraction to her filled his eyes, and yet he'd not let her in. "You're scared of women?"

"Scared of how they break. Scared of how I can't stop that."

She kicked at a runnel of snow on the side of the path and walked faster. "That again. Dinner is ready, Howard."

"Grandma wasn't always like this. How many whacks in the head does it take to change a personality?"

"And so, you'll not live either? You'll stay stuck in her past?"

He grabbed her elbow and pulled her into an embrace. "We'll talk later, after I take the others home."

She sighed into the pressure of his arms around her and let her head sink onto his chest. He could undo her, and she was a sucker for allowing that to happen. She pushed away, the separation wrenching. "So, friends," she said. "We'll keep it at friends." They walked slowly. "I know you'd gladly send me away, telling yourself Omaha is safer. But, friend, every location has its dangers."

"I tell myself that. 'Don't worry about her being here. In Omaha, she's likely to drop a book on her toe.'"

"Quit."

"Can't."

Eighteen

THEY SAT TWO on each side of the table, Mrs. Streamist and Dak on the ends, forming a perfect, corners-tight box. If Mina were home, Lauder knew, she would no more want to join them than she wanted to join the other three teachers when they ate in the mess.

Mrs. Streamist, with a bowed head and folded hands, mumbled under her breath what Lauder thought could be a very long prayer or a trek through a long string of words while she hoped a natural ending would pop into her head.

"Amen," Dak stopped her. He'd changed his shirt, added a string tie, and combed his hair. Lauder sat to his left, and he tried to act casual. He'd hurt her in the yard, and he was sorry for that, but goddamn, he struggled just to keep his hands solidly around the hour. Lauder deserved a better man.

Mrs. Streamist smiled at him, though possibly she believed she smiled at Howard; Lauder wasn't sure. As the woman reached and started passing the first bowl, the moist and wrinkled handkerchief tucked into the cuff of her sleeve fell onto the floor.

Bowls passed, and Lauder eyed the cordial in the tiny glass by her plate. She wouldn't be the first to drink. Spinster Salem had brought the raspberry liqueur in Mason jars tucked inside a basket. She poured an exact two-finger measurement in each glass, then made a show of setting the bottle back into the basket and putting both on the sideboard. There would be no second servings.

A platter of the goose Dak killed and carved rounded the table, but as Mrs. Streamist passed the potatoes to Dolly, alarm slammed her face, and she let out a little cry. Peeled and quartered, the potatoes were still raw and turning a rusty color.

Lauder opened her mouth, hoping a kind word would come out, but before she could speak, Dolly let go an ill-mannered huff.

"Help yourself," Dak told her.

Dolly threw him a look and passed the bowl to Greta.

Greta scooped out three wedges.

A saint, Lauder thought.

"Leave some for me," Dak teased, also grateful for Greta's sense.

At his comment, Greta's large hand pulled back the bowl she had begun to pass, and she helped herself to an additional two wedges. "Christmas manners, Mr. Dak. I am guessed."

He cupped his hands as if asking for the bowl. "I did the peeling." He spoke as if that explained not only why the potatoes hadn't been cooked, but why there was no need to cook them at all.

Mrs. Streamist's face remained slack, but she pulled back her thin, trembling shoulders. "I've had the cones hung in the church."

"What cones?" Spinster Salem asked. "I wasn't told."

"Thank you," Lauder said to Mrs. Streamist. For the first time that day, here was something positive. "When visitors were still expected," she explained around the table, "I had both Mina and my classes make decorative paper cones to hang in the church."

Her thoughts drifted back. Not a full week had passed since the day her class made the cones. Not yet knowing the delegation would cancel, Mrs. Streamist had been in a panic about their arrival. Lauder went to her office to offer encouragement. The woman's desk lay bare, neither papers nor books on top. Not so much as a pen to suggest she meant to do any actual work. "What can we do?" the woman cried.

Lauder had wanted to rush around the desk and wrap Mrs. Streamist in her arms. When they come, she'd wanted to promise, I won't leave your side. "My mother hangs China cones on our Christmas tree," she said, "and as a child, Nurse and I always made paper ones to hang across my bedstead. The children could make paper cones for the church."

She hadn't yet assigned Christian names or taught the children to recite a prayer, but pictures symbolizing Christmas would be something of a substitute, especially if they adorned the church.

"Children's drawings?" Mrs. Streamist had looked doubtful. "In the church?"

"Exactly. They'll win more favors there. My children and I could walk the delegation over. That would get the group out of the school, at least for a bit, and I could claim the pictures bring the parents into church and encourage them to stay for services." Trust me, there's no better liar than the one you're looking at. "The group will think you're brilliant."

"Nothing pagan," Mrs. Streamist wrung her thin, speckled hands. "Christmas images. No pagan symbols."

"I'll bring the cones to you," Lauder said. "You can approve them before they go to the church. You are headmistress."

Lauder had passed out half-sheets of paper, explained how she would add color to their drawings from her Winsor paint box. She'd taken the time to draw examples on the slate: trees, bells, stars, and candles. Little Rose finished first, leaving her brother's side, also a first, and raced to Lauder's desk. Her chin only inches above the desktop, and with nervous glances back at George, she beamed. She kept her picture behind her back. "Sunkawakan," her tiny voice hardly reaching Lauder.

Lauder's heart leapt. Little Rose had spoken. How to congratulate her, but not make such a fuss the child never wanted to speak again? "Please show me your drawing."

Little Rose put the drawing on Lauder's desk directly in front of herself and slowly pushed it forward.

With a dropped heart, Lauder needed a moment. "It's a wonderful horse." Like the endless others, the picture featured starving ribs. Mrs. Streamist would not allow the picture no matter how much Lauder begged.

"I'm sorry," Lauder said. She pointed at the objects on the slate. "Choose one of these."

Children watched. Lauder imagined them growing smaller in their seats, their confidence in their own pictures, their confidence in her, shrinking. "Beautiful horse," she tried again, but she couldn't let one drawing keep the whole project from being accepted. "George." His shoes were already turning for the aisle, his whole body looking ready to pounce forward. "Please explain to your sister she must draw something signifying Christmas."

Little Rose's eyes filled, her bottom lip curled out, trembling. "Sunkawakan."

"Most quiet," George nearly shouted. He ran to the front of the room, wrapped his arms around his sister. "Little Rose most quiet."

"Nothing pagan." Mrs. Streamist's words echoed in Lauder's ears.

"George, perhaps she could leave the horse, but add a big star in the sky."

He shook his head up and down, and looking panicked, ushered her away.

That night, Lauder had painted, rolled, glued, strung the cones with her gold thread for hanging. Several of the children had drawn large stars, which pleased Lauder. Their ancestors lived under the night sky. They knew endless stories of the constellations, and there was her own love of the armillary where she had stood for countless hours of her childhood, staring. The stars also reminded her of the scarf she had given to Mina, and of course, Mina herself.

Rolled, Little Rose's picture nearly buried the horse and left only the star. Lauder glued the drawing onto a larger sheet, which kept the horse, and she brightened the star with more gold paint. Little Rose's horse was saved. The refashioning made the cone larger than the others, an accidental but happy result.

At the Christmas table, Dak spoke directly to Spinster Salem. "We'll leave the cones hanging a couple of weeks. You should take your class."

"I do miss Mr. Maxwelt," she frowned. "He maintained order."

"You're having problems?" Dak asked. He was relieved to have the attention off his grandmother and her failure to cook the potatoes. Goddamned potatoes.

"Last day," Spinster Salem said, "I put a girl-squaw to the broom. She thought she could fool me."

Goosebumps rose on Lauder's neck. "What does that mean? Put her to the broom?"

Spinster Salem frowned. "Why, kneel on the handle. First time I turned my head, she's shuffling her weight, taking one knee off, trying to hide her lying by covering it with her skirt."

"Deceitful," Dolly said. "What did you do?"

"I hit her with the pepper stick." Spinster Salem's lips puckered sour. "They won't cry no matter how many times you hit them."

"You delivered just punishment," Dolly said.

Lauder nearly shouted. "Which came first the chicken or the egg?"

"I don't keep chickens," Spinster Salem said.

Dolly finished her cordial. "They don't have souls."

Lauder slumped against the chairback. Did Nurse move through the world knowing there were people who believed she had no soul? If without a soul, then by what force did she move? Lauder's students were too young to know the world thought them less than human. And when they learned of it, they'd need stricter discipline to tamp down the volume of their hurts. Would it be She-Stands-Brave who refused to kneel on a broom handle? And so, it would go on, the process of continually breaking their spirits.

She turned to Dak. His eyes were down; he had stopped eating and the fork he held looked ready to shoot from his hand.

What could he do? Lauder wondered. How many times a day could he walk through the school, making sure students were safe? He wasn't supposed to be wielding any power there. Mrs. Streamist was headmistress. Spinster Salem and Dolly held more power than he did. If they complained about him to Agent Moyer or wrote letters about his interference to the BIA, there would be trouble. Even if she and Greta wrote opposing letters praising the school, those letters, like her plagiarism apology, would be ignored. Those in power, with their eyes narrowed on one objective, would pick and choose and act only on what suited their purposes.

Spinster Salem with her skin cap and cabbage face and Dolly, painted and menacing, made Lauder wonder. Where did the roots of their hatred lie? Was it the abuse and rejection they carried as women, the dire circumstances that brought them to teach on a reservation, their low pay, the absence of any family to support them? There they were, stuck, and for all the cruelty they spit out, half of it blew back to ruin them. They carried it on their persons. Their future-less persons. Let them suffer, but the problem lay in the brutality they inflicted on children who would never throw off the darkness. I don't belong here, Lauder told herself. But the cruelest thing I could do is leave.

Greta watched the two women, her gaze slapping back and forth between them.

"What a lovely meal," Dolly said to Mrs. Streamist. "This is a lovely meal, isn't it Dak?"

Their eyes met, and though Lauder didn't know all that passed between them, she felt certain they lobbed wordless threats. The set of Dolly's cherry-red lips said she considered herself the victor.

"Where's Atlock?" he asked her. "Out searching for the missing Sioux?"

"As you know, the army sent troops and scouts to find the escapees."

"Escapees?" Spinster Salem crossed herself.

Lauder shifted in her chair. Her skirt brushed Dak's knee, sent a warm flush up his thigh. He speared and cut off a slice of his potato.

"Tell," Greta demanded of him.

"Close to a hundred and fifty fled after Sitting Bull's death. They're said to be troublemakers heading to the Black Hills. Another hundred and fifty took off with Big Foot from Cheyenne River and joined up with them. Word was they were going to be taken to prison in Pierre. Families separated. Pretty much a death sentence. Can't blame them for running."

"Is that true?" Lauder asked. "Not rumor twisted around a scrap of something real to sound convincing?"

Greta reached for the platter of muffins. "Sitanka."

"The two groups are traveling together," Dak said, "possibly heading here to meet with Red Cloud. They're mostly women and children, the elderly."

Lauder wondered at the name of the chief Greta readily supplied. Maybe she still had a secret Lakota lover.

Greta shook her head, took another muffin, and said what sounded to Lauder like "tree hunted."

"Three hundred?" Lauder clarified. She wondered about Greta's nervousness in grabbing a second muffin before tasting the first. She felt certain Greta wasn't frightened by the number of Sioux; she was frightened for them.

Spinster Salem looked ready to tip off her chair in a dead faint. "Hostiles on the war path and on their way here?"

"That can't be." Lauder wanted a second muffin herself; she would shove it down Spinster Salem's throat. "Three hundred are not going to walk into five thousand troops. What men take their elderly, their wives, and children on the war path with them? Besides," she turned to Dak, "why would they even come to Red Cloud? What can he do?"

"Little if anything. I doubt he can keep them out of prison."

A slice of goose breast, overly salted green beans, and raw potatoes lay on Lauder's plate. How could she get any of it down? Certainly not with her stomach clenched to the size of a walnut. "What does this mean for Mina? If the army is out searching, suppose they come upon the family? Considers them 'off their reservation.'"

"We'll be killed." Spinster Salem's fork dropped, rattled onto her plate. "We shouldn't be out here in the open." Her eyes flashed to the nearest window. "We must return to the agency immediately. The soldiers can protect us."

"You're safe." Dak lifted a hand, motioned calm. "The people are harmless, and if they get within fifty miles of here, they'll be seen and arrested."

"Sgt. Atlock," Dolly inserted herself again, "said friendlies have been sent to the Black Hills a number of times to try and talk the hostiles out. But the savages are vowing to fight to their deaths."

Lauder's cheeks burned. "You teach Sioux children. You know they aren't savages."

"All the years I've been teaching," Dolly's gaze fired at Dak, "I never thought the day would come when I'd be made to teach with one of them. How do we rid the Indian from the Indian with one of them teaching?"

"Where Red Cloot?" Greta asked. "Bat Lands? Take visiting Jesus?"

Dak suppressed a grin. If only Greta played poker; it'd be a hell of an evening. "Red Cloud's celebrating the holiday at home. He did go hoping to convince the fighters in the stronghold to come out, but they didn't listen to him."

"But he's considered a great warrior," Lauder insisted. "He closed the forts."

Mrs. Streamist looked down the table, smiled at Howard. He never aged. If one day they had a son, would their son be as handsome?

"Red Cloud's nearly seventy," Dak said. "Just as nearly blind. For all his fighting, in the end, he did sign the last treaty giving up Lakota land. Many resent him for that."

Lauder hated the thought.

"He was lied to about what he was signing," Dak said. "Threatened that his people would lose their annuities if he didn't. And he knew damned well that in the end the government would take the land with or without his signature. Sign, or his people starved. Maybe half of them killed in another pointless battle."

Lauder's head felt dizzy with a returned sense of hopelessness. "Then signing wasn't selfish or giving into whites. He tried to keep his people alive."

"Fighting to the death is a choice," Dak said. "Many think it's the honorable way."

"If they think Red Cloud a traitor for giving in," she paused. Dak's hand was just there, inches away, and she wanted to grab hold, feel his surety. "Then they think it of Plants Corn. Even Mina for teaching in a school designed to make students forget the ways of their ancestors."

"She isn't here," Spinster Salem said. "That Indian teacher. What's her name?"

"What's her real name?" Dolly asked. The repeated question aimed directly at Lauder.

"Mina. It means daughter."

"What's her Indian name?"

Lauder's hands dropped into her lap. Mina did very likely have a name longer than four letters. One with more meaning. She had not shared it, and Lauder had never thought to ask. How shameful. Raised to address the household staff by their role, she had not thought to ask any their names. They were Driver, Maid, Cook. Seeing them as only that. Their personhood only in terms of how they served her. Even

Nurse; she had never thought to ask Nurse her birth name. Didn't that deny their humanity? Here was the blasphemy of Lauder Ellison's life. She thought it of her parents, of Spinster Sarah and Dolly, but in truth, she was no different.

Greta grumbled something about a person's right to call themselves by whatever name they wished.

"That squaw came out of nowhere." Dolly's voice oily. "Our Miss Ellison came to us through General John R. Brooke, but that one?" Without taking a breath, she continued. "Miss Ellison, are you enjoying your accommodations? Dak worked hard to fix the place, cover up the fact," her red lips parted seductively, "that anything ever happened in there." She winked at Dak.

Lauder wanted to throw potato wedges at her. Then one at Dak. At such close range, she could hit them both between the eyes. It had been the place of the robbery, but was Dolly implying something more? Had the two of them? There in the storage shed between the harbored shelves of sugar, coffee, and cigars? Was that Dak's great secret and shame? She lifted her cordial, finished the glass. "My living quarters are quite satisfactory."

There were many nights when she forgot the stirring, falling deep into her reading or journaling. And as many nights, when she returned from her evening meal at the mess and in winter's early darkness dropped into her bed with exhaustion. Rushing to her dreams of Dak. She shivered. Still, there were other times when noises made her spin around as if to capture a glimpse of a phantom. Was it one of the two ghosted pieces: the music box or Mina's basket? "Sometimes," she found herself admitting, "it's like I'm not alone in there."

Mid-chew, Dak jerked as if he'd bitten a lead pellet still lodged in the goose.

"Do you fetter your mind with frightening, unholy books?" This from Spinster Salem.

That thing on your head, Lauder thought, could be turned over and work well as a spittoon.

Dak lifted the cordial he'd been sipping sparingly, as if choking down rotten fruit, and swallowed the last. He took the three steps to the sideboard, and as Spinster Salem watched, he poured himself a generous second serving. His back to the group, his shoulders expanded with a deeply indrawn breath, and he drank.

Nineteen

Dak stopped the wagon in front of the small house where the three other teachers lived. He helped each out of the wagon and wished them a Merry Christmas. For the next half mile, Lauder sat in the back alone, considering. After dinner, he'd ridden off as the women cleared the table, threw most of the food into the slop pail, and washed the dishes. Though not Mrs. Streamist. She paced and wrung her hands in her parlor as if something in the room upset her. Working in the kitchen, they kept one eye on the fretting woman, daring not even to whisper for fear the woman would misconstrue their words and suffer another attack. They also watched the window for Dak's return. Lauder grew so anxious, she feared she might run down the lane at the first sight of him.

She sighed with relief when he and a second rider came into the yard. A dark woman on a barebacked spotted pony looked old as Mrs. Streamist, but she slid off her horse with the grace of someone twenty years younger. This wasn't Richard's mother, and Lauder considered again the network of people in Dak's life. She wanted to stay and hear the woman's stories, spend hours in her presence, but Greta was carrying out chairs, and Dak needed to take them back. Again, he'd have chores on his return.

As they'd all crawled back into the wagon for the trip home, leaving the woman with Mrs. Streamist, Lauder asked no questions of Dak. The realization that he couldn't leave his grandmother alone again was new and how it would work likely puzzled and upset him. But for tonight, he had the woman's help. At other times, Richard's mother. A community, she thought again.

Rolling down Pine Ridge Road, she looked for the man Dak referred to as John. She shivered. His not being there only meant he was somewhere else. Unseen, lurking, maybe shapeshifted into a bear. Possibly even in her quarters.

Reaching her door, Dak stepped over the seat, untied the rope stretched across her stomach, and sat, leaving the space of an empty chair between them.

"So?" she said, surprised.

"So," he answered, unsure of how to start.

She motioned to her door. "If you'd like to come in?"

"If you're not too cold? It's a nice afternoon."

"Of course." The low afternoon sun gave no heat, but the wind was still, and she had her warmer clothes and a lap quilt. More importantly, she had Dak right there. His knees nearly touching hers. Though she also had the barb of his not wanting to go inside. Would he keep them in full view lest someone erroneously think he was interested in her? Given that his recognizable wagon would be outside her door. Army and civilians were about, but she couldn't see any movement through the window of the agent's office. "Agent Moyer isn't in."

Dak pushed his hat back an inch, opening her view of his face. "I know you've got a lot of questions about Grandma."

She straightened the quilt over her knees, each stitch placed by a woman's hand. Stitch by stitch, knowing the work couldn't be rushed, allowing the hours, days, months for a single quilt. Could she rebuild her life that confidently? Had she already begun? Dak was right; she did have questions about Mrs. Streamist, but most pressing were her questions about him. Dak, on the other hand, could think only about his grandmother and the long slide her wits had suffered that day.

"I've said Streamist ran off my brothers."

"Little boys." She loved all the little boys in her class, especially Badger and Much Wind with his irresistible smile. Their spinning tops and bright faces. "Each parting must have struck like a death, and I know what one death does. One of them might still return."

"I hope they've got the decency to stay away."

"You can't mean that."

"It's been too long. No interest in seeing their faces now. Tails between their legs, claiming how they've been busy."

The truth pained him, and she would not press him further. Let him tell her what he would. But she wondered if the brothers had memories so bad those kept them away, or if they blamed their grandmother too, and didn't care to see her again? Another cruelty inflicted on the woman. And Dak, the younger brother they'd left behind? Did they wonder what became of him or believe him lost, as well?

"You should know what happened," Dak said.

"Because of how your grandmother was today? You don't need to defend her condition."

"She deserves your understanding."

"She has it," Lauder said. But she waited. Maybe Dak needed to talk as much for himself as he did for his grandmother.

"I was ten. Streamist had been drinking most of the week. He'd ranted through a list of people who'd done him wrong. It was my turn. Time he ran me off. After 'he whipped my hide.'"

She sighed. "I'm sorry you experienced that."

"This isn't about me."

It wasn't about her either and how badly she did or didn't feel for him.

Dak hesitated, his gaze skating over Lauder's face. She was the prettiest thing he'd ever laid eyes on. But it was more than looks that grabbed him. She had an innocence and wide-open heart damn near beating out of her chest. However tough she pretended to be, her trust and looks were a magnet for trouble. The realization struck him every time he was with her, pounded him into the ground. He should have sent her back to Omaha the first day. Should have done the sending every day since.

"Are you all right, Dak?"

She roused his insides. Groin, gut, and heart. He wanted to tie himself into a knot so tight he couldn't so much as squeak out anything about himself. At the same time, he wanted to tell her everything. Well, not everything. Not about the two girls. He couldn't ever admit his role in their deaths and why he didn't deserve someone like her walking within fifty feet of him. But he did need to tell her about the bastard Streamist and Grandma. It needed explaining why a woman who couldn't bend a rule on occasion, who got her grandson confused with her first husband, and forgot to boil the Christmas potatoes ought to be allowed around the school. Though that was over. Somehow. Had to be.

"It's about Grandma," he started again, "shaking in her apron, fighting back tears, 'Yes Sirring' every time Streamist bellowed, knowing he'd follow through on his threats." Where to begin? "Thinking back, the first thing I see is Grandpa's watch."

How proud Grandpa Howard had been of the device, pulling the timepiece out of his pocket and flipping up the tooled, silver cover. Not caring about the time, the sun telling him everything he needed to know about the hour but relishing the watch.

"Grandpa loved his watch." Dak started again and lost himself in remembering. Grandpa's large hand pulled out the long silver chain, and then the watch itself appeared from his pocket and slapped into his palm. Grandpa looked from the watch face to the sun, grinning at the agreement in the hours. "Grandsons," he smiled at the four young boys. "She spent some pretty money, didn't she?" The gift from Grandma. And then, one or the other of the brothers rushing to be first with the line, to say, "You were really surprised, Grandpa."

They'd put their mother in the ground the fall before, and now the river ice had melted, and leaves budded on trees. Grandma could only force smiles when one of them wrapped arms around her neck, but she sometimes went whole days without crying, and Grandpa had a shiny new watch.

In a blink of time, Streamist's big hand pulled that watch out of his pocket. "You fucking muskrat!" he yelled at ten-year-old Dak. "Still hanging on your grannie's tit."

Not a full year had passed since Dak stood trembling, crying into Grandma's skirts, watching his last brother, Bennie, being run off down the road. Streamist roaring how if he ever saw the boy's mug again, he'd shoot it off. Bennie sobbing at the end of the lane, big goobers running onto his top lip, barefoot, only the clothes on his back, and the shotgun pointed at him. Grandma sobbing and pleading with Streamist. The boom of the gun firing. Bennie, realizing he was out of range, looking at Grandma, begging with his eyes for her to find a way for him to stay. Streamist reloading and marching down the lane to fire at closer range. And Grandma, knowing he would, shouting "Run!" Bennie turning slowly, slowly, not knowing where to go, then running.

"Dak," Lauder urged, "you don't need to tell me." He wasn't speaking, just studying his clasped hands, looking through them. "I know it's painful, and it isn't my business."

Now it was Dak's turn. He was the boy. Streamist smelled. Bad. He hadn't washed or changed clothes in a week or more–the length of what Grandma called a bender. The smell, as much as the red eyes and snarl, filled the boy with fear. Both were linked to the man's fist. "Get out of my house," he told the boy.

"Leave him be," Grandma said, dropping hands protectively onto the boy's shoulders.

Streamist's bloodshot eyes were slits. "You ain't gonna tell me what to do in my house."

Grandma's hands gripped harder. "Dak, run to the garden and bring back one of the onions I love."

The boy craned his neck, looked up at her. Grandma often went to the well for water in the dark, but they didn't go to the garden in the dark. Did she mean it was time? They'd come up with a plan: When she needed him to run and hide, she would send him for onions. Such an odd request, he couldn't forget its meaning.

The boy turned to go, but Streamist lunged half out of his chair, the strike of a rattler. Faster than the boy had imagined he could. He gripped the boy's twig-like arm, threatening to snap it, and would happily.

The boy howled in pain and fear.

"Dak?" Lauder spoke again.

"Sorry." He leaned back in the kitchen chair, rolled his shoulders. "I got to thinking about the last night with that bastard."

"Onions," the boy told himself as Grandma used her fingernails to pry Streamist's hands off him. Streamist cussed at her. "Goddamn clawing." The boy ran from the house, stood in the dark, peeked in a window. "Grandma, don't yell at him," he cried into the glass. "Don't fight back." She didn't normally when Streamist was dangerous. She went quiet, not talking back, and she found ways to disappear. Cleaning the barn, weeding the garden, checking pasture fencing. Always taking the boy along.

"I want that stinking little varmint out of here," Streamist's spit flew in the air. "Where's my gun? I'll pepper his skinny ass."

"No," Grandma's voice was strong, cold. "I won't lose him."

Standing at the window, stars whirled over the boy's head. Wolves howled. He trembled. Grandma had tried to keep his brothers too, but she was different this time, not pleading. Insisting. Was it because he was the last? Because she didn't need to consider any remaining boys and what Streamist might do to them?

Streamist saw the change in her. He'd kill her before he'd let her tell him how to run his household. He used his fists, dropped her, and when the effort of bending to the floor tired him, he used the toes of his boots.

The boy banged back through the kitchen door, jumped on Streamist's back. Then felt a blinding pain when Streamist flung him off, and he struck his head on the wall. The shotgun hung on pegs over the back door. He drew a chair, climbed, and snatched it down. A crack of the barrel told him it was loaded. His oldest brother, when he still lived under the roof, and each brother down the line, had taught him how to check the load, how to snap the barrel so that its weight locked it back into place. Now, fear kept him from yelling at Streamist, and the barrel shook when he pointed, but that didn't matter. At such close range, the scatter was sure. But Grandma on her knees, crying, "Dak, no. Baby, please. Fetch an onion."

Blood squished from the corners of her mouth and onto her chin, turned her teeth pink. Red along her gums. Streamist held her with a fistful of her hair. One eye had begun to swell shut, but even with that eye, she begged Dak to obey. Trust me, her whole wounded body said. A deep, grinding, heart loss. "Grandson. Please. Fetch an onion."

He'd always trusted her. She never lied to him. She loved him. And he couldn't shoot without hitting her.

He wouldn't leave the gun, but for the second time, he ran out into the darkness. This time, he didn't watch at the window but ran for the toolshed. Ran under the moonlight, ran faster, snot running from his nose, the loaded gun he carried across his body bouncing against him. Moonlight glazed the shed roof and slowed him. Inside, he'd stood with brothers who were old enough to learn from Grandpa the purpose of the tools. Hammers, wrenches, rasp. How to sharpen a hoe or scythe on a whetstone.

Lauder reached, put her gloved hand on top of Dak's. Leather on leather, wishing it were skin to skin. This grown man with his broad shoulders was sitting lost in the silence of memories he couldn't share.

"I took the gun," Dak said. Lauder's expression had grown more distressed. She pulled her hand back, tucked it under the quilt across her lap. He wanted to reach under, take the hand into his own, but he couldn't. He was guilty as any marked man. "I trusted Grandma, her telling me, 'not now.' Trusted I could kill Streamist another time when she wasn't around. I promised myself I would. One of my brothers, old enough now, should have returned and done it, but they hadn't. The job fell on me."

Lauder tried to piece together the scraps of information he had actually shared. He was remembering a night when he nearly shot a man. "Thank god, you didn't." His story wasn't finished, and she prayed he wasn't going to admit killing the man later.

"I spent the night in the shed on feed sacks, and in the morning Grandma came. I'd seen her with black eyes before, but I'd never seen her face so bruised and busted up. I recognized her only by her hair, the dress she wore, and the voice soothing me. She walked crippled, but she climbed a horse, and we rode to a neighbor's, some five miles away. She had me wait on the horse, strange behavior for her not having me come in. As the minutes dragged on, Grandma inside talking to the husband and his hired hand; the misses came out, brought me cool well water, and stood there in her kitchen apron watching me.

"When we returned home, Streamist was still sleeping. He hadn't made it to bed the night before, and he snored on the sofa, half hanging off. Grandma leaned over, took Grandpa's watch from his pocket, and dropped it into her own. He didn't stir. Late in the afternoon, a dozen men rode into the yard. Six white fellas, six Indians. I'm guessing they were Sioux. They'd painted their faces with white clay streaks running down over their eyes, cheeks, and chins. I didn't recognize any of them. The men drug Streamist kicking and bellowing from the house and hog-tied him over the back of a pack mule. Grandma stood hugging me, shaking so hard, I was holding her up. We watched them haul Streamist down the lane. Grandma staring him down, her watching and telling the bastard she wasn't running. Scared shitless, she stared him down. We could hear him still cursing half a mile away about how he'd be back, and how he'd kill her."

"She's a strong woman." Was Dak saying, his grandmother took the worst beating of her life, risked being killed by it, so that the men around her would finally be shamed into acting, and Dak's life would be saved? The neighbors, Lauder decided, seeing Mrs. Streamist often had black eyes, knew what was going on, but they hadn't helped. Probably loved the gossip but hadn't helped. Which must have told Mrs. Streamist they wouldn't come to her aid until she stood before them crippled and maimed. Only then did their cowardice shame them. "What became of the men?" she asked.

"I'll see one or other of the white fellows from time to time. We don't mention that day. Sixteen years have passed, and they're getting old. Same with the Sioux. I suspect most are close by." He shrugged. "With the paint they wore and my mind on Grandma and Streamist, I'm not sure who they are. There ain't a damn one of them that's ever felt the need to brag."

"It's a good thing the whites knew where to find them."

"What they knew was to keep their own white hands clean. If things didn't go as planned, they could blame red men."

Could one of the men have been Plants Corn? Lauder didn't ask. Plants Corn lived close enough and was a friend of Dak's. But sixteen years ago?

The sun had dropped even lower, and she shivered. Throughout Dak's story, men had ridden alone or in small groups down Pine Ridge Road and past the wagon. She had paid little attention to them, but now a pair of young men in hats slowed. They'd been riding in the middle of the road, but seeing her and Dak, they steered their horses close and stopped. The horses' haunches so close they nearly rubbed the wooden wagon sides. "The hell," one of them said, "you're too pretty for him."

Dak jumped up and swung his hat in the air. "Get outta here! Your ugly faces are scaring the lady."

Laughing, they steadied their spooked horses, tipped their hats, and rode on.

The light moment helped Lauder feel better about Dak's life beyond the agency and his grandmother. "Friends of yours?"

"Long as they stay lousy poker players." He remained standing, returned his hat to his head, and jumped off. "You're shivering."

She eyed the stool he'd set on the ground for her.

"Watch your step."

"When she married Streamist," Lauder said, looking over the wagon's edge to the stool, "her property became his. Divorcing him would mean losing the farm. And fleeing in the night, if escape had even been possible, would have the same result. In novels, poison is a great option."

"No doubt it crossed her mind," Dak said. "Not sure if they'd hang a woman."

"Leaving you without a guardian. Or worse, with Streamist."

Dak reached to take her hand, but she hesitated. If she feigned tripping, she could end up in his arms. In novels, heroines did that, too. Don't, she warned herself. You'll break your leg. You're embarrassingly clumsy enough without exaggerating the point. Her hesitation made Dak grab her about the waist and, without a word, lift her down.

"Did Mr. Streamist ever return?"

"No idea what happened to him," he said, letting go of her. "I hope they left him tied up in the Badlands. Gave buzzards something to chew on."

"Your grandmother must have been terrified he'd return."

"At first she trusted Streamist was gone forever. A few months passed, and she started having nightmares, believing he could return. Then would return. My friends helped for a while, but after they were taken, she boarded the windows on the inside, thinking she was more likely to hear if the lumber sticks fell inward. She got a couple of itchy, howling hounds, and she never hung clothes on the line without a gun in her laundry basket. Never rode into school unarmed."

They stepped onto the wooden walkway. "I couldn't do it," Lauder said.

"Some mornings still," Dak reached for the door handle, "she steps into the kitchen so ragged looking, I know she spent the night fighting Streamist in her dreams. The beatings, fear, it's been hard for her." He stopped at the open door. He'd been spilling his guts for too long.

Lauder wanted him to come in, but he'd refused her once; she wouldn't invite another rejection. "You'd better get going. Even with someone there, I saw how Mrs. Streamist clung to you, not wanting you to leave."

"Walking Back is there. Grandma knows her."

"If I'd thought for one minute you'd allow it, I would have volunteered to stay." She swallowed. "Stayed the night."

Her words sent ache through him. "It wasn't my bringing you all back that had Grandma so upset again. She loses hours, whole days, things. She thinks Grandpa's watch is gone."

Dolly's furtive action? Lauder wondered. She had no proof, and with Babette's music box just there, maybe she shouldn't be so quick to see the thief in someone else. Besides, Dak didn't need the additional strain of believing Dolly, a guest in the house, had stolen the watch. It was best to see if it was found. If it wasn't, then at a better time, she would share her suspicions.

"It's not lost," Dak said. "I'll find it." He took a deep breath, motioned her in ahead of him, and joined her. "Maybe I'll just warm up a minute. I've got a cold ride back." He looked around the room. "How does that work?" Books lay scattered. "Ten at a time? You can't decide on one?"

The strewn-about books did look funny. After burning Father's letter, she had gone from book to book, trying to find a place to settle her sorrow, anger, and even shame. She ignored them. "Why didn't your grandmother change her name? That's the first thing I'd do. Change it back to Mathis."

"See a judge, file a public document?" The fire had gone low, and though she had been handling the stove for a month, he opened the door to check the coal level. "Likely, she feared people would suspect foul play, wondering why changing her name mattered so much if he'd simply left."

"That's what she told people?"

"What choice did she have?"

"They believed it?"

"I doubt any of the six white guys told even their wives. Grandma had no plans of leaving the farm Grandpa Howard had built or quitting teaching. No matter what name she used, she wasn't going to hide. Streamist knew where to find her."

Lauder looked around her small place: The books were one thing, and thankfully, nothing intimate lay on her bed or over the back of her chair. "Were you afraid he'd return?"

"I trusted the Sioux. They'd come meaning to finish something, not see it drag on after they'd left. They wouldn't do half a job."

She removed her coat, hung it on its peg next to the burgundy and her hat with stampede strings after. She wished she had coffee to offer, though he'd likely refuse. "What does Mrs. Streamist say now about what happened?"

He shook half a dozen coal pieces over the top of the morning's embers. "Grandma has said a couple of times 'God stopped by that day.' I've never cared to hear how she figured it was God's working and not Grandpa's Sioux friends."

At the farm, Lauder had asked Dak if he carried guilt over his mother's death, and he'd claimed he didn't. "Do you carry guilt for Streamist?" Guilt would explain something more about him.

"There's plenty I'm guilty of, but not an ounce of that is for Streamist."

He looked ready to leave. Throughout the day, their relationship had stretched and contracted and stretched again. "You say women break in the West. After your mother and grandmother, I understand, but I'm neither of them. I'm not going to break."

His arms ached to hold her.

"I'm not," she insisted.

"You don't know what tomorrow will bring. What's likely to take you down."

She moved to him, wrapped her arms around his neck. "I'm not as weak as you think."

His hat hit the floor, and he held her. Kissed her. He moved her back just far enough to look into her eyes. She shouldn't be here in this goddamn place. He ought to have burned it down. "You're okay? At dinner, you said you're sometimes scared."

"I do often feel watched." She laughed. "But look at that desk. My dead sister's music box. The basket is Mina's and has her dead mother's hair woven through. This place is full of ghosts."

He let her go, took a small step away.

"I'm fine," Lauder said. Except for the fact that I'm not still in your arms. "I don't know what made me admit to fear. Dolly has a strange effect on me." Dak had let her go, and she wondered again of the possibility of him and Dolly. Oil and water, no possibility. Impossible. Was she so naïve? He was a man, and Dolly a woman more than ready.

"I should get back," he said. His mouth held words that wrestled with his heart. He couldn't spit them out. "Plenty to do and it's already getting dark."

She watched the pain in his eyes. He didn't want to leave, yet he would. Why? It wasn't the livestock, though they did need tending. And it wasn't his grandmother, who was being cared for. Was it to protect her or himself? "I'm stuffed with goose," she managed. "I'm so sleepy I'll be deep into it before you reach home. Thank you for the day, friend."

Friend? Christ. He loved her.

At his leaving, she dropped the bar across the door and faced the empty room. Christmas night, and her company would be the music box she wished she had never stolen and a basket she wished she had never accepted. No gifts, no new Christmas flock and slippers, no Nurse. She sniffled and slapped her fisted hands against her hips. No Mina and no Dak.

She forced herself to breathe evenly. In and out. In and out. She wasn't going anywhere, and neither was Dak. He'd told her much of his story, and they'd work out their relationship as she learned more.

With so many pitching emotions, including fear for Mina and her family, Lauder couldn't sleep or read. There was nothing in her books for her tumultuous feelings. Not even Thoreau had something to say to her. She sat before her journal, the eyes of Mina's basket and the music box watching. Dak had told her about Mrs. Streamist and the husband more fist than man. At times throughout the story, Lauder had wanted Dak to stop talking. For his own sake and for hers as well. But his story made her question her own. What had she kept secret even from herself for too long? Denial only served itself. Though her story wasn't anywhere close to what Dak experienced, what had driven her to plagiarize and then run to a reservation miles from home? Having grown up with a houseful of secrets? A household as two-sided as the moon. One part aware of everything Babette's death had done to her parents, but the other part secretive.

She turned to a fresh journal page, but for long minutes only stared ahead. Finally, she dipped her pen. *Nurse blamed Father for Babette's death.* She stopped, wound the key on the music box. Nurse had never actually said she blamed Father, or had she? *Babette was six,* Lauder wrote slowly, the music box chiming. Babette dancing. *Father made her try and stand on one leg during a carriage ride.* Of course, he had; he'd forced Lauder in the same way, though never in a moving carriage and he would not have missed the opportunity. Alone with Babette, the swaying, a daughter he needed to be sure ranked above other men's children. "Try harder," he'd scolded Lauder so many times. His voice booming and his eyes sharp. "You must be better." Why believe he'd treated Babette any differently?

Lauder picked up the music box — had she already turned the key? "I've known all these years," she said to Babette. "Father shouted at me, 'On one leg, balance. Balance. Do better than her!'"

She sat the box down slowly and began to write. *Babette fell against the door. Likely more than once. Striking the handle. The latch flew open. An accident…of sorts. Father wouldn't have noticed the door clasp slipping. He never meant to kill her. Only to kill the weaker, not-son in her.*

Lauder looked over the shaky script. She didn't doubt what she had written. The whole of it had been just there, buried seed needing the right conditions to break through the soil. She stood, sniffled, walked between books from one side of the room to the other, wanted to be done remembering.

Babette's hands settled on Lauder's shoulders, sat her down before the journal, and put the pen back in her hand. "Write."

Babette's death was horror enough, but added to it was the great, weighted secret of blame. And the inability of either parent to acknowledge that. Father couldn't. Nor Mother. What would it have required of Mother if she had done so? Divorce? Blame wasn't discussed. Mother couldn't forgive Father, not realizing it was herself she couldn't forgive. The blame of never having stood up to him. She had seen his treatment of Babette and, feeling guilty, she lavished the child with more attention, telling herself it was a form of love.

She bought me prettier things, Babette wrote with Lauder's hand. *Prettier dresses and dolls and a music box."*

Lauder reclaimed the pen. *Mother swathed Babette in lace and curls. Unknowingly made her the battlefield on which she and Father fought. She hadn't been able to stop Father, and she couldn't divorce him without losing custody of Babette. Mother, therefore, had to tell herself the situation wasn't so bad. Then, after Babette, she had to stay blind to the treatment of the second daughter as well. Anything less was admitting her failures with the first and the great catastrophe that resulted from her weakness. To survive, did she also have to convince herself the second daughter wasn't as worthy as the first? Telling herself, handling a chipped, plaster vase was different from the care necessary with a Ming.*

Father too. Treating the second daughter any less strict than the first was to admit his treatment of the first had been wrong. And admitting to the consequences of that.

I've never believed I was enough, Lauder continued, dipping her pen again, and starting a second page. *I've clung to that belief, proving it to myself with a thousand failures. My own sweet little galaxy of failures. It wasn't just my being inferior to Babette, her presence still clinging to the house like wall paint, I've never admitted my own guilt over her death. Had Mother not been bedridden with me, Babette would not have been off with Father.*

Nonsense. I am not to blame in even the most remote way. Why then, have I continued to carry the belief? Have I nestled and harbored and fed the thing because it matches the belief I'm not enough: my little nougat of candied pity?

Unable to sit still with her new realizations, Lauder rose, paced. Why did she have to see the truth about Babette's death today, an awful Christmas, and with Father's letter still wounding? Was she only now broken enough to admit the truth?

The music box sat in front of her, suddenly alive as a pushing, pecking older sister. "Mother's dear Babette," Lauder whispered. She used her pen, poked at the box, nudged the tribute an inch closer to the edge of the desk. "Twenty-two years of feeling unwanted." She nudged the box again. "That's the reason I stole you from Mother." A jab, more insistent, the box teetered. "So many years of carrying guilt, struggling to be more. I've swallowed hemlock in the way I've blamed myself and struggled to be found worthier. To the point of plagiarism. Even knowing it was wrong." The tip of her pen stabbed.

The music box struck the floor, gave a looping half roll and came to a stop. Whole. Rebellious.

Twenty

SUNDAY, DECEMBER TWENTY-EIGHTH, Lauder dressed and decided to attend morning church services. This would be her first time attending, and she didn't particularly care to go, but she had already paced for an hour and needed to get out of her quarters. Seeing the cones her students had hanging amongst the other Christmas decorations would be a nice relief. Maybe a couple of children from her class would be there. Badger and Much Wind had been absent the day of the drawings, but if they were in church, she would assure the boys they could make cones in the morning, when school resumed after the holiday break. In which case, Dak would see the cones were hung. The Christmas season, after all, wouldn't formally end until Twelfth Night, January fifth.

Tomorrow, the thought sent warmth spreading through her. Tomorrow, the children would all be securely under her careful attention. Though she had no idea what Dak planned to do about his grandmother. And Mina? Lauder clenched and unclenched her hands. Day twelve and Mina, Plants Corn, and Blackbird had not yet returned. She was certain. If they had, Mina would have instantly come. She knew how much Lauder worried, and their deep friendship would have brought her in.

A knock sounded on Lauder's door. She opened the door to a man with an untrimmed beard, standing not much taller than herself. A tattered coat, a soiled hat in his bare, thick hands, and the front half of one shoe wound in a glove of wire. "That feller 'cross the street there," he said. "That agency feller, said me ought to see you."

"Agent Moyer?"

He lifted his hand eight inches over his head. "Not the weasel, the bigger feller."

"Certainly." Her cabin was her home, but it was also her bedroom and dressing room. She felt squeamish about asking a strange male inside. But Dak had sent the man. "Would you like to step in out of the cold?"

He peeked in, pulled out. "Me boots happy here. There don't look big enough for a man and a woman ain't had a preacher hold up his Bible."

"Let me just grab my coat."

Ought she lead the man across the street to Agent Moyer's office? If Dak thought it was so important for them to speak, then he ought to be a part of the conversation. But several horses were tied along the rail. On a Sunday? And this early in the day? Something was happening.

"George, Little Rose, 'em's mine."

"Oh…" Get the surprise off your face. "Yes…I'm happy to meet you." His being white explained Little Rose's lighter complexion, though not George's darker one. He struck her as a meek but determined character. Not an abuser of children, but of course, looking at a person was not a doorway into their soul. Ought she admit to him she was worried about the children, and how George's dedication to his sister was unnatural? Would this man take that as an accusation? And maybe he should.

"She happened on me," he said. "She were struggling in a woman's way. Come limping down me lane, moaning, needing me help. Weren't no help with bringing in me boy, but me knew to tie off the string real good afore the knife." He slung his hat brim in his hands, watched it go around for a few turns, then lifted one hand as though it was worthy of Lauder's consideration. "Me hands the first to touch him. That's something."

"You're referring to George?"

"Maybe ain't to no one other. Me lifted him in a towel in me pitch. His eyes opened, and the first thing they laid on was me ugly face."

Lauder had chosen the burgundy and buttoned the coat to the top. Insecure next to the man, she fought an urge to cross her arms, hug herself, and hold on to the fur trim. Had Nurse's hands been the first to hold her? And Nurse's eyes the first to meet hers? "Yes," she managed, "that's something."

"She weren't but skin'n bones. Them first weeks after George's born … George me name." He looked to the right of her door, his gaze fixed there on a board of wood, but seeing something far different. "Feeding him left her plumb worn out. We struck a bargain. If she kept fighting to suckle that scrap of boy, me could keep a fire, feed her what there were. Beans, the bit of wild got snared in me traps."

The hat continued to round in his hand. "Winter long, she'd sing a bit o' song, and me'd sing back. Didn't neither of us know a dang word the other were going on about. Her right in me bed with the boy. Me happy on the floor by the fire. Best winter me ever lived." He sighed, looked up at Lauder. At her silence, his eyes dropped back to the spot on the wall. "Come spring, she still weren't walking away. Held me breath ever-day, me did, scaredt that'd be the one she'd leave me. The rivers thawing, ducks and geese a squawking overhead like the world were in celebration, and me can't hardly breathe. Half a dozen of her kin come riding down. Me wanting to run them off, lying how she ain't here, git away." He pleaded as if Lauder needed to understand. "That weren't me choice, were it?"

"No," Lauder managed, "it wasn't your choice. It was hers."

"She comes running out, and they's all howling and passing round me boy. Me went to the barn figuring to pitch dung 'til me back quit. Or me heart. Time the horses left, cow shit were slung from one side of the barn to the other. Waiting for me to sling it back." He shook his head, his eyes filling with the memory. "She stepped into the barn looking prettier than a bottom filled with flowers, holding our baby. Me carried 'em both, all the way back inside. Didn't let her feet touch ground fer three days."

"It's a beautiful story," Lauder said. She would add it to her journal, develop it, though she doubted she could capture this man with his fall-winter face and his love for his children. There were fathers who denied their own children. There were also men who looked upon the wonder of a child and, without a blood connection, were eager to parent.

"Little Rose come a year later," he said. "Spring again. Wild roses so pretty me brought a fistful to her bed. We called her Little Rose. She were a runt too, but she lived."

"She's a wonderful child," Lauder said into the man's pause. "She drew a horse that's hanging in the church. If you'd care to go and see."

"She's gone." He sniffled. "Ain't been a full moon since her dying."

"The children's mother?"

"Baby, too. She brung me another girl. Me buried them on the hill at me place."

"I'm terribly sorry."

"George and Little Rose, theys ain't close to crawling outta that grave. We ain't any of us close. We's all curled down in there with her."

"I'm sorry. Not a month?" She pictured the brother and sister walking into her classroom that first morning. Their mother must have died only a couple of days before. Was it any wonder George clung to his sister and she to him?

The worn hat continued its rotation in the man's hands. "It were yesterday. Last night. She died agin this morning. She dies agin ever morning we wake and she ain't there."

Lauder fought tears. "I'm sorry," she said again.

"Little Rose won't let go of George. They weren't in the pitch when she went. Three days dying. She weren't going to live. Me sent 'em young'uns off the afternoon knowing. Me slobbering like a bear in a trough. Could be, the two expect they ain't together, ones likely to go."

Lauder's original assumptions shamed her. George wasn't protecting his sister from another person, but from the great dragon itself: death.

"Day later, me done getting dirt on the grave, they's screaming. Their horse down. Both of 'em loved the old nag, followed Little Rose around like a pup."

"That's tragic."

"George doing better, he's thinking he's got Little Rose to big brother. Keeping busy at that. Little Rose ain't faring well without her mama. Crying about her horse like it's all that's gone."

"Transferring her pain as a way of coping?"

"Expect it's something like that." He shook his head and nodded at the skinny mule behind him. "This one's too ornery to trust with my young'uns."

Lauder heard the music box chiming on her desk. One note. Two notes. "Don't ever trust that animal. They could be thrown off. ... " Killed.

"If she'll rain a drop or two come summer, and me git a bushel or two of corn, I'll find a horse for Little Rose."

His shoes, one half wire, the other looking thin as cloth, shuffled. "Me come to tell you. You being schoolteacher. Ain't nobody taking me children, sending them off. Not whilst two legs be under me."

My god, no! "They wouldn't survive without you. Without each other."

"George goes to school, and if 'em are scaredt to be apart, they's both go. Ain't a dang word more to say about it."

"I understand."

"Come January, Feberary, trees exploding, 'em young'uns be home with me."

"Yes, Sir." She watched him mount his beast and ride away. Thankfully. She felt seconds from breaking down herself and slobbering like a bear in a trough.

Back inside, she paced. George was full blooded and living with a white man who considered him a son. If the school closed, could he still be taken away? And Little Rose with a white father? Did that keep her safe? Or being half red, did the government still consider her their property? Both children likely lived in more poverty than most Indian children who were removed because of their poor living conditions. At least, that was one of the excuses used. And who decided? Rich white men, their belts straining under their load.

The horses across the street still hadn't moved. She wanted them gone so she could rush across and into Dak's arms. Once again, she would shamelessly fling herself against him, make him hold her for a few minutes.

Twenty-One

SUNDAY SERVICES NO longer called Lauder. She spent the morning recording the story of George and Little Rose, motherless, and with a father who couldn't afford shoes but would throw himself on a blade for his children. She wished she had kept the letter from Father so that she could read it again. Why? Was there a purpose in comparing her father to the man who'd come to defend his right to be a father?

Do Not Return! Father had written.

She stood at a crossroads. She felt certain she knew now how Babette had died. Had known for a long time, though through denial, a well-practiced denial, she'd kept it hidden from herself. Now, with the baggage out in the open and gathered at her feet, the choice was hers. Leave off the trappings, the bags and boxes, the hoe and rake carried from Dusseldorf or keep dragging them.

Commotion outside drew her to the window. Reporters, always vying for the best position, camped in the street in front of Agent Moyer's office. General Brooke with a small entourage came and went.

She walked down the road, letting the cold fill her lungs. Seeing that the vagrant, in all his misery was nowhere in sight, she dared to go as far as the post where he normally sat. Then hurrying away from the spot, she came back up, using the other side of the road, passing in full view of the agency's window. Dak's horse hadn't moved, and she knew if he looked away from the barrage of men filling the office and glanced at the window, he would see her. Maybe come out to meet her. He didn't. She spent an hour alone in the mess for her midday meal and returned to her journal.

2:10. Dak's horse still hasn't moved. Is the Indian woman, Walks Back, still with Mrs. Streamist?

2:15 Sgt. Atlock arrived. Dismounted in a rush and entered Agent Moyer's office. What news does he have?

2:25, Dak, with his hat pulled low against the cold, and his coat collar high, hurried out of the office. Reporters surrounded him, but he answered no questions. He patted his horse's neck and looked my way, his whole person making my heart give way, but he did not cross to me. His thighs were covered in leather, the apparel looked buckled at his waist. I believe the word is chaps. Extra protection for his legs where the wind cuts most? How far was he being sent? What was so urgent that he couldn't spend a moment at my door?

4:05. Red Cloud walked down the street in no great hurry. I knew it was him by his height, half of it in his long face that wears years of winter and droops his eyes. Seven or eight men walked with him, all wrapped in blankets. A dozen women, wives, perhaps also daughters, walk ten yards behind the males. The men entered Agent Moyer's office, the women sat along the wooden walkway in front, huddled in their blankets. Reporters took endless pictures of them.

5:00 Red Cloud and the rest stepped back outside. The group retreated down the street in the same formation as they arrived. Men in front with Red Cloud in the center. The women trailed behind.

6:03. Horses thundered down Pine Ridge Road. Soldiers tall in their saddles, bundled in long navy coats and military hats. Five standard bearers, five war flags flying high from nine-foot ash lances. Five, the number of guidons Custer's men carried.

6:10. Everyone has left Agent Moyer's office. Only two horses remain: his and Sgt. Atlock's.

She put down her pen; she needed to know what was happening. With her coat and hat, her notebook and pen, she hurried across the road.

Agent Moyer stood over brown paper he had spread across his desktop.

Sgt. Atlock stood at his side. "Miss Ellison." He grinned as if he were her reason for coming. His eyes leered.

The wrinkles on the front of Agent Moyer's shirt proved he had spent the night, maybe more than one, sleeping in his clothes. Likely in his boots as well. "What's happened?" she asked him.

"We've got 'em pinned down here." Agent Moyer used his index finger; the nail, the color of garden soil, punched the paper.

Her heart rose higher in her throat. Could he possibly mean Mina and her family? "Who?"

"The whole lot of them. Over three hundred criminals." The cigar he kept perpetually between his teeth, as though he were an infant needing the comfort of a thumb, winked a red eye. "Thinking they can walk onto my reservation."

This wasn't about Mina and her family, but about the band of Sioux Dak mentioned on Christmas. She ought to feel relief, but she didn't. What would happen to these people whom Agent Moyer considered criminals? And where was Mina and her family? If she asked, the questioning would call dangerous attention to them.

"General Brooke," Sgt. Atlock said, his voice ripe, "sent out a barrel of whiskey to congratulate the men on the capture."

Jolly with information, Lauder thought. I'm still not impressed by you. "How many did you say were captured?"

"Over three hundred," Agent Moyer said. "Some of the nastiest scalpers out there. Armed to the teeth."

On Christmas day, Dak had said the band was mostly women, children, elderly. Agent Moyer well knew this, but his fear of that many Lakota, no matter their sex, age, or state of infirmity, coming down Pine Ridge Road had scared him into drawing up a map. He needed symbols fixed on paper to help him believe the threat was also fixed.

"Soldiers have them surrounded. The savages captured here." Agent Moyer's finger dragged an inch across the map. "Marched five miles to the creek here."

Lauder concentrated, taking mental notes. "What now?"

"Big Foot's being seen by a doctor," Sgt. Atlock said. "He's in a tent with a stove."

"One night," Agent Moyer's voice rose. "Only one. First light, the bastards'll be marched to the depot. Shipped to Omaha and prison."

"Prison? In Omaha?" The words had not wanted to leave her tongue. At what profit to the railroad? What fare would Father and his ilk charge the government for shipping three hundred people across the state in coach? Or would it be in open cattle cars? "Even children?"

"Anyone with that bastard, Big Foot," Agent Moyer said, "ain't mine. They got no right on my reservation."

His fear and superstitions of Indians festered like an open wound and made Lauder want to slap him. He wouldn't sleep again tonight, knowing the band of Sioux were so close. "Children," she said. Like the little innocents she spent time with each day. "There must be another option."

"General Brooke gave clear orders." Sgt. Atlock would contribute what he knew. "'Don't let them escape. If they fight, destroy them.'"

Lauder could still see General Brooke standing in Father's library, his uniform crisp and distinguished, appearing the noble gentleman. But he'd have three hundred "destroyed," in order to be done with the bother of them wanting to keep their land. Even children. She touched a shaky finger to blue lines on the map. "What are these?"

"Troops," Sgt. Atlock answered. Pride rode on the song of his word.

She hoped he could hear the disgust riding on hers. "And the soldiers will have their war." Her heart pounded. "They've been promised."

"Nah," Agent Moyer said. "With that renegade captured, it's over. Soldiers will all be going home."

Sgt. Atlock shifted in his tall boots. His spurs jingled, and he studied Lauder. "It ain't just soldiers. The whole damn country's been promised a war."

She tried to steady her racing heart and the threat of dizziness her pounding blood brought. "Promised?"

"For weeks now," Sgt. Atlock said. "You read the papers. We ain't still a divided country. Not like the war between the states. We all agree the Sioux need gotten rid."

The map morphed before Lauder, lines smeared, markings

representing hills and rivers wiggled, blended, bodies appeared strewn for miles across the surface. She gasped, clutched the stampede strings at her throat, and forced her attention back to the flat sheet of butcher paper. She straightened her shoulders. There was an easy explanation for that brief mental slippage. On Father's map table, hashtags had also risen and become carnage strewn across fields, acres of dead, many still only boys who'd enlisted believing war made them men. But she wasn't back in Father's library, and she hadn't seen dead rising from this map. She hadn't! She wouldn't give in to wild imaginings. "The blue lines," her voice tremulous, "that's a lot of troops."

Agent Moyer thwacked the paper. "They escaped once; they won't this time. We got 'em surrounded."

Sgt. Atlock had likely been the one to inform Agent Moyer of the troop placements, and Lauder hated him for it. Sitting in his saddle above the scene, he would have noted precise details. Like the reporters, he scavenged for fame.

A thin line scratched southward off a much thicker line running east and west. The White River, she knew, though she didn't know the names of the river's tributaries.

"Wounded Knee Creek," Sgt. Atlock said. "Hauled the Hotchkiss guns out there."

Lauder pressed her palm onto the desk for stability. There on the map, unnoticed until now, two demon eyes just north of the Indian camp. Cannons at the ready.

"Colonel Forsyth is on his way," Sgt. Atlock said. "Taking more troops, two more mountain guns."

"Four Hotchkiss cannons?" Lauder could scarcely breathe. They meant to murder them all. "If you were Big Foot," she strained to ask him, "and knew the army was coming for you, wouldn't you also try to get your family to safety?"

Agent Moyer studied his map like it spoke to him.

Sgt. Atlock's eyes pinned Lauder. "In war," he said. "You need to get them all. The ones carrying guns and the ones that will be in a few years."

She tried to match his glare. This was his justification for slaughtering children? Or sending them to prisons labeled schools, run by evil women and men in black robes?

"Big Foot is Sitting Bull's brother," Agent Moyer said. "Now, we've got 'em both."

"Buck's rutting with sister wives," Sgt. Atlock sneered. He hesitated until Lauder looked at him squarely. "I want them moccasins. Get me a price."

She wanted to say, impossible. She didn't even know where Mina was.

"You ain't seen her? She's in the mess."

Not bothering with goodbyes, Lauder ran out the door and down the road.

The hall bustled; the long tables held more officers and aides than usual. Pipes, cigarettes, cigars. Every man who'd finished eating had his tobacco. Others smoked between bites. The atmosphere was festive. Did they all imagine they'd soon be heading home, or was it the possibility of war that ripened the air?

Mina sat alone in the room's darkest corner.

Lauder rushed, paid no attention to the looks she received as she hurried past tables, brushed edges, and rocked cups. "You're back," she said reaching her friend. "I've been so worried. Why didn't you come and see me first thing?" She felt betrayed. "Because I didn't go to a Ghost Dance? I'm sorry for that."

"The trip was long," Mina said.

As Lauder took the chair opposite, her self-indulgent thoughts shamed her. Mina looked ill. Grey cheeks and haunted eyes. Even her fingers, chapped and thin on the fork she held, suffered. "I want to hug you," Lauder said. "If we were alone, I would."

"And I you."

Relief danced through Lauder.

"What is your name for us?" Mina asked.

"Not-by-blood sisters."

"Not-by-blood sisters," Mina repeated.

The scarf around her neck reflected the days of wind and wear in an open wagon, the nights in a hasty, poor tent. Silk threads had weakened, snagged, and broken, though the stars still held brightness.

The condition of the scarf didn't matter, but Mina's continuous wearing of it brought tears to Lauder's eyes. "Plants Corn and Blackbird?" she asked. "They are well?"

"They are well." Mina's eyes skated cautiously back and forth over Lauder's. "Mother?"

"The basket is safe and sound. I think it's begun to speak to me. If you had knocked on my door," she stopped herself.

"I wished to know what was being said here." She glanced at the crowded mess. "Men have big voices and imagine Lakota women do not have ears."

"Did you hear what you wanted?"

A shout and several quick bursts of laughter made Mina jump.

Lauder's throat tightened. Mina hadn't come to the agency to see her but to gather information about the captives. "Agent Moyer," she said, "drew one of his maps. I saw it."

"How many soldiers? What does the army plan to do with the people?"

Plants Corn, Blackbird, and Mina, had returned safely. No longer alone on a wild, winter prairie, three innocents without protection from angry whites or angry reds. The blessing mattered more than her suffering pride. "I don't know about the people," she lied. How could she admit those plans. "I only saw the map."

"You must come with me," Mina said.

"Dancing?"

"We will talk at your house."

Hardly a house, Lauder thought.

Mina stood without saying more. She clearly didn't wish to talk there and didn't wait for Lauder. As she passed a cook's serving board where ten loaves of bread cooled, she slowed.

Don't do it. Lauder's heart raced as she ran the few steps to catch up. She grabbed Mina's arm. "Meet me at my cabin. I'll bring a loaf."

Mina answered with eyes that said the theft was about much more than bread.

Chilled, Lauder waited until Mina was entirely out the door. "Sir," she called to an aproned man. "Your bread is delicious. Better than I've ever had." She smiled as charmingly as her lips would. "May I take a loaf? Later tonight with tea, it would make such a treat."

"How about I wrap it in a towel? Keep it warm."

Twenty-Two

EVEN EXPECTING MINA, as she had been for twenty minutes, the knock startled Lauder. She lifted the bar across her door too forcefully, then jumped back as it slipped from her hands and hit the plank flooring.

Mina stood on the walkway, motioned to the horse standing at the corner of Lauder's cabin, its large eyes staring. "I had to fetch him." She smiled. "You were hoping for Dak. That's why you threw the stick on the floor."

"Come in. I don't know where Dak is. He's got Agent Moyer ordering him around."

Mina wasn't listening. In a heavy coat with the shoulders drooping and the sleeves over her hands, she hurried to Lauder's desk and grabbed up the basket. She considered the open journal on Lauder's desk and took a moment before speaking. "What is it to be so wealthy? A belly so full, loved ones so safe, you fight boredom by fashioning the tragedies of others into stories?"

Lauder took the few steps to her desk and closed the journal. "It doesn't matter what I write. Supposing I'd ever write again for public eyes would be an irrational enthusiasm. My mother's favorite term for my plans or dreams."

"Irrational enthusiasm? What does that mean?"

"It means I don't think like her." Lauder studied her friend and how thin she had grown since their first meeting. The boarding school had not taken just Mina's childhood, the trauma sucked away her adulthood, too. Yet, in the school records, Mina would be counted as a successful graduate who'd returned to the reservation and schooled the heathen out of pagan children.

With the basket held close, Mina paced as if emotions burned in her and made her move.

"Maybe tonight you should take it." Lauder wouldn't mention how at times the nest of thatch made her nervous, and how, at other times, it made her feel companioned.

"If it's lost," Mina sighed, "Mother will not rest. And there will be nothing to prove she ever walked the earth. Dreamt. Wept."

Babette's music box sat just there and felt as haunted to Lauder: a memento full of sorrow and guilt. Which should not be returned. The thought surprised Lauder. Was it Babette suggesting Mother needed separation from what had become a yoke?

Mina continued to cradle the basket. "It's my mother's breast." Her voice caught. "It feeds me."

Lauder didn't completely understand how the reeds, thatch, and strands of hair mattered so much, but she also no longer supposed she should be able to understand Mina's faith. Or that she even had a right to. That sort of arrogance shut the doors on ever truly understanding another. She had sat reading in the library, and the hair of a boar had dropped into her lap. A whisper from the reservation? Some magic, conjured by Nurse or her wee folk? If she dissected the event, cut it open, analyzed it six ways to Sunday, it would die.

"Mother," Mina said, "braided her hair in as she was dying. I cannot have it taken."

Lauder didn't need to ask again why it sat on her desk rather than Mina's. "White women's possessions are safe," Mina had said in the wagon. "Not torn away from them."

Mina set the basket down, a hand lingering to trail an index finger around the top, then finger a loose bit of grass, fretting it back into place. Her eyes fell on the music box, and she turned the key. She listened to several musical notes before speaking. "In our beds on the third floor, we couldn't hear anything in the basement. But we could hear the piano on the first floor. When it was being played, we knew Sister Joseph was trying to block out the screaming she heard coming from the basement."

Lauder waited, her stomach beginning to clench.

Mina's eyes filled. "I knew the place. They locked me in the basement as well. In a box too small to lie down. Only darkness. A dirt floor. My water sinking away when I soiled myself, but the floor was never dry."

"Terrible," Lauder breathed.

"The worst?"

What was worse than shutting a child away in darkness, playing music to avoid hearing her screams?

"I believed I deserved it." Mina's hands began to tremble. "I believed because adults I'd been taught were holy and wise had forced me in the box." She interlaced her fingers, made a single fist of her hands. "I never tried the door. I didn't kick at it until it came off its hinges. I believed I was nothing."

Lauder wrapped her arms around Mina, felt the sting of her own tears.

"I was so small. They saw terrible evil in me. I had no way of making it go away."

Lauder couldn't speak. She couldn't say she understood. Hearing of another's loss did not qualify the listener to suppose they understood. A person couldn't compare their nicked finger to another's execution because both incidents drew blood.

"I spent the days pulling out my hair," Mina said against Lauder's shoulder. "One hair at a time." She struggled to make her words clear. "Pulling them out. A child's desperate way of surviving. At night, the quiet so deep I could hear a small snap tearing away with each hair I pulled. The sting promised I was still alive."

"Oh Mina."

Mina pulled back, looked down at her hands and the shiny marks like rings on her fingers.

Lauder had noticed the tiny scars before, imagined them the result of some ritual, and hadn't asked.

"One by one," Mina said, "I wrapped the strands of my hair around my fingers so I could keep them. When Sister Joseph let me out, my fingers were so swollen and blue, she needed a knife to remove the hair. She cut me. Called me an animal. Said I was filthy for pulling out my own hair. It demonstrated the demon in me the school fought to expel. 'No human child,' she swore, 'would do such a thing.'"

Mina's story, with its mistreatment, filled Lauder's eyes. Tears, too, knowing the abuse still dwelled in Mina, still tore at her heart, and would always be happening to her.

"My mother gave her hair. She was not a demon."

"She was not. She loved you very much. I know so little of your story. Where did you go after? Where were you before returning here?"

Restless, Mina moved around the room, eyed the books, stroked the fur on Lauder's burgundy. "I was seventeen. A man came to the school. His wife had died, and he needed help with four children. Many of the older girls looked away when he entered. I may not have gone willingly the day before. Perhaps not the day after, for I trusted no one, but that day, I stood. I wanted to go, and I believed that if necessary, escaping the man would be easy."

"At seventeen, couldn't you have left the school and come home on your own?"

"I did not belong to me. I was property of the nuns and used in the laundry. Also, I think now, there are many more things than walls to escape. I did not believe I was worthy of another life. I did not know people who might take me in. My parents were gone. I was afraid. The man paid the nuns money, and leaving with him, I was not a run-away. His children were small and easy to love. They showed me how with them I was good."

Lauder feared asking, but she couldn't stop herself. "Were you his wife?"

"I did not lie with him. He did not come to my bed at night and force himself on me. In his house, we spoke as friends. For two years, it was good. I taught his children to read and write. He married then, and yet for another year I was happy. I taught her to read and write as well. She was a good mother, kind to me and the children, but after that last year, I was not needed."

I was not needed. The words made Lauder shudder.

"It was time," Mina said. "I was no longer a child. It was time. He asked me where I might go. I would not go to another home to care for more children. I wanted to be with my people. I was here before I became nothing. It was here I had to come, but the man worried for me. He did not want me to return without employment. We wrote to Agent McGillicuddy. I studied more. Months passed, and he found Blackbird. She and I also wrote many letters. She wrote that the people are sick, and children are dying of hunger."

"At first you were told 'no,'" Lauder remembered hearing that part of the story. "Then the Ghost Dancing and people fleeing. I'm sure it was Dak who got the forms signed for your placement. He was probably the person who found Blackbird and Plants Corn for you."

"Seeing so many soldiers, I feared Mother would not be safe."

"Did you have the basket with you throughout your school years?"

"When I left the school, the nuns packed what I was allowed to keep. A single dress and change of under clothing."

Lauder glanced sheepishly at the two trunks and the dresser filled with possessions. More goods than she could lift.

"When I unpacked at the man's house," Mina said, "the basket lay at the bottom of the sack. I'd never seen it, but my mother cried out to me. The nuns had kept her from me all those years."

"I don't understand why they had it."

"Before I was taken, my mother made a small parcel for me. I've seen many children bring small bundles. Parents sending extra clothing, remembrances, and sacred objects for protection. The nuns take the bundles, save only what can be sold, destroy the rest. The nun who went through the bundle I carried at four years old knew the basket would not bring a coin, but she lacked the courage to destroy it. Perhaps," she glanced at the basket, "Mother hissed at her. When I left, they wanted it away also. To see my mother after such time. To know the years she was kept from me. I wept many days with sadness and joy."

"How does a person put so much behind themselves?"

"Blackbird is most unhappy with me."

The information surprised Lauder. At the depot, the family had fallen into each other's arms. "I'm sure it's just some misunderstanding." What else to say? The hurt in Mina's voice cut too deep for platitudes.

"As my mother's sister, Blackbird is mother to me as well. She sees my schooling has made me foolish."

"It's not true. You aren't foolish."

"The boarding school cost me much. The years of pain there and the years lost not being here, not witnessing the hardships or learning the wisdom of my elders."

The books Lauder had left scattered, suddenly felt unwelcome, guests too proud of themselves. She gathered them up, off her bed, two on the floor, another on her desk, and returned them to the book chest. It wasn't that they lacked value, more that they were the wrong medicine for this case. Or were they? "You've been given something in return for what you lost," she tried, "you can read and write English."

"Something better in the service of my people, or better in the service of whites?"

"You can't return to the old ways." What of those even remained? "And you can't believe in Ghost shirts to protect you."

"As your priests believe in their vestments. Ghost shirts demonstrate our faith in being protected by the Great Spirit. When two or more are gathered."

"Don't believe it."

"You suppose a god that recognizes only your form of worship? That the mind of the Great Spirit is so small it holds no more than your own? Only fools suppose such."

Lauder had been taught exactly that. That after billions of years of evolution, the white man had arrived, the pinnacle of eons of shifting plates and geological ages, which saw the extinction of thousands of less worthy creatures. But the white man had evolved to such a state he was now perfect and complete and would therefore remain for all eternity as fixed as the stars. This white man could now address God on His level. The two could barter, make deals, and they now agreed on how to handle the lesser beings: Bring them to their knees. Or destroy them.

"I'm no longer sure of anything," Lauder said.

Mina plopped down on Lauder's bed. "There's much to be unsure of."

"You're kind. Why do you bother with me?"

"Because with you, I'm smart." She gave the quip a moment, a breath of lightness in the gloom. "Come with me. Tell Blackbird what you saw on the map and what you know of the army's plans."

Lauder longed to go but discussing the army's positions? Would that make her a spy, a traitor? Agent Moyer would say yes. Possibly consider such actions treason. Going, she also risked her job, and if Dak was right, that meant she risked the school as well. "Can't I just tell you what I saw? It would be wrong, but if you destroyed it, I could draw the map."

"Please," Mina said. "People are in much danger. Blackbird must be told. You must convince her."

"Convince her of what? Why would she listen to me over you?"

"You have information."

Lauder, uncertainty weighing her, sank onto her bed beside the person she considered a sister. If she redrew the map, which she could do with more expertise than Agent Moyer's original, then why the necessity of going?

"You'll come?"

How could Lauder refuse? She had refused Mina in not attending a Ghost Dance and regretted it every day since, worrying herself into a winter sweat of recrimination. She would not deny Mina this. "I'll come."

While Lauder pulled on a second pair of bloomers and a second pair of stockings, Mina went back to the basket, cradled it in her arms. Whispered to it.

The heavy set of her shoulders frightened Lauder. "I'm ready."

"Where is your other hat? The one a clown wears while riding a horse backwards."

"Very funny."

Mina waved with an elaborate gesture at Lauder's attire. "Your clothing is no longer silly. What would your mother say of this?"

Lauder pulled on gloves. Mother would be far more upset by

Lauder's association with Mina than the new attire. "Mother would say I'm damaged and no longer welcome under her fine roof."

Mina touched the scarf of stars around her neck. "White families do not welcome their wounded into their homes?"

The question seemed as much about Mina's own family. But Plants Corn and Blackbird weren't guilty of ignoring their wounded. Nor was Mina. They'd all helped a filthy and broken man climb into their wagon, and Mina had sat beside him as the wagon rolled away. No one in Lauder's family, not even one of the staff, including herself, would have assisted the creature. Respectable people didn't even make eye contact with such wretchedness. Nurse, she amended the thought. Nurse would come to the man's aid.

"Was there no love in your family?" Mina's dark eyes still asked broader questions.

"We didn't talk about love. The word wasn't used. I think silence carries less pain." She glanced at her closed journal. "And denial serves a purpose."

Dressed to leave, she turned out only one of her lanterns, thought again of Nurse and how the woman who lost her family to a fire would not have one in her room. "Too easy knock over. Lanterns make fire wings."

Lauder's fear, greater than fire, was returning and having to enter the place shrouded in darkness. There was the scratching, and there was John.

Mina opened the door, paused. "This is a place of sorrow." Her eyes fell on the basket, then on the music box. "It doesn't want to be here."

Lauder's breath caught. At the same instant, she had thought the same. It wasn't the basket or the music box, though, that accounted for what Mina sensed as sorrow. An otherness lived there; a negativity Lauder hadn't brought. On the first night, stepping through it, had taken will. "There was a robbery here."

"And death?"

"There's been no mention of a death. Though if you ask Agent Moyer, he'd tell you he's afraid his reputation kicked the bucket that day." She handed the loaf to Mina. "Don't say a word; I know what you're thinking: White women can take all the food they want, and they aren't considered thieves. That truth shames me."

"Take the music box." The words rang in Lauder's head as if this time they'd come from Babette, who didn't want it returned to Mother. Lauder shook her pillow out of its case and used it as a knapsack. "A gift for Blackbird," she said. "I'm expected to bring a gift, aren't I?"

They stepped into darkness as deep as the cold. A bitter dark, full of omen, Lauder thought. Lights from lanterns inside buildings threw out blocks of pale yellow onto the frozen and snowy surface. Agent Moyer's office where Dak worked days lay dark. "I'm sorry for this," she whispered in that direction. Both Agent Moyer and Dak would be upset with her going.

She groaned when they rounded the side of her cabin and Mina clicked her tongue. The horse, having strayed a couple of yards, came close. "I wish you'd brought the wagon."

"You could walk, but maybe your white legs can't walk three miles."

"That's very far."

"And we haven't got the time."

"You knew I'd come. You should have brought the wagon."

Mina tucked the loaf of bread inside her coat and stroked the horse's long muzzle. "Too slow. Wagons must stick to roads. Are you afraid of horses?"

The reins dangled, leaving the animal untethered, able to charge or rear at any provocation. "They're fine harnessed to a wagon or carriage and a strong man has the reins and the brakes."

Mina's brows lifted. "Do you fear falling off?"

Lauder hadn't thought that far ahead. Now she knew that if she ever got on, she would certainly fall off.

"You've never been on a horse?"

The trip from the depot with Mina and Plants Corn had been Lauder's first wagon ride. "Carriages. With a driver."

"Oh." Mina's voice sounded full of mock pity. "You don't know animals at all?"

Lauder took a nervous step closer, a far too skinny horse with unblinking eyes full of dislike. "I do know animals." She spoke to both the horse and Mina. "Mother has a Pekingese named Pou-sa. She's white and harmless. Have you ever had a dog?"

"More often than you."

Lauder struggled not to grimace, not to imagine Pou-sa turning on a spit. "I'll get my chair."

"If your chair is left sitting outside," Mina lifted a sarcastic brow, "some thieving Indian is going to come along and steal it."

"Very funny."

Mina ran a hand down her horse's long nose. "His name is Hahepi, and we're wasting time."

"Ha-he-he-pie?" Lauder faltered.

"Hahn-hay-pee. It means night. Use that."

"I shouldn't be doing this," Lauder said, "it's dangerous. I wouldn't do it for anyone else in the world."

"Riding Night, or telling Blackbird the truth?"

"Leaving the agency in the dark. Telling your family about the map. Agent Moyer could have us sent away. Worse. Maybe court-martialed. And Dak? I don't know what he would do."

"Tell them you went seeking adventure for your books." She motioned Lauder to step closer. "A man mounts from the right. A woman from the left. A man must keep his left eye closed, but a woman, her right."

Lauder took another hesitant step closer, her knees shaky and her right eye tightly closed. "Now what?"

Standing at the horse's shoulder, Lauder expected Mina in her long skirt and leggings to do some bit of fancy leaping. Some whole body flip upward that would have her landing on top of the horse, her skirt and coat perfectly organized beneath her.

Mina tucked the bread high under an arm, held the reins in her left hand, and gave them a gentle downward tug. Night lowered his head, and she tapped his belly with her right hand. The horse shuffled, moving his hind legs slightly forward under his rump, folding his front knees, and lowering to the ground. He sat sphinxlike, the ridge of his backbone at Mina's waist. She put her leg over, sat, and gave Lauder a wry look.

Twenty-Three

THEY STARTED FROM the darkness behind Lauder's cabin, avoiding those leaving the mess and those milling about, looking to begin the night's carousing. They would go unseen lest someone report them to Agent Moyer or General Brooke. And for what supposed crime? Two females riding back-to-back? Lauder leaving the agency under the cover of darkness with a Lakota? Mina being a Lakota moving under the cover of darkness? None of which were crimes, all of which were crimes enough.

The rear of the buildings had no hanging lanterns to light the way, no wagon ruts or horse trails to follow. Winter-dead grasses whispered around the lower legs of the horse Lauder thought of as Night. He trod through the scrub; his hooves crunched the frozen surface beneath. Three miles. She cringed at the thought. Anything could happen over three miles. And there was always her fear of John, a person so damaged she was sure there was no help for him.

The agency receded behind them, and cold wind blew unimpeded by buildings. They'd gone half a mile when Mina pointed. "John lives through there. Deep in those trees."

Lauder, already shivering, kept one arm around Mina and with the other hand gripped tighter to the pillowcase containing the music box. She coached herself not to flinch at every low, crouching form they passed. Bushes, rocks, she promised herself, not evils lurking, lying in waiting. "In all those trees? He's in there now? You're sure? He's not at your house?"

"He's not at my house."

"He scares me."

"John mourns his two sons."

Lauder kept one fearful eye over her shoulder and on the trees until they were far past. "His sons died?"

"Sent away to school. It's been a decade; perhaps they are dead by now."

The news settled on Lauder. She thought of the friends Dak had lost, and she wanted there to be more reason for taking children than whites needing to fill their expensively built schools. "Were they taken because of their father's drinking?"

"Taken because they were happy. It's not good to be a proud Lakota boy."

They rode on. Despite the wool scarf Lauder wore wrapped high on her cheeks, leaving only her eyes uncovered, her cheeks burned. She leaned down onto Mina's shoulder, shielded one side of her face and rested it on Babette's scarf. The silk wasn't as warm as her wool, but so much richer in other ways, and connected her with Mina. Their cultures were separate as trees, but underground, weren't their roots the same? They both wanted to live in peace and to pursue their dreams. She couldn't speak for Mina, but for herself, there was a love and respect that bound the two of them together like the clasped fingers of sisters. "I understand your empathy for John. You and his sons being taken, sent to boarding schools, his drinking, which will soon kill him, your parents' drinking that did kill them."

Mina jerked, her shoulder pulling from Lauder. "Not every Lakota dies from drinking."

They rode in silence.

"Was I mistaken?" Lauder finally asked. "I assumed your parents—"

"You did. My parents died of white man's illnesses. Coughed blood, became skeletons while their hearts yet pumped."

Lauder, you are a fool. You astonish yourself with the extent of your stupidity.

"Fifty thousand a year," Mina said, "traveling across our land. Littering the hills with trash they no longer want, killing our food, sickening our water with disease." She drew in a breath. "Alcoholism is another name for sorrow. Whites brought that too."

"I'm sorry." How many times since arriving at the reservation had she needed to apologize for false assumptions? How deep was that barrel before her apologies amounted to nothing?

"Had my parents died of whiskey poisoning," Mina said, "I would not be ashamed. And John does not sit there every day. When the sadness rears so high over him he cannot endure, drinking helps him catch hold of the fantasy that his boys are on the road home. He goes to wait for them."

Lauder dared not speak.

"My return gives him false hope."

"You did come back," Lauder was happy to agree. "Maybe there is hope."

Mina bent deep and lay her head a moment on Night's long neck. "If they live," she straightened, "they are no longer John's sons."

The words carried such weight, Lauder wondered if something more had happened to Mina in her ten-day absence. She wouldn't ask. She couldn't bear another story like that of a little girl locked in a box, a nun on the floor above playing the piano so as not to hear a child screaming. She searched for easy conversation. "You walk this distance to and from school every day?"

"If I run, I'm warm."

Superficial chatting. Avoidance of the real. All that Lauder did not know about Mina carved a distance in the twinning and sisterhood for which she ached. She knew again that she couldn't meet Mina in her place of sorrow. She could pity and weep for her friend, but no one ever fully experienced the height and depth of another's pain. Now Mina was turning away from her, turning more into what Agent Moyer would call a troublemaker. Lauder couldn't let that happen. "All I'm saying is that there's too much drinking on the reservation. Not everyone has lost children. There was this drunk woman, lifting her dress to a soldier."

"There are many things to lose."

"How does John," the civil name felt awkward in Lauder's mouth, "get money to buy liquor?"

"Maybe he works. Maybe he raids."

"You mean steals? Stealing is wrong."

"Do you have another term for taking a man's land, his food, his livelihood, his children? Ah, I remember now." She reached skyward, her arm falling across the cold, white moon, the orb appearing to crack. "Manifest Destiny."

Night's hoofs rang on frozen ground and at other times the sound was only the shush of hoofs punching through snow. Distant hills shouldered and bunched like sleeping, prehistoric animals, and hungry wolf-howling rolled eerie and sonorous.

"The ancestors are speaking," Mina said.

"That's wolves."

"Ancestors, wolves, land, it's all one." She paused. "How do you get your money?"

"I tell clerks, 'Put it on Father's account.' Please, don't answer that. I hear myself. I'm only suggesting John's drinking isn't helping."

"Perhaps it helps him." Mina glanced over her shoulder. "Would he be better sober so white men can pat him on the back and tell him he's a good Indian?"

"You don't mean that." Holding tight to Mina's waist, Lauder promised herself that despite the teeth in Mina's bantering, they rode twinned. She was sorry for assuming Mina's parents had died from alcohol abuse. Sorry for having mentioned drinking at all. Every day, she saw parents coming and going from the school in the morning and again in the afternoon, and none of them appeared drunk. And of course, there was Father and his guests who were handed a drink the moment they arrived at the house, and their glasses were refilled steadily until they stumbled out hours later and headed home for a nightcap before bed.

They rode on, the rocking as steady as the cold weaseling up the cuffs of Lauder's sleeves, through the buttons on her coat, down her collar and through every inch of wool and leather she wore. Clouds became a dirge, a heavy and silent rug across the sky, that at times blocked out even the moon's weak light. Night's reins rubbed against his rough, winter coat, and the longer they rode, the closer they were to reaching Mina's family where Lauder would need to confess the lines of troops on Agent Moyer's map. The Hotchkiss guns. She felt her stomach lay somewhere miles back. "I hope you still consider me a friend," she whispered. A sister.

"Wasicu."

The word and the power behind it stung. "You don't mean that. You know I'm on your side."

"When an over-loaded boat is sinking, only a fool climbs in and cries, 'I'm here to help you.'" She shook the reins, encouraged Night to move faster. "It's time my people are left in peace."

"You know that's not possible. The world will not revert centuries, no matter how you wish it. We are fools, but don't give up on us. On me. I'm learning Indians are holy people."

Mina shuddered. "All things are holy. Even warriors who raise guns to try and save their land and their families."

Lauder shivered as much from Mina's chilling attitude as the winter cold. "When you talk that way, you scare me. You'll get yourself killed."

Mina didn't answer.

They rode, silence a winter between them.

Lauder considered the music box inside the pillowcase she clutched. She had been wrong to take it from Mother; wrong to suppose she knew best how Mother should undertake her mourning and healing. And yet, now, it was Babette herself who would not have it returned. Has the loss, Lauder wondered, made Nurse's companionship necessary to Mother again? A much healthier option, but poor Nurse. A life stretched between others' needs.

"I believed my return would be different," Mina said. "The reservation is a churning tempest."

"And whites see only that. I'm beginning to understand something. The anger, the illnesses, the starvation, the dancing, the poverty — those things are all visible and the blame appears to fall on the Lakota. What's not visible are the whys. The broken treaties and the governmental policies are invisible." She paused, wanted to sound encouraging. "It's a bad time, but the soldiers won't be here forever. It's too costly."

"Then they must hurry to wipe us away."

"Have you thought about going back to the family? I mean if you were happy, they may still have a place for you."

"I do not wish to grow old as a servant. I will not leave Plants Corn and Blackbird. They have survived much loss and pain. For them, I wish to be a part of good world making."

"You're doing that now."

"Am I?"

Lauder's fingers and toes burned, and their conversation was sad and desperate. "How much farther?"

"A couple of ridges."

They'd ridden what seemed an hour, and "a couple of ridges" didn't tell Lauder much. Suppose the sky opened and dropped six inches of snow before they reached safety? Suppose Night tripped in the dark and broke his leg? Dak had warned about the cold that year after year killed numbers of people. If he knew where she was, he'd rake his hand back through his hair, slam on his hat, and ride out after her.

Finally, they climbed a dark rise, and Lauder saw the squat form of a low cabin with faint light buttering a window. Reaching the yard just outside, and sliding off the horse, Lauder's body rocked with cold, her feet so numb she couldn't stomp them to bring blood back into her toes.

Holding Night's bridle, Mina led him into a three-sided structure of loose and weathered lumber, hardly larger than a closet, where wind moaned between the rotting boards. He nosed an empty trough.

Skeletal, Lauder thought. The horse wouldn't survive the winter. Holding the music box, she found the courage to run her free hand over the corrugated bones and thought of the gaunt horse Little Rose drew.

Mina whispered in the horse's ear as a tear rolled down into the scarf of stars high on her cheeks.

Caught, Lauder thought of the tear. Preserved. She didn't know what Mina had said to Night, only that the words held love and pain. She considered what losing the animal would mean to the family. Crush them. Just as it had Little Rose. Emotionally and physically. They'd need to gather wood and hunt on foot. Walk to the agency for rations — pittance though the rations were — carry them back through the snow. Become beasts, travoises yoked to their shoulders.

They started for the cabin, but Mina grabbed Lauder's hand, stopped her in the windy yard, and drew her into a tight embrace. "I want to start fires and stick knives in white men. White women too, for acting innocent of what they let happen. I want to drink until I can't stand on my feet. I want to lie beneath the entire army and pass their diseases man to man until they all die of syphilis."

"You don't mean any of that. What would all your destructive acts do?"

"They will have been mine. Mine! I will be killed for acting so, but for the moments before, I will have been alive."

"You can get away from here. There can be a future somewhere else."

Mina hugged Lauder again, her lips at Lauder's ear, her words garbled, sobbing, ending with the word "sister."

Lauder held tight. "Sister."

Twenty-Four

L AUDER, SO COLD she couldn't control her shaking, nearly fell into the one room cabin. The only light came from the stub of a flickering candle sitting on a table in front of Plants Corn and Blackbird. The air smelled of burning wood from an iron stove in the center where faint orange seams bled through the stove's grates.

"Good evening," Lauder said, passing rockers, one flanking each side of the stove, and stepping around a man asleep on the floor. She didn't wait for an invitation to sit, could only stumble onto a chair at the table.

Plants Corn lifted a heavy face; his hands worked on hard, cream-colored objects in front of him. He nodded a greeting.

Blackbird looked at Mina with anger or disappointment, Lauder couldn't be certain which.

"Hau." Blackbird's acknowledgement was civil, but no more welcoming than the woman had been to Lauder weeks earlier when they'd met at the depot.

I've been invited, Lauder would not say aloud, and I can't make the trip back tonight. Where would she sleep? On the floor beside the man who had a blanket rolled under his neck and a hat covering his face? She doubted he slept, but he obviously didn't care to meet her. Didn't consider her worthy of removing his hat and greeting her.

Blackbird rose from the table and the candlelight to stand at a dark window. Her chin and jaw had grown sharper since the first afternoon when they'd all ridden in together from Rushville. She looked meaner, older, her neck ropey, and her eyes sunken. Pink-rimmed now, her eyes proved either she hadn't been sleeping or like Mina, had been weeping. Lauder supposed the first.

Mina set the loaf onto the table and crossed the room to hang her coat. She kept her scarf of stars around her neck.

Lauder pulled the music box from her pillowcase. "For you," she said to Blackbird. "A gift." Now that she was there, looking over the sparseness of their lives, and seeing Blackbird so gaunt, it shamed her that she hadn't thought to bring coal or some other gift of value. Given this family's meager circumstances, there wasn't a more useless item in the world than the music box. She prayed Blackbird could see beyond the nonsense of the item and to the goodwill intended. She gently pushed Babette's likeness two inches closer.

"Listen." Mina had come to the table, and she wound the key.

The tiny, internal drum turned, the tines on the comb bouncing, sending out musical notes. The ballerina performed.

Plants Corn watched, but Blackbird looked down at the sound and the twirling as if she saw nothing.

Lauder's throat burned. The figurine rotated on the toes of one foot, a fixed pirouette, the spectacle so out of place it felt garish and offensive. She had obeyed the urge to bring it, and on the ride out, considered how the box might celebrate the family's safe return. The box would make a gesture toward bridging their cultures. Failed, all of it. "It's not the music," she tried, "my sister." She stopped. Mentioning Babette felt equally wrong. The box had been stolen. How could it then be considered a gift? Likely the reliquary — how else to think of it — was bad luck. She wanted to grab the token, run with it out the door, and chuck it into the first ravine she found.

Mina and Blackbird spoke in low voices. Argued in Lakota.

Lauder looked away. A cradleboard hung on an otherwise bare wall. At least one of Blackbird's children must have spent their infancy in the board, looking out on the world while riding their mother's back. Traveling with her strides and the dips of her knees. Living with the motion of her bones. Perhaps Mina had spent time in that cradleboard. Only a few feet back from the table, a bed hugged the wall. Narrower than Lauder's bed in Omaha, she was certain Blackbird and Plants Corn shared the sleeping space. Across one corner of the room, a blanket thrown over a rope acted as a curtain. Beneath the hem, just visible, the spindly legs of an army cot. Mina's bed? The bit of space between the fashioned drape and the cot left only space enough for Mina to stand and change clothes. If she knelt to pray for her people, her heels would stick outside the enclosure.

In Omaha, each member of the Ellison family had their own large bedroom. Each lavishly furnished with ornate carvings on mahogany bedsteads, desks, wardrobes, winter curtains of lush velvet, and imported rugs. Mother's room with a blue, elephant hide settee. Objects Lauder knew wouldn't interest this family even if they had the means.

"Your coat?" Mina held out a hand.

"In a minute," Lauder said. She would keep her coat, protection now, not against the cold but with a need to keep bundled against the smallness she felt in front of the family. "My hat," she said, at least that. She drew out the long pin, watched as all eyes noted the slow removal and seemingly endless length. She shrugged, jabbed the thirteen-inch-long pin back through the top of the hat, and handed the whole to Mina. "Don't hurt yourself."

"Warrior white woman," Mina said.

The word "warrior," and the room's spareness helped Lauder understand the loss she felt. Where was the long arm of their history? Buffalo hides, pottery, bows, beadwork leggings and belts all absent. The cradleboard had survived, but had everything else been burned, stolen, or in some other way destroyed by the army? A purposeful destruction of spirit that Lauder feared would never find its way back. She wanted to believe Dak that the people would rise again, and she wanted to turn and promise Mina that on her life she would keep the mother's basket safe. So long as Mina needed. Was this one of the reasons Mina so often wore her beaded moccasins, not letting them off her person? Not letting them out of her sight?

The man on the floor remained still as death while Plants Corn continued working, a piece of tin serving as a cutting board. With a short knife, he nicked off the ends of hard objects the length and color of wax beans. He worked with precision, removing the sharp barbs on what Lauder decided must be porcupine quills and scraping those from the tin to a pile on the table. The phrase "skin and bones" was inadequate. In the flickering candlelight, he looked foreign, not the man who'd brought her to the agency that cold November afternoon. Then, he'd had lines flaring from his nose and carving down around his mouth, but they hadn't been this deep, the cheeks this hollow.

Lauder tried to smile so broadly that neither he nor Blackbird would notice her shock and heartbreak at how gaunt they'd grown. Had there been no food on their travels? None to pack, no berries or roots to find, no rabbits for his gun?

Mina and Blackbird resumed their conversation, though Lauder thought it sounded more like an aunt scolding.

"Aunt wishes," Mina said, "to know why you come here and bring your ways for our children?"

The question, and Blackbird's use of Lakota through Mina rather than asking herself in English, made Lauder's tongue tighten. Because I'm welcome nowhere else. "My students are happy."

"Mr. Washington most happy," Blackbird said.

Now the English, Lauder thought. The woman hated the language, but she would use it to make her point. Her condemnation of teaching also referenced Mina, who'd turned and left the table. Attack me, not her. "Taking children is wrong," Lauder said. "It's why we must keep the school open. Mina is helping to prove to Mr. Washington the children can learn at home."

Blackbird's thin hands quivered. "Mr. Washington most happy."

The repeated phrase made the tips of Lauder's ears burn. She shrugged out of her coat with hardly an awareness of doing so. "The children must be taught. It's a new world." She sighed at the stupid things she continued to say. Did she suppose Blackbird wasn't aware of the changes? The woman likely met a long string of murdered loved ones in her dreams. She likely woke at night and found them crowding around her bed. They likely whispered in her ears, told her to fight.

At the stove, Mina lifted the lid off a kettle and took from her leather pouch the foodstuffs from the mess. She had been served two ribs along with her beans and potatoes, and she dropped them in. Then six or seven rib bones nearly picked clean. Lauder's heart drummed. Bones discarded by well-fed whites who considered what remained on them scraps to be thrown out? Had Mina dug through garbage thrown out the back door of the mess? Was that the reason for her slow arrival at Lauder's cabin? Finding Night but also picking up bones thrown out to four-legged scavengers? Would taking bones thrown to animals, considering she was an Indian, be considered robbery?

Mina leaned over the rocker to the right of the stove.

Gooseflesh needled up Lauder's back and tattooed curlicues across her shoulders. The rocker was occupied. A tiny body. A second shrunken figure sat in the chair at the stove's far side. Even swathed in thick blankets, the pair looked smaller than Badger or Much Wind. Two ancients with wrinkled and leathered faces the color of wet oak bark, threads of white hair in braids thin as pencils. Determining their sex was impossible.

"Grandmothers," Mina said to Lauder's surprised expression. She knelt and squeezed the hand of the nearest, then moved to squeeze the hand of the second.

The shock of not having seen the women straight away made Lauder even more uneasy, as if the creatures had at that moment materialized from some liminal plane. Perhaps a graveyard.

The chairs rocked ever so slightly. Ghost rocking, Lauder thought. The women's feet, wrapped in rags, failed to reach the floor. She rose. With each step closer, the pair looked more conjured from a wooded fairyland. "Greetings," Lauder said.

The crones, how else to think of them? They stared straight ahead, not acknowledging Lauder's address. Their eyes, nearly closed, were little more than slits. And inside, the pale of egg custard.

"Grandmothers are blind," Mina said.

"Good evening," Lauder tried again, louder this time.

"Deaf as well."

Blind and deaf, yet Lauder believed the women knew she was there. Like Nurse, they used senses few people bothered to develop. They'd felt the draft of two people entering the cabin, the vibration of two walking with varied gaits across the floor. They knew exactly where in the room she stood, and she felt their uncomfortableness in having her there.

She turned to Mina. "Does Agent Moyer know you've brought them here? Will he say they are here illegally?"

"They are here by every legality," Mina answered.

Lauder glanced at Blackbird and Plants Corn, lowered her voice. "I'm only questioning if we need to protect them from Agent Moyer. If they are off their reservation, and he learns they are here, he's likely to notify the army." Mina might also lose her job for harboring criminals, but Lauder wouldn't speak it.

Mina pursed her lips. "Hostiles crossing reservation lines."

"You know what I'm saying." Lauder followed Mina's example, kneeling in front of the first grandmother. How like kneeling in front of Nurse with her Creole blood, though this woman felt even darker and more mysterious. She had no right to touch the woman's elfin hand as had Mina, though she longed to do so. Perhaps doing so would startle the woman or uninvited touch was taboo.

"Closer," Mina said.

On her knees, Lauder edged up closer.

The woman's body dipped forward, and she lifted a twig-like hand from beneath the folds of her worn blanket. She reached and trailed fingers across Lauder's face, cheek, nose, cheek, a narrow face: a Wasicu. Then a finger around the rim of Lauder's chin. Female, Lauder imagined her thinking, no facial hair. She dropped her hand on Lauder's shoulder, gripped through the dress sleeve, and let her hand slide down Lauder's thin arm. Weak, no threat.

Lauder had a sense the woman knew far more about her than her cover. She had opened the book of Lauder and read its contents. Compelled to be as honest with the second woman, Lauder rose and knelt in front of her.

The wrinkled nose twitched as if a gnat had suddenly climbed a nostril. She sneezed. Sneezed a second time.

"She thinks you smell good," Mina said.

Lauder had grown accustomed to bathing from pails of water heated on the stove, but she had not forsaken the bars of scented soap she'd brought from Omaha. She stood. "She thinks I stink."

Returning to the table, feeling even more unwelcome and out of place, she waited for what would come next. Mina had brought her to inform Blackbird of the troops, but likely Blackbird already knew everything. Still, they would sit awhile, broach the subject slowly while a man on the floor, his face hidden, continued to feign sleep.

"She wishes you to remember," Mina said, first listening to Blackbird in Lakota and repeating in English, "our people have lived on the land more days than stars in the sky." With her emotions visibly torn, Mina continued translating. "Your people try and teach us how best to live on our land. You are fools. Wolf and coyote do not speak to you."

Lauder hoped Mina saw understanding and love in her eyes. None of this was Mina's fault. At the first opportunity, Lauder vowed, I'll confess everything. Even tell Mina about the plagiarism and confess the wealth and privilege I have enjoyed. All of which was bound up in Mina's need to pick bones from trash heaps.

"I've killed a hundred buffalo," Father's bragging rang in Lauder's head. "Shot them from train windows. Bulls weighing a ton. When they go down, the ground shakes for twenty yards. You never heard a sound like that huffing and moaning."

The first time Father told the story, Lauder had flown and found herself on the train with men shooting out windows. She had heard the animals huffing and moaning, even bellowing in pain and fear. There had been the thud and suck of bullets through hide, flesh, and bone. Blood flying out in red cloudbursts and long strings ribboning in the air.

"Stupid animals," Father spoke from dead eyes. "They make good sport. Easy to pick off. Too stupid to run. Man's got time to reload while they sniff and low around the dead like they've the brains to mourn."

Plants Corn's knife rapped on the dented tin sheet.

Drawn back to the room, Lauder found her voice. "Tell her in Lakota," she said to Mina, "in Blackbird's language." The respect of that. "I am sorry the white man has overrun the land. But it is done. I will teach in the way life-saving medicines taste bitter." She could not imagine the little ones she taught surviving after being pulled from their families, sent hundreds of miles away, treated with cruelty. "I will do everything I can to keep the reservation day school open."

The sorrow in the room thickened as Blackbird spoke again. Mina turned to translate, her eyes misty and one hand absentmindedly winding a scarf end around the fingers of her other hand. "Aunt believes teaching for Mr. Washington is not teaching. To clean buffalo, to instruct the young on how to find medicine to save a sick child, to store food for the winter. That is to teach. Aunt also wishes you to know you do not save the people. The Lakota will die, or they will live by saving themselves."

The man feigning sleep continued to do so.

"Your schools and churches are not for the people." Mina translated again. "They are statecraft."

Lauder dropped her eyes. Blackbird knew better than Lauder that the children no longer had a need to learn how to clean buffalo and there was no food to store for the winter. But knowing didn't relieve the woman's pain.

Mina unwrapped the loaf of bread. She sliced slowly, reverently, and put a slice in each of two shallow bowls. From the pot on the stove, she ladled on broth. She set one bowl in front of Plants Corn, who nodded with solemnity, and the other before Blackbird. Using a third bowl, she repeated with the bread and broth. This she took to the grandmothers, breaking off soggy bits of bread with her fingers, and lifting small dripping morsels first to one woman's lips and then the other's.

At the table, Plants Corn and Blackbird ate.

Lauder felt as if she watched something so private, she should turn away. Mina had asked her there for a reason, but there'd be no hurrying the conversation. She shuffled her numb feet, looked for a distraction. "How long are the grandmothers staying?"

"Winter here," Plants Corn answered.

Blackbird's expression faltered around her skeletal cheeks. She swallowed the food in her mouth and looked off as if seeing into the future. "Short time."

For Lauder, the words carried prophetic weight though she knew it wasn't Blackbird's wish to have the women gone. "Which one is your mother?" she asked Plants Corn. She would at least try and make polite conversation.

With questioning in his eyes, Plants Corn looked to Mina.

"Both are mother," Mina said. "A woman's children are also her sister's children."

Blackbird finished eating and stood. Her soft, unadorned moccasins whispered on the floor as she moved once again to the night-blackened window as if she wished to be out there. A pair of women's hard leather shoes sat beside the narrow bed, the toes under. Blackbird's hair, free and unbraided, with more white than black, shifted as she turned back. A patch of bare scalp the size of a coin winked and disappeared.

"Tell Aunt about the map," Mina said.

"Too many," Plants Corn's voice rose in sudden anger. "Buffalo Bull Sitting gone. Enough."

"Was that the chief's real name?" Lauder asked. "Buffalo Bull Sitting?"

"No more!" Plants Corn's angry words fractured into the room, slid across the battered floor, and reached the deaf mothers. Their throats released long, high-pitched cries.

Lauder's eyes widened in Mina's direction. "They heard that?"

"They witnessed Sitting Bull's killing," Mina said. "Though they were many miles away." She rubbed the top of one grandmother's hand. "They felt a great crack of light as the bullet slammed into his head. They witnessed his son's cry when he rushed after his father and bullets tore into his body."

Lauder didn't ask how that witnessing was possible. Or how Mina knew of it. Many things had happened to her that the world would call false. She knew too, what had happened after the killings, how many of those from Sitting Bull's camp feared more fighting and began scattering. Even Spotted Elk had started off from his reservation with a couple hundred. "When you heard the grandmothers were traveling," she asked Mina, "you all went after them?"

"The band moved only under the cover of darkness. The grand-mothers," Mina looked from withered face to withered face, "are too weak for such a long journey in the cold. We could travel day and night, bring them here in much less time."

Lauder didn't know where exactly on the wide plain they'd met up with Spotted Elk and rescued the grandmothers, but this explained why Mina hadn't wasted any time riding in to tell her goodbye. "I'm sorry for Sitting Bull's death," Lauder turned to Blackbird. "Especially how it was his own people who killed him."

Blackbird muttered under her breath, seemed to pace even though she had returned to her chair, and sank again. She stared at the music box and made a slight hand gesture as if in the next instant she meant to sweep the offending thing across the room and into the far wall.

I'm wrong, Lauder thought. Again. The story I've been told isn't the whole truth.

"Killed by his own people?" Mina said. "An agent sending out forty red policemen to do his murderous deed. Exactly how your white history wants the death reported. Like Crazy Horse, dead by the hands of his own people. Savages who kill their holy ones."

Outside, the wind rumbled and rocked against the cabin's walls as if roused to sudden anger.

"Men fight to survive," Mina said. Her voice strained, exhausted, and sorry at having to explain the obvious yet again to her friend. "Many do as ordered to keep jobs, so the bellies of their children will have food. Many others choose to fight, also so the bellies of their children will have food."

Lauder bit the inside of her cheek to keep from crying out. Agent Moyer had told a half-truth, and she had been gullible enough to accept it as whole. Papers too, reported Sitting Bull was killed by his own people. As a bonus, the story painted the Sioux as foolish savages. She had trusted Agent Moyer and the dailies like the *Bee Newspaper,* even as she knew the press was often little more than fiction. It was hard not to be sucked in by the papers, which looked important and official: a reporter's byline, bold letter screaming in black ink, *Sitting Bull Killed by His Own People.* Forever in history, written that way. Yes, a red hand, but a great white army controlling the red hand. And a white press to inform the nation of what they wanted to hear.

Mina left the grandmothers to cross the room and stand behind Blackbird's chair. She looked over the woman's head. "Tell her what the army plans for the people when they reach the agency."

Reach the agency? As if Agent Moyer might requisition food from the stockade, and send men out to buy heads of beef from local farmers? As was done for the troops?

"The soldiers are honest men," Lauder said, as much to reassure herself. "They play games with the children in my classroom."

"The army's function," Mina's lips tightened, still standing as one with her aunt, "is to kill. Is it not?"

Lauder took a deep breath, strove for calm. "They aren't human," Dolly had said of all Indians. But it was 1890, and regardless of the foolish few, no modern army officer would lead an attack on a band of mostly women and children who were already suffering horribly from four bitter days and four bitter nights in the cold. "The people will be safe. They will be sent to Omaha. Mr. Washington's feelings toward the Miniconjou and Lakota are honorable."

At the news of the people being sent to Omaha, Blackbird's expression darkened more. "Wasicu carry no honor."

Hardly words, Lauder thought, more like four hurdled stones. She did feel sure no captives would be killed, but once they reached Omaha? Would families be broken apart, husbands sent to prison, wives shipped east? Children sent to far-off boarding schools?

"Our leaders will no more touch pens," Blackbird said. "They will die on the backs of ponies. Not on their knees."

Plants Corn had let off his work when the conversation began. Now, he dropped his hand on the table, the knife hilt still fisted. "Much trouble."

"Aunt," Mina came around the table, sat again, pushed aside the music box, and reached across to squeeze Blackbird's hand. "Uncle is right. Going is too dangerous."

"Going where?" The nerve endings in Lauder's fingertips fired. "To where the cavalry is holding Spotted Elk's band?"

"Soldiers are distracted," Mina said, "drinking whiskey and celebrating their great capture of a hostile chief and his fierce warriors."

The man on the floor shifted, his heels dragging an inch left, an inch back. He kept his hat over his face.

Listening now, Lauder thought. Was he the one who'd brought the news of the people's capture?

Blackbird leaned forward, the patch of bare scalp showing again.

Loss, worry, starvation, Lauder thought, is robbing her even of her hair.

Blackbird turned as if Lauder had spoken out loud. "Show."

Plants Corn huffed a breathy sound of anger, but at the sound Blackbird drew back her shoulders. "I wish husband's favor, but I will obey the wishes of my ancestors."

The evening long Lauder had felt the queasiness of dread. "I don't understand what's going on."

"She wishes to rescue people," Mina said.

What? Sneak people away from under the noses of hundreds of soldiers? Impossible. "You'll be trapped. Or arrested. Maybe even shot."

"Much trouble," Plants Corn swore.

"I save one. Two," Blackbird said.

Lauder sucked in her cheeks, wishing Dak were there. They'd listen to him.

"Show." Blackbird's voice more insistent this time. She used a small, blackened shovel to remove half-burned cinders from the stove. With a finger, she poked here and there in the ashes and retrieved a sooty two-inch stick. On the table, she scratched a line, darkened it with a second ashy swipe. Off that, she drew a thin line, black dust sifting down. Her dark eyes fixed on Lauder. "Creek."

Lauder accepted the warm cinder with reluctance. She wanted no part of this, unless it was to thwart the whole impossible idea. She held the stick, considered. Blackbird knew the region far better than any late-arrived, white, pretend cartographer. She knew where the people were being held along a tributary of the White River. What she didn't know was the number of soldiers and how they surrounded the Miniconjou. Did the man on the floor not know this, only knowing that the people had been captured? "The soldiers, if I remember correctly," she marked the table, "are here, here, here, and here." She bit her lip, searched her mind, conjured Agent Moyer's map. "And here. Five lines of troops. The people are surrounded." She could not bring herself to make more markings, noting where the artillery guns sat on a small hill, pointed at the captives.

Plants Corn, his skin the texture of old boots and seamed with suffering, lifted his eyes skyward. "Much trouble," he said again.

"Uncle is right." Mina's fear tightened her lips, but she spoke softly, less sure. "Aunt, if you cause a soldier to fire even one shot, fighting will break out. Many will die. One woman, too dangerous."

"Trust in the army," Lauder said. "They have Spotted Elk in a tent. With heat and food." She wasn't lying, so why did her tongue feel thick and false?

"Mr. Washington," Blackbird said, "have cities of men for soldiers. Mr. Washington see soldiers die, no care. Mr. Washington see soldiers are," she searched for an English word, "cheap."

"No one wishes harm to any of the people."

"Prison is much harm," Mina said. "Grave harm."

Lauder wiped soot from her fingers onto her sleeve. Mina's quick anger frightened her. "They'll be fed. They'll have trials." Would that be ushering fifty into the courtroom at a time and pronouncing them all guilty in mass for leaving their reservation? Therefore, guilty of an act of war against the United States?

"There will be no trial. Psst!" Mina flicked the air. "Three hundred starving and ragged Indians. A courtroom shouting, 'hang them.'"

Her heart remains torn out, Lauder thought. There's nothing that can soothe it back into place.

Reaching in Lauder's direction, Blackbird extended a thin, outstretched hand. "Greetings, friend."

The odd action and the comment made Lauder hesitate, but she leaned forward to accept the offered hand of peace.

Blackbird pulled back quick, changed her hand to model a gun, and with her index finger pointed at Lauder's chest, lowered her thumb. "Pow!"

Lauder gulped. She was seen as an enemy. She felt like weeping, but she needed to keep focused on them, not herself. "You can't rescue anyone. It's impossible. There are five hundred armed men surrounding them."

What had Mina said? When an over-loaded boat is sinking, only a fool climbs in and cries, "I'm here to help." Wasn't that what she proposed to do now? "Don't the people," Lauder stressed, "have a far better chance of sneaking away on their own?"

"Some may try," Mina agreed. "Trauma will hold most. They are weak after their travels. They don't know where to go. This house," she motioned to the stove and its glowing heat, "they would not find. It's too cold to flee into the night without tents and sleeping robes. No mother takes a child into such a night without knowing safety is near."

Through the course of the conversation, Lauder had feared Mina was changing her mind, deciding in favor of Blackbird's action versus Plants Corn's wariness. Now, she was sure. "You don't need to do this." She looked from the gaunt face of Blackbird to Mina's. You both should be eating that loaf of bread and eating what meat is in that pot, not taking off on a suicidal mission. "Hunger is addling your minds. Your deaths aren't going to solve any problems. What would Red Cloud tell you?"

"It is my aunt's wish to go," Mina said. "She does not look to others to slay what arrives at her door."

The words held such despair, Lauder felt choked. "There must be someone else who can go."

Avoiding the man on the floor, Mina gave an exaggerated look under the table and peered into her small sleeping corner. "Where is someone else?"

Blackbird spoke in Lakota to the prone man. He stood and not meeting Lauder's gaze, hurried to the door. The room came alive, Blackbird reaching for a warm coat and blankets, Mina following suit.

"If this is some sort of trial by fire," Lauder nearly shouted, "a quest or Sun Dance? It's crazy. It has no purpose other than to get yourselves killed."

Blackbird and Mina continued, donning coats and wrapping themselves in blankets.

"Mina, stop," Lauder said. What had Mina said in the yard about being willing to die if for a few minutes she lived? "This is not the way." When Mina pulled down the blanket separating her sleeping space to take it as well, Lauder fought an urge to push her into a chair, pin her down. "You can't even walk in all that."

"We ride with him," Mina said of the man. "Blankets for others."

Plants Corn muttered to himself, perhaps prayed, long and quiet.

The man at the door asked something of Blackbird. When she nodded, he stepped out. A rush of sweeping cold rolled into the room. One of the grandmothers made a throat-deep guttural sound, and Blackbird looked back to where the elder woman had moved aside a fold of her blanket, exposed a brown, twig-thin forearm, and drawn out a short knife. Blackbird grasped the dome of the woman's hand in a moment of connection, then slid her fingers onto the knife hilt and took the weapon. The knife disappeared into the layers of her clothing.

The second grandmother, as if her blind eyes had seen the exchange, also lifted a thin wrist, exposing her forearm as her sleeve slid back. She ruffled and pulled out a knife.

Having knelt in front of the women, supposing them feeble and sweet, Lauder shivered at the sight of the keen blades. At the same time, she wanted to cheer their fierceness. Even in ancient age, they were willing and prepared to defend themselves. Their arms proved the chilling reality of what they'd borne: red cuts tracked down their forearms. Warriors despite the loose and leathered skin draped over bones as thin as twigs.

Mina accepted the second grandmother's knife in the same way as had Blackbird. First placing her hand on the grandmother's, squeezing, then hiding the weapon away in her own clothing. The swiftness saddened Lauder. The knives on the grandmothers had felt like means of defense, but Mina's actions felt rooted in offense. In just a month of being returned to her people, Mina gladly armed herself.

Twenty-Five

T HE DOOR CLOSED behind the man, Blackbird, and Mina. Whether the man who'd been resting on the floor was a relative, friend, or hired hand, Lauder didn't know. And it didn't matter. She was glad they had a male accompanying them, but the fear creeping over her the evening long still burned a hot reed down her back. Plants Corn in his chair hummed his prayers, and the grandmothers stared into a realm Lauder could not see. But she had seen the red slashes on the women's arms. They'd cut themselves and the wounds, not yet healed, spoke of how recently they'd been inflicted. Very likely after Sitting Bull's death. She wanted to weep and wasn't sure of any of the hundred reasons. She grabbed her coat and her hat where it hung and ran out the door. She would not abandon her sister.

Blackbird, with a determined, upright stride ahead of Mina, rounded the side of the cabin and disappeared.

"You shouldn't go." Lauder ran and caught Mina by the arm. "I have a terrible feeling about this." In a softer voice, hoping it carried no farther than Mina, Lauder went on. "Your aunt isn't strong enough to be out here. She's as weak and starved as those she thinks to rescue."

Mina pulled away. "Trying matters as much as success."

"Are you trying to get yourself killed? End it all tonight?"

"You do not understand."

"I want to. Send Blackbird back inside. You and I will go." Would they? What an unbelievable thing to say.

Mina unwrapped the silk scarf, held it out to Lauder. "Go to Dak."

"No, it's yours. Don't sever everything between us." As they rounded the corner, she stopped Mina again to tie the silk back around her neck. A second and third knot. "Sisters still."

"Come," Blackbird called as she climbed into the wagon, and the unnamed man took up the reins.

"Lauder, you don't belong here," Mina hissed. "I don't want you here."

"You're lying. I belong here because you're my friend."

"Go back," Mina said.

"To what?"

"To your own people. To where you belong."

All her life, Lauder had tried to find a place where she belonged. In Omaha, that had been only in Nurse's tiny room, but even that was over. Do Not Return! Father had written, though the words might have been from Nurse. Save yourself: Do not return. "This is my home now," she said.

She followed Mina and climbed into the wagon. The children she taught were family. Over time, with or without Dak, there would be more people to befriend, more people who would become family. If they would have her. She didn't blame any Lakota who wished to stick a knife in her. If the tables were turned, she would also want to stick a knife in her. But, this moment, she was a white woman. If that and her father's connections to General Brooke were all she had in the way of helping Blackbird and Mina, then she would use the privileges. However odious it was wielding them.

Mina pulled out the knife given to her by one of the mothers. "If you must, take this."

"You keep it."

"I have another."

"Of course you do," Lauder lifted a hand as if to push it away. "I'd never have the courage to use it."

"Take it, foolish woman." Mina kept the knife extended while they rolled out of the cabin's yard. "Take it. Whatever you're thinking, that's not the real world."

"But—"

Mina leaned close, pulled open Lauder's coat, grabbed a fistful of her dress, including the waists of both bloomers, and stabbed the knife through.

"Geez!" The coldness of the blade stung Lauder's hip, and the near stabbing took her breath. "I think I'm bleeding."

Mina patted the hilt. "Something for your next heroine."

Shaking, Lauder closed her coat and pulled the collar higher. She sat mute, rocked with the wagon and wondered if Blackbird meant to rescue someone specific. She might be trying to rescue a sister or a daughter. Days earlier, when she met up with Spotted Elk's band and extracted the mothers, for whatever reason, someone dear, perhaps several, must have elected to stay with the group. Now everything had changed.

"I'll talk to the commanding officer," Lauder said. "Introduce myself. Tell him I'm a friend of General Brooke, and we'll house women and children at your place until morning."

Blackbird gave a disbelieving head shake.

"The army will not give up prisoners," Mina said. "Even children."

"But I know important, wealthy men."

"The army," Mina stressed, "will find you a foolish woman bothering in man business."

Lauder, sitting on the floor of the wagon, huddled into herself against the cold. The wheels rolled on and on, one with a squeak that yipped, went silent, and yipped again. Mile after mile, the yipping and creaking wood. She trembled with cold before she finally spoke again. "How much farther?"

Neither Blackbird nor Mina answered, and Lauder wondered if they prayed. She shook, breathed into her gloved hands for the warmth of her breath, and tried to move her toes up and down in her boots though they had gone numb.

The wagon finally stopped at a river's edge.

"We walk from here," Mina said.

"How far?" Lauder asked. Was she the only one who cared about distance?

Mina's eyes widened as if to say, 'What does it matter?'

They climbed down after Blackbird, who'd instantly started off.

Mina turned to the driver. "Wait here."

In the dark, his dark skin, and his winter clothing blocking most of his face, Lauder only saw a slow nod of his head. "Do you trust him?" She whispered to Mina as they started off. "If he leaves, we're dead."

"Quiet," Mina hushed. "Voices carry in the cold."

A quarter of a mile ahead, Lauder gauged the distance, a glow spread across the horizon. Campfires. "We can't do this," she pleaded yet again.

"Hush. Voices carry."

Walking, stumbling, Lauder's feet burned as they followed the river. The temperature was so cold it made a thick substance needing to be fought through, and the scarf covering her mouth and nose had crystallized with the moisture in her breath. They walked, the distance beginning to feel like a dream, the lines between sky and earth vanishing.

Blackbird stopped, swung an arm out from under her blankets, and motioned for her and Mina to walk faster.

Lauder tried to keep up, promising herself that the pain in her hands and feet did not matter, that in going to help, step by step she filled a hole in her soul.

They moved down a shallow but wide ditch and Lauder wondered where they had left the river. She gasped at a quick motion that darted across in front of them. Too small for a wolf. A coyote then, night-cloaked, it stopped several paces away. Crouched low to the ground, its peering eyes slanted and icy white, it stared. Starved and hunting.

"Your knife," Lauder gasped at Mina shoulder.

The animal turned and disappeared.

Mina hissed a whisper. "That scared?"

Lauder was too cold to make it back even to the wagon. The only hope was for them to keep going forward, reaching tents and warmth. Dak had warned her. Even in ugly boots, a warm coat, hat, and wool scarf, only a fool stepped into a winter night in the Dakotas.

Plants Corn had warned as well. "Too dangerous."

Wind scraped the frozen ground and tall snow drifts, dragged dead leaves, dried seed heads, and gloom. Lauder stumbled and fell twice, her feet, burning and cumbersome as bricks. She couldn't feel them hitting the ground. Her chest smoldered with rasping lungs.

When at last the fires were no more than a city block ahead, Lauder nearly cried out in thanksgiving. Blackbird and Mina dropped to the ground and, when she didn't follow their example, Blackbird yanked her down. Camp smoke, kept low by the cold, hung above endless tent tops. On both ends of the camp, hundreds of dark silhouetted shapes moved around the fires. Soldiers with sticks, stoking the flames, tossing on more fuel to showers of sparks. They tipped back tin cups, talked, laughed. Celebrated having captured the renegade band.

Not wanting to even sniffle, Lauder wiped her nose on the cuff of her sleeve. The soldiers were her people: white men like General Brooke and Dak. She could work back to her feet, stumble into camp, sink in front of a fire, and speak to the commanding officer. She would be housed in an army tent with a stove, be warm again, be saved.

Blackbird and Mina rose only to squats. Lauder tried to move as they did on half-folded knees. Her wanting to enter the camp to save herself shamed her. If she did, a hundred questions would be asked. She couldn't mention Mina and Blackbird. They might be arrested, bound, put under heavy guard.

She followed as Blackbird led them around to the right of the camp. This was the impossible part. Impossible. They couldn't get in, find Mina's relatives, gather the strength to leave, then actually find a way out. The people were surrounded. There was no way to rescue anyone. The truth drummed in Lauder's head. Mina and Blackbird were out of their minds with fear and grief, and they hadn't seen the awful map. Despite Lauder's charcoal scratching on the table, they hadn't under-stood the full extent of the situation. This was her fault; she should had done more to convince them of the numbers.

Crouched at the rim of a dry ravine, Mina waited for Lauder still a few feet behind.

We can't do this, Lauder wanted to say, but Mina touched Lauder's numb lips through the wool scarf, signaled silence.

Sound came from behind. Lauder spun, saw the dark shape of an approaching horse. She turned back to whisper a warning and found herself alone. Blackbird and Mina had been just there, but they'd disappeared. She had not seen them go down into the dark maw, but they must have. Blackbird knew where they were; she knew the depth of the fall, and she had chosen it. Lauder dropped her legs over the ledge and sat a hesitant moment on the edge. Her heart pounded. She was a stupid white woman who ought to have her head measured, the shrinkage recorded. With no certainty of the depth, she slid on her bottom. Dirt clods loosened and rolled down the bank after her. She landed, her feet hitting, and her upper body toppling over knees too cold to catch her.

"Stop!" A man's loud command.

"Who's there?" A second male voice.

Soldiers. Clear English. "Don't shoot," Lauder shouted. She stood and faced the single lantern coming at her. "I'm a reporter."

Three men stood directly in front of her, the alcohol so strong on their breaths, she wondered the lantern flame didn't catch it on fire. The barrels of their rifles fixed on her. On the bank above, a horse whinnied, and a fourth man on horseback looked down on them.

The man nearest her jabbed her ribs with his rifle. "Stick up your hands."

She pulled down her wool scarf, revealing her face. "I'm a woman," she cried. "I'm white." She winced at having added the fact. Blackbird and Mina had certainly heard. No, not that, she wished she could tell them. I'm not claiming to be better, only that I'm not one of their captives trying to escape.

"The hell?" The speaker spat. "A woman. What ya doin' here?"

"My name is Lauder Ellison. I teach at the Pine Ridge Day School and report to Agent Moyer."

As if he'd heard nothing or nothing of it mattered: "You armed? Open yer coat." His eyes leered. "Give us a peeky."

The smell of whiskey wafted again. Her heart banged. "I will not. I'm not hiding weapons."

Beneath the drab, army-issued hat, his brows furrowed at her refusal. "Take it off."

The lantern, a godless eye, pinned her. She had feared being shot without a chance to identify herself, but now she had stated her name, her sex, her occupation, and her race. None of which mattered to them. She crossed her arms across her chest and hugged herself. "I won't tolerate mistreatment. Please, take me to your commanding officer."

The one on horseback remained silent. She didn't know if that made him less dangerous or more dangerous. Another kept his rifle pointed at her while the two others lowered their guns, the stocks to the ground, the barrels leaning against their groins. Using both hands, one yanked open her coat. She had thought herself too numb to feel any colder, but chill blasted deeper into her bones. They jerked her coat off her shoulders. Leered at her chest as if they could see through her dress front to her bare breasts.

She felt sick. The men's speed and savagery towards her was shocking. She was in a place they believed she had no right to be. Where a woman ought not be. Disobedient women were a threat and deserved to be taught a lesson. She struggled to pull her coat back up over her shoulders. When she couldn't, she kept her hands at her waist, covering the knife hilt.

"I'm Lauder Ellison," she tried again, fighting her shivering and the shaking in her voice. "My father is an important railroad man. A scientist. I'm a friend of Agent Moyer, Sgt. Atlock, and General Brooke. They'll see you all court-martialed for this."

She had called out three names trying to save herself, but the only man she wanted to ride up at that moment was Dak.

"I'm George Washington," the first man said. He looked around at his cronies for assent to his wit.

"I be Abe Lincoln," the second chimed in like a dunce.

"I'm a friend of Jesus Christ himself," the third slurred. Every word he spoke puffed white into the cold, and each tiny cloud firing onto her face was laden with whiskey fumes. "That there," he nodded at the man on horseback, "be J.C. himself."

She hated the man's well-fed horse, too. What right did it have to feed when Night starved?

"Better search for weapons," George Washington said.

"Yes, sir." Two began patting her down, their hands slow, cupping and groping the contours of her breasts. She cursed them, but the more they assaulted her, the more she refused to scream. Blackbird and Mina couldn't be more than a few yards away? A scream would bring fifty men, more — their lanterns lighting the length of the ravine. As it was, there were only the four, their attention absorbed with her while Blackbird and Mina hopefully got farther away. I admire you, she thought of the pair. You're heroines worthy of literature.

The knife hung at her waist, but even if she could work it free, what good was wielding it against four? Only an hour earlier, she thought the weapon unnecessary because she was Lauder Ellison, above the sort of banality that made carrying a weapon necessary. Now she knew she was above nothing, and the knife wasn't defense enough.

The drunken men continued their assaults. They had the cover of night, a woman alone, and brains fettered on whiskey. George Washington's hands rubbed down her leg, then up beneath her skirt, snaked up her calve, her thigh. She slapped at him, tried to jerk away, only to be knocked against the back wall of the ravine. The other two pinned her, a man on each arm, sneering, enjoying themselves.

George Washington pulled on the fingers of his right glove. A slow methodical removal that soured her stomach. He went to one knee and his hand started at her ankle, underneath her bloomers, crawling up to her knee. She fought against fainting, swallowed her screams, and hissed down at him. "Go ahead. Enjoy yourself. I'll enjoy myself at your hanging."

He rose, his hand flew to her throat, knocking her head back against the frozen embankment. He yanked her dress front and the fabric ripped. New cold scraped her skin. He slid his naked hand into her chemise. Lust descending to anger. Anger circling back to lust. Righteousness. License.

She spat, her spittle hitting the face of the man breathing on her. "That," she said at his flinch, "is something you can never remove. For all time, you are a man in whose face a woman spat."

He opened his mouth, roared whiskey fumes, and drew back his fist.

"Stop," J.C. said. "She could be Brooke's fucking granddaughter. I ain't looking to hang for you assholes' fun. Bring her up out of there."

George Washington stepped back. "Hanged?"

Getting her coat back over her shoulders and closed nearly took more energy than she had. "Too bad for me. I looked forward to seeing you swing."

With a man gripping each arm, they dragged her up the ravine wall. She wanted an opportunity to spit in each man's face, to scratch at eyes, no matter the beating they gave her. She couldn't, but she hoped she had saved Mina and Blackbird. Though she didn't know for how long.

Pushed and prodded every time her knees buckled, they hauled and herded her into camp. Soldiers not trying to sleep in tents looked up from their cups, their whittling, or their card games to stare or whistle or catcall as she passed.

"What's this?" A man, clearly their leader, rose from a camp stool.

She twisted free of her captors, the jerking nearly tossing her into the fire.

A tall black hat with an eagle badge, a long navy coat, and the fire reflecting off his shiny gold buttons. An officer. A full beard and dark eyes, each holding a tiny, reflected blaze, glared at her. Three others, similarly attired, each with his pipe, that symbol of wealth and power. For what lowly soldier could afford imported tobacco?

"I'm Lauder Ellison." She meant to speak with authority, but it sounded like a near shout. Standing before a circle of those judging her, men all, the volume in her voice was all that remained of her courage. Behind her, George Washington and the others shuffled away. Ought she accuse them in front of their superiors? She couldn't admit to what they'd done, and she didn't trust this newer bunch anymore. Would they laugh at her distress, consider her mistreatment warranted, drag her into a tent for their own pleasure?

The camp's noises continued: Horses neighed, boisterous men with booming voices who would be heard over their companions, and campfires that crackled, spat, and blackened the night beyond them. And wind. Always the wind. She wobbled with cold, all but yelled for the second time. "My name is Lauder Ellison. I need to speak with General Brooke." Either weep or throw back your shoulders, she told herself. The latter. "Immediately."

The bark of a chuckle. "Is that right?"

In her peripheral vision, a flap lifted on a nearby tent, but she feared letting her eyes drift from the commanding officer. "I was sent to Pine Ridge by General Brooke, and I work with Agent Moyer."

"Lauder?" Dak stepped up alongside her, still pushing on his hat, and his brows scowling with skepticism. "What the hell?"

Her lips burbled with relief.

"General Brooke," Dak addressed the men, "will be looking everywhere for her."

"If I ain't seen it all now." The man was in charge, though Lauder didn't know his rank. He took his time looking her up and down, then to Dak, "You vouching for her?"

"Sir, she's telling the truth. She's on the reservation per General Brooke's order. She teaches at the school and works with Agent Moyer."

"He sent her, too?"

Dak tugged Lauder's elbow and started her away. "No, Sir. She can find trouble all on her own." By the time they'd chuckled, their gazes taking in the chuckles of each other, he'd pulled her ten feet away. "I best get her back to the general. He's likely spitting fire." Five more steps away and before more questions could be asked, he called back over his shoulder. "Don't concern yourselves, this matter is for General Brooke."

The officer sat slowly back onto his stool. He stretched gloved hands out over the fire. "I don't want to see either of you again."

Twenty-Six

LAUDER RODE IN front, wrapped in the bedroll Dak pulled from his tent. Sunk against his chest, her head on his shoulder, she struggled to stay upright. Her muscles were pudding.

"Moyer sent me," Dak was saying. "My orders were to stick around the camp. Keep my eyes open. Offer the agency's assistance."

Fighting to stay awake, Lauder tried to make sense of the situation. She felt sure, given the size and capability of the army, no officer on the site needed or cared about Agent Moyer's support. Agent Moyer had sent Dak as a spy, giving Sgt. Atlock some rest. Dak was to report back immediately if the army started the prisoners toward the agency. The army had tolerated Dak's presence because Agent Moyer was a governmental appointee. And just as quickly, they were happy to see him go. Taking the problem of the woman with him.

"Agent Moyer is that afraid," Lauder said.

Dak kept his horse at a steady, even trot. "Damn near outta his drawers. But I was happy to come. I know some of the people. I thought I could make sure translations were truthful; help keep tensions down."

Drifting into sleep, she wanted to apologize for pulling him away, and to tell him Blackbird and Mina were somewhere out there. She couldn't. If they were successful, then Dak never needed to know. It was better he didn't know. She also thought to tell him about the soldiers in the ravine and how they'd treated her. But that treatment shamed her. She would never admit it.

She stirred awake when Dak stopped his horse in front of her cabin. He dismounted, lifted her off, and helped her inside. "Give me a sec," he said and stepped back out. She used the moment to take off her coat, pull the knife free, and hide it in her top drawer.

He stepped back inside, carrying his rifle and dropping the bar across the door. His eyes landed on her torn dress, and he came to her, held her. "Are you hurt?"

She appreciated his first asking about her welfare, not instantly demanding to know who'd assaulted her. "I'm all right." She was weepy with anger, exhaustion, and the blessed relief of being safely back in her own place. "I'm alright," she said again. "It's just a dress."

At the foot of the bed she crawled into, he lifted the covers and began massaging her feet; strong hands rubbing and forcing blood to circulate.

Her eyelids were too heavy to lift. "Stop, please. That hurts."

"I'm trying to save your goddamn toes. What were you doing out there?" Working on her feet was the only thing keeping him from riding back out, demanding to know who'd torn her dress, and putting a bullet between the asshole's eyes. It had to be one of the soldiers who'd found her and dragged her into the camp. Since reaching the creek, he'd been watching the soldiers celebrate, believing after weeks of hard camping in the cold, they were going home. Then the whiskey arrived, and men crowded around the barrel. For some it meant more partying; for others, the whiskey sailed them right through celebration into meanness. "What were you doing out there?" he asked again. "Suppose I hadn't been there?" His fingers worked. The next question came slower. "What happened to your dress?"

She couldn't answer his questions without betraying Mina and Blackbird. And if he knew, he might be obligated to report them. He might be court martialed if he didn't. Court martialed if he did. Lauder, she asked herself the same question, what were you doing out there?

As she sank into sleep, she wanted to insist he hadn't saved her. Her threatening the soldiers with her connection to General Brooke had gotten her to safety, and she would have been put in a tent with a stove. Dak had only brought her back. Nor was she to blame for the vulgarness in the men. But that last felt untrue. They'd attacked her, proved her vulnerability and her insignificance. Only their fear of a higher-ranking male stopped them, not her worth.

She dozed, woke fitfully a few hours later with her feet itching. Dak slept slumped in the chair by her desk. He'd left a single lantern burning, but he'd turned it down to little more than a glow, leaving the room in shadow. "Dak?"

He stirred, his eyes opening, and his neck rolling out a kink.

"What will people think? Your horse in front of my place?"

He stared at her, his grief over her attack manifesting as anger. "There were fifty ways you could have gotten yourself killed."

She rolled onto her side, turning away, and facing the wall. He'd never wanted her on the reservation.

"What do I need to know?" he asked. "For the fifth time, what were you doing?"

"You don't want to know." She rolled back to face him, scrubbed tears, sniffled. "Sleep here with me." Make the whole night go away.

He didn't move.

With the stove and her blankets, she was warm, but she trembled. Why had she gotten herself stranded with four drunk males? She felt erased, had been erased. She sobbed. "Make love to me."

"You don't know what you're asking."

"Always that, 'I don't know you,' or now 'I don't know what I'm asking.'" She balled fistfuls of sheeting under her chin. "I hate it." She was beggarly, raw, and indecent. She was as crude as Sgt. Atlock, yet, she couldn't stop herself. "Make love to me."

He stood, came to the edge of the bed, his weight making the springs squeak. A boot clunked on the floor, then a second later the other. He stretched out beside her but remained on top of the blankets and put his arms around her. "Not tonight. Not like this. Not with our minds a hundred miles away."

A few days earlier, he'd kissed her, confided in her about his grandmother. That was back when she had been Lauder Ellison. She closed her eyes, dizzy with fatigue and shame, her mind drifting into sleep.

"Put me in that wall with the ghosts," she mumbled. The statement so foreign it might have come from Babette. Or had.

When she woke again, her window was still dark, but she knew dawn was nearing. Dak still lay on the bed, his arm still around her, and she felt certain he'd never closed his eyes, only stared down the night.

"Two girls," he whispered. "No more than ten. Twins. Scared and fighting for themselves."

Lauder's heart quickened. She didn't want to hear another sad story, could not carry another of the world's weights.

"Years ago," Dak said, "when Grandpa Mathis lived, Grandma would have befriended the girls, admired their spunk and vinegar." He stopped, cleared his throat. "You need to know she didn't mess up; I did."

Lauder dared not speak.

"They were from Dolly's class. She had them kicking and screaming."

"Had they refused to kneel on her broom? Or maybe refused to cry when she struck them?"

"Dolly went to Maxwelt for help, but his rough handling only frightened and angered them more."

"Maxwelt? He was mentioned on Christmas."

"He's one of the teachers who left. He and his wife. Dolly and he were likely sharing sheets. She isn't so particular that she cares about someone else's marriage. Grandma heard the commotion, but I couldn't say whose idea it was to get the girls out of sight. The troop of them burst into Moyer's office, Maxwelt's big fists locked around the girls' skinny arms. Them still kicking and screaming."

"Your poor grandmother."

"Two school inspectors had spent the night in the hotel and were expected any moment at the school. Grandma wanted the key to here."

Lauder sighed.

"She'd never asked before; the thought never crossed her mind. Maybe it was Maxwelt's idea. Doesn't matter whose. Moyer was off, and my giving out the key was against a heap of rules. At the time though, it seemed the best answer. I wanted the girls away from Maxwelt and his manhandling them. They needed saving but telling them to go home didn't mean they would. Suppose they ran to the inspectors screaming about abuse? They had the grit for it. I wanted Grandma to calm down, and of course, I didn't want anything negative written about the school."

Sensing where the story was going, Lauder stiffened.

"The best thing at the time," he repeated, "seemed to be just separate everyone. I gave Grandma the key, knowing the men wouldn't stay long. Then they were off to Red Cloud's for pictures and fry bread like it was some kind of French delicacy. I figured once she let the girls out and brought the key back, I'd return it to Moyer's desk without him even knowing. I told myself if Moyer were there, he'd give Grandma the key himself. Him being a new agent, he wouldn't let the girls' behavior reflect on him."

Dak took a deep breath. "The day turned plum crazy. Another wagonload of reporters arrived, flies swarming, wanting scoop on the dancing and trying their best to create a havoc they could write about. Temperatures were already freezing, but they plummeted more, Moyer returned and sent me ahead to Red Cloud's. Given the cold, the inspectors would have to meet the chief inside, and I was to make sure his place was warm with no one drunk or naked. I was to see everything went off without a hitch and get the men headed back to the train on time." Dak stopped. Rested. "If I thought of the girls, I must have let myself believe Grandma or Maxwelt had sent them home. Damn, it's all excuses. It was dark when I got home. Grandma had been brought back, and by the time I finished my chores, it had to be near midnight. Grandma asleep, I ate a few bites still on my feet and dropped into bed.

"Near morning, Moyer's banging on our door. A Lakota couple stood behind him, and he demanded to know any information she had about the missing girls. The parents had been searching for hours, had drawn up a search party to help walk ditches, and check homes across the area. They feared the worst, that white men had nabbed them for sport. Moyer quaking in his boots, thinking about angry Lakota, him at the top of the white food chain."

"My god," Lauder said. She didn't need to hear more. She knew where the girls had died: Their spirits still rustled there.

Dak's chest rose and fell. "The agony on the parents' faces. That pain." He swallowed. "Moyer, scared shitless of the couple and not knowing how many others were combing the agency, wanted Grandma to promise the girls had left school on time. Grandma swore she knew nothing about them; she was telling the truth. I stood right there, knowing if my fears were true, it would push her over the edge. I couldn't slam that anvil on her. I prayed she, Dolly or Maxwelt, maybe Moyer himself wanting another cigar, had come in here and let the girls out. Or the girls themselves had broken the window or door and escaped.

"Moyer didn't know the family, and he turned on the couple. Threatened them with jail if they didn't go home. Said he couldn't be responsible for every girl who got it in her head to run off. He said when the girls did come dragging in, he had a mind to lock the whole family up for a few days. 'Teach them a lesson.'

"I counted the hours since I'd handed over the key. Sixteen, Seventeen. Two skinny girls without heat, half-starved, no meatier than the dresses they wore, the temperature below zero. If they were still in the shed, they were likely dead. Moyer left, I stood a minute with Grandma. Fully awake now, her head clearing, her face began to pale. White as death, she stumbled to her coat. She turned to me, her hand shaking so hard the key she held hit the floor. She screamed, then went down cold.

"I got her to bed, saddled a horse and rode in. I planned on taking the blame; I'd handed over the key. I prayed Grandma's mind wouldn't let her remember a thing. I'd swing if necessary, keep it all from her. Though whites don't hang for killing reds. They get medals. When I reached here, the sun had risen. Moyer, Atlock, and a dozen police were gawking at the busted-out window. Moyer foamed at the mouth, rabid about how much goods had been stolen. Not a word about the girls. They were trivial when it came to the theft of what he considered his property. There was no mention of bodies, which meant none had been found. At first, it seemed like a miracle."

Lauder pressed her lips; there was nothing to say.

"Moyer," Dak went on, "ordered Atlock and every man there to hunt down the thieves. He wanted names and swore he'd have them 'strung up.'"

Lauder pressed her lips harder.

"Admitting the girls had been locked in the shed," Dak continued, "would have been giving Moyer the names he wanted. It would have put a target on the parents' backs, marked them as thieves though there wasn't a speck of evidence. I'd have slung a death sentence on them. They would have been found and hanged. If they'd gotten away, there'd be mercenaries today still hunting them."

"No forgiveness even if their daughters were dead?"

"Taking government property is a crime. The deaths of two skinny red girls wouldn't even be factored in."

Lauder wanted to weep for the world's darkness. For herself, for Mrs. Streamist, for Dak, and for two little girls who'd died just feet from where she lay.

"If the parents had lost their daughters," Dak continued, "though I was still praying the girls were alive, but if they weren't. If the parents had taken the bodies, they deserved to bury their daughters in peace, to be free, not to spend the rest of their lives running." He stopped again, took a breath. "Maybe they didn't take a goddamn cup of sugar. It could have been anyone. Whites are mad that the government gives Lakota even the pittance of the crap it does. Anyone could have thought they had as much right to what was here as did a Sioux."

Lauder watched the back wall, listened. It was quiet.

"It doesn't matter who broke in," Dak said, "blaming reds would be quick and clean. I didn't dare mention the girls. Grandma and I would never have been charged with a crime. Locking up red children is a legitimate discipline. Moyer would likely have congratulated me for two less Lakota."

"A horrible accident," she said, "if it happened." What was she saying? She knew it had happened. "Why didn't they scream and pound the door?"

"I've asked myself a thousand questions. Had Maxwelt threatened them with their lives if they did? Had Maxwelt banged their heads together and left them unconscious? Had they screamed until they couldn't, but no one heard, or heard and didn't think it was their business?"

"You aren't responsible. This isn't like the fatal beating of your friend."

Dak let out a tight breath. "Murder by neglect is still murder."

"You had too much on your mind."

"You can have a hundred things weighing on you, but you've got to have the sense to line them up, keep the most important ones up front."

This was the secret she sensed in him from the first day. And why he shied from a commitment to her. "You can't spend a lifetime trying to pay off what happened."

"Two died. It would take two lifetimes."

"This is what Dolly referred to on Christmas. Is she threatening you?"

"She's never asked what became of the girls. I hoped she believed the family up and hauled somewhere else, or the girls were sent to a boarding school. Now, I'm not sure."

"I wish you could get rid of her."

Dak lay unnaturally still. "If she's fired, I don't know — she's dangerous. Suppose she goes to Moyer with her suspicions."

"That's a kind of black mail."

"If she gives names, the army will flood the reservation hunting the couple down."

The wall was still quiet, and Lauder tried to send love across the room to spirits she imagined sitting there. Two small girls, black hair flowing over their thin shoulders and down ghostly gowns, their faces wet with tears, shivering with cold, loss, and disbelief. "Who do you suppose found the bodies?"

He shrugged. "The parents? Searchers holding a torch to every window in the agency? Maybe the ghosts made it home, told where their bodies could be found."

"It was an accident."

"Grandma's forgetting them was medical, an accident. I handed the keys over, abandoned the girls."

"Maybe Maxwelt killed them."

"Put them in here, kicked them in the head before leaving? If I believed him that much of an asshole, then I'm guilty still for leaving them with him. The man who ignores a fellow dying in the road is as responsible for the death as the one who pulled the trigger."

She thought of how she could ignore John and shuddered.

"For a few weeks, I walked up and down the pasture. Just me and the hills. Out of sight of anyone, shouting to any Sioux. 'I'm here. Come get me like you did Streamist.'"

"For weeks? While I've known you?" She fumbled with wanting to say something helpful. "You haven't had time to get over any of this. You've been hurrying to chores and hurrying to get yourself slaughtered."

"A couple of nights ago, I realized what a goddamn coward I am. Suicide by Lakota. A chicken shit, easy way out. They aren't interested in helping me, and I haven't earned the right to die. Grandma doesn't deserve my deserting her. I need to pick up my shame like a goddamn man and carry it. Focus on saving the school. I don't know any other way of pulling my boots on in the morning."

"Are you afraid one day the parents will come?"

"They don't know one person to blame. They blame the whole white race, and another dead white won't help their loss."

"So then," Lauder needed to understand, "Maxwelt fled even though no bodies were found?"

"I rode out to his place. I wanted him gone. If he stayed around, he'd squeal the girls' names the first hour, knowing it wouldn't mean any trouble for him. I told him the girls were dead, that Lakota had seen him lock them up, and a war party was on its way. The only chance he had was to run to the largest city he could and disappear."

Lauder listened to how Maxwelt loaded his wagon and his wife and headed out that very morning. When Agent Moyer asked if Dak knew anything about their leaving, he speculated on the growing fear around the Ghost Dancing.

Twenty-Seven

LAUDER AND DAK lay together another hour. With the windows brighter and the first of a few horses clopping down Pine Ridge Road, Dak rose. He stood at the bedside, tall, narrow-hipped, and sleepy. "I'm riding back out to Wounded Knee Creek. You stay here. In bed."

She grabbed his hand. "I don't want to be alone. Stay with me." She flung back her blankets. "On this side of the sheets."

His eyes softened. "I'm a goddamn fool for not snatching that offer. But things aren't that simple."

"Why can't they be?"

"Lauder, making love to you right now," the thought warmed his groin, "I can't. I'm worried about what's going on out there. I got to get back. Greta, Mina, someone can take your class. I mean it. Stay here."

This second refusal squeezed her throat. If he left, he left her with the ghosts, the memory of the men mauling her, the shame of having asked to be made love to, and the shame of his refusal. "What about what I need?"

He kissed her. "I have to go. I owe plenty, and my guts are telling me I need to be there. No telling what's happening."

She drew her knees up, curled into a ball, and pulled the blankets over her head. "Go. I don't need you here."

His boots sounded on the floor as he crossed to the door. He removed the bar, leaned it in the corner, then faced the bed again. "How'd you get out there?"

That again. She couldn't bring the blankets down and look at him. "How do you think? I rode my unicorn."

He opened the door.

"Dak," she flung the blankets off her face, nearly screamed. "I went with Blackbird and Mina. If they're caught, you need to save them."

He closed the door again, his eyes narrow. "What did the three of you think you were doing?"

"They had to go."

"And for no more reason than that, you had to follow?" He lifted the hat he'd just put on his head, ran his fingers through his hair, and set it back on.

"I know what you're thinking," Lauder said, "but I can't go back to Omaha. I belong here."

"Stay in bed. Greta will handle the school."

Lauder dozed another hour and woke feeling trampled by dreams of abuse and rejection. She turned her thoughts to Blackbird and Mina. Had the pair managed to get a single person away? Had they saved themselves or been forced to hide amongst Big Foot's people? In which case, they'd be marched onto cattle cars with the others. Agent Moyer could likely save them, but given the chance, would he? And if they didn't need saving, she couldn't risk reporting them. She wouldn't do anything that risked having Mina disciplined. Or that exposed herself to expulsion. She had told Dak, and he'd be more effective in saving them than a trembling-in-his-boots agent.

She wanted to do just as he'd said: Stay in bed. But she needed answers, not sleep. And she needed the children. They needed her, too. She would muster the courage to be present for them.

At the wall, standing on trembling legs, she dropped her forehead onto the surface and stretched out her arms. With her hands splayed, she pressed her fingertips into the seams between boards. "I'm sorry. And you know how sorry Dak is." She wanted to tell them to rest in peace, but that seemed empty. Who was she to give encouragement?

She took a step back. Dak wanted her to remain in bed, but what had Blackbird said to Plants Corn? Something about what fell at her door mattered more than his wishes? She couldn't remember exactly, and it didn't matter; she was Lauder Ellison, and this fell to her. At the dresser's mirror, she saw tangled and hanging hair, red-rimmed eyes, a ripped dress front. Foolishly, she had thought herself above the treatment the soldiers demonstrated, believing such treatment didn't happen to women in her rarified realm. Shame at having thought so clutched her throat, sank her spirits. One woman's experience could as easily be every woman's experience.

After school she would scrub every inch of her skin until she no longer felt like a bug under a dirty heel. At the moment, she didn't have the time for weakness and self-pity. The children were returning from the holiday break. Little Rose, Badger, Much Wind, She-Stands-Brave, and the others.

She rolled her dress and shoved it under her bed with the abandoned craniometer. She wasn't sorry for going with Blackbird and Mina, foolish as that had been, but she ought to have used her knife with the soldiers, drawn at least a little blood.

She stepped outside. Foreboding hung in the air as it had on the day of Sitting Bull's death. Heavy clouds in the west sagged and dragged along the horizon. The armillary in Father's library proved the planets were charted, but life on earth orbited, spiraled, and exploded beyond a pattern she was capable of understanding.

She rushed up the hill, chased by the clamor of noise rising from the nearest military field, then forced herself to slow; she wouldn't act on her fears even if they coursed through her. She would hold as fast as a five-year-old she thought of as She-Stands-Brave.

Finding Greta had unlocked the school door, Lauder's knees nearly gave out in gratitude. Sounds of Greta preparing her room were there, but Mina wasn't in her classroom. "Don't panic," Lauder whispered. Mina might have returned home so late she was still asleep. Or she might at that moment be running down Pine Ridge Road.

Lauder's own classroom felt colder than the air outside. A locked-in cold that over the Christmas break had suffused into the walls and flooring. She knelt at her stove, struck a match to kindling.

"A woman on her knees," Dolly stood at the door, nearly sneered. "Where's your lover boy?"

Lauder sighed. She lacked the will for a retort.

"Still in your bed?"

"Which means you saw his horse at my door when Sgt. Atlock sent you away from his. I'm sorry your visits with the man are so short." She gave a cloying smile. "Men like him are always in demand."

With Dolly having swished away, Lauder finished at the stove and wiped down the slate in front of the room, though she had done so before the Christmas break. She straightened chairs that were already in lines as straight as flagpoles. There was the strain of last night with the vulgar soldiers, a residue left on her person she could not lift, but heaviest was the ghosts of two girls and fear for Mina and Blackbird. Were they at that moment being marched to Rushville where cattle cars waited? Dak would try to save them, but if they'd been arrested, he likely couldn't free them. She wished she could speak to Nurse and ask Nurse what gave her the courage to trust and maintain an internal fortress against whatever came her way?

Students began arriving, and Lauder followed the other teachers out to greet them. She-Stands-Brave, George, Little Rose, and many of the tender faces she loved were there, but again the happy faces of Badger and Much Wind were absent. She turned to the clouds in the west, crouching even closer, bunching like great beasts thundering toward them. The approaching blizzard, she promised herself, was the cause of the boys' absence. Their parents were taking precautions.

Mina still hadn't arrived, and the group of students standing in her area was smaller than usual. "I'll take them," she said to Greta. "They know me."

Greta rang the bell. Her thick arm rising and falling, the gong ringing out, and Lauder felt sorrow. Mrs. Streamist would not be returning, and what that meant for the school was yet to be decided.

In the classroom, with both classes combined, she counted only thirteen. She forced a smile, promised herself the absences were due to the storm, not numbers of children getting so sick with hunger and disease over the week off they were unable to return.

"Let's begin today with a song. Who would like to sing?"

"In Lakota?" Richard asked.

Her little orator. Always the first volunteer to read or recite in front of the class. "Yes. In your tongue." They needed a song all could join. That, Lauder told herself, or pulling up the old plank flooring and coaxing them into crawling deep underground with her.

A sound thundered. The noise startling. Then a continuous, great bellowing and vibration rumbling through the air. Loose windows rattled as percussions roared and lumbered through the room. Chalk lying in a tiny trough at the board, the wooden flag on the wall, and struck faces trembled. She knew the sound, had heard it flying, and witnessed men on a train firing non-stop into a buffalo herd. Heard it, too, standing over Civil War battlefield maps and flying to the slaughtering fields. But this blasting wasn't happening somewhere in the past. This firing of rifles and Hotchkiss guns was happening at that moment.

Children screamed, some froze, others hit the floor. Under their desk, Little Rose pressed her face into George's chest. A child from Mina's class reached for She-Stands-Brave, the pair clung, burying their faces in each other's neck.

"Everyone down," Lauder shrieked, her arms in the air, her order unnecessary. These children, primed by lives of suffering, were vigilant to danger. The thundering continued, sounded as if a mountainside of rocks and trees raced toward them.

She ran to the window, kept a foot back from glass that might explode with the percussion. She couldn't judge the distance to the uproar. A mile, half, only a quarter? Last night, they'd ridden north to reach Plants Corn's cabin. Later, travelling to Wounded Knee Creek, they'd gone back south and east. Returning from there in Dak's arms, her eyelids too heavy to open, and her body collapsed against him, she had had no sense of direction or distance. She ought to have paid more attention; she ought to know if the children were in danger of being struck.

Two boys from Mina's class came running to the window, then suddenly all the children were there, their tiny bodies shaking and sobbing in front of the trembling glass. First one, then a second boy from Mina's class broke from the group and bolted from the room.

"Stop," Lauder cried. She ran into the hall after them, but they hit the front door, pushed it wide, and jumped off the stoop. Before the door banged closed behind them, they raced across the yard. She yelled again. With her longer legs, she could chase them down, but the children behind her were crying, and if she left, going and wrestling back two, several were likely to run off and into danger. "Go straight home," she shouted. A gulp of air. "Straight home!"

She hurried back, slammed her classroom door, and fell against it. "Come away from the windows." The boom of guns and cannons drowned out her voice. "Everyone, on the floor!" They turned to her, crushed faces, eyes full of tears and terror. She slid down the door, feeling as though her body pooled there, and reached out. "Get down. Everyone, come. Quick."

Children dropped to all fours, crawled to her, huddled around her like a bevy of quaking doves. She shamed herself, this inability to mask her fear. She was shamed too, by the fear she saw in the children. They'd lost family, seen parents and elders weeping. For them, tragedy lived close, weighed their steps, stunned their sleep.

Rifles continued firing, cannons continued exploding, and children continued screaming and slapping their hands over their ears. Lauder cursed herself again for not having paid more attention to the topography of the surrounding lands. This was coming from Wounded Knee Creek, and she ought to know if there were sufficient hills to absorb the bullets, and if not, how far bullets flew through the winter air? Would the shooting stay far from these innocents? Didn't extermination of a race mean everyone?

"It's all right," Lauder tried even as her heart fought in her chest, and she knew they couldn't hear her over the noise. Some still screamed at each boom, some sobbed, and still others quaked so much they were incapable of making sound. That silence too, wounded the air. She pulled them closer, cupped cheeks, lifted chins, squeezed shoulders, her shaking hands — the pittance of them — was all she could offer.

Little Rose crawled through others, pulling George along with one hand. She squirmed into Lauder's lap and curled into a tight ball, never letting go of her brother. As frightened as the boy was himself, he kept his hand in his sister's. They'd just lost their mother, and Lauder wondered how many other children had recently lost a loved one. How many were losing loved ones that minute?

She leaned down over Little Rose, one arm around her, and the other around She-Stands-Brave, who on the first day had known that when big trouble came, it came from white people. The panic in every child bore into Lauder, cried for her to make it all stop.

I can't. Children kept crowding against her, down the length of her, her shoulders, her lap, her legs. She smelled clothes scrubbed with soap made of lye and grease, small bodies, hunger on young breaths. She smelled sulfur, gun powder, and fear.

"Everyone is all right. We're safe." How many times had she shouted it, though they couldn't hear? And were they safe? Her heart banged up through her temples. Maybe they ought to be in the farthest corner of the room in case someone fired through the door. But moving, if soldiers came, would only be delaying the inevitable for a few seconds.

The ruckus, the sounds of what must be killing, went on and on. Children screamed and cried out, and Lauder shouted over the racket, trying to calm them.

The thunder finally rumbled away, echoed off. The windows settling in their casements. An eerie quiet. Had the murdering lasted twenty or thirty minutes? Had it lasted as many hours? "It's over." She tried to offer smiles around. "It's over."

Traumatized faces wet with tears watched, unbelieving.

What had happened, Lauder knew, would never be over for them.

A rifle shot cut the silence. A wasp sting. Then others, the buzz and zip. Lauder struggled not to cry out. The sporadic and sinister lone shots carried their own macabre truth. They sliced and ripped. Quick and hot, followed by a breath of silence, then another icy tut-tut. The moments between them saying, studied shots, aimed, picking out targets as though firing at a warren of fleeing rabbits. What other possible explanation but soldiers with steaming rifles and carbines walking amongst the fallen, shooting anyone who still moaned, twitched, or begged for mercy? The native men would be dead. They'd have rushed to the front, fought to save their fleeing wives, mothers, and children. They'd have been the first to die. This late shooting was picking off those they'd hoped to save, the weak, the helpless.

Fear and the sounds of dying roared through Lauder, lifted and carried her. She was there. Women ran, the thunder of charging horses bearing down on them, beasts in saddles kicked horses' flanks, fired guns. Tongue-thickening, breath-sucking fear bellowed through the women and the bodies of children too big to carry, shorter legged, whose hands mothers tugged and begged to "Run! Run!" Old women fell, crying out for their daughters to leave them. "Run! Run!" Daughters refused, dropped to their knees, huddled around their aging mothers, taking the first bullets.

The classroom lay in shocked silence.

"Good morning," Richard screamed suddenly. "Good morning," he tugged on Lauder's arm.

The others remained huddled around Lauder. She had clenched every muscle and bone until now her body was limp, collapsed onto itself, her bones in layers. They waited through long minutes of quiet, Lauder not certain what to do. Children sniffled, twitched. A foot moved, knees jerked, hands lowered from ears, small shoulders fixed in terror began to loosen into shaking. The motion frightened Lauder. She reached, grabbed a foot, a sleeve, pulled it back into the huddle. "Stay here. We'll wait until someone comes for us." She had no idea who would bring the all-clear. Was anyone still alive out there? She prayed for Dak. "He'll come," she said. Afraid again that she lied.

What felt like another hour passed. Little Rose urinated in Lauder's lap. Feeling the warmth run over her hip, seeing it spread onto the floor, a silver thread snaking to an inch of She-Stands-Brave, Lauder wiped it with her hand, swiped it back into her own skirt.

Shouting rose in the school yard. Indian voices, male and female, wailed and cried out. Lauder couldn't see this new commotion from the floor, and it held such anger she wouldn't risk going to the window. The children would follow her there again, standing completely exposed.

"What do they want?" She looked over the group, twisted mouths, tear-filled eyes.

"They want us to come out," Richard said.

"Lauder!" Dolly banged on the door. "The savages are going to burn down the school. They'll kill us. Don't let the children outside."

Many had just been killed, many more were dying from their

wounds. Nothing else could result from that much shooting. If only one in ten bullets had hit its mark, which was fantasy, then still, hundreds lay dead. Who could blame those in the school yard for wanting to incinerate every implement of colonization and the genocide it brought?

But keep the children as hostages? To save themselves?

Hearing the whooping and shouting, children who'd managed to calm even a bit were afraid again. Little Rose trembled so hard Lauder feared the child would seizure. George snuggled closer to his sister, pressed his head against her back, whispered. She-Stands-Brave sat upright, her hip against Lauder, her body rigid. A young boy hugging Lauder's knees shook so hard his shoes hummed against the floor.

Lauder wiped wet cheeks, hugged small bodies, tried to smile. "Richard, sing."

"They won't," Richard said of the shouting. "They won't hurt us." He began to sing in a frightened and reedy whisper, then his voice gathered will and rose.

Others picked up the song. Lauder wished she knew the words and could take the sounds into her mouth, hold them like live coals, and use them to cast safety over the school.

The shouting outside continued, but Richard's singing held their little knot tight. When the commotion finally drifted off, Lauder's racing heart banged on. What had drawn the people away? She tried to think rationally, to thought-by-thought bead a string of logic. The parents must have decided their children were safe in the school. A confidence that let them address a second issue. The battlefield? Rescuing wounded?

Racing wagons came down Pine Ridge Road. From her place on the floor, Lauder knew nothing but the pounding horses and the groan of iron wheels rolling over the frozen ground. Then shouts filling the agency courtyard.

"Lauder," Dak banged on the door. "You all right?"

"Yes! We're all alive."

"Hang on! I've gotta check the other rooms."

Lauder held her shaking bottom lip between her teeth. Felt how it wasn't just her lips, but her cheeks trembled as well. She wanted to cry in relief, but wouldn't. Not in front of the children who might misinterpret her tears for fright. She slid Little Rose's tiny feet off her lap and onto the floor. She tried to straighten the panic out of the knees of She-Stands-Brave. "It's all over. It's all over," she said again to each pair of frightened eyes. "Mr. Dak is here."

Children wiped their faces, thin hands pushed snot and tears across their cheeks. Others went on weeping. Little Rose tipped from Lauder's lap and fell into her brother's arms. Helpless to do more than drop towards him, knowing he'd catch her.

"Lauder?" Dak knocked again.

She hurried to get everyone on their feet, and as she opened the door, every child rushed on her skirts into the hall and around Dak.

Snow melted on his hat and the shoulders of his coat. His cheeks and nose, wet and flushed, said the storm had arrived and he'd ridden hard, the wind and snow in his face. His eyes spoke of sorrow and disbelief. She stepped into his arms, felt how they trembled across her back, and his heartbeat against her ear. She had a thousand questions, but none to ask in front of the children.

"My god, you're safe." Dak released a fisted breath. His hands slid up and down her back as if to assure himself she was whole. "Okay," he said, more to himself than Lauder. "You're all right. They're bringing in the wounded. I need to go and help."

Twenty-Eight

THE SCHOOL'S FRONT door opened and a woman, her eyes wild as Dak's, rushed through. Richard ran into his mother's arms. "I sang," he told her. "All the time I sang."

"He did," Lauder took a respectable, teacherly, step back from Dak. "His singing saved us."

"We need every available pair of hands," Dak said, his voice urgent. "They're bringing in wounded soldiers."

"Soldiers?" Lauder had imagined only Sioux died. "I can't leave the children, they're so frightened."

"You'll stay?" he asked Richard's mother.

She nodded.

"No," Lauder faltered. Richard still clung to his mother, and she bent over her son, relief at having him safely in her arms. "Take her," Lauder said. "I don't know anything about nursing and bandaging wounds." The children need me.

"I'll take scalps," Richard's mother said to Dak, the look in her eyes steamy with warning. "Best I stay, kill no one."

He gave Lauder an almost imperceptible shrug, and she understood. Richard's mother would not work to save any white man's life. Nor would soldiers trust an Indian anywhere near their wounded.

Lauder wanted to insist again she must stay, but Dak was heading for the door, expecting her to follow as soon as she could. The shooting had stopped, but suppose it started again? Suppose an angry mob returned? She looked at Richard's mother and over the children still huddled around her. Little Rose with her face pressed against her brother. "She's so small."

"Little Rose," Richard's mother said.

"You know her name." In a wordless gaze, Richard's mother said much: Little Rose was a child of her people, not a child of the white woman who believed herself a savior. Shame burned the back of Lauder's throat, and she did her best to smile and nod.

The children trailed behind Richard and his mother and back into the classroom. They sang a slow, sad-sounding song Lauder did not understand. She watched them go and fought back tears.

Snow hit her face, watered her eyes, stung her cheeks. The quickness and the strength of the storm's rise, building to a near white out, on this morning of all mornings, felt like a diabolical addition to the horror. Another wagon rolled down the agency road. How many was that now? The driver yelled at the horses, slapped reins over their backs. Men lay stretched out in the wagon bed, snow settling on their bloody uniforms. Coming abreast of Agent Moyer's office, she saw the line of wagons in front of the mess hall. She ran and tried to hold the door open for two soldiers carrying a stretcher with a wounded man. A soldier burst through from inside, pushed her back, and held the door himself. Not meeting her gaze, he barked. "Move away, ma'am. We're treating men."

When the door closed on her, she clamped her jaws, opened it again, and stepped inside. She meant to find Dak, but the scene stopped her. Mayhem. From everywhere the cry for medics. "Over here! Over here!" Able-bodied men scurried, carried cots, sopped wounds, pressed wads of compress. Wounded men moaned, cussed, or lay silent as death. They covered tables and stretched across the floor. Nowhere a Sioux. She wouldn't let herself think about what their absence meant.

A man carried two pails of water, bumped one against Lauder's hip, splashed cold down her leg. Dak worked over a table, cutting the coat sleeve off a man, the arm beneath hanging at an impossible angle. He wasn't a doctor, but he could help bandage until one arrived.

She started for him.

"My boot!" A soldier on the floor in front of her worked himself onto his elbows and bellowed at her. "Cut off my boot."

George Washington! One of the men who'd accosted her the night before. The one who'd slowly pulled a glove, finger by finger from his vile hand, knowing his anticipated vulgarity frightened her as much as the act would wound her. He didn't recognize her now, or thought what he'd done so insignificant, done to such a non-entity, it didn't warrant remembering.

"Goddamn, my boot!"

She found a cook's knife and hurried back. To avoid cutting his leg, she fitted the tip of the knife just inside the boot, the sharp edge of the blade pointed away from his flesh. She sawed upward while he moaned. Again, half an inch lower. With each inch opened, she could pull the leather wider and go deeper. He moaned and cussed at her with each sawing motion. She continued, pushing the tip through like an awl, a bit lower each time, slicing her way through leather tough as a saddle.

"Damn you!" he roared. "You chewin' it off?"

She stopped, her hands shaking.

"Cut it!" he bellowed.

Five inches into the boot, blood squirted up from the bottom. The combination of sweat and coagulating blood reeked, covered her hands, and made the knife hilt slick. She wiped the stink from her palms down her coat front and labored on. She prayed for Dak or a man with stronger hands and a sharper knife to rescue her, but every able-bodied man worked at other tasks, and every bloody body needing attention looked just as wounded or worse than this man.

George Washington's fists banged the floor. "You idiot!"

She held the knife an inch from his nose. "We meet again." Turning the blade, she wiped the flat side down his cheek, smearing it with blood. "May I suggest you shut your mouth."

His eyes widened.

Had she actually done that? Threatened a man with a knife? Where was the old Lauder Ellison? She went back to work. When the side of his boot lay nearly open, she gripped the muddy heel while he grabbed his leg at the knee and pulled. The foot peeled slowly from the leather with a sucking sound. At the sight, or maybe it was the pain, his eyes rolled, and his body flopped back in a dead faint.

Lauder gagged. Bones protruded through the blood-soaked wool sock. The foot crushed like a melon.

She rose from her knees, scrubbed her hands again on her coat, and looked over the wounded. Men, not boys rushing to join the army thinking it a grand adventure into manhood. These were men, muscled and bearded. They knew the horror of war, but they'd enlisted to kill Indians. Thinking they defended country and family, or believing dead Indians meant more spoils?

Dak, his shirt sleeves rolled up his thick forearms, worked farther across the room now, bandaging a man's head. She would reach him, tell him about the man who'd passed out, give off the man's care.

"Ma'am," a second soldier begged in a whisper. Blood pooled on the floor from his right cheek and shoulder. His hand was mangled, his eyes glassy. "I gotta piss."

She didn't have the strength to support so large a man out to the latrines, and he was far too wounded to move.

"A cup." He pressed together blue lips.

She wanted to insist he relieve himself in his pants. His uniform was already ruined, and he was dying. Surely, he knew that. But he wanted this, a last wish that when he was carried out by men in his company, it would not be with his pants urine-soaked. She wanted to hurry away, but she felt compassion: He begged her with his eyes. Tables had been swept clean with flailing arms, and Lauder retrieved a dented tin cup lying a few feet away.

He used his one working hand, managed to open the buttons on his trousers, and she held the cup. She had never seen a naked male, though everyone knew the two parts: scrotum and penis. And she knew sex required tab A be fitted into slot B, but still, the sight was shocking.

His urine stream rang into the shallow bottom of the tin, splashed back and out over her hand. He lost the strength to hold himself, and his hand fell away. A sob.

His sorrow struck Lauder, again. She held the cup with one hand

and used the other to both hold his member and cover the top of the cup. "There," she said. "Finish up."

His urine stream dripped, he sank back, his breathing labored, his uniform bloody but with little urine soaking the front. She set down the cup, tucked him inside his trousers, and hurried for Dak before another man could cry for her.

Shouted orders and moaning continued from every corner. "More beds! We need doctors!"

General Brooke entered, his hands clean, his uniform pressed. His face flushed with anger.

Lauder turned her back to him. Her hair had lost its pins, her clothes were covered in urine and blood, and he wasn't likely to recognize her, but she would do her best to keep hidden. The last thing she wanted was his attention.

He looked over the mess. "Men lost?" he demanded.

"Twenty-five confirmed casualties," a man called. "Near forty wounded, wagons still coming in."

General Brooke's face set. "Twenty-five," he bellowed the number. "Hostiles?"

A man waiting medical attention spoke from his place on the floor, hunched against a table leg. "We got 'em. We bloody well won the battle."

"Then," General Brooke shouted congratulatorily over the men, "we bloody well won the war." He turned and left.

The news made Lauder's heart sob and alternately shriek. She hurried on to Dak. "There are no wounded Sioux in here." His eyes were both empty and full of shock. "Is it possible?" she asked. "Everyone killed?"

He kept his voice low, his hands winding white bandaging, the front of his shirt soaked with blood. "A few are being brought in, but the snow's too bad to send out more wagons."

The sound of the cannons and rifles still echoed in her ears. "Survivors of Big Foot's band are being left to die in the cold?"

"Some are being taken to the church."

"That's not what I asked."

"There's nothing more to do."

"Wounded Sioux are being left to die in the blizzard? Agent Moyer needs to organize a search party. You need to do it!"

Dak turned from the man, pulled Lauder a few steps away. "Look out there." He pointed at a window and the falling snow thick as a white curtain. "Nobody can go searching in that. Wouldn't make it out there, wouldn't make it back."

"And Agent Moyer wouldn't send anyone if he could. He's happy to leave them to die." Dak didn't answer, and she closed her eyes to keep from screaming at him.

"If you'd rather go to the church, help there?" he said. "I'll come as soon as I can. Army surgeons will be there soon as they're done here."

"Hey!" The man they'd stepped away from looked at Lauder with hate-filled eyes. "Bring the bastards in here. I got something more to say to them."

She ignored him and looked over the hall. Nearly forty bloody men, some dying, needed treatment. "It'll be hours before army doctors are done here."

He plunged his bloody hands into a nearby pail of clear water. The water pinked.

Lauder did the same, then pulled open her coat and wiped her hands on the cleaner lining. She grabbed Dak's hands and dried them as well. She didn't want to leave him, but word had spread, and several helpers were entering the mess including women: Spinster Salem, officers' wives, merchants' wives. Were as many helpers rushing to the church?

"I'm going up there." She gathered her nerve. "Mina and her aunt? You didn't see them?"

"I saw them after the shooting," he said. "Plants Corn rode up before hell broke loose, and they were looking for him."

Lauder couldn't imagine how Mina suffered having witnessed the scene, but she was alive. "Thank God." She took a step back, glared at the man with his head wound. "I'm going to the church. Good people may need me."

"Wait," Dak grabbed her arm before she had stepped completely away. "What you'll see in the church isn't pretty."

"I'll be alright."

Twenty-Nine

L AUDER RUSHED FIRST to her cabin, grabbed up petticoats that could be ripped into bandages, her blankets, and burgundy coat that could serve as another blanket.

On any given day, the church, with its weathered whitewashing, looked ghostly. Now, as she ran through the blizzard, the otherworldly effect was heightened. She knew the church's pastor, half Native, was said to be an honorable man who loved his people, and that he gave his people hope and a thin ledge on which their old beliefs could merge with Christianity. Still, Lauder didn't understand why any Sioux entered the church voluntarily when its sole purpose was the destruction of a culture whites deemed inferior. Nay, evil. And how was that different from the school?

She halted just inside, the air so solid with the pall of death, she might have hit a wall. The shock made her keep her eyes lifted, giving herself a moment before entering. There was no vaulted ceiling, though a bare cross hung on the wall in front, a symbol that represented as much victorious pride as the flag.

An infant wailed.

Boughs of green firs hung in swags across the ceiling. The paper cones from her classroom looked to weep from them. Her eyes traveled down: wainscoting, thin-glassed windows that moaned in the wind. Or was the sound that of people suffering and dying? Pews were shoved right and left to the walls. The bodies of what looked like nearly fifty women and children lay strewn like stones in a riverbed. A thin layer of straw was scattered about the floor beneath them, but too slight to offer cushioning or warmth against the cold seeping up between the floorboards. A stove had been started, but with no heat in the building since yesterday's church service, some thirty-six hours earlier, the building was still so frigid Lauder could see her own heaving breath.

Hoping to see Blackbird and Mina working amongst the wounded, the scarf of gold stars tied securely at her friend's neck, Lauder searched. The pair wasn't there, but Dak had seen them alive; he wouldn't lie to her. She moved around bloody bodies with torn-open flesh, some with the stench of bowels ripped and spilling feces. Blankets wet from the storm and stained with crimson hid wounds she could only imagine. Children cried in pain without parents to comfort them. Somewhere, an infant still wailed.

What need of hell, Lauder's emotions raged, when there is war?

Two men in uniform, stood guarding the door, rifles at the ready. "Don't be scared ma'am," one said. "We've searched them. No weapons. One moves, we'll take her down."

She had no words. In disgust, she turned sharply away. The ghosts in the room were those two standing men.

The woman closest to Lauder clawed the floor in pain. Her broken nails bleeding onto the straw. A bit farther on, a child lay dead in a woman's one whole arm. The woman, a string of red rolling from beneath her blanket, tried to sing. Six feet away, another child, the face tender as any of the sweet children in her classroom, was also dead. The child's body had been lain straight, her arms and legs positioned as if she only slept. The side of her head bashed in.

"Help them," a woman, painfully breathless, cried.

Lauder bent, took up her hand. "Rest. We will help them." The woman's eyes closed as she lost consciousness. Lauder wondered if her request in English meant she had spent years in a Christian school where she was taught reds were barbarians, whites civilized?

Feeling worthless, Lauder straightened. How to help? She had no knowledge of nursing. She struggled just to stay upright, and despite

Dak's assurances, her eyes still searched the prone victims, praying not to see Blackbird or Mina. Given they weren't in the church, they could only be back home. Probably nursing wounded. And Plants Corn? He wouldn't let the blizzard stop him. He'd be at the site helping victims into his wagon.

Unlike the hastily pulled together forces to save the soldiers' lives, only three people bent over victims. Her heart screamed with relief, seeing one of them was Greta. She rushed over. "Tell me what to do."

The church door flung open, and Dr. Eastman, the reservation's new physician, hurried through.

"Go with him," Greta said.

Lauder feared there was little he could do, and yet his being there gave hope and placed someone in charge. He needed bandages, and Lauder ripped and tore long, white strips, and followed his instructions as he went from patient to patient, assessing. He bent over the wounded, lifted blankets, evaluated, and decided within seconds which he would return to, and which were without hope.

Lauder had no notion of the passing hours and little of the baby still crying, the sound scratching through the cacophony of suffering. Until they reached a young woman lying so still she might already be dead but for a flutter of lashes. Propped against her was a cradleboard and inside the wailing baby Lauder had been hearing since first entering the church. Dr. Eastman spent a moment assessing the gash in her side, sighed, and went on.

The woman's eyes fluttered again.

When Eastman lifted the woman's blanket, Lauder had seen the dampness spreading across the front of her calico dress, a growing wet, her breasts lactating in response to her infant's cries.

She couldn't leave the mother who looked younger than herself and who must also be hearing her baby's cries. She sat behind her, reached under the mother's arms, and drew her close. With the woman propped between Lauder's legs, her head at Lauder's cheek, she opened the mother's wet dress front and exposed a breast. She drew the infant from his cradleboard and held him along the length of her arm, his tiny head no larger than her palm. She cupped the breast, nearly weightless, and put the baby to the nipple. The infant latched. Suckled. Milk filled the corners of the tiny mouth.

The body in her arms trembled, and Lauder imagined the flood of emotions the woman must be feeling: grief, loss, fear. Maybe thanksgiving too, that her child was no longer crying.

"You're going to be all right," Lauder lied. "Dr. Eastman is coming back to you. You aren't hurt so bad; others need him worse. He'll be back. Soon. He'll be back soon." When she felt the death, a heaviness sinking in her arms, she struggled not to cry out. She wiped her face on her shoulder, keeping the baby to the breast, letting the baby suckle the mother he'd never know.

Over the next hours, Lauder completed one assigned task and then another, not thinking, scarcely aware of what her hands did. Staggering with fatigue, she felt the grab of strong hands steadying her. Sgt. Atlock. His was a familiar face, a man alive and whole. He often angered her, yet his being there at that moment, tall and sure, holding her amid the carnage, there when Dak was not, made her want to fall against him. "It's terrible," she said.

He looked over the room, scowled at the work being done, and Dr. Eastman. Wordless, he lifted a whiskey bottle to his lips.

"Have you seen Mina?" she asked.

"Hostiles running scared. You won't see her again." He looked over the victims on the floor. "Christ, the place stinks."

She drew back. "Then leave."

"Wouldn't choose to set a foot in here. Moyer wants you."

"So, I can document how none of this is his fault? Tell him I'm helping Dr. Eastman."

"That foul witch doctor." Looking in the doctor's direction, Sgt. Atlock's face warped in revulsion. "I'd rather die than have his red hands touch me." He took another swig. "Moyer's waiting."

"Tell him I'm busy."

Sgt. Atlock studied her. "I'll tell him." He motioned with his bottle. "That squaw down there, on the end. It's Big Foot's wife."

"What's her name? Is her husband here?"

"Took a bucketful of lead."

Minute by long minute Lauder felt she moved deeper into dream. "Does she know?"

"She'll be joining him soon enough." He started for the door, tipping his bottle as he went. "White Hawk."

"People are in pain," Lauder said. "Leave us the whiskey."

Wind squealed through a loose window, the sound an unearthly shriek.

"You're a woman," Sgt. Atlock squinted. "You help 'em."

Susan LaFleche, the reporter Agent Moyer had grumbled against, came sometime in the night. Lauder studied the famous woman who had been several miles away at the time of the massacre. Her account, therefore, would only be secondhand.

Later, a burly man rushed in, threw down his coat and rolled up his sleeves with such speed and surety, Lauder believed him also a doctor, arrived from a nearby town.

In the early hours of the next morning, the church finally quieted. Both doctors operated, but they were assisted by people who knew how to help. Some victims lay quietly, thankful their wounds were tended, others whispered prayers waiting for their deaths, and still others had already died. She approached the woman Sgt. Atlock had identified as Big Foot's wife, the straw beneath her too thin to give cushion or warmth and Lauder wondered if it had been strewn to help patients or to help protect the floor. Soiled straw could be swept out and burned.

White Hawk's eyes were closed. Whether unconscious or simply unable to look out on what the world had become, Lauder didn't know. A few feet from her, a man with a weathered face much like Plants Corn's, sang-moaned, the sounds striking on hard letters and rounding on strings of vowels. His voice riding the waves of his waning strength. The chilling sound scored up Lauder's spine. Was there anything braver than singing one's death song?

Lauder dropped onto the floor, drew her knees up, and rocked beside White Hawk. She had no comfort to offer, wouldn't offend with worthless apologies, less than puffs of air against this loss, but she would sit, not turning away from the suffering. She would witness. Sgt. Atlock was wrong; White Hawk did know her husband was dead. She knew all the family members who had died that morning.

The bitter irony of White Hawk lying under symbols of Christian love and peace made Lauder ache for distraction, any distraction she could offer the woman. "Let me tell you about the paper cones," she leaned closer to White Hawk. "The children in my classroom made them. There is a little girl...." Her eyes tracked along the first fir swag hanging overhead, looking for Little Rose's cone. Then trailed along the second swag. Given its larger size, Little Rose's drawing ought to be easiest to find. There was Richard's and George's, She-Stands-Brave's, each cone bringing a child to mind and the fear that child suffered during the shooting. How eternally damning to them. Even at a remove, every child on the reservation was a victim.

Not finding Little Rose's horse, Lauder started the search again, her gaze combing the first swag then the second. A cone she had not noticed, given it was only a quarter the size of the others, struck her. Little Rose's! A scrap of a star, the horse nearly torn entirely away, the drawing mangled.

She slapped hands over her mouth to smother her sob. The disrespect of a child for what? For what hellish gain? If Mrs. Streamist was the cause, even with half a mind, it made no difference. Here was one more desecration. One more! She had to move before she struck something. A few feet away the blue feet of a small child stuck out the bottom of a blanket. On hands and knees, she crawled, reached the feet. Ice cold. She began massaging, working the toes, pressing her thumbs into the soles, around and around, harder, and sobbing when the feet neither warmed nor changed color.

"Lauder," Dak squatted to her. "I'll take you back."

She continued kneading. "He's cold."

Dak put his hands on hers, slowly peeled off her fingers, fisted them inside his own. "There's nothing to be done here." He pulled her up, held her. "You've been here for hours."

"His feet. They're so cold."

"It's almost morning. You can come back tomorrow."

Dr. Eastman and Greta talked in a corner. Other workers quietly tended patients, and this child — she realized now — was dead. Though her entire body screamed with fatigue, she struggled against Dak who had her coat in his hands and was working her arms into the sleeves. He didn't understand. She pointed at the fir swag and the small paper cone. "Little Rose's horse is ruined."

With an arm around her, he coaxed her toward the door.

The cone didn't matter; she could see that. But couldn't he see it was more of the same, taking the defilement down to the very youngest? "Little Rose's cone is ruined," she tried again. "Don't look at me like that. I'm not crazy like your grandmother, not crazy like you for always defending her, no matter what she does." Her body screamed fatigue, but she fought to pull away. "You've no idea how much I can do." Her raised voice caused Greta to turn and give a pitiful look.

"Enough for tonight," Dak said. She was also a victim, and the only one he could help at the moment. "You need sleep."

"The cone. I'm trying to tell you something."

"We'll fix the paper in the morning."

Said exactly as he'd speak to his crazy, mad grandmother. "You can't fix it. Her horse is gone."

"She is goot?" Greta was there.

"I'm right here; ask me. And yes, I'm goot."

"She's had enough," Dak said, "I'm taking her back."

Lauder heard fear and loss in his words. And in all his small talk as they made their way to her place through darkness and blinding snow. She kept one side of her coat front wrapped across her chest, and the other side held high, shielding the snow and wind from her face. Her head on Dak's shoulder, his arm around her as they trudged on.

Thirty

THROUGH THE FEW remaining hours of darkness, Lauder and Dak held onto each other, whispered, cried, dozed fitfully, but nothing more intimate. The fabric of the world had been so savagely ripped, their bodies were stunned.

Dak sat up first and pulled on his boots. "I have to go home for a bit. It's been over seventy-two hours since Grandma has seen me. Just as long since the livestock has had feed or water."

"She's not alone?" Lauder asked.

"I left her with Walks Back," Dak said, "but with the killing, maybe Walks Back's family came for her, or she had family at the site, maybe Grandma is … hell, I just don't know." He drew her into his arms, motioned to her books and journals. "I know you won't listen to me, but you ought to keep busy here."

"I'm all right. Last night, that was fatigue, not madness. I'm all right."

"I should be back by noon."

"Promise?"

He kissed her. "You have my word."

Pine Ridge Road was crowded with gawkers, reporters from across the state, military officials like General Miles, military ambulances, troops moving, departing, others on high alert after there'd been another battle, albeit smaller.

Entering the church, Lauder hurried to check on the baby she had helped to suckle. The infant and the mother's body were gone. She found Greta. "The baby? Did family come?"

Greta was bleary eyed. "General Colby take."

"To where?"

"He take infant for wife."

"What?" Lauder cried. "Are there no free puppies around?"

There was nothing to be done about it, and Lauder knew if she was to help anyone, she had to let the matter go, not crumble as she had the day before.

She worked with others applying fresh bandages to wounds that had bled through, carrying out waste, carrying in pails of fresh water, fetching food for the doctors, and feeding soup to wounded too weak to help themselves. She swept up piles of soiled straw and spread out fresh. The number of victims stretched across the floor grew smaller through the hours. Some wished to die at home and were carried off by family, but the greater number were passed out the door and carried off by grave diggers.

Big Foot's wife, White Hawk, suffered fever. Her eyes were closed, her wounds infected despite the efforts to clean them. The rattle in her lung spoke of advancing pneumonia. The hand Lauder touched burned.

As Lauder worked, she knew she had to record as much as she could. She would write about all that happened even if her reputation meant few would believe her. The largest hurdle lay in herself: fear of condemnation. Who was she to think herself worthy of writing about the massacre? How could she tell the story of all this suffering? She was only an observer. The real story lay in the hearts of the people. She had only a white perspective, which was, therefore, if not overtly flawed, seriously lacking. There would be outrage against her, but she wouldn't let that stop her. If one person believed, if one read her account and did not dismiss the carnage, that was worth all her efforts.

A single reporter with his camera was allowed in. A throng of others were blocked from entering. Red Cloud came wrapped in a blanket, his gaunt, brown face drooping like sorrowful candle wax.

Lauder's heart ached for Dak and for Mina. School was closed until things calmed, hopefully only that long, and Mina had no reason to come into the agency. She, Blackbird, and Plants Corn were likely busy nursing wounded, along with the mothers. She wished Dak would ride out and check on the family, but he had too much needing tended to, and maybe he shouldn't go. If he didn't know numbers and names of those being nursed there, he broke no law by not reporting them.

By evening, she sat slumped and exhausted again on the floor beside White Hawk, who'd suffered through another day. The church, despite the stove, remained chilly, but every time Lauder touched the woman's hand it burned hot as a stove plate. Unable to eat or drink, a slow and agonizing death stalked her. Lauder imagined images fluttered through White Hawk's mind like wind-whipped birds, memories winging in one direction to her childhood years, valleys of flowers and game. Winging in the other direction to the diseases, starvation, and now this massacre.

Near midnight, Lauder made her way back to her cabin. A low fire burned in her stove, telling her Dak had visited hours earlier, but he was off again, pulled from duty to duty. Not thinking about her, though he must know how badly at that moment, she needed him. She opened her journal: *25 soldiers. Over 300 Miniconjou and Lakota dead.* Her pen heavy in her hand, she wrote. *Hour one: Anguished loss, pain.*

Hour two: Anguished loss, pain.

Hour three: Anguished loss, pain.

She could not stop her pen or the way it tore her paper. Giving each hour its own line, and though her script was nearly unrecognizable through her tears, she worked on. Reaching *Hour eleven: Anguished loss, pain.*

Hour twelve: Anguished loss, pain.

Turning the page, she did so with such force the paper ripped. She couldn't stop. Who was she to stop, unable to even write the hours that others were living through? Shuddering in pain. She worked on, a few minutes later reaching *Hour twenty-five: Anguished loss, pain.*

Hour twenty-six: Anguished loss, pain.

She had filled two scribbled pages, and her hand was numb. She went on, finally reaching, *Hour thirty-six: Anguished loss, pain.*

And still, White Hawk lived, suffered.

Lauder's pen dropped. Not having eaten in forty-some hours, her stomach ached, but she was too tired and upset to see if anyone minded the mess and could give her a bit of food.

She paced. The ghosts in the wall were quiet but thankfully, she had the company of Mina's Mother basket. She wanted to be with Mina and her family, but she had no means of getting there and even with a horse, if she knew how to ride, she could never find the place on her own. And what could she offer? Her sympathies would only be an idiot crowding onto that damn sinking boat. Mina suffered too much to be burdened with useless words. Not all pain could be shared like luggage handed off to others. Most pain, like White Hawk's and Mina's, was stone and could not be entered by anyone else. Going to Mina at this moment, needing self-assurances, would be an act of aggression.

The trunk of books was shameful. How smart she had thought herself. Believing she reigned above the uneducated. Believing book knowledge provided a height from which to better look down on the masses.

Loud knocking roused Lauder. She needed moments to wake and reorientate herself to the cabin. She was at her desk, her journal open, and ink trailed down the page where her pen had faltered mid-sentence. The knock came again. Dak? Mina?

Sgt. Atlock looked wobbly and grinned at her with glassy eyes. He wore his hat, but he'd walked the short distance from the hotel, not bothering with his coat. At his hip, hanging from his hand at groin level, a bottle of whiskey. He'd left off his gun belt, and lantern light winked off the glass bottle. "Pretty boy ain't here?"

A statement, a question, an accusation? She was too tired and depressed for the bother of him. "What do you want?"

"He ain't told you?"

Her stomach clenched. "Told me what?"

Sgt. Atlock stepped through and closed the door behind himself. He smelled of day-old pomade in his unwashed hair, body oil and sweat on his collar band, Dolly's henna under his fingernails.

"Told me what?"

He gave her a fatherly look. "You best take a swig of this. Nothing out of me until you've calmed down."

Her heart raced. His whiskey breath stank. What hadn't Dak told her? And where was he? He wasn't there, and she needed him. She took a sip from the bottle Sgt. Atlock kept extended, a barrier to be crossed before the man would speak. She coughed at the heat rolling down her throat. "What news?" her mind moved past him. Was it Mrs. Streamist, something to do with Dak? Mina?

He took the bottle back, tipped it to his own lips, and reextended it.

Her hands shook, and she swallowed the next offering without noticing the taste. His news was terrible, the panic rising in her told her so. She took another swallow.

"Whiskey." He saluted with the brown bottle. "Better than smallpox. Disease'll cut down one generation, but let the next go. Now likker, that'll roll right on down from one litter to the next, like shooting a row of bottles."

Her mouth opened, "All's fair in war, right?"

"Now you're getting it." He put the bottle to her lips, tipped it against her resisting, tapped the bottom, making sure she got a mouthful.

Her head began buzzing, less from the whisky than from the pounding fear roaring in her ears. "What hasn't Dak told me?"

"Jesus." He crossed to her bed like a man invited and sank onto it. "The army got even the nits hiding in the wool."

She wouldn't beg again for what he knew. Now that he would talk, she didn't want to hear. "Please leave. Dak will be here any minute."

He dropped his hat on the floor, drew his feet up, stretched out, and propped his head on her pillow. His wet boots, still in spurs, crossed at the ankles, shed snow and mud onto her bed. "Jesus," he said again, tipped his bottle, brought it down.

A tear of whiskey wept over the lip, rolled onto her gripping fingers as she accepted the bottle again. He circled a vision that even he, this soulless man, needed whiskey to tell. She shook so hard the glass rattled against her teeth. She swallowed. "Do you know where Dak is?"

"Our mercy boy? He rode out hard, working the reins like there's no tomorrow."

"To where?"

"Away."

Away? Always away. The world had sunk to a new nadir, and Dak wasn't there. She took another drink. "Tell me what you've come to say."

"You want to share the rest of that?"

Her mind knew a horror approached; it rode at her hard and was about to show its deadly face. She took another sip before handing back the bottle.

"Two of 'em," he said. "After the shooting stopped, soldiers called everyone out, shouted the all clear to anyone hiding." He uncrossed his ankles and recrossed them in the other direction. The brown spot beneath his boots widened.

Lauder's heart pounded. She tried to stay present, the acrid smell of his shoes, the two burning oil lamps, cloying fumes of alcohol.

"Roaches hiding in the dark," he said, "waiting until everything went quiet. Every man had missed 'em, but sure as shit, there they were. Two boys, five… six years old. Bawling, tears smearing their faces, hopping around, screaming at all the bodies. They ran right up to soldiers like the men were passing out fry bread. Sobbing 'Happy soldiers. Soldiers much fun.'"

Badger and Much Wind. They'd seen it all. They needed her and she them. "Where are they?"

He lifted a hand, mocked firing. "Pow! Point blank. Blew 'em back three feet. Their clothes smoking."

The air left Lauder's lungs. Invisible hands pummeled her shoulders, boots kicked out her knees, dropped her to kneeling on the floor. She shook, seeing the happy faces of the boys, remembering how they'd feared soldiers, but they'd trusted her, trusted she would do nothing that would put them in danger.

"Do not teach children to play with snakes," Mina had begged.

"I did," the words whispered.

"That ain't all. The worst I saw…" Sgt. Atlock's eyes glistened with whiskey and the glory of his tale. "Two squaws, one old, one young." He looked over the bed at Lauder on the floor.

She couldn't move.

"The old one humping from body to body, turning them over, squatting close to get a good look at the bloody dead faces. Keening like the devil slammed his toe in a door." He used his sleeve, wiped his mouth, one corner of his mustache. "All of 'em cousins and inbred. The young squaw you're so friendly with, those fancy moccasins."

Lauder panted.

"She kept close to the old one, the two of them crazy as a couple of drunks hunting a bottle." He took a swig, swung his feet off the bed, and reached down for Lauder.

Her knees scraped the floor two feet as he hauled her onto the bed, across his body, putting her between him and the wall.

"The old one found her dead buck. Goddamn, nothing human sounding in all that racket, sucking air, tearing at her hair. I tell you, it weren't human. Jesus Christ, that sound weren't human."

Lauder lay in shock. The rim of the whiskey bottle, moist with his spittle held to her lips, liquid burning her tongue.

"That teacher," Atlock went on, "standing over the old squaw's shoulder, screaming that devil's howl. The two of you eating together, won't be no more of that. She slapped her hands over the old one's eyes. I thought she didn't want her to see grandpa there in the snow, but quick as a card shark, she whipped out a knife." With a drunken hand, Atlock made a slicing motion. "Slit the old nag's throat."

Lauder's brain screamed, went blank. She wasn't there. Wasn't anywhere. Wasn't.

"You okay, girlie? Come morning, you best write all this down. You write Sgt. Atlock saw it all. Sitting right there on my horse, saw how the young one held the old squaw, a hand still slapped across the witch's eyes, the blood running down her front. The squaw finally went over. Dropped to her side dead as a sack of feed."

Lauder looked down from somewhere ceiling high. Two lamps burned. One on a chest of drawers, the other on a desk. An open book, a dropped pen, a woven basket.

"The one with the fancy moccasins weren't done," Atlock went on.

"She lifted that knife, blood running off the blade, rolled her eyes up, and drew it across her own throat."

A guttural scream came from the back wall. No, this time the sound rose from the heart of the woman on the bed, rose up through that throat.

Atlock shook his head. "I been around 'em a long time, and I ain't never seen anything like it. Slicing right through a dirty, knotted scarf. Sounded like scraping jam across toast." He tipped the last drops of the bottle into Lauder's mouth. Watched her slim white throat, felt his groin swell. "People think they ain't savages."

He let the empty whiskey bottle drop and roll a few inches on the floor. He worked open the buttons on the bodice of Lauder's dress. Bared her breasts. Young things. Not floppers like Dolly's. He'd taken young red recently, but he ain't had young white in too long. She lay limp as ribbon, wasn't fighting him, wasn't telling him to stop. Even lifting her dress and working off her bloomers, she wasn't protesting. Not even as he spread her legs and mounted.

Whimpering came from the woman down on the bed, her white legs splayed wide, moved apart by rough hands, a man groaning on top of her. Looking at the blank face over the man's shoulder, Lauder saw empty eyes, the soul absent.

Thirty-One

DRUMS ROARED IN Lauder's head. A beetle in a cotton bale, she struggled to claw up through layers of folds and weights. She shivered with cold. Shivered harder at a door opening and the strike of a freezing draft on her exposed legs. A voice. Her eyes fluttered to a spinning room. Dak stood beside the bed, looked down on her. Saw not just her nakedness, but her nakedness with Atlock. The vile man who'd left not bothering even to cover her.

She slapped wildly at her dress, wanting it down over her pubis and legs. The motion bringing on new dizziness. Stale dregs of alcohol filled her mouth, rose from her reeking pillow.

Dak pulled her blankets up, the dropped weight as heavy as the expression on his face.

"Dak," she tried through the drumming. He wore disappointment, hurt, and something foreign to the situation — shame.

He toed the empty whiskey bottle, paced angerly, cussed under his breath. After a minute, he stepped out, slamming the door so hard the bottle on the floor rocked.

Alone again, she curled into a ball, pulled the blankets higher under her chin, and wept.

She woke an hour later. Fully awake, she stumbled to the dresser, would not look at the monster in the mirror, drank water from the pitcher only to feel her grief rise up over her head and drop her back onto the bed. Badger and Much Wind. She had taught them to trust soldiers. Her stomach jerked; she leaned over the bed gagging and lost the water she had drank.

And Mina? What depth of despair must she have been feeling when she slit Blackbird's throat? Then her own, a hand so determined to leave the grizzly world it did not falter. An act so gruesome even Sgt. Atlock had been appalled.

She slept, jerked awake screaming and gasping for breath. In her dream, Badger and Much Wind held knives, lifted them in a synchronized choreography, and ran the blades across their delicate throats. Only a nightmare, but the real was more than a nightmare. The men who killed them, likely with children of their own, had watched them come, heard their crying, and waited until the boys were so close their clothing burned with the firing.

There was no humanity in the cruelty. Evil that sinister had no reckoning.

She lay curled on her side, wishing for more of Sgt. Atlock's foul liquor and the blessed stupor it brought. There was no relief. She slumped from her bed, crawled to her chest of books, pulled them out and started ripping pages. She tore and shoveled and screamed, stuffing them through the open stove door. Flame, brilliant in its flashing, rose and filled the stove's belly. The excessive heat wafted wings of burning paper into the room. Magnificent orange and yellow birds flew, landed on the floor, on the desk, her bed. Frantic, she threw in a whole book, but that only sent up puffs of ash, not catching as did loose pages. She ripped and stuffed in the paper, cried with the splendid birds and butterflies rising, wingtips curling and flaming, falling around her.

Dak burst through. "Lauder!" He slapped at her skirt and two coin-sized holes burning.

"Go away," she screamed. "Leave me alone."

He dragged her back across the floor, left her braced against the foot of the bed as he hurried to slam the stove door and kick the air lever closed. He stomped out live cinders twisting on her floor.

"Burn them all, I don't want them," she howled and crawled back for another book. He caught her, sat on the floor with her, held her as she trembled and fought against him.

"I got you," he said, holding her tight. Again and again, "I got you."

On the floor, they rocked for nearly an hour before Lauder could form a sensible string of words. "You didn't tell me. Sgt. Atlock told me everything. The boys, Plants Corn, Blackbird, Mina. You didn't tell me. They're all dead."

"I'm sorry." He was sorry for letting her stay at the agency, for not being the one to bring her the news, for leaving her alone while Atlock prowled. "I didn't see everything that went down once the cannons quit firing. Bodies were scattered across a couple of miles. It was chaos. I don't know how far from the camp the boys were hiding. I saw Blackbird and Mina frantic, but there wasn't a soul who wasn't frantic. I only heard yesterday what became of them."

"You didn't tell me."

"Yesterday, I got back here about noon. Went first to Moyer's office and heard what Atlock had witnessed. At the same time, a telegram came about medical supplies arriving in Rushville. Much of it for the army, but some of it for Dr. Eastman. A couple of tired, angry, and Sioux-hating soldiers were going by wagon to get them. Snow drifts are ten, twenty feet high across some of the roads. I was afraid they'd make it a two-day trip, maybe needing a week to get there and back. They aren't from around here. They don't know the hills, the ravines. I knew I could get there and back in five, six hours with a string of saddlebags full of chloroform and morphine. I came across here hoping to find you first, but you were still at the church. I headed out."

"You looked for me?"

"I decided against going to the church." He wiped tears from her cheeks. "I couldn't give you news like that and then just ride off. I wanted to tell you when I got back, and I had hours to sit through it with you. Of course, the goddamned train was hours late."

She wanted to grab her remaining books, open the stove. She would burn the place down, the two of them sitting right there.

"I thought," Dak went on, "I'd see you when I returned. I never imagined that bastard Atlock," she hadn't said the name, but he knew, "would rush over. I never wanted you to know the details of their deaths. Learning they were dead would have been enough."

"It's the end," Lauder said. "How can anyone go on?"

"This is how," his arms tightened, "by holding onto each other. It's all we've got."

She pulled back. "I taught Badger and Much Wind to trust the soldiers. They might still be alive today. I came here with my big ideas and books—"

He pulled her back against his chest. "You might have asked me about the books."

He meant to be funny, but levity was the moon's distance away. "I can't ever return to that classroom. I can't face the children when I brought in the soldiers. I can't face the empty desks where Badger and Much Wind sat."

"Never?"

"Never. Never."

"Yeah," he agreed softly. He readjusted his arms around her. "The thing is, the school can't wait for your 'never' to be over."

"Stop being a goddamn optimist. Families don't want me. I never came to teach children. I came for myself, to hide after plagiarizing an article."

"Tell me."

She confessed it all. "In the end, I think the journal did receive my letter of apology and retraction. I think the editor ran the piece anyway to teach me a lesson. Shame and silence me forever."

They sat with their legs outstretched and Lauder sunk against Dak. "That's it?" he asked. "That's your big crime?"

"It was in my world. Back then." Now there was Sgt. Atlock, the boys' deaths, the deaths of Mina and her family. White Hawk enduring terrible suffering, death everywhere.

For a long moment Dak said nothing. Then slowly, "It's not optimism that keeps me going. It's terror."

"You were right. I shouldn't have come."

"White greed has destroyed pretty much everything. Keeping the school open is us trying to clean up some of the mess."

"I didn't clean up one thing; I was more of the problem."

"I know it looks impossible." He kissed her forehead, cradled her cheek against his shoulder. "But the government's policies aren't going away, aren't even going to lighten up anytime soon. This is where we are. This set of problems."

"You are a damned optimist. And Atlock, I—"

"Forget him. I'll put a bullet between his eyes."

"You can't do that."

"It's quick. There's times discussion's a waste."

She closed her eyes and let fresh tears run from under her lashes. "I don't know what to say about him. I don't know how to try and explain."

"Then don't try."

"I want you to know the truth."

"I know the truth," Dak said. "The bastard brought his gruesome news knowing I wasn't around, knowing it would break you. He plied your shock and grief with his whiskey. You were likely passed out."

Lauder sucked in ragged breaths and let them ease from her shaking lungs. "I took his whiskey. But I wasn't passed out." She didn't want to go on, but prayed Dak was man enough to let her. "I was drunk, but it wasn't the booze; it was the deaths." She looked up to the ceiling. "I was somewhere up there. This morning, thinking back, I realized I wanted him to take me crudely, to crush every last bit of stupid Lauder Ellison. Punish me. More. Finish me off. I wanted to die. Suicide by depravity."

Dak held her.

"But here I am," Lauder said. "I'm still alive. He couldn't even do that. Mina and her family, those two precious little boys, all the others dying in the church. It's all still here. Atlock hasn't made any of it go away. If bullets were free," she pulled back enough to look at Dak squarely, "you putting one in his head would still be a waste. He's less than nothing."

"Then no one will notice when he's gone." She needed to talk, and he needed to be careful, plan how to take Atlock out. No matter how much he longed to do so, he couldn't walk into the hotel and gun him down. He couldn't be hauled off to the state pen, hanged. His own need to see the man dead ranked somewhere around fourth or fifth in line. There was the school, Grandma, Lauder. Still, there were ways. He'd take care of Atlock.

Lauder drew up her knees, curled closer to Dak. Kind as he was being, what had happened with Atlock had put a dagger straight through any hope of a real relationship with him. They would never be more than friends.

"The massacre," Dak spoke slow, "unbelievable. It proves we need to grab up life. Live every single minute we're given."

She raised her head, searched his eyes, the set of his mouth. Did he still want more than friendship? Were his standards so low? "After all I've done, I'll never forgive myself."

He kissed her. Long and slow. "I love you. I've loved you from the first time I saw you, but being with you felt impossible. I was scared you'd get hurt, end up swinging in an empty barn like my mother."

"Or burning down my place?"

He didn't answer, only looked across the floor strewn with ashes and scraps of charred paper. "I should have sent you back."

"My being here was never your decision to make. And neither is my staying."

"You'll stay?"

"If we sit like this through eternity. If you promise to never forgive all my mistakes."

"I'll never say I forgive you. You're not needing my forgiveness."

"That leaves me to doubt your character." She took a deep breath. "I'll never get over the deaths. I'll be an emotional cripple forever."

"Aren't any of us walking on two whole legs."

She shook her head. "There's nothing you can say to make this better. Quit trying."

"Hasn't Thoreau got something to offer?"

She looked to the stove. "He's cinders." Her lungs shuddered, her breath still uneven. "How do we go on?"

"A day passes and another comes. Time carries us."

"There is a little girl, She-Stands-Brave. There's not a day she doesn't hang back, not a day she doesn't have to find the courage to enter the classroom, and not a day she doesn't do it. But can I do it? Enter the classroom with half my being carrying shame for those little boys' deaths and still teach?"

"Do that," Dak said. "Give fifty percent to your shame. Then you can teach at fifty percent, be fifty percent available for the children."

She'd been regaining a bit of composure, but at his words she wept again. "You're very obvious." If only she could climb into one of his pockets and ride his hip. "I'm still shaking inside. Another five minutes and I would have had this whole place blazing."

"Burning paper flew from your chimney."

"You were watching?"

"One way or another, I think you're determined to get yourself killed."

"What about the bodies? What cemetery will they be taken to? I want to be at the burials. Buy headstones."

He kept his arms tight, holding her close. "They're being buried right now in a mass grave."

"A mass grave?" She pulled back, wanted to shriek. "That's wrong."

"It's over," Dak said. "They're gone; the people are dead."

"It's wrong. You know it's wrong. The army is trying to cover everything up as quickly as possible. It's wrong."

"I'm not saying it's right."

Thirty-Two

SHE HAD BEGGED Dak to bring her to the site. Now that they'd arrived, seeing lifeless bodies strewn over the frozen ground, she changed her mind. She wanted to ride back to the agency, but she must stay, bear witness, learn what must be witnessed. As they walked toward a group of both spectators and military, she kept her arm through Dak's for support.

He pulled up suddenly, shouted. "Get the hell away from there!"

Ten yards away, a man's body had been stripped of its leggings, and a photographer stood over the victim, his camera posed, not bothering to cover the man's nakedness, but hurrying to get his picture before someone stopped him. Profit over decency.

"Let him," Lauder managed. "Let all the barbarity be recorded. When the bodies are all buried, and the records are falsified for history, the pictures will remain to tell the truth."

They reached the group crowded around the burial pit. The grave was a hole so deep the dirt walls rose above the heads of the two civilian men standing inside. Other men pulled bodies from wagons and handed them along to the men in the pit who stacked them one on top of the other like cordwood. Frozen bodies. No drooping arms or lulling heads, but arms and legs stiff as branches. Children dropped in; adults dropped on top of them.

The taste of blood made her release her bottom lip from between her teeth. If spectators had wanted to see three hundred dead Sioux, they had it now.

Thirty soldiers posed at one end of the mass grave where another photographer could capture both the bodies in the hole and the men in full uniform, erect and proud. Rifles either over one shoulder or in their hands, standing over their kill. A triumphant picture for the press and their families.

There were no bouquets of red roses, no loved ones over the bodies saying prayers. This quick burial, too, was the work of statecraft.

"Sir," she heard a soldier address an officer. "There's a wagon over yonder."

"How many dead?"

"Hard to say. A dozen or so. They took a direct hit. The scraps oughta fill one box."

"Fill the wagon with brush. Burn the whole thing."

"I've learned white men are not above the Sioux," Lauder said to Dak in a low voice. "But I didn't know so many were lower than dogs."

"Indian lover." A woman directly behind hissed at Lauder's shoulder.

The woman's face, contorted in hate, wore Father's eyebrows, Mother's resentful lips. Lauder clung to Dak, alternately clutching her eyes closed and peeking again at the bodies being lowered. She prayed not to see Badger and Much Wind, even as she prayed for the strength to give the little boys the respect of having been seen. She was faint and wanted away, but she wouldn't allow herself the privilege of flight. The privilege of leaving her body or the site as if she were so refined she was incapable of witnessing. Not again, not ever again.

A man began pulling another body from the wagon, jerking it forward by its bare feet. A young woman, a frozen body now, its knees folded, as if the woman had died while kneeling in prayer. An indistinguishable face black and purple. With the body pulled free and held over the pit, a scarf around its neck fluttered. Caked with dried and frozen blood, but a single gold star still untouched on one end.

Lauder's knees buckled.

Dak caught her, held her half-upright.

The men in the massive open pit laid Mina on top of the jumble of dead. Lauder tried to grab breath as another body was reached for and placed on top of Mina.

"You've seen enough," Dak said. He turned Lauder, kept her upright as he pushed them through the crowd. He needed to get her out of there. She had seen Mina, and she understood the burial situation. She didn't need to see the bodies of the little boys she loved so much; he would spare her that.

"Monsters," Lauder sobbed, looking back. "They are all monsters."

Dak nodded in agreement; his face stricken. "But any man with red blood is capable of this."

Something ruffled the corners of her awareness. Like the wind lifting the manes of horses, scrubbing icy flakes off the ground and pushing her skirt against her legs; there was something she wasn't seeing. Suddenly, she knew: Mina's beaded moccasins. They had been stolen, and that theft was an attack as sinister as photographing a murdered man's nakedness. As if death were not enough. Even the bodies needed assaulting, stripped of clothing that would bring a few dollars on the black market, clothing that mattered more than the wearer.

Atlock. He'd admitted watching Mina take Blackbird's life and then her own. Sitting on his horse, he'd not bothered to try and stop the tragedy. In his mind, he might only have been watching the struggle of caught animals. But with Mina dead, he'd dismounted and pulled off her still warm moccasins.

"The army doesn't know what it's creating," Dak said. "This spot right here, people'll still be visiting here in a hundred years. There'll be healings here, prayers answered. It'll be powerful." He looked back at the mass grave. "This place will make warriors."

By the time they reached her lodging, the sun was setting. He helped her inside. She wasn't speaking. Hadn't spoken a word in the ride back. She'd left all the talking to him and he was no good at it.

"Come home with me," he said. "It's been a hell of a day. We need to stay together."

She pulled the long pin from her hat, dropped it and the hat onto the dresser top. "Tonight, I need to be alone."

He took her in his arms. "We need to hang on to each other."

She had allowed Atlock into the lodging where she and Dak stood;

two young girls had died there; Mina's body lay amongst other dead, and somewhere under that weight lay the frozen bodies of two innocent boys. Along with how many other children? "Tonight," she stressed the word, giving hope that tomorrow would be different, "I need to be alone. I need to just sit or maybe pace all night. Please understand."

"Leaving you alone hasn't worked so well."

"Please. I'll drop the bar, and no one will get in. Besides, you're no better off. You're dead on your feet. Go home. You've got hours of work waiting and a frightened grandmother who probably thinks you're dead."

"Come with me. I swear I won't force myself on you."

"That, Mr. Thomas, is the least of my worries."

"I can't talk you out of it?"

"I need to be alone. Please understand that. I promise not to burn the place down."

Dak stepped out, stood on her cold stoop, the wind funneling down Pine Ridge Road, threatening to take his hat. He hesitated. "I'm coming back; I'll sleep here. I'll get things settled, make sure Grandma is all right. You'll have a few hours, then I'll be back."

Nothing sounded better. "Please don't," she begged. "I ... I don't want you to come back. For three days, you've had no more than a few winks of sleep. Mrs. Streamist needs to see your face when she wakes in the morning. I need to write and try to wrestle out in my head and ..." she fisted a hand, struck her heart, "and in here, some peace. Being with you tonight will only postpone the argument with myself."

He studied her, then stepped back in, and kicked the door closed with a heel.

"I'm fine," she said. "Believe me."

"Why should I? Because I can trust you to stay safe?"

"Because I need you to."

He pulled her close. "I love you."

"Tomorrow," she whispered, her lips brushing against his ear.

He checked the stove he'd already checked twice, kissed and held her a final time. He didn't understand her wanting to be alone, only knew this decision, too, wasn't his to make. They were both strung to their limits and relief was nowhere in sight. He'd keep moving. Do the thing closest, then do the next closest thing. He climbed into his wagon, God, he was dead, and looked over the agency. Wounded soldiers had doses of stabilizing medicine and those able to be transported were on their way to hospitals. People from Big Foot's band, those who still lived, were under Dr. Eastman's care, and had medicines.

He wanted to see a string of people hung, including Atlock, and in the morning with a clear head instead of a drum between his ears, he'd figure out a way to deal with the bastard.

He looked back at Lauder still standing in her doorway, her eyes rimmed pink as her lips. He didn't need to remind her to drop the bar. What had been done to her and what she'd seen sickened him. Somehow he'd make it up to her. "I love you."

She mouthed affection in return and shut the door before she lost her nerve and ran through snow after him.

When she was sure he was off, she headed back to the church. White Hawk had died. The news sent her back down the hill.

She waited until full darkness before she stepped out again. The night was sunken in a mean and deep cold. Nature cowered. Not a nightbird or wolf cried. Even the streets and soldiers' camps were quiet, leaving her to wonder how many of the troops had already left. Beasts fleeing.

She hurried to the hotel without being noticed and entered wrapped in a blanket over her head. Men were in the bar just off the foyer to her right. A haze of tobacco smoke, noise, and a hundred odors associated with men clouded the doorway. To her left, a staircase led up to the rooms. Straight ahead, a man stood behind a counter watching her.

"I'm looking for Sgt. Atlock's room."

He hesitated, his eyes asking who she was and what type of woman came alone at night seeking the man. After studying her a moment, he shrugged and nodded at the staircase. "Room six, but I wouldn't go up there right now."

"He's not in?" Could she be so lucky?

"He's in. Entertaining a lady."

Dolly is not a lady. But, of course, the woman in his room could be anyone. "May I wait?"

"Might be some time."

Unlikely. Atlock would grope and satisfy himself and leave for the company of men and whiskey. She grabbed the chair the proprietor pointed to, dragged it to the back corner of the lobby, nearly under the stairs. She rewrapped the blanket, making sure her hair was covered and the wool came forward enough to hide both sides of her face. When Atlock came down, he'd go straight into the bar, not bothering to look around. And if he did notice a figure in a blanket, hopefully, he'd suppose it a sleeping Indian and not give it so much as a single thought.

A short time later, footsteps rang on the stairs above her head. "He'll be expecting it," Sgt. Atlock's voice.

"I'll mail it tomorrow," Dolly answered.

"Good girl."

Lauder kept her chin on her chest, her heart racing. If she so much as pulled in her feet, the motion would draw attention. She had not begged the proprietor behind the counter to keep her presence a secret, though he could see she didn't want to be found out. She hoped he was a kinder man than the editor who published her article, a kinder man than Father and his ilk, a kinder man than the soldiers who'd hunted down women and children for sport.

Atlock and Dolly hesitated a moment at the door, whispering to one another, a cold draft tumbling in. Dolly left, and Atlock took several steps toward the bar, his boots striking the floor, his spurs jingling, and stopped.

Lauder, her heart in her throat, dared not look up. Was Atlock standing at the bar entrance, looking over the tables, or turned and looking at her? She forced herself to remain still and nearly cried out when the spurs started again, and the noise faded. She peeked. He was gone. She waited a few minutes more, imagining him taking a seat, and ordering a bottle. She rushed to the counter. "I need the key. Please. Quickly."

Bushy, gray brows came together.

"He stole something that belonged to my friend. I have a right to take it back."

The man hesitated a long minute, then slowly laid a key on the counter, used one finger to push it to her, his face hard. "It's all nasty business."

In a rush up the stairs, she found number six at the far end of the hall. Despite her shaking, the key slid in, and the knob turned. Too easily. "Mina," she whispered, "stay with me."

A room with red flocked paper on the walls, a chair with his abandoned gun belt draped over the back, a half-empty whiskey bottle, a rifle leaning in the corner, a blanket hanging off the end of a tangled bed, a lantern burning at its side. The lamp's flickering threw light on the exposed white sheets, and Lauder gasped as the memory of her rape struck her.

She spun away. Struggled to draw an even breath back into her lungs. Mina. She was here for Mina. Her skin prickled suddenly, and she felt watched. Shadows, less than vapors, flitted, disappeared. Nothing there and yet life, formless, restless. The room lay a world apart from the killing field of that afternoon. There, the ghosts of the dead would always remain for those with the consciousness to witness. There, children would never stop screaming from the rocks and the grass. But here? Was all of Pine Ridge haunted? There'd been enough killing, and what had Mina said? "Spirits do not rest while their sacred objects are in the hands of thieves."

She opened the wardrobe: shirts, a couple of pairs of pants, a long, India-rubber coat. Nothing there even to touch. Fear wrapped fingers around her neck, squeezed her throat, and reached down to her heart. What was she doing? Where was the old Miss Lauder Ellison who'd never have had the courage to do such a thing? Deep inside, that woman still existed and feared she would puke, but the new Lauder Ellison wouldn't stop until she found Mina's moccasins.

She dropped to her knees, peered under the bed. A long flat case that might hold a rifle or two. At least one of Atlock's rifles stood in a corner. She pulled out the case and opened it slowly. Over a dozen objects: a pipe, bear claw necklace, two small leather pouches, a turtle fetish, a pair of long beaded strips about two inches wide and nearly a yard long, a doll. A pocket watch. She closed her eyes and took a steadying breath. Mina's moccasins. She picked them up along with the watch and doll. It was unlikely the doll had been left behind. More likely was that Atlock had taken the doll from a dead child's arms. If not dead, he'd likely seen to that.

Holding the objects, Lauder sank onto the end of the bed where the blankets were less disturbed. The leather on Mina's footwear had been cut down the back and along one side of the footbed to the toe. Holes had been punched with an awl, and a three-inch band of newer leather partially stitched in. Had Atlock thought he could somehow make Mina's moccasins fit his feet? Had he planned to wear them without shame? If Mina had not taken her own life, would he have done so to get the moccasins? Was her body still warm, blood still pulsing from her neck when he pulled them from her feet?

"The hell!" Atlock stepped into the room roaring. He slammed the door, causing it to shake on its hinges.

"The man downstairs told you."

His grin showed teeth. "It's a man's world, ain't it."

"You're evil. A thief." Once thinking him handsome, now she saw only cruelty. "I'm taking these. The doll, Dak's watch, and Mina's moccasins."

"The hell you are!"

The bellow and his expression chilled her. He was a dangerous man, and she had gotten herself into another impossible situation. He wouldn't let her go, wouldn't have her going to Dak or General Brooke. Even if he received no fine, his black-market scheme was lucrative, and he had no intention of giving up his dealings in stolen goods. He wouldn't hand over the moccasins he'd coveted from the first time he saw them. "You're breaking the law," she said. "The Repatriation Act was signed in October."

"You think I'm the only one picked up a few trinkets? Every soldier out there took him some goods. Grabbed up 'em Indian rifles like it was Christmas."

She swallowed, angry at her shaking and his pleasure in seeing it. "That's the army's problem. I'll take only these. What you do with the rest is your business. If you don't let me take these, I'll tell General Brooke what you have." She motioned to the open case, mentally catalogued the items. "You'll lose it all."

He smirked.

She stood.

His smirk remained. As did his wide stance and his loose arms ready to fly out and grab her when she made for the door. "It ain't that simple," he said. "Now is it?"

She dropped the items and stepped away from the bed where he could too easily push her back onto the mattress and rape her again. Before he killed her. His arms lifted, his hands out as she worked around the nightstand, leaving a foot between her and the wall. The door an impossible distance away.

"It's a big country out there," he said. Easy, confident. "Bones might never be found. Coyotes and wolves starving. Finding the skull of a dead schoolteacher, three, four years from now, no way of proving what happened. An Indian needing strung up to teach 'em all a lesson." He pointed. "Those pretty little things will fetch some money."

Her shaking increased. "You're a pig."

"You weren't calling me that last night. I had you singing, screaming for more."

Pig had already said it all. He would lunge at her. She saw it unfolding slowly, time warping a second ahead of itself. He'd knock her back against the hard wall, just as the man in the ravine had pushed her, pinned her, the full weight and force of his heavy body slamming into hers, knocking the wind out of her.

It happened. He charged her, his heavy body hitting and slamming her into the wall. A hand on her throat, muscled, squeezed, blocked her air. Five seconds, ten, she couldn't breathe, strangling, the pain incredible. He'd break her neck even before she died of suffocation. Then his eyes grew wide with disbelief. His hand dropped as he slumped back and looked down at the knife stuck hilt-deep two inches below his shiny belt buckle. Blood seeping.

"You god damn…" He came at her again, but slower, disbelief and pain sucking strength.

She twisted away, grabbed his gun belt with its row of shiny hard bullets, and whipped it across his face. The force turned him, bloodied his nose and mouth, but he remained on his feet, came at her again.

She rammed him, knocked him against the bedside table and the lantern. The glass shade rose with the force, floated to the bed, a long wavering ribbon of kerosene tailed it. The gold snake landed, slithered, and bellied across the mattress. Exploded into flame.

Atlock on his knees, fell over, curled and cussing.

"Fire," she screamed. "Fire!"

She stepped around him and his spewing obscenities. Danced out of his reach as he tried to grab her ankle.

"Fire!" she screamed again, this time at the open door and down the hall. "Fire!" She had seconds to grab everything and bundle them in the blanket from the bed.

The stairs thundered with men running in a double-wide mass, including the proprietor who'd gone into the bar and informed Atlock of her presence. Wrapped in her original blanket, she pressed herself to one side and let the charging males pass, their yelling and issuing orders to one another, none paying attention to the Indian woman stepping out of their way. Outside, she stood in the cold, smelled the burning, and looked up through the window of number six to see men slapping blankets, coats, rugs, against the flames. The window opened, and two men heaved the flaming mattress onto the street. The room went dark.

She ran through the cold for her cabin, shoved the bundle under her bed where the craniometer and her torn dress still lay, and back to her door to peek through a crack. Four men carried Atlock out on a rug.

"Take him to the infirmary," a man shouted.

"No. The doctors are busy with our men." A deep and breathy voice Lauder recognized as General Brooke's. "Army doesn't want anything to do with that one. Take him to the church. Dr. Eastman's there. Maybe he'll care enough to take a look."

As they started slowly up the hill, struggling with Atlock's weight, Lauder dropped the bar across her door, and fell onto her bed. Her body shook so hard the bed on its four legs stuttered, but her eyes were dry, and a tiny smile worked its way across her lips.

She lay awake, staring first at the wall, then at Mina's basket. The hours went on, her room quiet. Her stove still sent out warmth, her lamps burned, and she could hear the wind sliding over her roof, knocking on the back, north-facing wall, but something was different. Despite the reality outside, inside, her place had changed. She rose, walked her hands across the painted surface where a window had once been. The ghosts were gone. Had they traveled away with the spirits of three-hundred others, the sweep and drag of that many souls? Had it been Dak's confession and hearing the story of what happened that released them? Was it the recovery of so many items?

"Rest in peace," she whispered.

Thirty-Three

NURSE STOOD OVER Lauder's bed. In the liminal space between dreams and wakefulness, Lauder knew she was there. The visit was one of night's small benedictions when the mind was quiet and the spirit allowing. She opened her eyes, fully awake and alone. But touched. The gift of a visit. The gift of Nurse. The fortress of her, despite her small stature. She had lived through heartache, grew wizened and determined. Mystical. Able to put the hair of a boar where Lauder would find it, answer the call. How like the mothers of Plants Corn.

Her stomach sank. The mothers! Had someone rescued them? She tried to think, turn the days page by page. Mina and her family had arrived home on the 28th with the women in hand. Blackbird and Mina had gone with her that very night, wanting to rescue others from Big Foot's band, leaving Plants Corn with the mothers. But Plants Corn had left them the following morning to find his niece and wife, supposing he'd be back in a few hours. Did anyone else know the women were there? There'd been the man sleeping on the floor who'd driven them close to the encampment, but she had no idea what became of him. Had he gone back to Plants Corn? If he hadn't spent the night there, he'd have no idea that Plants Corn left early the next morning. Or if he did know, did he also leave, supposing the family would all be home again in a few hours?

Lauder tossed. Turned. Punched her pillow. She couldn't help the poor women. Given the passage of three days, their fate was already sealed. Wasn't it? There was nothing she could do. Mina's moccasins had been saved along with several other valuables, and Atlock? There was no way of knowing what might happen to her over the stabbing. Or what was happening to him. The mothers weren't hers. In the morning, when Dak rode in, and he heard about them, he'd know what to do and where to go.

She tossed again. Turned, finally rose from bed and sat in front of Mina's basket. What had Mina said of Blackbird? "She does not look to others to slay what arrives at her door."

"Noo," Lauder let the moan fill the room. "Noo, this isn't mine."

She tried to reason responsibility away. In that moment, before Mina drew the knife across Blackbird's throat and then her own, with Plants Corn dead at their feet, wouldn't she have considered the mothers? Had she known they were tended? Or with bodies all around her, grief so deep it blinded her, nothing else had existed?

Lauder paced. She hadn't thought of Dak or the children or anyone else when her body separated from her mind and Atlock raped her. She, mind, body, and soul, had been in shock. How could Mina not also have been in shock? In the deepest part of the well there was nothing but darkness. And the mind was unable to consider a future. Somewhere in all the dying Mina had just witnessed, stacked upon her suffering at boarding school, her fatal wounds had welled up, consumed her. "The mind," Dak had said, "goes the same as a heart, a leg. The dead can't be blamed for suicide."

If Mina stood there now, what would she have Lauder do? The answer headlined in Lauder's mind. Help The Mothers.

Dak was exhausted, but he'd somehow muster the energy to ride out to Plants Corn's cabin. But she couldn't find his place even in daylight. Darkness made the possibility an impossibility. And she had no horse. Nor did she know where Red Cloud or Agent Moyer lived, and she doubted Agent Moyer would care enough to pull on boots. The two old women were not his wards, and again she couldn't take him there in the dark even if he'd go intending to arrest them. The same was true of going to General Brooke. If he ordered a few soldiers to investigate — soldiers hating Indians because of the army's twenty-five dead, and even more injured — she couldn't show them the way in the dark. She regretted again not having mapped every location. *How safe is a woman*, she would write in her journal, *if she doesn't even know where she is?*

She could think of only one person who knew the way, even in the dark. One person indebted to the family. The thought of going to him threatened the need for her chamber pot. She would puke into the porcelain and then lift her skirts with the need to sit.

Her fear was a beast, but that didn't matter. That monster could be wrestled with after the task was done. For now, she needed to act. She yanked open a dresser drawer for any warmer clothing she hadn't ripped into bandages. Cramping in her abdomen made her hesitate. She pulled the string on the bloomers she wore and looked into the crotch. Her monthly course had begun. Given the horror of so much death, she had not considered the oats Atlock had sown, but now she knew not even a hull survived. Over the next two days, her female body would expel every remaining trace of him. She smiled. Mother had been right about how the reservation would change her. When she ought to be considering the possibility of Atlock dying, her body's rhythm, sound as the courses of the planets on the armillary, flushed her clean.

She dressed hurriedly. If Mina's moccasins were whole, she would have pulled them on for spiritual help, but they'd been sliced open to fit an ape's foot.

She went around her cabin to the rear and into deeper darkness, passing the back of the mess, the hotel, the livery, and the post office before stepping back onto Pine Ridge Road. Unseen, or at least unapproached. Everyone on the agency grounds was either in exhausted sleep, or consumed with patients, and uninterested in a dark form wrapped in blankets, leaving the grounds. Half a mile farther, she stopped. She took deep breaths, prayed to Babette and Mina. She stepped off the road, crossed the narrow field, and entered the thicket of spruce and fir. The undergrowth reached waist high, and she stepped and climbed over fallen branches and tree trunks, sank into snowdrifts, and kept herself going by playing a game in her mind: She was working through King Minos's labyrinth. Theseus must also have been afraid, but he'd had advantages she did not: daylight, a warm season, and a string to follow.

She struggled on, not even certain she was going in the right direction. The farther she went, the more the going felt like entering another realm. She wasn't just a quarter mile from Pine Ridge Road, rather a dimension away.

The thicket of trees had never been cleared of its dead fall, but the going was so hard she wondered if John had dragged in additional broken limbs from wherever he found them. Barricades to keep trespassers like herself away. John likely had a smooth open trail that wound through, but it was well hidden even in daylight. She could see nothing in the dark. Climbing over another downed tree trunk, she stepped on an icy branch, slipped and went to her knees. She was a fool. There was nothing to do but try and find her way back to the road while she still had the energy.

A waft of wood smoke touched her nose. Had Nurse sent it? She went on, the smoke growing stronger, and finally parting branches to a wavering blush of firelight bleeding through the skin of a hide teepee.

Standing in the clearing, she prayed for a lightning strike, a flash flood, the four horsemen from the apocalypse, anything to end this. She took a deep breath. "John! John!" Another breath. "I'm a friend of Plants Corn and Blackbird. Only a woman. I'm alone and unarmed."

She waited while a mule brayed from deeper in the shelter of the trees. The animal heard her, and the sound of its approach grew louder, but she had no idea if it was tame or fierce as an attack dog.

The tent flap parted no more than a slit. Two eyes, reddened by the fire burning inside.

Her knees shook. A stench. She gagged. She would not run. Atlock, with his sculptured good looks, proved evil. John, for all his supposed evil looks, might not be a better man, but unless he stole dolls from dead children for the dollar they brought him, he wasn't worse. "I want to hire you. I have money. Take me to Plants Corn's cabin."

He stepped outside. She had not seen him standing before and imagined a shorter man. Given the night, and with his dark face, she couldn't see much of his features, but the hair that had looked matted when he sat by the post now seemed only two flat braids hanging over his shoulders.

He grunted. "Dead."

"Plants Corn? Yes, he's dead, but his mothers were at his cabin. I'm not sure…" She also wasn't certain he understood her English, but he continued to stand, just outside the warmth of this teepee, staring in her direction. Surely, living so close to the agency, he'd been around English speakers, if only whiskey traders, long enough to understand the language.

"I pay you."

He made a disinterested gesture at her offer to pay and stepped back inside.

"The mothers need help."

After a moment, he opened the tent flap again, made a scooping, invitational motion with one hand.

Her stomach screamed. "I can't come in there." I'm too small. Spiritually, emotionally, by every scale, I'm too small. She grabbed at breath, repeated the phrase again that had caught his interest. "The mothers need help."

She waited, eyeing the animal that had come and stood beside the tent like a watchdog. It was shorter than Mina's horse and with larger, hairier ears, almond shaped eyes, and with a shorter mane more like a scrub brush running down his neck. A donkey, a mule? "Stay there," she said. "Stay." She wished again she could turn and fight her way back through the trees. Suppose John could still be talked into taking her, but he was so intoxicated he couldn't find his way to Plants Corn. They'd wander around in the dark until they both froze.

John reappeared in a coat and hat with several fur tails of varying length hanging off. He patted the mule's neck, addressed the animal as he'd not done her, and put on a rope halter. He mounted first, his worn boots hanging only twelve inches above the ground and motioned her to get on behind him. No sign of extending a hand.

She had to concentrate to make her feet move. Left foot, right foot. Reaching him, he tipped his elbow out, and she grabbed the aid.

She closed her eyes in disbelief as his hand came around her waist and lifted. She found herself atop the mule and sitting close to the man she once thought not fully human. With the mule's first step, she nearly slipped off the back of the rump and had to grab John's coat, making a handle of each side. The animal started out of the thicket on a narrow, winding trail while she bounced precariously on its haunches. She scooted up, tight against John, her body pressed into his back, her arms around his waist.

They rode. Lauder remembered how she had righteously told Mina that the Lakota drank too much. John was as sober as the cold they moved through. His hair, or was it his fur hat, carried an odor she couldn't name. A scent as earthy as it was foreign. Mostly, he smelled of wood smoke. Had the horrid odor she'd once associated with him been more imagination than reality? Had her brain, based on all her judgments thus far, produced smells in her head? Could prejudice work that amazingly?

They rode without speaking. He'd spoken only a single word to her, "dead." And reserved his additional conversation for his mule.

She watched stars for an hour. Plant's Corn's small place was dark with not so much as a penny-dip light touching a window. The chimney top sans even a tendril of cold-looking smoke. John didn't move, and Lauder suspected this was the first time he'd let himself fully believe his friend, and his friend's family, were gone. Would he wish to know exactly what had happened? If he wanted to light the stove and sit with her, she would tell him what she knew.

"We must go in," she said, "we've come this far."

The mothers sat in their rockers. Lauder sank to her knees before the first one. Touching the woman's hand, she reared back. The women had frozen, staring straight ahead as they had in life, seeing nothing. She remained sitting there, her legs crossed in front, her head and shoulders bowed. Hardly aware of John, she knew only that he moved around in the dark. There was a scrape of wood, the clank of the stove's metal door, but none of it mattered. She crawled from in front of the first mother to sit in front of the second. Equal respect.

"John," she said his name, though his real name likely wasn't in reference to a biblical character. His real name held a more personal meaning. "We're too late."

She expected that at any moment he'd motion it was time to head back. Instead, after several minutes of getting the fire going, he sat down at the table and lit the candle. The music box caught his attention, and he drew it close. Turned it over and over in his hands.

Lauder went to him, stood at his side, and when he looked up at her, she said, "May I?"

His hands parted over the box.

She wound the key.

He jerked with surprise on hearing the first notes, but he didn't take his eyes off the twirling ballerina. When the music stopped, he wound the key a second time.

Lauder went around the table and sat across from him. He looked to be a man in his fifties. A straight nose, broad cheeks. Eyes piercing and intelligent. No scars, no fangs, just a man. He could be any of the fathers who brought their children to school.

Listening to the music, his mouth moved in such a way she thought he might cry. Instead, his chin lifted, and he let out a deep, belly laugh. An infectious laugh that made her laugh as well. The more times he wound the key, the harder they laughed. Until Lauder bit her bottom lip and fought back tears. There was so much space between their lives, and sharing the box was so layered and rife with stories, there was nothing for it but tears.

John rose, took the box with him, and stretched out on the cot where Mina had slept.

Lauder watched his back, certain that he'd fallen almost instantly asleep. Minutes passed in which fatigue struck her like fists. With John asleep, there was nothing to do but go to the other bed. She wouldn't sleep, though. How could she with two bodies and a Lakota man who spoke no more than did the corpses?

One mother jerked, moving the rocker, then the other. Lauder jumped up, nearly screamed, "They are alive." She rushed to John, hesitant about waking him, her eyes on the stilled but haunted forms of the women. An arm moved, only a fraction of an inch, hardly more than a pulse. She knew then. As the room warmed, they were thawing, limbs loosening. The fact did little to settle her nerves. She hurried back to the bed, a squeak and bounce as she jumped in, and pulled blankets over her head. The chuckle she was certain she heard came not from one of the women but from John.

When she woke, the sun had risen high enough to suggest midmorning. John's bed and the rockers were empty. Afraid of having been abandoned, she ran to the door, yanked it open. John was in a tree, roping a bundle to branches. The two mothers together. She knew the ground was frozen too deep to attempt a grave, just as she knew John would bury the bodies in the spring when digging a grave was possible.

Late afternoon, Lauder rode down Pine Ridge Road behind John, her arms tight around him. The music box tucked securely inside his coat.

General Brooke, Greta, and Dak stood outside the office, watching as the pair rode in slowly on the mule. General Brooke looked full of purpose and issued orders. Greta's facial expression revealed nothing, but Dak, his mouth slack left the two without a word and rushed across the street. "Thanks, John." He lifted Lauder down and shook John's hand. "I owe you a beef. Come any time."

He ushered Lauder into the privacy of her cabin. "Where the hell have you been?" He held her. "No, don't tell me. Christ, you're going to kill me."

"John took me to Plants Corn's place. We had to check on two elders."

"John, first name? We?" He shook his head. "I don't get it."

"I'll explain everything. But what's going on with General Brooke and Greta?"

"Greta is taking over as headmistress. General Brooke has agreed. After the massacre, of course, he's not calling it a massacre, he's making the school a priority."

"An olive branch?"

"He's given Red Cloud his word it'll stay open."

"What about the soldiers? Will the killers be court-martialed?"

"He's going to propose they receive medals." At the disbelief striking her face, he went on. "He claims it's for the families of the dead. Hell, the whole damn country wants to claim innocence and have returning war heroes."

"I could scream all over again, but I have my notes," Lauder said. "And I know what I saw."

"You're planning to write about it? You sure about that?"

"If I've learned anything, after all that's happened, it's how small I actually am. Given the size of the universe, I'm less than a speck. So how big can my sin be?"

"You'll be a target."

"It was one blunder in a long life. If the world never forgives me, well, there's a lot for which I'll never forgive the world. I'm not saying my plagiarism wasn't wrong; I'm saying my little sin isn't bigger than the rest of my life. Isn't bigger than the lives of Mina, Badger, and Much Wind."

Dak shook his head. "Plenty will make noise, wave that plagiarism charge."

"If I don't write, my silence will be the biggest lie I ever told."

"I love you."

"What else?"

"Out there?" He glanced at the window, back, and hesitated. "Moyer is leaving. It'll take a couple of weeks, but he's history."

"And?" Lauder asked. "What do I see in your eyes. You aren't telling me something."

He leaned back onto the corner of her desk, pulled her between his knees, and took up her hands. "Atlock got into a fight last night, ended up stabbed. Dr. Eastman fixed him up enough to travel, and this morning, Brooke put him in a horse ambulance for Rushville. By nightfall, he'll be on a train headed to a hospital in Omaha, but he'll likely be dead by the end of the week." He considered her expression. "I'm just sorry it wasn't me. Someone cheated me out of it."

"That's all General Brooke knows about the fight? Just that Atlock had been stabbed?"

"The knife was Lakota, had an antelope horn handle, and an Indian woman wrapped in a blanket was seen coming from his room. It looks like he got what he deserved. Brooke isn't going to make any inquires beyond that, and Atlock isn't talking. Of course not. Anything out of that liar's mouth would incriminate him."

"And he didn't say what happened?"

Dak shook his head. "Dolly's with him. Good riddance there, too." He studied Lauder's face. "You don't seem all that surprised." When she pulled her hands free, he stood. "Lauder?"

She turned away, took a breath, and turned back to face him.

"No," he said. "Not you? He didn't come back here?"

"He didn't touch me." She pulled the bundle from beneath her bed, set it on top, and unfolded the corners. "I had to get Mina's moccasins. Your grandfather's watch was there."

He looked down at the items, then lifted the timepiece by the chain, letting the case swing solidly into his palm. He closed his fingers around the silver.

Lauder dipped her head to his shoulder. "You're welcome. I'm sure Dolly stole it from your house on Christmas."

He shook his head, his unsettled gaze roaming over the other items. "You could have been… Why didn't you wait for me?"

"With everything going on, all the inquiries and accusations, I was afraid Atlock would take what he had and run. I needed to get the moccasins for Mina."

"She's gone. She wouldn't have wanted you risking your life."

"I wanted her to rest in peace," Lauder said. "At least that."

Dak pulled her close. "Jesus," he said again, "I don't know what to say."

"I know I've gotten myself in another mess. I'm scared because I went to Atlock. He didn't come here. Before I'm arrested, I want to give everything to Red Cloud. He'll know best what to do with it."

"Okay." Dak had been shaking his head since he first saw her with her arms around John. "Dr. Eastman expects Atlock to live, though he'll be crippled up for a long time."

"Which is it? He'll die, or he'll live?"

"I wanted you to believe he was a goner, but now, knowing it was you, I want you to know he'll live."

"So that I'm not haunted with guilt?"

"Brooke warned him if he's ever seen near a Sioux reservation again, he'll have him arrested."

She put a hand on Dak's chest, felt his heartbeat against her palm. "I'm not afraid of Atlock. He's nothing. Though slime is a thing. Sooner rather than later, a rope, a gun, or another knife stick will put an end to him. See?" She smiled at Dak. "My wheels are not going to come off."

He took her in his arms again. "Tell me about the elders."

"Two women. Plants Corn's mothers. John has tended to the bodies."

"Pack your things. I'm not leaving you alone again. What do you need for the night?"

"You're sure?"

He kissed her. "I've never been surer of anything." He dropped to one knee, took her hand. "Miss Lauder Ellison, would you do me the honor of becoming my wife?"

She nodded, grinning. "I accept your proposal … though a date—"

"That's all I need to hear. I'll wait days, months, years. Pack. In the morning, we'll bring in the wagon, haul those crates out to the farm. For now, can you ride?"

"It's time I learned."

"Pack. I've got a surprise for you. I'll be right back."

"We need to see Red Cloud before we go anywhere." She took up Mina's basket. "But this? Would it be wrong to keep it?"

"Let's let the chief decide."

Half an hour later, Dak returned on his horse, holding the reins of a second.

"Night." Lauder's eyes filled. "Where did you find him?"

"On the way back from Rushville, I saw him off on a hill pulling Plants Corn's empty wagon. I'd seen him and the wagon enough times to know who he belonged to. I got Dr. Eastman his supplies and went back out to find him. When I did, I unhitched him and put my rifle to his ear thinking he needed help out of his misery. I couldn't do it."

Lauder set down her bundles, stroked the horse's long nose, unable to speak the words tumbling in her throat.

"With the number of dead," Dak went on, "I thought he needed a chance. A couple of days of solid food and stabling, he's looking better.

No more than you weigh, a ride will do him good. You looking to own a horse?"

"This horse?"

"I'd talk to Red Cloud about that, too, see who and how much he'd like us to pay. I've got plenty of horses, but if you maybe want this one? Him belonging to Mina."

Lauder stroked Night's long face, laid her cheek against his. "I'm sorry you lost her," she whispered in his ear. "She loved you."

"Here," Dak said. He'd come around Night and cupped his hands, "Step in, I'll give you a leg up."

"Wait." Night watched her with wide eyes, but Lauder no longer feared him. Like so many of her initial worries and beliefs, fearing this horse was foolish. She tugged on the reins, coaxing Night to look down, then tapped his belly.

"The hell," Dak said as Night folded to the ground.

She stepped over, seated herself, and clung both to the reins and the mane as Night stood. "That's all I know," she nearly shrieked. "What do I do now?"

Dak pushed his hat lower, picked up her bundles, and swung onto his horse. "Just stay in the saddle. The horse'll teach you the rest."

She would learn to ride, though she would not keep Night. She knew a little girl who needed the horse.

Acknowledgements

A SPECIAL THANKS TO Pen Women Press and the wonderful Lucy Arnold, who steered me through the publishing journey with knowledge and graceful encouragement. Thank you, Nancy Dafoe and Laura Jo Brunson, for your editing extraordinaire. Sally Nimmo, you were with me from early on, thank you. Faith Colburn, thank you for your wonderful feedback. Mary Hines and Cindy Krafka, thank you for your wisdom on all things Lakota. Gail Weiland, writing buddy, thank you for your wisdom and support. No writer delves into history without finding a long list of books lighting the way. Four of the most helpful were: *Bury My Heart at Wounded Knee*, Dee Brown; *Sting of the Bee*, Samuel R Russell; *Eyewitness at Wounded Knee*, Richard E, Jensen, R. Eli Paul, and John E. Carter; *Wounded Knee: Party Politics and the Road to An American Massacre,* Heather Cox Richardson.

About the Author

Margaret Lukas is a native of Nebraska. She received her MFA from Rainier Writers Workshop in Tacoma, Washington. For over a decade, she taught writing at the University of Nebraska-Omaha. Her award-winning short story, "The Yellow Bird," was made into a short film, which premiered at Cannes Film Festival and was then shown at film festivals around the world. She is the author of *Farthest House*, 2015, BQB Press, *River People* 2019, BQB Press, and *The Broken Statue*, 2021, BQB Press. *Spirits Do Not Rest: Heartbreak at Wounded Knee* is her fourth novel.

Lukas has won several awards, including a Nebraska Arts Council Fellowship Award, an International High Plains Book Award, and a National American Pen Women Literary Award for 2024. She is a long-standing member of the National Association of American Pen Women, Inc. and past president of the Omaha Branch. She lives in Omaha with her husband.